"We're Surrounded!"

Throughout the night Grantin had become accustomed to the clatter of the leaves. It was the absence of that sound which caused him to awaken. Sitting up sleepily, he needed a moment to remember where he was. Strange . . . he could not recall bedding down so close to the woods. Twisting his head, Grantin was surprised to see that he and Chom were surrounded.

"Chom!" he called. Chom awakened instantly. As soon as his eyes cleared the Fanist stood, turned a brief circle, and addressed the crown of the largest and oldest tree.

"What do you plan to do to us?"

"Who are you talking to? What's going on? Where . . ."

"These are not ordinary trees. I sensed something last night but could not interpret what I was feeling. Obviously they have some plans for us. What is it that you want, friend trees?"

A smooth, deep bluish vine terminating in thick palps which wiggled like a nest of worms slipped from the gnarled tree and snaked toward the Fanist.

"Pull back your arm before we are forced to employ our magic against you," Grantin warned in a nervous voice. . . .

FANE

DAVID M. ALEXANDER

A TIMESCAPE BOOK
PUBLISHED BY POCKET BOOKS NEW YORK

Another *Original* publication of TIMESCAPE BOOKS

A Timescape Book published by
POCKET BOOKS, a Simon & Schuster division of
GULF & WESTERN CORPORATION
1230 Avenue of the Americas, New York, N.Y. 10020

ISBN: 0-671-83154-2

First Timescape Books printing August, 1981

10 9 8 7 6 5 4 3 2 1

POCKET and colophon are trademarks of Simon & Schuster.

Use of the TIMESCAPE trademark under exclusive license from trademark owner.

Printed in the U.S.A.

To Jack Vance, the writer whose prose
and imagination I most admire

Racial/Political Groupings on the Planet Fane

Hartfords
(descendants of the human colony group led by Amis
Hartford)

Greyhorn
Grantin

Gogols
(descendants of the escaped human criminals led by
Gogol, a master necromancer of the Black Church
on Abraham V)

Hazar and the other lords
Mara (half-Hartford/half-Gogol)

Ajaj
(descendants of former crewmen of the colony ship
Lillith, natives of the planet Ajagel; short, furred,
pacific humanoids; servants of the Hartfords and the
Gogols)

Castor

Fanists
(natives of the planet Fane; large, bipedal, four-armed
hairless humanoids)

Chom

dog'd soldier running toward us. He walks through the

Chapter One

Man had crossed the void, spread out, split up, and dispersed like water through a grate. Perhaps somewhere commerce still flourished and spaceships went forth serving an organized community of man, but not here.

On the far spiral arm at the eastern edge of the galaxy only suns swung through the void. No ships sailed the star lanes, and what men there were had almost forgotten life beyond their narrow realms.

Out in the mist of the Great Dog Nebula the nearest stars were occluded by dust and debris. Almost alone in the center of the interstellar storm rode the great orange sun Pyra. Around it floated a single planet, Fane.

Fane's night sky was a gray, faintly glowing blanket pierced here and there by the pinpricks which were all that could be seen of the far glories in the heavens.

For unknown reasons, perhaps the interaction of the storm with Fane's peculiar modulating magnetic field, the relationship here of man and matter was changed. Mechanized society rapidly broke down—machines disintegrated and power packs ran dry. Magic, sorcery, and spells built a new technology to fill the void. A skilled wizard could become a wealthy and powerful man. Grey-horn was such a wizard.

Greyhorn paused a moment and cocked his head. What was that? A noise in the hall? He sensitized his mind but felt no unauthorized presence. Then, at the edge of his awareness, he sensed his nephew Grantin, down the hall near the library. At least that wastrel was performing his lessons for a change. Greyhorn shrugged and turned back to the bulging plate of glass balanced on the desk in front of him.

The object was neither clear nor frosty, but at the same time both watercolored and confused. It seemed filled with a thick, clear, swirling oil which, while having no color of its own, distorted and puddled the image of anything that might lie behind its surface. The plate was a foot in diameter and five inches thick at the center, tapering to a half inch at the edge. The front was flattened, while the surface away from Greyhorn bulged asymmetrically.

Under the sorcerer's gaze flecks of color sparkled and congealed in the center of the plate. To Greyhorn's eyes, a three-dimensional simulacrum of a man's head and shoulders occupied the center of the disk. In an instant the picture became sharp, though if Grantin had stood at his uncle's elbow he would have seen only a formless swirl. In reality the scene was not in the plate but in Greyhorn's mind, the device functioning only as a focusing mechanism for the thoughts of the men who used it. Hundreds of leagues away in a similar room the man whose image filled Greyhorn's lens stared into a companion device in which he thought he saw Greyhorn's image.

The forces of the lens—or, better, the forces of the planet Fane which were controlled and focused through the lens—concentrated and intensified the principal qualities of each man's visage. A face long and narrow with sunken cheeks and a bulging, puffy structure under the eyes stared out at Greyhorn. The skin was of a sallow, glistening copper hue and was adorned above the mouth with a coal-black, downturned mustache. Bushy black oily brows lay above the eyes. The hair was also black and gleaming and full. It rose in fluffy crests from the center of the forehead and at each temple. The pupils, as well, were black, while the whites seemed to glow with a sickly yellow tone. From the man's neck hung a crude copper necklace centered with a smooth red stone. On his left hand glowed a golden ring likewise bearing at its center another bloody, polished jewel.

In his associate's face Greyhorn detected lust, greed, power, envy, cunning, malice, and, above all else, unbridled ambition: a lovely man, a perfect man, the ideal man for Greyhorn's needs.

"Your deacons and underdeacons are dedicated to our purpose and ready to act?" mouthed the face in Greyhorn's lens.

"No worry as to that, Hazar. I have picked carefully and well. They will follow my every order."

"When will they be fully trained in the spells I have revealed to you?"

"Soon, very soon. Another few days at most. No more than that. They are strong and determined. The weak have already died. Now remains only the job of directing the power with subtlety and fine control. Those who were soft have long since been consumed by their inability to direct Fane's mighty energies. Have no fear; all will be ready. We can move as soon as I receive my ring."

"Ah, yes, the ring. That may prove a bit of a problem. Full control of the stones has not yet been placed at my disposal. My associates are jealous of their powers and they know me to be a man of action. In order to avoid delaying the plan, we may have to move before your ring is available."

"Not at all!" Greyhorn answered with cold finality. "My cooperation and that of my deacons, underdeacons, associates, informers, coconspirators, powers, energies, and spells are all contingent upon the tendering to me of the bloodstone, without which our association is at an end."

"My dear Greyhorn," Hazar responded with an oily smile, "if I did not know you better I would think that you failed to trust me. Surely you realize I cannot rule Fane alone. From the instant that we take power you shall have dominion until your dying day over every person within a hundred leagues of your manor house."

"That I will, Hazar, with or without our association, and I shall also have the ring. And, by the way, before

3

you think upon our arrangement with the mind of a shyster, I will remind you that my dying day is a long time hence. Now, with these minor details out of the way, when and how will I receive the ring?"

An insincere smile split Hazar's lips. He nodded his head in an expression of acquiescence.

"I will send a courier to Alicon, someone special, someone who will not look as though she comes from me."

"She? What will she look like? How will I recognize her?"

"You should not meet her yourself. These things go better with a bit more mystery. There is no need for her to know for whom the bloodstone is intended. And"—Hazar paused meaningfully—"there is no need for you to learn the identity of my operatives. Send a trusted associate to Alicon. Have him wear your amulet. She will recognize him by it and make the exchange. She will comment on the stone, and your courier will say that his father once had a ring with a gem of that type. She will offer to sell him the bloodstone for five coppers, which he will pay her upon delivery of the ring."

"When should I expect the messenger?"

"Perhaps tomorrow afternoon. If not then, the next day certainly."

"Agreed," Greyhorn answered.

Hazar's visage nodded solemnly, then faded; the lens cleared.

Greyhorn's left hand involuntarily twitched in the direction of the plate. It was only through the exercise of conscious effort that the sorcerer restrained himself from hurling a spell at Hazar's vanished form. *You will have power until the day you die.* If Hazar had anything to do with it that day would be soon indeed. Greyhorn was not fooled. If he did not conceive a plan to eliminate the Gogol sorcerer his life would be in constant danger. No, it would soon come down to one or the other of them—but first to get the bloodstone!

Whom to send to Alicon to pick it up? Werner? No; Werner's eyes were too close together, his face too feral, his soul too thin. Maurita? No; Maurita had her advantages, but the bloodstone might tempt her to break her solemn oaths. Greyhorn considered each of his deacons and subdeacons. He concluded that none of them was sufficiently trustworthy. Well, one does not expect to find selfless loyalty in the hearts of those who are willing to sell their fellows into slavery.

Was Grantin up to the chore? Perhaps his worthless nephew would at last be good for something. Up to now the wastrel had only shown an aptitude for womanizing, sleeping, and creating debts. Grantin, son of a sorcerer, nephew of a master sorcerer, grandson of an expert sorcerer—and still he possessed the talents of a field hand. Everyone said the power was in the blood, yet Grantin seemed determined to prove the theory wrong. Well, no matter; perhaps he would at last make himself useful. Certainly he could successfully reach a village only two leagues distant, pick up a bauble, and return it to the manor in reasonably good condition. He knew little enough about magic to understand the power of the ring.

Greyhorn again cocked his head and let his senses roam the hallways of the second floor. Yes, remarkable though it seemed, Grantin was still in the library apparently hard at work. Greyhorn decided to look in on him. Perhaps later in the day he would charge Grantin with the errand. He slipped from his workroom, sealed the door behind him, and padded to the library where Grantin studied the forbidden history.

Chapter Two

Grantin pulled back the cover and began to read the first page of the Ajaj's journal. The ink was of a brownish umber tone. The edges of each letter puddled and ran, as though the fluid were unusually thin. When Grantin concentrated on some of the broader lines he was able to detect in the strokes a shading of pale chocolate at the center of the lines darkening to a deep brown-black hue at their edges.

The paper was an aged, mottled tan which popped and crackled as he turned the pages. Nevertheless, the script was precise and demonstrated a fine expressive flair. The Ajaj who had penned the book was a master scribbler indeed.

Grantin turned another rattling page, then halted to listen for sounds from the corridor beyond. He remembered the last time his uncle had caught him trying to read the book.

"Here you are," Greyhorn had screamed, "the nephew of a master wizard, and you can't even pluck a flower out of the ground without bending over to pick it up. Now, instead of studying your spells, I catch you wasting your time with this nonsense. You're deficient, and every day you become a worse embarrassment for me. Remember, this is not some sparkling dream planet. This is Fane, and I, as master wizard of this locality, have a reputation to uphold."

Now, Grantin held his breath. The house was quiet enough to let him hear the beating of his own heart. He exhaled. With another crackle he turned the next page and continued his study of the history of Fane.

The *Lillith* was of acceptable construction and of the type often seen on our sad world Ajagel. Great blocks of metal and glass were fused as needed. From the outside the starship appeared as a tumble of interlaced blocks, cubes, and rectangles joined haphazardly at sides, top, or bottom. In some ways she resembled the old, broken city of Alnarth built by our ancestors in the days of water before our sun grew red. Now we, the faithful Ajaj, are drawn from Ajagel like blood leaking from a wound.

Time period by time period the gray, twisted space slipped behind us. One after another the planets we investigated were rejected by the colonists who had chartered the *Lillith*.

One planet, 4-Clarion 4312, was passed because its gravity was twice what the humans were used to bearing. They did not wish to carry too heavy a load. Another, 2-Marissa 1847, had a trace too much chlorine in the atmosphere. Our passengers claimed that this would irritate their noses. It, too, was rejected.

Captain Marvin had made an unfortunate charter arrangement. In an expansive moment he had agreed to take the colonists out along the great spiral arm, eastward to the very edge of the galaxy, until such time as they found a suitable planet. Here he had erred. Often we of the Ajaj, as well as the human members of the crew, disputed what might have happened had the contract contained the word "habitable" instead of "suitable."

The voyage continued farther and farther until, at last, we approached the Great Dog Nebula where the near stars were occluded by dust and debris. Beyond was only interstellar fog and then the vast empty void.

Each time period that the *Lillith* pressed on increased our captain's unhappiness. Farther and farther he departed from his course for our next stop at New Ossening. Truly he was cursed that trip. He had also agreed to transport criminals to that bleak world, so much was Captain Marvin in need of riches.

In the center of the mist of the Great Dog Nebula, almost alone in the heart of the interstellar storm, rode the gigantic orange sun Pyra and its single planet: Fane.

Captain Marvin drove the *Lillith* toward this world. As senior apprentice empather, I was summoned to my dials and nodes to test the flavor of the orb. The long-range scanners reported it not only habitable for human life but lush and fertile. Still, I tasted a strangeness about the world. This I reported to the captain, but it was news he did not wish to hear.

The second officer, an Earthman named Barth, contended that the world had a strange fluctuating magnetic field. He decreed that the core of the planet was of such an odd constituency that it generated an electromagnetic haze. This he assumed to be the natural cause of the disturbance of our amplifiers and our instruments.

Without incident we landed in a meadow surrounded by pale green trees and tall plants with leaves of striped blue and yellow. After the analyzer pronounced the atmosphere free of toxins, plagues, and noxious elements the convicts were shackled waist to waist and sent out first to test the air. Remote sensors monitored their blood and sweat. When they passed the test the colonists and the Ajaj and much of the crew were allowed to leave the *Lillith*.

Once outside, teams of colonists commenced gathering samples of plant and animal life in an effort to determine if they were healthful and nutritious. By the end of the watch the biologists had decided that all was well.

Once freed of their roles as guinea pigs the prisoners lay in the long grass, backs against humps of soil and upthrusting trees. Here they took a last sweet rest before their shipment to bleak, bleak New Ossening where there are only clouds, damp, and death.

The criminals numbered sixteen and were of mixed and varied backgrounds. Included in their number were three zombiests, a gamemaster, a handful of expurgators, four housebreakers, and a master necromancer of the Black Church on Abraham V. The necromancer, Gogol by name, was accompanied by his chief helper, Windom, both of whom had been sentenced for a too energetic dedication to genuineness in the staging of human sacrifices. According to rumors Windom had procured the subjects, while Gogol, at the height of the Black Mass, performed dark deeds to the rapt approval of his faithful acolytes.

By midafternoon Fane had been adjudged salubrious. The stevedores commenced unloading the colonists' supplies. The task was almost complete when, from between two piles of duraplast crates, there appeared a strange creature.

Four-armed, smooth-skinned, and hairless, the biped was dressed in a seamless green fabric which extended in the form of trousers from just above the midpoint of his legs upward across the hips, groin, and stomach to cover his chest, shoulders, and back. The arms were sleeveless and the feet and ankles bare as well. No seams, clasps, or fastenings could anywhere be detected.

The creature's skin was a medium gray, with the dome of his skull deepening to a slate or almost charcoal color. The being's forehead seemed permanently wrinkled. The brows above the large round eyes were ridged with gristle.

The Fanist calmly walked to the center of the camp and with mild courtesy watched the exertions of the colonists and crew. The creature seemed neither hostile nor concerned.

One thing above all must be said about our Captain Marvin—he was not a timid man. In fact, he was often referred to by the human crew members as possessing that emotion which they termed courage.

He approached the Fanist with a weapon prominently displayed at his belt, but his hands were empty. In the background all work stopped. The human crew soon armed themselves and formed a perimeter guard about the camp and ship. They found no other natives, nor could they discover how this one had entered our midst unseen.

Captain Marvin went through the standard procedure for communicating with a strange being. He recited a list of nouns, emphasized by gestures with his right arm.

"Marvin—rock—tree—ship—"

The Fanist stared at the captain but made no attempt to reply in kind.

Next, Captain Marvin attempted to demonstrate the personal pronoun "I," then to introduce a series of simple verbs.

"I run," he said as he pranced a few feet forward and back. "I sit," he announced and flopped down onto the ground. An instant later he arose while declaring: "I stand."

The Fanist remained impassive, watching everything but speaking not at all. Finally, to our amazement, he uttered two Terran words, "Talk more," followed by a sweep of one of his hands in the direction of the captain, colonists, and crew. Immediately all conversation ceased. The humans stared at the Fanist with open amazement. Angrily the captain shouted: "He said to talk. Everyone start talking."

For ten minutes the Fanist stood quietly in the midst of the babbling colonists and crew; then, at last, he held up his upper right hand.

"Enough. I understand now. You are accepted."

"This is your world?" the captain asked.

"We are here."

Captain Marvin pondered that statement for a moment and then replied: "We wish to be here, too."

"You are here," the Fanist answered.

"You have no objections, then?"

"The world is as it is. Destiny shapes itself. Everything will set itself in proper order. You are here. You are part of the order. What will you do?"

Amis Hartford, the leader of the colonists, now strode forward.

"We will build our city here," he declared. "We will grow and multiply and found our world."

"The world is vast and there are limits. You are mistaken."

"With our things," Hartford continued, pointing to the bales and bundles of equipment which had already been unloaded from the ship, "we will build a great city. If you will let us, we will work with you and help you and we will be friends."

"You will not build a great city."

"You intend to stop us, then?"

"Things are as they are. If you tell me that you will drop a rock and that it will fall upward without the words, then I tell you it will not happen. I do not stop it, but it does not happen."

"What will stop us? What words?"

"The words are necessary. Everything must be done with the words. My words will not work for you. Each life has its own way. You will learn."

"Do you mean spells, incantations, witchcraft, mysticism? We are civilized men. We do not believe in such things. We know better. The machines will serve us well."

The Fanist looked around the clearing. He stared intently at the crated equipment, then looked back to Marvin and Hartford. With an almost human expression he shook his head.

"You will see. You will find your own way. It is all one. Destiny will take you where it will. I say back to you your own words: 'Good luck.'"

The Fanist turned, walked to his left, weaved through the piles of supplies, and apparently without exiting from the other side disappeared.

Grantin jerked his head as he heard his uncle's slapping steps. He slammed shut the oversized volume and shoved it under his arm. Greyhorn was close now, almost to the right-hand angle of the corridor. Grantin whirled and ran for the shelves on the far side of the room. There he replaced the Ajaj history, then grabbed Hedgkin's *The Magician's Constant Companion and Source Book Compendium*. Opening it at random, he settled in a chair with the volume on the table in front of him.

Grantin tried to suppress his harsh breathing and will his heart to slow its pace. His eyes barely had time to focus on the page before his uncle entered the room.

"I hope you're doing something useful for a change, nephew," Greyhorn announced in an accusatory tone.

Grantin looked over his shoulder in a pathetic attempt to appear surprised. Greyhorn's expression remained unchanged, the winter-gray eyes open, unblinking; the tip of his short, narrow nose pointing at a spot in the middle of Grantin's forehead; hard lines running from each nostril to the corners of his mouth; and a hint of angry furrows marring the sorcerer's brow.

Grantin swallowed and replied in a breathy, nervous tone.

"You'll have to excuse me, uncle; you startled me. Yes, I was just now reading the, uh—*Magician's Compendium,* trying to sharpen up my skills."

"Skills!" Greyhorn exclaimed. "Harrumph. I've seen cross-eyed, one-legged virgins with more skills than you possess. You couldn't conjure up a tip of your hat if your life depended on it. Why I've been cursed with a nephew like you . . ." Greyhorn halted in midsentence, his cunning eyes looking past Grantin, across the table, and down to the lower shelf where the Ajaj scribbler's history now lay slightly askew.

Greyhorn strode around the table, his wide cuffs and cape flapping behind him in the wind of his passage. In an instant, he bent and examined the volume for signs of recent use. Greyhorn's suspicions aroused, he stood and turned to face his nephew. Leaning forward across the table, he placed his hands on the planks and angled his great triangular head down and forward until his nose halted only a foot in front of Grantin's now nervously darting eyes.

Greyhorn stared at Grantin for a long minute, as if he could divine his nephew's thoughts by mere mental concentration. Even though Grantin knew that his uncle's skills were those of a high manipulator, master sorcerer, and workmanlike prestidigitator, he still felt a rippling chill course through his spine, as though Greyhorn now possessed the talents of a telepather as well.

One great, white, bony, long-fingered hand shot out to cover the page that Grantin supposedly had been reading. Greyhorn's bone-white member protruding from his midnight-black sleeve seemed like a skeleton's hand thrust out from a freshly dug grave.

"What were you reading on this page?"

"Why, I—I—*The Magician's Compendium*—"

"What were you reading on this page?"

For an instant Grantin's eyes flicked downward to scan the right-hand sheet.

" '—and so with the tri-finger and arm upraised one pronounces, in the fourth voice and at the intermediately high volume, the incantation—'

"It's the spell . . . the spell for warding off noxious mendicants and—and—other such people," Grantin suggested in a querulous tone.

"A Traditional Spell to Clear One's House of Demonized Politicians and Other Odious Creatures," Greyhorn announced as he read from the book.

"Well, uncle," Grantin suggested with a weak smile, "that's more or less correct. I can't be expected to memorize the titles of all of these things. As long as I get the spell right, that's what really counts; isn't that so, uncle?"

"Bah! One more time, Grantin, one more time that I find you wasting your days instead of working to make yourself worthy of being my nephew and I will evict you from my home. Only my solemn promise to your father has allowed you to stay here this long. As you know, in one month you will be twenty-two and so, in law, my debt will be discharged. Take care that I do not on that day send you out to make your own fortune. No doubt you would end up as little better than a barkscraper or toothbuilder. Heed me, nephew: put this nonsense behind you or else there will be dark days ahead!"

With a slap of his hands Greyhorn stomped out of the room like a great black bird of prey. Grantin again looked down at *The Magician's Compendium* and, remembering some long overdue debts, he attempted to read one of the pages. The words seemed to shift beneath his gaze, and by the time he gained the bottom of the page he had forgotten what he had read at the top.

Well, perhaps the fair at Gist two weeks hence would provide a solution to his financial problems.

With a thump Grantin closed the *Compendium* and began to plan how he might return to the library after dinner and finish reading the ancient Ajaj history.

Chapter Three

Wearing soft moccasins, Grantin crept noiselessly into the library. An oily black night coated the manor house's windows. As was customary for this time of the month, Greyhorn was away from the house, off on some wizard's business which he refused to discuss or reveal.

Grantin carried a blanket in his arms. He closed the library door behind him and then carefully hung the cloth over the window. When he was certain it was secure he ignited a crude oil lantern and then removed the scribbler's great masterpiece. Settling himself into the softest chair, he opened the book and began again to read:

Amis Hartford stared for a moment at the spot where the Fanist had slipped between the crates. By some unknown method the native had disappeared. After a moment Hartford slowly shook his head and turned back to the captain. Clearly the colonists must be allocated guns. Captain Marvin disliked passing out arms to passengers, but these were strange circumstances. He hesitantly agreed to honor Hartford's demand.

The colonists went back to their duties. Those without specific tasks relaxed in the warm afternoon sun. Several of the criminals borrowed decks of cards from the crewmen. Only Gogol and his assistant, Windom, remained aloof. Standing at the edge of the clearing, Gogol seemed to fidget. He turned this way and that and scented the air like a predatory beast.

A few minutes later crewmen bearing boxes of weapons left the ship. One of the crates was opened and pistols were brought forth. They consisted of hundreds of long, slender rods bundled together side by side, polished and shiny on each end. The cylinder of glass rested upon a thick, rigid baseplate, underneath which a metal handle extended downward.

One by one the colonists marched up to receive their weapons. The sixth man in line was a laborer named Blotho who, having gotten into trouble on the docks of his native world, had joined the *Lillith* as an apprentice colonist.

Blotho was large, even for a human, and towered more than twice my height. His skin was the color of copper. Curly black sprouted from between the openings of his garments, the wirelike tendrils protruding at his throat, hands, ears, eyebrows, and toes. Blotho grasped the pistol firmly in one great fist, then walked toward the edge of the clearing waving the weapon back and forth like a scythe. Amis Hartford noticed his reckless behavior and shouted to Blotho to stop playing with it as if it were a toy.

At the sound of the order Blotho suddenly turned. Catching his foot in a root, he fell forward, landing in an ungainly sprawl. The gun flew from his hand and smashed against one of the rocks which marred the face of the meadow. Showers of pulverized crystal erupted from the barrel, in response to which Blotho uttered a roaring oath:

"Damn the demon idiots who gave us guns of glass! Blast them and all their broken toys!"

The words had hardly left his throat when his body seemed to change. The colonist's skin began to harden. It glistened even as he struggled to his feet. Barely had Blotho arisen before his joints froze and

16

his voice strangled into silence. His flesh became like polished mail. Light danced in shimmers through his arms. In a few minutes every inch of him, even his hair, teeth, and eyes, had become a glowing crystalline statue. His ship-issued clothes were the only aspect which remained untainted; his few pieces of clothing rustled free in the breeze. Blotho's head was as hard as diamond, his fingers as unbreakable as steel. All of us sensed, in that instant, that what the native had said was true: Fane was a very special world and we did not know the words or the way.

Grantin sat up straight and thrust back first his left shoulder, then his right. He arched his neck and lolled his head around in a counterclockwise motion. The book was too awkward to hold in his lap. He had huddled over it, like a miser counting his gold. Awkwardly he twisted his torso in an attempt to quiet a host of complaining aches.

Grantin leaned forward again. One by one he lifted the lower right-hand corners of the remaining pages, counting as he went. Only a few more and he would be finished with volume one. He adjusted the chair until his stomach was only a foot and a half from the edge of the table, then slid the book toward him until it lay tilted, one edge resting on his belt buckle, with the spine against the table's edge. In this condition he pressed on, anxious to finish before Greyhorn's return.

All of us crowded around Blotho's statue. A few of the more adventurous persons walked close. Hesitantly they slid their palms along the surface of his cheek. There the flesh was cool, hard, and slick like finely polished marble. Dr. Milton, the geologist, closed his hand into a tiny fist and rapped lightly three times against Blotho's temple. The knocks produced a sonorous *thump, thump, thump,* as though Milton had been rapping on a solid piece of soft, light wood. Experimentally one of the crewmen brushed a questing palm across the top of Blotho's head. He yipped in surprise and yanked back a bleeding hand. So hard and sharp were the individual strands of hair that he might as well as have petted a cactus. Small drops of blood oozed from the tips of two of his fingers. At the sight of this injury the crowd retreated a pace or two, then halted in a frightened, nervous circle.

One of the crewmen ran to fetch the captain. In a few moments Captain Marvin shouldered his way through the spectators. He looked first at Blotho, then turned an inquiring gaze to Dr. Milton.

"What in the bloody blue blazes happened to him?"

"As best I can tell he's turned to stone, or, more accurately, a crystalline substance similar to diamond," the geologist responded.

"He smashed one of the pistols," Able Starman Norberg volunteered.

"Just before it happened he cursed the glass," Mary Allen chimed in.

"It's witchcraft, just like the native said," another voice whispered from the edge of the crowd. "Sorcery."

"Nonsense!" Amis Hartford pushed his way to the captain's side. "Don't let your imagination run away with you. There's no such thing as spells and witchcraft."

Captain Marvin stared quizzically at Blotho, then strode forward and gave the head a backhanded rap on the point of the nose. Blotho remained as insensate as a tree while the captain pulled back his hand and thrust a skinned knuckle between his lips.

Marvin looked truculently around the clearing. He saw only golden afternoon sunlight slanting through the trees and dappling the heavy grasses with yellow specks.

"Everyone back in the ship," he called. "Tomorrow I'll decide what to do."

Reluctantly, the colonists climbed the gangplank. Inside the *Lillith* they split into pairs and returned to their bare metal cubicles. In the meadow, crewmen armed with rifles mounted a watch where the grass met the trees.

The next morning the colonists arose early. Without consultation with the captain Amis Hartford ordered them to finish unloading. So determined was

Hartford to complete the job that even the criminals were pressed into service. The work was done quietly; few words were spoken. After the incident with Blotho, each person took care with what he said. No shouts or arguments or curses marred the early-morning silence. All worked diligently, even Gogol and Windom, although these two were often seen muttering softly to each other.

Shortly after breakfast Captain Marvin left the *Lillith*. Descending the gangplank, he was amazed to see such furious activity. He wandered through the camp until he found Amis Hartford chairing a meeting with his subordinates.

"Hartford, I want to talk to you," Marvin said brusquely.

Hartford spoke to his associates, then turned to join the captain. The two men walked to the edge of the meadow to a point where they could converse more or less in private.

"Hartford, I don't think this planet is going to do for you. All taken with all, I suspect that the best thing is to load your people and proceed to New Ossening. After we've gotten rid of the criminals I'll let you off at Clarion or Marissa on the way back."

"Captain, we're all quite satisfied with Fane," Hartford replied. "The climate is harmonious; the water sweet; the air pure; the land fruitful; the produce nourishing; the natives friendly."

"Listen, Hartford, I've been talking with my chief engineer. Between you and me, the equipment is beginning to deteriorate. The magnetic field seems to shift in some kind of harmony with Pyra's sunspots. Certain of the frequencies are able to penetrate our shielding. It's getting worse. Already systems are breaking down. If we don't get out of here in the next ten hours we may never lift the ship at all. Mussman thinks that sooner or later every engine and electronic circuit you've got will decay into a worthless pile of junk. Your colony doesn't have a chance here. In a week you'll be back to the Stone Age."

As he talked the captain's eyes darted back and forth, checking to see if anyone were near enough to have overheard the conversation. Amis Hartford, though, seemed calm, serene, after the fashion of an admiral in command of a battleship which is about to attack a rowboat.

"Captain, it is to be expected that no planet will be perfect. We assume that there will be little problems here and there."

"This isn't a little problem. In three months standard you'll be plowing the ground with a sharp stick and living in a mud hut. Brute force is the only thing that will stand between you and starvation. This isn't a suitable planet."

"Captain, as you well know," Hartford replied, "the colonists decide what is and is not a suitable planet. We're staying here. If you're worried about our not having enough muscle power, perhaps we'll keep the criminals as indentured servants. I am sure they would choose to stay here in preference to New Ossening."

"Those men are cargo!" Marvin shouted. "They are my responsibility, and nobody takes . . ."

The captain halted in midsentence, speechless with astonishment and fury. Quiet, well-mannered, precise Amis Hartford stood there pointing a pistol at the captain's stomach. Without spoken orders other colonists appeared at the captain's side and relieved him of his weapons. As if by a common signal the crewmen guarding the meadow were also disarmed. Within a few moments captain, crew, and criminals were herded into a tight circle at the foot of the ship's ramp. Amis Hartford addressed the entire complement.

"The captain has decided that for the good of his ship he must depart immediately. I, and those who follow me, will remain. Yonder is the ship, and here is the site of the first city of the New Reformed Orthodox Credentialists. Those who wish to help us found our world come to me. Those who wish to return to space, and perhaps New Ossening, may board the *Lillith*."

The captain's anger had now transformed itself into a cold frenzy. He said not a word, but it was clear from his expression that he was determined to return and send everyone, colonists and criminals alike, to New Ossening. No one contravened Marvin's commands or hijacked his cargo.

The colonists moved to Amis Hartford's side. Next, hesitantly, one of the expurgators arose and slowly walked toward Hartford as well.

"Come back here, you scum!" Marvin shouted. The expurgator stopped and looked back at Marvin uncertainly. Then he turned and studied Hartford. In his years of strife and travail the expurgator had learned one thing: always take orders from the man with the gun. He turned his back on the captain and crossed the meadow to stand a few feet apart from the ranks of colonists.

"The rest of you transportees, if you wish to stay, must spend the next ten years as our indentured servants. After that time you will be freed. If this does not please you, go back aboard the ship."

The rest of the criminals crossed the meadow, and a few of the crewmen as well, myself and six of my brother and sister Ajaj among them. In a few minutes it was done. The captain and two thirds of the crew boarded the ship; the ramp slid away; the hatch began to close.

A few seconds later the whine of the *Lillith*'s generators filled the air. As the great cryogenic magnets began to fill with charge, she slowly bucked her way through Fane's oscillating magnetic field. While the colonists focused their attention on the rising ship I sensed a new source of power and wandered toward its focus. There at the edge of the clearing stood Gogol and Windom, waving their hands in a complex pattern of interwoven circles.

With the *Lillith* a pinpoint two thousand yards in the sky, Gogol and Windom simultaneously clapped their hands, pointed their fingers, and uttered a great curse. The *Lillith* fragmented and shattered like a bullet-blasted mirror; a twinkling rain of metal fragments cascaded across the sky. The colonists stood transfixed by the disaster.

In that instant Gogol, Windom, and three of the zombiests seized five guns, four women, and three Ajaj and fled into the forest. Though chase was given almost at once no sign of the fugitives or their captives could be discovered. All had fled into the heartland of Fane to found their own empire.

So it began. This is the history, the source, the genesis, of the Gogols and the Hartfords, the twin camps which inhabit our world. There is much to tell of my brother Ajaj, the Grays, who serve the Gogols, and my people, the Pales, who share Fane with the Hartfords, and of the Fanists. Always the Fanists; but the story is long and I must rest. Later, later, perhaps I will tell the tale.

Grantin pushed the book away from him and stretched his arms above his head. He had finished volume one. The flame on his lantern popped and flickered and seemed ready to sputter out. It was late, later than he had meant to stay.

Downstairs, he heard the creak of the great front door opening under Greyhorn's hand. Grantin stumbled about the room in a flurry of sudden activity. He replaced the book, blew out the flame, and took down the blanket. Now, stoop-shouldered, bent, and sore, only a few seconds ahead of Greyhorn's tread, he tottered off to his bunk.

Chapter Four

Grantin yawned, stretched his arms, and attempted to burrow his head into his pillow. His nostrils filled with the odor of the pillow's ticking, a fragrance like the mixture of burlap and wet hay. Regretfully he forced open his eyes, sat up on his bunk, and stared around the room.

A clock stood on the dresser. Grantin rubbed his bloodshot eyes and strained to read the glowing numbers. A beam of light penetrated a hole carefully drilled in the far wall. As the sun arose the shaft of light inched its way down the tall column of etched glass. The front of the clock was studded with hemispherical bulbs of black-painted crystal. On the surface of each dome a number was etched through the paint. As the light struck the back side of the dimples the figure glowed and so announced the hour. The Hartfords had long ago decreed that each day would be twenty hours long, to be divided into two sets of ten hours each. Sunrise was at the first hour B. D. (Before Dark); lunch typically at the fifth hour; dinner at the tenth; midnight at the fifth hour A.D. (After Dark); and sunrise at the end of the tenth hour.

Grantin stared incredulously at his clock. The beam

was between the third and fourth hours—no, almost to the fourth hour. Could someone have moved the instrument and so impaired its accuracy?

Grantin threw wide the covers and leaped from his bed. He pulled on a pair of rough woven pants, a white homespun shirt, and the same soft shoes he had worn last night. Without washing he slipped from his room and raced downstairs.

First he went behind the manor to lay in a supply of firewood. After a few minutes of swinging the ax he regretted his deficiencies as a wizard. Had he merely practiced a few simple spells he could have added insuperable keenness to the blade, strength to his shoulders, and lightness to the ax, not to mention steellike toughness to his now blistering hands.

Grantin worked with a will. Shortly he tottered back to the house beneath an enormous pile of rudely cut kindling. After storing the firewood he cleaned the dishes, then swept the floor. Mercifully, this morning Greyhorn was occupied in another portion of the house and did not enter the kitchen until almost the fifth hour, by which time Grantin had completed his chores and was beginning to lay the table for lunch.

"Good morning, uncle," Grantin said politely. "Did everything go well last night?"

"What do you know about last night?" Greyhorn growled. As he spoke he turned his head sideways and studied Grantin with a mean, squinty glance.

"Nothing, uncle. I don't know anything about what you did last night. But obviously you did something last night, because you weren't here and because you got up late this morning, and I just wondered if whatever it was that you were doing that I don't know about, if—"

"Stop your inane babbling! Just listening to you makes me forget half of my spells." Greyhorn turned an inquisitive eye to the kitchen and then nodded slightly, apparently satisfied with what he saw. "Well, at least you've been working this morning, doing something constructive for a change. Perhaps you have a skill after all. With a little work you might qualify as a fourth assistant wife. Well, let's see if your cooking measures up today. Bring me lunch—and none of those wretched boiled root whistles either. While we're at it, I'll thank you to never again make snail gravy. The last batch turned my throat the color of a Fanist's hoof."

"We have cold broiled chicken and seedbread," Grantin suggested, "and I could make us a red-leaf salad."

"Fine. Set the table, and bring a portion for yourself. Hurry, now; I have an errand for you."

Grantin returned in a moment with the meat, bread, and salad and, for good measure, added a slab of fine white cheese accompanied by a bowl of sugared berries. Not to Grantin's taste, however, was the beverage. Greyhorn insisted on plain spring water. The wizard claimed that alcohol dulled his senses and inhibited his powers.

Greyhorn relaxed during the meal and some of the surliness seemed to leak from his person. Sensing a mellowing attitude, Grantin attempted to turn the conversation to a discussion of the approaching fair at Gist.

"Is the meat cooked enough for you, uncle?" Grantin began.

"Quite satisfactory," Greyhorn allowed.

"You know, uncle, I've been thinking about what you said earlier, about my skill as a cook. Perhaps I should enter something in the fair. What do you think?"

"Fair? I have no time for such things."

"Oh, come now, uncle; you must remember the fair at Gist. It's the biggest of the year. Yes, there are many opportunities at such doings. With just a bit of help I think quite a few triumphs might be arranged."

"What kind of help?" Greyhorn asked as he fixed Grantin with a suspicious glare.

"Well, uncle, you know that occasionally, from time to time, a man makes a few unfortunate enemies—persons of low social status who resent their betters—and these petty jealousies sometimes get in the way of true advancement. There is, for example, the small matter of those peasants, the Bondinis. I paid some slight attention—out of common courtesy, no more—to their daughter. Those ruffians have blown the matter all out of proportion until it now assumes the pattern of a blood feud. They have no sensibilities at all. Imagine attempting to lay hands on the nephew of the great wizard Greyhorn.

"But I have just the plan to settle with them. One or two of your minor spells would render my person inviolate—perhaps something that would discharge balls of green fire to blast the fingers of any who might accost me during my trip to the fair. Ha, ha, that would be a lesson to them, would it not! Those Bondinis would learn to trifle with—"

"Stop, nephew. I perceive where this discussion is going. Perhaps you might like a talisman to bring you good luck at the doughnut toss. The ability to read playing cards from the back sides would be helpful at the fair, would it not? And, of course, a love potion or two for some wandering maiden who is lonely and needs your caress? Are these the sorts of things that, perhaps, you thought might be appropriate baggage for your planned expedition to Gist?"

"Why, uncle, what a marvelous suggestion! I had no idea—"

"Shut up, you imbecile! Of course you had no idea. You never have any idea, you twit! Do you know what magic is?"

Grantin half closed his eyes and dredged up the catechism phrases from the corners of his memory. " 'Magic is the method by which the powers of the heavens and the earth are used by men for—' "

"None of that nonsense prattle! You don't know what magic is, but I will tell you this one last time. Try and get it through your thick head. Magic is the control of the power. The power is not in me. It is not in you. It is not in the Fanists or the Ajaj or the Gogols—or anyone. The power is in the world. It is part of the very stuff of Fane.

"Our spells, our amulets and potions—the words, the motions of the hand, the aspect of the body and the eyes, the tightness of the muscles, the pumping of blood through our veins, all points and parameters of our being—are only a means to control the power. I am a great sorcerer because I have great control over the power. I am a conduit, a conductor. The power flows through me at my bidding like sparks through a lightning rod.

"Do you know why there are very few master sorcerers? Shut your mouth—of course you don't know why. It's because the more powerful the spell, the more energy which the wizard must channel and control. The slightest mistake in the pronunciation of a powerful spell, the minutest deviation from prescribed ritual, will cause the power to go awry. Then it will no longer be conducted through the wizard and onto the object of the spell but will dissipate inside his own body or in some unpredictable locale with an unknowable result. The wizard or his house or family may then be blasted by the energy which he has sought to use.

"Few men wish to take such risks, and of those who do, the incompetent are soon killed. Only the finest wizards, the most powerful men, are able to survive their apprenticeship. That is why no apprectice wizard is allowed to marry. The weak ones are killed without fathering children. Those experts, such as myself and your father and our grandfather, are preserved to pass along the traits of success.

"Were I to throw open my books to you or even allow you to attempt some of my most elementary processes, you would no doubt instantly blast yourself to kingdom come. That is why most men, most creatures on this planet, stick to the simple spell. There the powers which are invoked are so weak that the chance of harm is small. And that is also why, year after year, sons follow the professions of their fathers—because history has shown that their fathers had the skill, the innate, inborn, inbred instinct, to safely manipulate the incantations native to their craft. So the chances are higher that the son will also succeed in that same occupation.

"Now, you ask me to manipulate a few simple spells for you as if it were no more effort than pouring a glass of water. You idiot! The greater the energies which I control, the more of my own energy I must expend. Spells are not free. It is effort; it is work to achieve the desired goal. Each time I call upon the powers I tire myself, I weaken a bit. If someday I strain myself too far I may weaken to the point where I make a mistake and become the instrument of my own death.

"So, therefore, my lazy nephew, my ignorant nephew, my incompetent nephew, there will be no love potions, no good-luck fetishes, no power of penetrating vision, and for the fair no spell of physical protection.

"Now"—Greyhorn brought Grantin to a state of attention with a buffet—"pay attention. There's work to be done. Wake up! Look smart! I do have an important task for you. Against my better judgment I am going to give you the opportunity to make something of yourself. As you've no doubt discerned, I've already resigned myself to the fact that you'll never be a wizard. However, from time to time, you may make yourself useful. You may, if the powers be willing, in some time derive into your full occupation as my factotum, majordomo, and chief lackey.

"Now listen to me, Grantin. Things are on the rise. A new wind nips through the trees. Events shape themselves under the hands of strong men such as myself. If you perform well and prove yourself worthy, you may yet bask warmly in the reflected glory of my success.

"Here, take this amulet and hang it about your neck. It will be a sign to the one you will meet of whom you represent. You are to travel to Alicon, past the Hall of the Fabricators and into the Street of the Artisans. I will give you a spell of protection for the trip.

"Wear the necklace in plain sight, but do not part with it. Give it to no one, no matter what anyone may offer you. By and by, after admiring the amulet a stranger will tell you of a ring which contains a stone of the same material. When you see the ring say: 'My father had a ring that was so.' The person should answer: 'Then you should have this to complete the family treasure.' The person will offer to sell you the ring for five coppers. Buy the ring and return it and the amulet to me. Now, is all clear to you?"

Grantin fondled the pendant, which was welded to a heavy gold-alloy chain. The object was a dull copperish color, round, heavy, and uneven, the workmanship crude. In the center of the disk was mounted an oval red stone polished to a silky smoothness. In the light the gem glittered with bloody highlights. A nice enough gimcrack, Grantin thought, but not of surpassing value. It might be worth a silver or two but not much more. Grantin studied the amulet for a moment and then looked back at his uncle.

"I do have a few questions, uncle, now that you mention it. Who is it that I'm going to meet? What do we do with the ring once we get it? How long—"

"Silence! A lackey doesn't ask questions. He follows orders!"

"But you asked if I had any questions."

"I didn't mean it. Now go! It is already approaching the sixth hour. If by chance you are not met today, remain in town and return to the Street of the Artisans to-morrow. Stay there until you get the ring. Guard it with your life. Here are a silver and two coppers. That should be sufficient to cover your food and lodging, provided that you are prudent and invest in medium-grade straw for the pallet and nourishing gruel for your evening meal. Now, be on your way."

Grantin retrieved his brown leather jacket from the closet and slid the amulet into his pocket. He opened the front door and, slinging the coat over his shoulder, walked out into the early-afternoon sunshine.

A lovely day, a protective spell guarding him from the Bondinis' wrath, a trivial task, and money in his pocket. What could possibly go wrong?

Chapter Five

From his workshop window Greyhorn watched his
nephew pace the trail toward Alicon. A vague anxiety
began to pervade the wizard's vitals. Grantin was an in-
dolent, irresponsible spendthrift, but what could go wrong
with so simple a task?

Greyhorn watched Grantin's departing figure until it
reached the bottom of the slope, then he turned back to
his workbench. He had been experimenting with a contrivance of glass and steel which he hoped would operate
as a focusing mechanism for his more powerful spells. In
a few days it would be ready for a test. The subject?
Hazar's form immediately sprang to mind. Yes; this device would possibly slow the villain down a bit.

As if his thoughts of the Gogol prince had tripped a re-
lay, the black wizard's form suddenly called to Greyhorn
from the lens. Greyhorn pushed his psychic condenser to
the side of the table, then positioned himself in front of
the plate. Palm outward, Greyhorn moved his right hand
in a sweeping pass in front of the lens. Immediately
Hazar's visage appeared.

"Hazar," Greyhorn called. "Have you called to tell me that your fellows have at last agreed that you shall be their chief?"

"Not yet, Greyhorn, but soon, soon. No, I merely wish to inform you that my messenger has been delayed and will not reach Alicon until tomorrow morning. Your courier may delay his departure until sunrise."

"Departure? I don't believe I indicated that my associate lived outside of Alicon. In any event you are too considerate, Hazar. My messenger will be ready to receive the ring, be it tonight or tomorrow or even the day after."

"Excellent, Greyhorn; I'm glad you are so well organized. I'll tell you this: your associate is a lucky fellow indeed. The person whom he will meet is a rare beauty."

"Assuming that my subordinate is a man, I accept your assurances of the lady's beauty," Greyhorn replied frostily. Grantin to meet a lovely woman! He'd rue the day he was born if he let her get the better of him, Greyhorn promised himself. He turned his attention back to the lens. "So, Hazar, what other news have you for me? Does all go smoothly with your plans? Everyone is ready for the attack? No little inconveniences or difficulties?"

"Well, in these things there are always minor snags here and there. Hardly difficulties worth mentioning."

Greyhorn's interest was instantly aroused. "Little snags? Perhaps you should describe them to me so that I can watch for similar problems arising among my fellow Hartfords."

"Small chance of that. One of our Grays is being a bit obstreperous, but he'll be settled with shortly."

"A Gray causing trouble? I thought they were the most spiritless, docile creatures in existence. I have always been given to understand that the Ajaj Grays follow your every command. It would seem that an Ajaj voicing complaints is truly an extraordinary act."

"Perhaps extraordinary, but not at all important. The Ajaj take little interest in our affairs. Certainly your Ajaj Pales will have no role in the coup. No, this fellow is obviously one of those random mutants who prove the rule. I'm sure the slightest reproach from the lowliest of my subdeacons will have him cringing in abject obedience."

"Still," Greyhorn replied, "one must tread warily with the Ajaj. They have their own powers. My ancestors found that those who had molested them often disappeared without a trace."

"Possibly true of the Pales, but the Grays accept our rule. We assign them tasks which they perform without complaint. They are controlled by their own leaders."

"No doubt you are right, Hazar. In any event the Grays are your problem, not mine. I will have the ring tomorrow, and seven days hence I will order the attack on the defenders of the mountain pass."

"Yes, Greyhorn," Hazar said as he broke the connection; "soon you will have all the power you can use."

But what's power to a dead man? Hazar gleefully asked himself once the screen was clear. That arrogant, flint-eyed popinjay Greyhorn would never live to be one of the lords in Hazar's empire. Already Maurita, his dear Maurita, had supplied Hazar with a bit of Greyhorn's hair and a fragment of dead skin from his left big toe.

Hazar chuckled at Greyhorn's cold reception of the probes regarding the identity of the courier. That would keep the old fool guessing. Hazar already knew that it was Greyhorn's worthless nephew Grantin who went to receive the ring. Now, if only Mara played her part, beguiled him, seduced him, and then smeared a drop of Grantin's blood upon the bloodstone. The blood which flowed in Grantin's veins was like that which flowed in Greyhorn's. Together with Mara's enchantment it would cause the ring, once in Greyhorn's possession, to lose its power within a month. Then, with the hair and skin and blood which Mara would bring back to him, Hazar would destroy both uncle and nephew as easily as a lumberjack squashes an ant. Except for that ridiculous Ajaj Castor, all of Hazar's plans proceeded apace.

What to do about that troublemaker? First he must be isolated from his own kind. Without the support of his fellows, Castor's death was far less likely to cause annoying repercussions. Hazar crossed his workroom, opened the door, and stuck his head into the anteroom beyond.

"Rupert, come in here; I have a task for you."

Rupert urged his sweaty, dumpy body to its feet. With surprising quickness he crossed the office and entered

Hazar's private study. The deacon's skin was a pallid, waxy white and glistened softly under its sheen of oil. The brown, thinning hair was greasy and combed straight back in limp chestnut strands.

"Rupert, I have a job for you," Hazar said. "I want you to get yourself over to the Ajaj settlement and straighten out one of the Grays. Word has reached me that one of these fellows has been urging his associates to resist my lawful orders.

"You talk to the chief of that race of sheep—the chief decision maker or random factor or whatever it is they call her—and tell her to take steps to solve this problem. You make sure that she orders this Gray, this Castor, to cease his seditious propaganda and to withdraw all his previous remarks. Be sure she understands that if she does not silence Castor herself we will take steps to do so. Further, she must realize that there is to be no unpleasantness in the event that we are forced to take matters into our own hands."

"I am to obtain the promise of the decision maker to deal with this fellow, then?"

"Nonsense! One doesn't trust a sheep to do the job of a huntcat. First talk to the decision maker, then secret yourself in a likely spot, recite the appropriate incantation, and observe how she handles the problem. If the matter is concluded, all well and good. I will then reduce Castor to the position of a scullery assistant or garbage picker for his impertinence, and that will be that. On the other hand"—Hazar now fixed Rupert with an intent steely gaze—"if for any reason this Gray continues in his treason, you are to kill him in a most spectacular method. Nothing ordinary, now—no drops of poison or clean slash of the knife. Turn him into a human fireball; explode him like an overinflated bladder; cause him to pull free his legs and beat himself over the head—something to make an example of him."

"It shall be as you command, Hazar."

"Of course it will. Now, get to it!"

Rupert hurried from the room with a strange rubbery grace. Hazar closed and locked the door behind him. In a moment the wizard had forgotten Castor and the Ajaj, and Greyhorn as well. Instead he turned to his workbench and commenced even further refinements of the spell which, when augmented by the powerstones which he would soon possess, would be sufficient to amplify his army's power to the point where it might conquer every being on the planet, Hartford, Gogol, Ajaj, and Fanist alike.

Chapter Six

Orange pinpoints glittered from the veins of mica which ran through Castor's walls. The translucent tissue which normally covered the window had been rolled out of the way, allowing the midafternoon sun to enter through the grate. Hewn from the center of a monstrous boulder, the room was spacious by Ajaj standards—a full ten feet on a side, with a ceiling six feet high. Behind Castor a narrow passageway connected the main room with a large, circular, rock-walled bath. On one side of the hall a crevice five feet long, three deep, and two high had been hollowed out. Here Castor passed the nights on a thin straw mattress hidden behind a woven screen. Now the Ajaj sat before his window, apparently enthralled by the view ahead and below.

Beyond the walls of Castor's apartment could be seen huge boulders, slabs, and blocks tumbled each about the other, the whole field of stone sloping downward into a narrow valley some three hundred yards below. It was within the crevices, hollows, caves, and hideaways formed by these stones that the Ajaj Grays made their home.

Am I the only one who knows what should be done?

Castor asked himself. *Am I so different from my fellows? Perhaps I am mad, or cursed.*

The view was incomparably lovely. So easy to relax in the serenity of Fane, to block out the world beyond the valley. In these very apartments there was room for the other two members of a triad. Castor was of the proper age to begin a family. It would be no great task to cut two more niches in the wall and add a small fertility closet for the appropriate rites. Impossible, impossible. Destiny pulled him in another direction. Well, that was the Ajaj way. Castor shrugged and gave himself to his fate. He would visit the decision maker and make one last attempt to convince her of the need for them to flee or, failing that, to oppose the Gogols.

Stooping, Castor negotiated the zigzag narrow passage which led between the boulders. His three-foot form slipped effortlessly between the crags. In a few moments Castor had reached the entrance to Obron's lodgings. He made chirping sounds. An instant later two more chirps sounded from within, and he entered Obron's apartment.

"Castor, I thought it might be you," Obron said when Castor moved into the light. "Your suggestions have disturbed many people. The Gogols themselves are enraged."

"The Gogols? How have they become involved in all of this?"

"How could they not be involved? Your remarks bear directly upon our relationship with them. Surely it was inevitable that one way or another they would be consulted."

His people were slaves of the Gogols, and when someone objected their masters were asked for their opinion on the topic! Incredible. Yet it should have been predicted. He was so unlike his brothers. Perhaps he was indeed mad. Castor waved his hands in inexpressible frustration.

"I must admit that I had not considered that possibility," he said at last. "Naturally the Gogols were not pleased with my suggestions."

"Naturally not."

"Well, then, now that they are alerted, all the more reason for us to flee. Come, Obron; surely you must see that. You are the soul of the Ajaj—the average, the stereotype, the representative of our common hopes and desires.

Surely the random factor would not have chosen you if you did not feel what must be felt and see what must be seen."

"Castor, I feel that it is you who are out of step, not I. You know the Ajaj way: retreat from danger, accept our lot, protect ourselves, and bend with destiny. Here we are safe and secure. Our duties to the Gogols are not overly burdensome, and they offer protection against marauding bandits and rapacious animals."

"We could handle the bandits more easily than we can control the Gogols," Castor replied. "This is Fane. Here there are few beasts to threaten us, no slavers to drag us to some far star. The Gogols provide nothing that we could not provide for ourselves. Each year their service becomes more demanding, their lusts and perversions more repellent."

"No, Castor. Our duty is to protect the race, the tribe, the Ajaj. I've cast the stones five times, and each time they have picked a different member of our company. To each of these I have put your suggestions. Your ideas have been unanimously rejected. The random factor has not failed. We are all of the decision that we will neither fight nor flee. You, of course, may do as you wish, but I warn you that we cannot intercede on your behalf should the Gogols call you to task for your statements."

"I must do what I must do."

"We all do what we must do. Still I am duty bound to beg you to cease your arguments. Already Rupert, assistant to the great Hazar, has demanded that you be taken in hand. There is no doubt that if you fail to change your ways Rupert will have your life. If you continue the rest of us will not, cannot, intercede on your behalf."

Castor arose stiffly and nodded in Obron's direction. The day was waning. The room's diffused orange light turned his silver-gray fur to charcoal black. Castor slid from the room while Obron shook her head in silent despair.

Four hundred yards farther up the hill Rupert also shook himself as he broke from his trance. A shiver passed through his body as he opened his eyes. Below, he could see Castor making his way back up the hill to his apartment. Clearly the insolent creature had to be dealt with.

Rupert fingered the knife at his belt. It could be over in five minutes—but no, Hazar had commanded otherwise. Hazar was a man whose orders one did not defy.

Rupert wrapped his cloak more tightly and resigned himself to an all-night vigil. The required spell took time and patience. Throughout the night he would build a field of energy around the Ajaj. With the dawn he would lead him forth from his apartment, center him on a sun-warmed rock, and then, with the final syllable of the spell, explode his body like a rotten gourd.

Chapter Seven

A dirt trail split the lawn and led to the village two leagues away. Grantin hummed as he walked. The air was filled with the scent of growing plants and a faint hint of woodsmoke from the luncheon fires.

Ahead the trail zigzagged through a farmer's meadow in order to take advantage of a small area of infertile ground. Off to the left stood the farmer, engaged in the traditional rites preparatory to planting his next crop. Above his head he held a diamond-shaped piece of heavy metal wire. One prong projected from the upper apex of the wire, curling and ending in a hook. This contrivance was clenched in his right fist while with his left hand he moved his index finger in a slow counterclockwise motion. His lips chanted the ancient words. With his eyes closed he began to walk forward, legs moving of their own accord in an apparently erratic pattern. Mounted on the farmer's back was a sack of chalk. A hose ran from the bag and down his left leg, terminating in the hollow heel of his boot.

As the farmer walked the chalk recorded the pattern of his movements. At the conclusion of the trance there would exist an outline of the most fertile area in which to plant the seed.

Knowing that a greeting would only startle the farmer and force him to begin again, Grantin maintained his silence and went on. At half past the seventh hour he neared the edge of the village which straddled the River Out. A community of some one thousand people, it maintained a full complement of servitors, magicians, factorers, artisans, scribblers, and even three warriors who functioned as the town police.

The buildings on the outskirts of Alicon seemed, at first glance, haphazardly set upon their foundations. This appearance derived from the fact that the structures were sited by members of a subclass of the Wizards' Guild known variously as builders, structors, or tectors according to their skill. Each construct was located, designed, built, and adorned according to plans derived through secret guild spells. Grantin knew that by and by the open spaces between the buildings would be filled with structures of a suitable construction and shape.

Occasionally one saw vacant fields of the most peculiar proportions, filled with flowers and wild grasses, in an otherwise densely populated portion of a town. Now and then hardheads would decide that this was pure waste. Sometimes they sought to appropriate these lots and build their own edifices. Invariably the structures toppled, sometimes with great loss of life. Usually the catastrophe was due to inherent weakness of the soil, latent quicksand, or the sudden appearance of geysers and springs. While a few disgruntled people occasionally claimed that these disasters were precipitated not by natural forces but by the wizardry of the Structors' Guild as punishment for disobeying their edicts, most of the populace, being reasonable and intelligent citizens, ignored the charges.

When Grantin passed the first few such isolated structures he remembered his uncle's command to wear the amulet about his neck. He had taken to carrying his coat draped over his left arm, and now he reached into the pocket. His fingers touched only air, leather, and tiny clumps of lint. The amulet was gone!

Grantin looked up with a start, his face pale, his body suddenly as hollow as a dried gourd. He whirled and studied the ground. There was no sign of the necklace.

Grantin raised his eyes, trying to decide what to do next. At his left was a building two stories tall, the first floor of stone, the second of wood. Grantin chanced to read the emblem which hung above the doorway. It said:

HOUSE OF GUILDLESS LABORERS

Below the sign, tacked to the post at the left-hand edge of the portal, was a printed notice:

Today's Availables:

Beet Pullers and Potato Diggers (3 male & healthy)
Moderate Quality Young Virgin (slightly used)
Apprentice Clown

Positions Open:

Journeyman Cartdrivers (2 needed)
Advanced Barkscraper (experienced help only)
Toothbuilder (1—will train to suit)

With a sick feeling in his belly Grantin recalled Greyhorn's evaluation of his abilities. If he didn't find the amulet, here lay his future: apprentice toothbuilder—trained to suit.

With his left hand Grantin held the coat in front of him while he searched the garment. Hadn't he put the amulet in his right-hand pocket? But now that one lay slack and empty. But wait, the coat was facing him! He had checked the left pocket!

Grantin thrust his fist into the left-hand pocket as the coat faced him. There, at the bottom, tangled with the lining, lay Greyhorn's necklace. With a great exhalation of breath, knees weak and shaking, arms limp, Grantin removed the amulet, checked the clasp, then placed it solidly around his neck.

Ahead the road continued straight for a hundred yards, then began a series of zigs and zags all according to the dictates of the tectors. Occasionally, at apparently random points, side streets joined the main highway. By the time Grantin reached the Hall of Fabricators, no open spaces were left on either side.

41

Some of the structures were tall and narrow, others low and wide. An odd mixture of shapes assailed the eye: conical buildings with exterior spiral staircases, squat cubes whose ceilings towered some thirty feet above their floors; a confusion of materials and styles was presented. The left third of a structure might be of wood and brick, the center of quarried stone, and the right-hand edge white stucco with timbered beams.

A peculiar mingling of odors penetrated Grantin's nostrils: scents from the perfumers, from the inns the fragrance of honey and spice and boiling gruel, and occasional whiffs of the garbage pits at the far end of town, all intermixed with the underlying stench of the leavings of the carthorses and the occasional unmannered dog.

Now, past the eighth hour, dinnertime was approaching. The villagers were making a last attempt at completing their business before supper. The road ballooned unpredictably, forming areas where merchants, fabricators, and artisans had set up stalls. A yard or two ahead it narrowed to but a few feet in width, then swelled again. Looking down on it from above, one would have imagined a tangled stretch of beads on a string.

These widenings in the highway formed the many specialized markets of the city. The narrow paths between allowed the constabulary to keep close watch on all who patronized Alicon's businesses. Footpads had little chance of threading their way through the narrow sections of the road. Such men would find short shrift with the sturdy citizens of Alicon. Were they captured, at best they would complete their lives less the tips of their noses and the lobes of both ears; at worst their organs would make a fine contribution to the sawbones' always understocked apothecary.

Just beyond the Hall of the Fabricators the Street of the Artisans cut away from the main road. The new avenue formed a round, bulging loop which rejoined the highway a hundred yards ahead.

Grantin turned to his left, elbowed through the crowded passage, then entered the first of the artisans' alcoves. Here stood the stalls of the leatherworkers. Belts, coin purses, coats, and saddlery abounded. Toward the end of the cul-du-sac stood the wares of a small subgroup of the guild, the taxidermists. Here were displayed stuffed dogs, boars, and occasionally a well-established citizen's favorite relative.

At one of these booths Grantin chanced to pause and examine the handiwork of a master craftsman. Grantin's eyes were arrested by a small, spindly, mean-faced, squinty-eyed old man who stood in a menacing position. Lank, stringy, oily black hair drooped down either side of the long, narrow head. The mop framed a sallow face from which protruded a thin, beaklike nose and a pointed, outthrust jaw. The eyes were narrow and stared menacingly ahead. The figure's right hand was raised, index finger pointed forward, as though the old man had been frozen in the midst of a vengeful, bitter threat.

So menacing and clearly evil was the creature that Grantin pulled the finger and pinched the cheek to assure himself that the villain was indeed dead.

"A true work of art, is he not, sir?" the taxidermist whispered in Grantin's ear.

Grantin jumped back, startled, then relaxed as his eyes focused on the artisan.

"For a fact he does seem most unusual," Grantin allowed. "Is there much of a market for items such as this?"

"Oh, yes, sir, to be sure. A rare find is old Theleb. Notice the narrow, beady eyes, the blackened teeth, the thin-lipped, leering smile, the hand caught the instant before the fingers clench, then open again to fling poison into the face of his enemy. Oh, yes, indeed, Theleb would make a fine addition to any manor house. Why, equipped with a simple spell from almost any medium-grade wizard, his presence would keep away poachers, trespassers, burglars, footpads, mendicants, and tax collectors. And for you, sir, whom I see to be a man of rare discernment and high standards, I would be willing to part with Theleb for the price of a mere two golds and four silvers."

"Two golds and four silvers for this stuffed old reprobate!" Grantin replied in amazement.

"Why, sir, in the first year alone Theleb would save you that much in flowers trampled by ill-mannered children. Surely you recognize a bargain such as this when you see it."

"That vile-smelling old heathen isn't worth a—"

Grantin snapped shut his mouth. The blue eyes seemed

to hold an even more malevolent cast. Had Grantin noticed a slight twitch at the corner of the mouth? And was it not the index finger which formerly had been pointed outward?

"Careful, sir; I am a true craftsman if I do say so myself. Much magic is wrapped up in my creations. Though he may be dead, Theleb is still a sensitive man and sometimes given to extremes of conduct."

"Perhaps you are right. On second thought Theleb is probably worth every iron of two golds and four silvers, perhaps more. Alas, I have but a few coppers in my pocket, and those reserved for a modest dinner."

"Well, sir, don't let that stop you. Never let it be said that Adolf the taxidermist was a difficult man with whom to deal. I see you wear a crude, but somewhat interesting, amulet. I might be induced to trade Theleb for the necklace and five silvers, the coin to be paid one year from today. Further, if you are not satisfied at the end of that time, you may return Theleb for a full refund."

"Ah, Master Adolf, you do present a tempting offer. Unfortunately my castle is not nearly grand enough to warrant such an imposing figure. In fact, if the truth be known, the roof leaks, and the fine old fellow would no doubt be drenched in the first rain."

"Sir, you do yourself an injustice. I am sure that your manor would do honor to my creation. If the only thing that stands between us and the bargain is the five silvers at the end of the year, why, then, forget them. Let no man say that Adolf is not magnanimous with his art. Here, take Theleb in fair exchange, an even trade across the board for your amulet. Merely throw the old gentleman across your shoulders and take him home. To show my true colors, should he mildew, stain, or rot at any time during the next ten months, I will take him back and happily give you a full credit of two golds in satisfaction of your purchase price."

"Adolf, you make a tempting offer. Theleb might well serve as a grand adjunct to my poor home. I am almost of a mind to accept your proposal. Let me do this: I will go through yonder passageway and relax myself with a cup of wine and, perhaps, a hot sausage or two. When I am refreshed and unburdened, like as not I will return and accept your kind offer."

So saying, Grantin smiled at Adolf, curtly nodded in Theleb's direction, and then, vowing to exit the Street of the Artisans without again passing the taxidermist's shop, pushed onward into the next marketplace.

This new bulge in the street was filled with the stalls of the potterymakers and stonemasons. Not merely purveyors of goblets, cups, and plates, the members of this guild made anything and everything which might be constructed of clay or stone. Grantin saw not only household crockery and decorative statues but also pendants, rings, bookends, tiles, and simple mechanical parts.

One by one Grantin traversed the markets of the Street of the Artisans. He passed through the shops of the glassblowers, toymakers, painters, and scribblers. By half past the ninth hour he was tired, footsore, and hungry. Ahead of him still lay the metalworkers, jewelrymakers, clothiers, weavers, rugmakers, cartographers, and woodcarvers.

On one side of the glassblowers' market reposed three food stalls and a modest, though appealing, tavern. A few chairs and tables had been set beneath a great awning in front of the public house. Serving the diners was a young woman, nicely rounded in all the proper places. At one table she set out a jug of frosty purple-black wine.

Grantin detected a dry, rasping ache in his throat. No doubt the dust from the market also had found a home in the lining of his nose. Yes, there was no question that Grantin needed a tonic to refresh himself. Perhaps also a bite to eat would be helpful before completing his uncle's errand.

Grantin edged through the crowd and found himself a comfortable seat beneath the tavern's striped awning. Behind him at the far end of the dining area, the serving girl joked with one of Alicon's substantial citizens. She turned to reenter the building. A moment later another female came to the patio and headed for Grantin's table.

This new waitress was far different from the first. Her face was square and solid. A wart adorned her right cheek an inch below her eye. Her bust was flat, her hips wide, her legs like the stumps of two trees. The woman's age was indeterminate, somewhere on the far side of thirty-five but not so old as fifty.

"You wanted something?" she asked Grantin in an almost accusatory tone.

"A cup of throttleberry wine and perhaps some dinner if your menu is to my pleasure. What do you have to offer?"

In half an instant the waitress had appraised Grantin's form, clothing, and demeanor. She replied in a flat tone: "Hot fried gruel and salt crackers."

"Gruel is not to my taste. If that's all you have perhaps I should seek dinner elsewhere."

"We also have sliced steak cooked in wine with boiled tubers and peas, but such a meal comes dear, four coppers—plus tip. On the other hand, for merely an extra iron we could add some of the trimmings from the roast to the gruel."

"How dare you suggest that I appear to be a man who could afford only gruel! I'll have the meat and all the trimmings, and don't forget my throttleberry wine. Be quick about it or there'll be no tip!"

The waitress anxiously nodded her head. Perhaps thinking of her tip, she even gave Grantin a slight curtsy which caused her ear-length black ringlets to bounce like corroded springs.

Now the sun was nearing the horizon. Its rays shifted from gold to a deep orange red. By some trick of perception, the shadows appeared tinted in shades of bluish green. The air was filled with the scents from the food booths. Around Grantin swirled the fragrance of good eating and vast comfort.

The waitress, one Flourice by name, soon returned with a clear crystal goblet of plum-colored wine. Grantin examined the rays of the dying sun through the fluid, then treated himself to a healthy swallow. Bittersweet, with a sharp, full, fruity flavor, it slid down his throat in thin, burning rivulets. In its wake the wine left the spicy warmness for which it was so renowned.

Grantin finished the beverage just as the innkeeper ignited the torches which surrounded the patio. New sounds now textured the twilight—the sputtering snap of the flames, the sizzles and tiny squeals of the night moths who flung themselves into the fires, there to be incinerated and fall to the earth in broiled husks. At the end of the evening, Grantin knew the innkeeper would salvage mounds of the little bodies and add them to his larder as a protein enricher and extender for the gruel.

Grantin turned back to the steaming sliced steak and side dishes which Flourice had now set before him. He popped a small morsel into his mouth. It was excellent— hot, rich, juicy, and full-bodied. Grantin reached for his goblet and, to his dismay, found it empty. Detecting Flourice at a table a few feet away, he waved his hand, then pointed to his glass. In a moment she set another portion of wine to hand.

Four coppers for the dinner, two more for the wine, perhaps one more for Flourice herself . . . but what matter, he had more than that in his pouch. Where would he sleep that night? A worry for a later time. No doubt something suitable would suggest itself.

Grantin speared another forkful of meat, washed it down with a heavy swallow of the tart, sweet wine, and reflected that his life was not so unpleasant after all.

Chapter Eight

Though Pyra had long since fled the sky Castor still sat at his window gazing at the moon-tinted rocks below. An unseen ghost-storm was building, gathering its energies like a dirty psychic wind. Castor could feel its power barely held in check. The forces derived from the Gogol city of Cicero half a league away. If something were not done, and soon, the maelstrom would sweep up everyone, humans and Ajaj like. What could he, one lone Ajaj, do to prevent the catastrophe?

Reluctantly he rose, swung the window grate into place, fastened it, then pushed the granite slab across the narrow door. He set out his warning bells and pronounced his spell of protection. Convinced that all was secure, he crawled into his sleep niche and slid closed the curtain.

Castor lay on his back, hands crossed at his shoulders where they could be quickly moved to guard his throat in case of attack. Tonight, sleep eluded him. Perhaps it was tension brought on by the decision maker's warning. The fur along his neck rippled as if to a static field. Castor twisted uneasily on his thin mattress. His arms and legs distracted him with sudden itches. With conscious effort he ceased his movements and willed his breathing back to a regular steady beat.

At last a heavy suffocating sleep seemed ready to descend. Castor welcomed it, concentrating his attention on counting the purple-black star bursts which sparkled in the gloom of his inner eye.

Involuntarily he watched these flickerings. Almost against his will, he strained his pupils to focus upon their shape and distance. What were these strange lights within his brain? His body now heavy and constricted, Castor kept alive a spark of consciousness for the sole purpose of pondering that question. With a start the answer came to him. The itches, the tingles, the chills, the points of light behind his lids could have but one explanation: he was the victim of a powerful and deadly spell.

Fighting silken bonds, Castor struggled back to a state of full awareness. With great effort he found that he could still move his arms and legs, although they felt as if they were made of lead. He rolled to his left and tumbled from his sleeping niche in an ungainly sprawl. He lay on the stone floor for a moment, then, gathering his strength, struggled to his feet. Using the wall for support, moving only a few inches at a time, Castor managed to reach his strongbox, set beneath the flagstones of his parlor chamber.

For ten minutes his clumsy, blunt-edged fingers struggled with the inlaid bits of stone until at last the key piece came loose. Awkwardly Castor pulled up the metal box, mumbled his spell of release, and opened the lid.

Inside were his papers of heritage listing all of his ancestors back to the founding of Fane and beyond. Beneath them lay two golds, six silvers, and three coppers, his entire life's savings; a prayer band set away against such time as he might form his triad and conceive an heir; and lastly, in a carved wooden box on a pillow of satin and silk a round-cornered cube of milky, green-hued emerald.

This was his source stone, his inheritance, passed down from generation to generation of master empathers, the gem originally having been found, cut, and blessed by his remote ancestor Marmet, a crewman on the *Lillith* and an original slave of Gogol himself.

Castor clasped his hands together, the stone in the hollows of his palms. He felt the psychic warmth spread through his hands.

This was the source stone, the concentrator and amplifier of those energies normally controlled by the mind alone. Its particular shape, color, and lattice structure when brought into contact with Ajaj flesh enormously increased the user's ability to use the power of Fane.

Now Castor squatted on his parlor floor, legs tucked beneath him, hands joined in front of him as if in prayer. He concentrated his attention first on freeing his body from the immediate effects of the spell. In a few minutes the power of the stone enveloped him. Urging his consciousness through the lattice of the gem, he reached outward in ever increasing circles until he located the source of the hex that sought to envelop him.

Castor detected the huddled, chanting figure of the Gogol assassin on the ridge above the Ajaj city.

Emboldened by the power of the stone, he focused all his energies upon Rupert's form. In spite of the chill night air sweat had begun to bead the killer's forehead. Tendons strained in his arms, wrists, and legs. Clearly Rupert was aware that his power was insufficient to achieve his goal.

As long as Castor held the stone he would be safe, but how long could he do so? A few hours? Perhaps a day or two? Even if he survived he could not spend his days in hiding with the stone always within easy reach. If nothing else it was dangerous to experience too long a contact with the gem. Its powers were great. Like fire it could burn as well as warm.

Perhaps a fast and sudden bolt of energy at the base of Rupert's skull or the muscles of his heart. Quick death and another deacon of evil down the well. Castor steeled himself to form the killing bolt, but in vain. His teachings were too strong, his empathy with life too great. He could not take a life, even one as corrupted as Rupert's. Instead he constructed a softer blow, one which would stun the sweating Gogol but no more.

From his crevice Rupert struggled, calling forth every particle of energy which his skill could attract, but all his talents were unable to breach the shield which had suddenly enclosed his victim. Rupert readied himself for another straining attack but was unable to complete his chant. Without warning a numbing daze overtook his mind, and he fell over like a stone.

With great care Castor assured himself that the assassin was truly unconscious. He then replaced the source stone, secreted all his treasures, and unbarred his door.

Navigation was easy by the light of Dolos's full moon. He retraced his steps to the decision maker's home. It took several minutes for his calls and raps to bring a response from within.

"Who is it? Who calls at this time of night?"

"It's Castor on an urgent mission. I must speak with Obron at once."

"It's late; come back in the morning."

"This will not wait until morning. There's a Gogol killer in the hills above our homes."

A moment later a scrape of stone signaled the opening of Obron's door. Castor entered. Behind him the stone returned to its place. Obron and the other two members of her triad stood on the far side of the room, backs against the wall, a glowpod in each left hand and a knife, a spear, or a club in each right.

When the light was sufficient for Obron to make out Castor's features, the weapons were lowered and the decision maker came forward to greet her guest.

"Castor, I thought that we had finished the matter of the Gogols. What has happened to make you shake us from our beds at this time of night?"

"It appears, Obron, that your warning was most accurate. Tonight as I prepared for sleep a Gogol spell enveloped me. It was only with the greatest effort that I was able to overcome the assassin. For the time being he sleeps in a cleft at the top of the ridge. By the second hour he will awaken. A decision must be made before then."

"Castor, you put us all in a most unfortunate position. You offend our masters, and even when requested by your own brethren to cease these efforts still you persist. Now, having brought down the vengeance of our lords, you come to me for advice."

"Not advice, Obron. I do you the courtesy of telling you what is taking place. As for solutions, there are at least three.

"One, I can continue in the future as I have in the past,

kill the Gogols who attack me and, sooner or later, die at their hands—"

"And bring ruin to all of us in the bargain," Obron interrupted.

"To continue: secondly, I could dispose of the assassin who haunts me and flee to the east, seeking sanctuary with the Hartfords across the mountains."

"And again bring ruin on your brothers, for we all know the penalty which will be exacted against us if even one of us is so impolite as to shirk his duty to our masters and leave the village without their permission."

"Thirdly," Castor continued, "I can retract all that I have said, keep my protective spell strong, and at the same time admit the error of my ways. In this way the village, and perhaps even I myself, will be spared the ultimate penalty for disobedience.

"Before you offer your suggestions let me tell you that I have decided to take the third path. I hereby, now and formally, retract my suggestion that we should rise up as a group against the Gogols. It was foolish advice; none of us is skilled at war. Besides, I now realize that none of my fellows would stand with me."

"And . . ." Obron prompted.

"And I hereby agree to make no further statements with regard to our masters. Again, it would be a waste of time and wind. Further, I authorize and request that you consult with this assassin when he awakes and tell him the news of my recantation and promises of good behavior."

"On the surface, Castor, your words are proper and correct. They warm my heart; yet, for some reason, they seem to contain a chill of obstinacy and sarcasm. You will obey your promises to the letter, of that I am sure. But I sense that your mind is in ferment, teeming with other plans against which you have made no oath. No, tell me nothing further—I do not want to know. I wish you fortune and health in whatever you do, but I warn you to be careful, for neither I nor any of your fellows are strong enough to stand between you and your fate."

At the conclusion of Obron's statement Castor bent his head, lower than a nod but not so deep as a bow, an implied admission of the truth of Obron's prediction. Castor turned on his heel, bent low upon entering the passage, and picked his way back to his own apartment.

Chapter Nine

In the narrow streets of Alicon the night took on a murky complexion. Orange torches flickered here and there but gave off little light. In the randomly situated swellings of the road the thin pink light of Fane's first moon, Dolos, tinted the earth. The second moon, Minos, would rise full and pale yellow in another hour or two.

Grantin now wandered the streets somewhat at loose ends. After a few less than subtle hints from first Flourice and then, later, the tavern keeper himself, he had settled his score and left the comfort of the tavern's patio. In payment he had been required to give Flourice the silver entrusted to him by his uncle. A moment later she returned with four coppers in change. In recompense for her somewhat haughty attitude Grantin would have been satisfied to leave a tip of five or six irons, but he had none in his purse. Flourice's insistent glare deterred him from asking for change. He left one copper on the tray and dropped the other three into his purse. Now the change from the silver, together with the two coppers given him by Greyhorn, left Grantin with a total of five.

Coincidentally Greyhorn had instructed him to pay five

coppers for the ring which he had been sent to fetch. Well, perhaps by reason of the force of his personality, some spirited haggling, the exercise of his enormous powers of perception and persuasion, Grantin supposed that he might convince the fellow to let him have the ring for less. And if not, well, he could always give the messenger a copper or two as a down payment and return later with the additional money.

Unfortunately Grantin had no other money. Could Greyhorn be persuaded to advance the rest? After all, it was Greyhorn's ring. No, that was not a good idea. The silver and two coppers also had been Greyhorn's. He might be a bit perturbed to find that Grantin had spent them on steak and wine and lodgings, leaving his errand unperformed.

In the past Greyhorn had displayed unpleasant habits when angered. In such situations he often gave free rein to his darker proclivities. Grantin, in particular, remembered the unfortunate gardener who had foolishly cut down Greyhorn's dragonthistles, mistaking them for weeds. The last time Grantin had seen the fellow, in place of hair there protruded from the gardener's head four clumps of dandelions.

Grantin decided it was definitely a bad idea to return home lacking both the money and the ring. But if the ring cost five coppers and Grantin only had five coppers, then that left no coppers for a bed tonight or breakfast tomorrow. Clearly a disagreeable situation all the way around.

Ahead of Grantin and to his left flamed two torches marking the entrance to one of Alicon's three hostelries. The inns, named in order of their comfort, were the Weary Traveler's Rest, the Savoy, and Master Percival's Renowned Out Inn. The sign between the torches proclaimed this to be the Savoy. Grantin went inside.

"Good evening, sir. What is your pleasure?" the innkeeper's wife asked him.

"One of your excellent rooms for the evening, if you please," Grantin replied politely.

"Of course, sir. We have one available on the second floor overlooking the river. Only last week we fitted it with a new mattress and pillow."

"Just the thing. I'll take it."

"That will be three coppers and five irons, sir, in advance."

"Naturally I understand your very reasonable precautions, but in this case they are unnecessary. I am Grantin, nephew of the great wizard Greyhorn, whose magnificent manor house lies a mere two leagues down the road. Through an unfortunate set of circumstances I find myself forced to remain in town this evening instead of returning to my own luxurious quarters. This being all unplanned, I naturally am a bit short of ready cash; but fear not, there is no problem. I am here on business for my uncle and I assure you that as soon as I complete it I will fetch your coppers and return . . ."

In the midst of Grantin's statement the innkeeper's wife began shaking her head. Now, unable to hold her peace any longer, she interrupted him.

"No credit."

"But my uncle—"

"No credit. That is our policy, as unalterable as the mountains and the seas. If Amis Hartford himself were to appear here this evening he would have to pay cash like the rest or sleep in the street."

"Perhaps some job—a minor service—a task or two? . . . Can't you do anything but shake your head? All right. All right, I'll take my trade elsewhere."

In a fit of pique Grantin strode across the small lobby and outside. A breeze ruffled his hair. In the distance, to his right, a Rex lizard cried. There lay the livery stables of his uncle's nemesis—Dobbs, the town's current mayor.

At dawn the next morning Grantin dreamed that he was being attacked by two men armed with knives. Unmercifully they stabbed his tender body. Grantin awoke with a start to discover the triple prongs of a stableman's pitchfork rhythmically puncturing the seat of his pants. Grantin leapt up, grasped his neck to make sure the amulet was still in place, then raced from the stable, only a foot or two in front of Dobbs's fork.

Five minutes later Grantin was still shaking straw from his hair and dust from his ears. Alicon began to awaken. Again the odor of food rode delightfully on the breeze. This morning Grantin was so hungry that he would even settle for gruel. In his right pocket his fingers nervously sifted several handfuls of oats which he had borrowed from Dobbs's supply.

Well Water was available at the pump in the square Soon the Street of the Artisans would be open for business. Undoubtedly among the stalls reposed the booth of an ironmaker who possessed a copious supply of pots. Certainly among so many implements one of them would have an odd color, texture, or trace of scale. One did.

"This pot seems odd," Grantin told the artisan. "I have in my purse five coppers, but I don't wish to buy something which will make the food taste strange."

"There's nothing wrong with my pot " the ironmonger exclaimed. "It's the equal of any other pot in the whole town, probably better."

"Perhaps, perhaps; but what if I take it home and cook my lunch only to find the food has an unusual flavor? I might even get sick and die."

"This is all nonsense. Here, take it and try it for yourself. Old Rasco across the way has a nice fire going. Tell him I sent you. Take the pot and cook your breakfast with it."

"Well, I hadn't planned on having porridge. I usually dine at the inn. Coincidentally, however, I do have a few oats in my pocket left over from feeding my Rex. Understandably I wouldn't normally eat that sort of thing myself. Over in the corner, however, you seem to have a bit of dried meat. Perhaps a small fragment or two to season the oats and I would be able to solve once and for all the questions of the healthfulness of your wares."

"There is no question as of healthfulness of my pots! How dare you even suggest such a thing?"

"Well, you know how rumors are. . . ."

"Here! Here! Take the meat and a handful of wheat, too. No rumormonger will sully my reputation!"

Oh, well, gruel did have its advantages. It filled the belly and eased the mind. After breakfast and a nice nap in the warm morning sun Grantin would be ready to locate the accursed ring. In a few hours he would be home for lunch.

Grantin seemed to have barely reclined in the lush bluegreen grass when something awakened him. Groggily he lifted his head. As he was massaging the back of his neck a loud bong sounded from the tower across the square—the village clock marking the second hour. So late already?

Grantin stretched his arms and came to his feet. Around him the industrious citizens of Alicon bustled about their affairs. Again Grantin ambled back to the Street of the Artisans.

For half an hour Grantin strolled through the shops and booths, Greyhorn's amulet on prominent display. Standing in front of the silverworkers' arcade, he sensed that he was being studied. To his right stood a middle-aged, brown-haired peasant. Wearing neutral clothing and of an undistinguished guild, the fellow seemed to be peering at Grantin from the corners of his eyes. Could this be the contact? Best that he acquire the accursed ring and be gone. Grantin wandered next to the man and pretended to examine the rings in the silversmith's tray.

"Lovely workmanship," Grantin suggested.

"Yes, absolutely first rate," the man replied, turning toward Grantin. The peasant's eyes drifted toward the amulet and then, self-consciously, lifted to Grantin's face. "That's an interesting bit of workmanship you've got there," the man said, nodding at the pendant dangling from Grantin's neck.

"Yes, it's been in our family a long time," Grantin replied. Now was the time for the fellow to mention the ring.

Instead of giving the code, however, the man stood silent and nervous, apparently unsure how to proceed. The peasant's odd behavior, coupled with the appearance of a more attractive customer, caused Grantin to rapidly lose interest in the conversation. Behind the stranger Grantin spied a lovely young woman who now looked frankly in his direction.

Dressed all in black velvet, she had tawny hair that flowed in waves down below her shoulders. Her face was strong; her eyes sparkled with golden fire. Beneath the soft folds of her gown twin swellings of a voluptuous figure were apparent.

". . . I said, would you like to sell it?" the man asked.

"What was that again?" Grantin asked.

"Your amulet—would you like to sell it?"

"No, it's not for sale. Excuse me; I think I see a new friend." Grantin approached the girl.

"Miranda, it's so good to see you again," he began. "It must have been——"

"You have mistaken me for someone else," the girl replied sternly.

"Someone else? I don't see how. . . ."

"My name is Mara, not Miranda," she continued in a businesslike tone. "That certainly is an interesting amulet you are wearing."

The cursed necklace again! Why did he bother showing his face at all? He might as well wear a sack and twirl the pendant over his head on a string.

"A mere trifle, not nearly so pretty as you. You live around here——"

"The gem in the amulet is very unusual," Mara interrupted, as though she had not heard a word Grantin had said. Did she seem the slightest bit afraid? Could such a lovely and self-assured creature be insecure? Never; Grantin would not allow such a thing.

"I . . ."

Mara grasped Grantin's left arm. She pulled him to the corner of the booth. Taking a deep breath, seeming almost as if she were speaking against her will, Mara continued in a throaty whisper.

"The stone in my ring seems to be the same kind as in your pendant."

From a slit in the side of her robe the girl removed a golden-yellow metal ring inset with an oval, blood-red stone. She was careful not to touch the band with her bare flesh; instead she held it wrapped in a bit of velvet.

Gratin stared at the object, transfixed by the highlights glimmering from its surface. Mara watched him expectantly. After a moment she prompted:

"Your family has had the amulet a long time?"

Oh, the code, the silly code.

"Yes, my father had a ring that was so," he recited, feeling foolish.

"Then you should have this to complete the family treasure," Mara volunteered. "I will sell it to you for five coppers."

Grantin removed the coins and placed them in Mara's outstretched hand. When his fingers brushed her palm he felt an almost electric tingle.

Ignoring the black velvet upon which it rested, Grantin

picked up the band. Fearing that he might lose it if he merely dropped it into his purse, he slipped the bauble over the index finger of his left hand.

For a moment or two Grantin concentrated on adjusting the ring so that the stone might be displayed to its best advantage. With his eyes averted he failed to see a look of astonished fear wash across Mara's face.

This couldn't be the lackey whom Hazar had ordered her to beguile. Only the most powerful of wizards would dare place a bloodstone in contact with his flesh. In only a few minutes Grantin's sweat would penetrate the metal and the ring would be bonded to his finger forever. Obviously the wizard must have distrusted all his cronies and decided to come himself.

So this was the great Greyhorn. What an excellent disguise he had chosen. He looked just like a moderately attractive but soft, lazy, and ineffectual youth. And to think that she had almost been so foolish as to attempt to enchant him with a simple spell. That would have been disaster indeed.

I've done as much as I can, Mara told herself, and was possessed of an overwhelming desire to flee. She turned her back on Grantin, breathed a sign of relief, and walked out into the Street of the Artisans.

"Wait! Just a moment—there's no need to hurry off!" Grantin shouted. He sprinted up to Mara's side. She ignored him and continued her brisk pace to the end of the lane.

"Our business is done," she said without turning.

"We may have new business. You're an absolutely enchanting woman. I'm sure that we have many things in common."

"You have your mission, wizard, and I have mine. My job is completed. I have a long way to go. Surely you realize that I am but a small part of this plan. Besides, we both know it is not good for such as us to become involved with each other."

"Such as us? What do you mean?" Grantin trotted now to keep up with the girl's pace. He ran beside her with his head turned so that he might catch yet another glimpse of her lovely features. Suddenly he collided with an old woman who had been carrying a sack of meal. Both went sprawling into the street. Amid curses and demands for payment for the spilled grain Grantin struggled to his feet. Even as he managed to stand he saw that Mara had disappeared.

Unconsciously he looked down at the ring. He fingered the band and sought to adjust it a little higher on his finger but was unsuccessful. For some reason the metal seemed welded to his flesh. Grantin strained, but despite his efforts the ring would not come off.

Chapter Ten

Seedbirds trilled their undulating call. Hopping from branch to branch, they followed Grantin's progress on the trail below. The beauty of the day had lost its edge. In his mouth was the subtle taste of ashes. Pyra's rays no longer dappled the grass with warm ale-colored light. Instead, to Grantin the beams appeared as harsh orange blotches against a sickly pea-green lawn. The seedbirds' song became strident. The road itself seemed more than usually filled with rocks and roots.

Sweat dribbled down Grantin's brow and cheeks. One by one drops of perspiration leaked from his fingers and dripped to the road. He tried to dry his hands against his trousers but without success. The palms remained slippery and damp. Every few yards, almost by reflex action, he grasped the bloodstone with the tips of his fingers. Perspiration coated the band. Despite repeated attempts he was unable to obtain a firm purchase.

As Grantin labored up the hill toward the manor house a slight breeze swept across the trail. He shivered in the wind, as though it carried a penetrating chill. Perhaps he had caught some disease in Dobbs's stable. He cursed himself for his magnanimity in accepting Greyhorn's assignment without sufficient recompense. His generous nature had obviously played him false again. Nothing to be done for it now, however, except crawl into bed and sleep until the fever passed.

Grantin plodded on the last few feet, lifted the latch, and pushed back the massive front door. To his right, stone steps marched upward to the second floor. No mountain crag could have presented a more imposing sight. He doggedly attacked the stairs one by one. When he had climbed halfway up a voice called from the sitting room on the first floor below and beyond the stairs.

"Grantin, is that you? Come in here at once and bring me the ring!"

Grantin halted his ascent, panted, and leaned against the wall. His left hand waved feebly in an attempt to dissipate the subtle tingling which had begun to creep up the arm. Had the ring pinched off the flow of blood? In a fit of pique Grantin grasped the bauble and tried to wrench it from his finger. Instantly his arm numbed. Small white dots swam in blackness before his eyes. His left hand slipped unnoticed from his grip and dangled limply at his side. Kaleidoscopic fragments of color glittered in his mind.

Slowly his vision cleared. Again Greyhorn's summons echoed from below: "Grantin, stop dillydallying around! If you want to remain my factotum you must learn to perform your duties promptly. Now, come in here!"

Deciding that it was easier to go down than up, Grantin descended to the entranceway, then turned along the passage and into Greyhorn's parlor. The wizard sat in the center of the room, reclining in a massive leather chair, a tablet of paper and a stylus across his lap. As Grantin entered Greyhorn turned and stared at him peevishly. Sickly yellow light from the room's only window toned the tip of Greyhorn's nose, the jut of his chin, and the left half of his visage. In harsh contrast bluish-gray shadows filled the sockets of his eyes.

"So you decided to return at last, did you?"

"I . . ."

"No stories. Tell me just one thing: do you have the ring?"

"Yes, I . . ."

Grantin's answer caused the tenseness to leak a bit from Greyhorn's muscles. His features softened ever so slightly and he exhaled with a low whoosh, as if he had been holding his breath.

"Well, perhaps there is hope for you yet, Grantin. I confess no small degree of amazement that you've avoided making a botch of the whole thing. But you have the ring, you say?"

Grantin nodded his head vigorously. He opened his mouth to speak, but Greyhorn continued along with hardly a pause.

"No money left, I suppose?"

"No, you see . . ."

"Not surprising. I suppose one should not expect miracles. Well, we're just going to have to count that against your allowance. Very well; let's conclude the business." With surprising energy Greyhorn maneuvered his lanky frame out of the depths of the chair, turned sharply on his heel, and approached Grantin. He extended his right arm.

"Give me the ring."

Grantin shuffled his feet slightly, his earlier discomfort now all but forgotten.

"Come, come now, Grantin; I'm a busy man. I don't want to spend all day listening to your exploits in the village. A simple errand, a simple answer, a simple delivery of the object, and the matter is closed. Now, put the ring right here." Greyhorn tapped the center of his palm with his left index finger.

"Well, uncle, you see there is a problem with . . ."

"All right, Grantin; let's take this in order. Firstly, you met the courier?"

"Yes, but—"

"No buts, just answer my questions. You met the courier and she gave you the ring? True or false?"

"True."

"You brought the ring back here with you, correct?"

"Yes."

"You have the ring with you at this very instant, then?"

"Yes, I do."

"Then I see no difficulty. Just put the ring in my hand and get out."

"I can put the ring in your hand, uncle, but if I do so then I can't get out."

"Grantin, have you been drinking? You know how I feel about overindulgence. Here, let me smell your breath."

Grantin obligingly exhaled a large waft of air into his uncle's face. Greyhorn winced as he was enveloped in the remnants of the steak dinner, the throttleberry wine, oat gruel, and the fragrance of Dobbs's stable, but he could detect no present intoxication.

"Perhaps I expect too much of you. Could it be that you're not my nephew at all, just an addlebrained idiot who was slipped into the family over the back wall? Give me the ring!"

Grantin turned his head a bit left, then right, seeking to avoid his uncle's gaze. His fingers entwined themselves like a mass of hypertensive worms. Finally, with a shrug of resignation, he lifted his trembling arm and dropped his left hand into his uncle's waiting palm.

Greyhorn stared at the member for a moment, nonplused by Grantin's action. Then, in the dimness of the sitting room, he detected the scarlet gleam of the bloodstone and the deep golden highlights of the band where it sat fixed upon Grantin's finger.

"It . . . it won't come off," Grantin mumbled lamely as Greyhorn stared at the proffered digit.

As if in a daze, Greyhorn touched the ring and gently tried to slip it from Grantin's hand. It refused to budge.

"Uncle, I've tried everything I could think of, but it won't come off. With all the tugging and pulling I'm sure my finger has swelled. Perhaps if we waited a few days . . ."

"A few days!" Greyhorn yelped. "A few days! A FEW DAYS!" With a fierce surge of energy Greyhorn grabbed Grantin's wrist with his left hand and the ring with his right. He pulled with all his strength. So energetic was his attack that Grantin was jerked from his feet. Both men tumbled to the floor. Greyhorn rolled himself into a sitting position and commenced a new attack.

"*Give me my ring!*" he screamed. Greyhorn placed both his feet against Grantin's torso and with maniacal strength strained to pull off the bloodstone. Grantin's world exploded in electric pulses of color and waves of pain. His senses reeled; visions pulsed luridly in syncopation with the beating of his heart. With all his strength he willed himself free of Greyhorn's grasp.

Sometime later, perhaps a few seconds, perhaps minutes, the throbbing faded and the sitting room slipped back into focus from the multicolored fog. Grantin found himself sprawled on the floor, his back propped against the couch at one end of the room. Some twenty feet away, arms and legs knotted in an intricate tangle about the legs of his desk, Greyhorn lay, twitching feebly.

Grantin shook his head once, twice, to clear it of the vestiges of the disorientation which had descended upon him. Greyhorn's movements he now discerned to be more organized. Bit by bit his uncle disengaged himself from the desk.

"What happened?" Grantin wheezed.

Greyhorn staggered to his feet like a man possessed. In the dimness of the parlor his eyes seemed to glow. He advanced upon Grantin.

"Uncle, it wasn't my fault," Grantin pleaded. "I didn't do anything, really. Uncle, get hold of yourself, now. You don't want to do something that you'll regret later. Uncle, uncle . . ."

Cringing, Grantin raised his hands to protect his face, the ring pointed outward. As Greyhorn approached he noticed that the bloodstone seemed to glisten with a phosphorescent fire. The ring's bloody glimmer sent notes of alarm through the wizard's sinews. Mustering the last particle of his self-control, he managed to bring his body to a halt two feet from Grantin's cowering form. So great was the power of the bloodstone that further attempts to pry it from the finger would be suicidal. Greyhorn closed his eyes and wheezed ten long, deep breaths before allowing himself to speak.

"All right, Grantin," he said at last, "you can get up now. It's obvious that we're going to have to think our way out of this problem."

Hesitantly Grantin struggled to his feet.

"Don't worry, uncle; I'm sure that with perhaps some cold water and lots of soap we can get it off. If worse comes to worst, I can saw through the band and pry it away from my finger."

"The first blade that tries to scratch that ring will destroy itself and the arm that wields it. Perhaps, however, an appropriate elixir might, through the force of my power, insert itself between the ring and your flesh. Failing that, there are other, less tidy, but nevertheless dependable alternatives." A death's-head grin split Greyhorn's face as he contemplated the latter possibility.

"What do you mean, 'other alternatives'?"

"The possibility of a mild solution of liquefier cannot be overlooked. Skillful injections would rubberize the bones and joints of the affected digit. With a minimum tearing of flesh perhaps the item might be removed."

Grantin's face went slack and white.

"And, if that doesn't work, there is one final alternative which is guaranteed to solve the problem."

Grantin stared expectantly, now even afraid to breathe. Greyhorn caressed the knuckle and index finger and studied the ring.

"What alternative?" Grantin whispered.

"The answer is, of course, quite simple and direct. If we cannot remove the ring from the finger then we must remove the finger from the—"

With a shriek Grantin pulled back his hand and stumbled backward against the wall. "No, no . . . my finger . . . you can't—you wouldn't! There must be another way."

"Perhaps, perhaps; we shall see. Come; we will go up to the workroom. You can assist me in preparing the unguent. Who knows, it may work; and if not, what's one finger more or less?"

"But . . ." Grantin mumbled as Greyhorn paced toward the door.

"Come along, Grantin, come along. There's been too much dillydallying already. We'll try the unguent, but remember this: one way or another I mean to have that ring!"

Chapter Eleven

A steamy wisp of smoke curled from the beaker cupped between Greyhorn's skeletal hands. The thick gray-brown walls of the container hid the substance from Grantin's view, but judging from the stench which emanated from the flask the material was vile indeed. Grantin had been sprawled on a small stool, his legs widespread, elbows on knees and chin resting in his cupped palms; but now this latest of his uncle's concoctions brought him to a state of weary attention.

For the past three hours Greyhorn had subjected him to one horrid treatment after another. His hands had been soaked in solvent, encased in jelly; his finger poked, punctured, scratched, smeared, rubbed, chilled, and burned. Spells of amazing force had been hurled at him in Greyhorn's fevered attack upon the ring. But all to no avail. It still sat innocently upon his left hand and glittered and glowed in a most virginal appearance. In fact, it almost seemed to Grantin as though the bauble thrived upon the rigors to which it had been subjected.

Now it pulsed firmly in time with the beating of Grantin's heart. When he dared to look within the stone he thought he glimpsed shadowy images, fleeting visions of strange beings involved in disturbing acts. These phantoms became more substantial as Pyra slid from the sky. In that lazy time between twilight and full dark, scenes glowed with a life of their own and minute by minute became ever clearer and more frightening.

After all he had been through that afternoon, Grantin was surprised to find that Greyhorn's latest potion was still able to raise in him a new knot of fear.

"No, uncle, not again," Grantin whined.

"None of your complaints, Grantin; I don't like this any more than you do. It's all your own fault anyway. I'm the one who should be upset. Haven't I spent half the day trying to save your stupid finger? Haven't I exhausted myself with spells and incantations? Haven't I emptied my larder of supplies of many coppers in value all in your behalf? You should get down on your knees and thank me for my kindness and generosity in going to all this extra trouble in your behalf, so stop your whining!"

"Yes, uncle; but at least could you tell me what this one is supposed to do?"

"It's supposed to get the ring off your finger, idiot!" Greyhorn replied as he advanced an ominous step or two closer to Grantin's seated form. "Here, Grantin; hold this under your nose and breathe deeply, then hold your breath while I pronounce the spell."

Trembling, Grantin accepted the cup, but the stench was so vile that he held it at arm's length.

"I said breathe deeply. . . ."

"I know, uncle, but I could breathe deeply with greater peace of mind if I knew what this was supposed to do. Couldn't you just give me a little hint?"

"All right, if you're going to be a baby about it. This is a unique substance of my own devising, a combination of the sorrel stasis incantation and a soup of boiled mummy plant."

"Mummy plant! Isn't that the one they use to shrink corpses so that your loved ones can be carried in your pocket?"

"Full strength, yes, it is sometimes used for that purpose, but this is a much milder batch. A lungful of my compound will only reduce you to about four feet in height, three at the most. While you're shrinking I will pronounce a spell which will keep the ring the same size. Naturally, the finger of someone three or four feet tall is much smaller than that of someone six feet in height, and so if the ring remains the same size we should be able to remove it easily."

"Well, uncle, don't get me wrong. I'm not complaining, and of course I have complete faith in your abilities, but will you be able to expand me again once you've removed it?"

Greyhorn hesitated a moment before answering, then turned a somewhat distracted gaze to the ceiling. At last he replied in a roundabout fashion.

"Well, I suppose something or other could be done if you want to be picky about it. I'm sure that I can bring you back to more or less your previous size."

Grantin sucked in his breath, then, tasting the harsh fumes of the mummy plant, tried to halt his breathing, choked, and coughed. The spasm jerked Grantin's arms. The beaker slipped from his hands and crashed to the workroom's stone floor. As the liquid contacted the granite blocks it foamed and exuded a sudden cloud of dense white smoke. In an instant an acrid fog enveloped the room. Hacking and coughing, both at least half an inch shorter, Grantin and Greyhorn fled the laboratory.

Wheezing, the men staggered down the hall, finally coming to rest at the massive oval window at the end of the corridor. There they sucked in great drafts of cool air until, at last, the spasms subsided.

"Cursed . . . why am I cursed with the likes of you?" Greyhorn wheezed. "Now, with victory almost within my grasp, you bungle everything."

As inconspicuously as possible Grantin attempted to retreat from the window and slink back down the hallway toward his room.

"Where do you think you're going? Come back here— come back here with my ring!"

"Uncle, you're tired and upset. You should rest. I'll go and fix us some dinner; then you should take a nap. When morning comes you'll be fresh and able to think more clearly. Perhaps there is a solution that we haven't considered."

Still weakened from the potion's noxious fumes, Greyhorn hesitated a moment, then leaned wearily back against the wall and nodded his assent. The wizard trudged down the front stairs and into his study while Grantin made his way to the rear first-floor kitchen and prepared a light meal.

After dinner he cajoled Greyhorn into reclining on the parlor couch, whereupon the wizard fell into a deep sleep. Now Grantin had only a few hours to make his plans and, if necessary, flee. First he must scour the library for some reference, some hint to the nature of this strange ring. Possibly in some dusty volume was recounted a spell which could free him from its weight.

Grantin first checked the common references: *A Thousand and One Spells for All Occasions; Hancough's Compendium of Useful Chants; The Wizard's Guide to Advanced Magic*—all to no avail.

Hours later, Grantin turned the last page in Ruffin's *Quaint Spells I Have Known and Used* without finding so much as a single useful passage.

Beyond the library windows night surrounded the manor in purple black. Grantin's single lamp glowed feebly, and as the charge slowly ebbed away it flickered with an almost hypnotic rhythm. Overcome by the day's events, Grantin slumped forward, head on his hands, the bloodstone pressing hard against the center of his forehead. Reluctantly he surrendered to Morpheus's blandishments, all the while promising himself that he would only rest for an hour or two and then awaken refreshed to finish his search or, if necessary, flee into the woods.

Chapter Twelve

A strangeness pervaded the scene, but Grantin had to concentrate to determine the nature of its peculiarity. It seemed as though images approached from a great distance, danced in front of him, and then roared past him and disappeared. With a start Grantin realized that a colored fog shrouded these scenes until they were quite close to him.

The visions themselves were composed predominantly of reds and oranges, yellows and tans, but the fog that surrounded them, without actually touching them, was itself a pale pearly green.

Each succeeding vision persisted for a longer time. Grantin began to catch fragments of entire scenes, all of a uniquely frightening nature: dungeons, cells; humans, Ajaj, and Fanists in chains; storms, blood, and torture. In spite of his revulsion Grantin stared fixedly at each picture, trying to drink in all of its details before it flickered away. More and more he thought he discerned a common link between all of them—in each vision he detected the hint if not the actual presence of a bloodstone such as that affixed to his own left hand.

Grantin was intrigued by one apparition in particular, one that he realized he had been watching for some time. This picture filled his entire field of vision. Grantin avidly watched the events silently unfold.

A small, chunky, baldheaded man, childlike in size but bearing the grizzled face of age, tramped down a gray-walled corridor. Bandy legs moved pistonlike beneath the folds of his wizard's gown. In only a few paces the magician reached a wooden door broken in the middle by a small barred window. The portal was flung open by his touch. The room beyond was brightly lit by several glow-pods. The chamber was circular. Down its center was a line of floor-to-ceiling bars spaced only a few inches apart. Imprisoned in the right half of the room was a four-armed creature, a Fanist of a clan unknown to Grantin. The native's hairless, pebble-gray hide did not yet bear the network of wrinkles and seams which distinguished the elders of the tribes. This native was young, barely into adulthood, although even after five hundred years of cohabitation humans were unsure what his age would be as man reckons time.

The wizard's mouth worked angrily and he shouted in silent frustration at the impassive Fanist. An instant later bolts of red and green leaped from the wizard's fingertips, passed through the bars, and discharged themselves into the native's flesh. The Fanist writhed in agony but refused to answer the wizard's questions. Another bolt struck him, and, as the Fanist crumpled to the floor, the scene began to fade. In the last instant before the vision failed Grantin saw, or sensed, affixed beneath the tough flap of skin which covered the native's forehead a glowing milky blue jewel set there in an indentation of the skull itself.

With a snap, like a spark of static electricity, the scene pulsed brightly, then went dark. Grantin awakened to find himself still sprawled in the library, with dawn beginning to tint the far horizon. Soon Greyhorn would be stirring, looking for Grantin. With him he would bring his knife.

Chapter Thirteen

Grantin raced from wall to wall, shelf to shelf, searching for a book, any book, which might provide a clue which would save him from his alternatives of amputation or penniless flight. In desperation he yanked volume two of the Ajaj history from the bottom shelf and as fast as his eyes were able began to read.

So the first human city, Integrity, was established on the banks of the river the humans called Resurrection some two miles east of the site where the *Lillith* had first landed. Under Amis Hartford's direction the colonists pooled their efforts to construct the first rude settlement while we, the Ajaj, withdrew to the pinnacles on the far bank of the river. Crops were planted and the first year's harvest was . . .

No, no—that was no help at all! Grantin madly flipped the pages forward, reading a line here, a fragment there. The sun was now halfway above the horizon. Grantin turned the pages in a mad dash for some clue to the nature of the bloodstone.

. . . Thus the Gogols were forced to retreat far to the west and to halt their attacks on the newly established Hartford villages.

Wait a moment! How did the Hartfords force the Gogols into retreat? Grantin flipped back to the preceding page and read the ensuing paragraphs with great interest.

. . . Edgar of Illum, the first of the great Hartford magicians. By rumor Edgar's grandfather was a learned colonist of the tribe known as geologists. That ancestor passed down special knowledge to his heirs. Edgar himself refused to reveal the nature of the device by which he hurled energy bolts back at the attacking Gogols and so saved the Hartfords from domination and slavery. It was commonly believed, however, that Edgar through the use of his grandfather's teachings discovered a rock or crystal which somehow amplified the power of his spells. Edgar would neither deny nor confirm the rumor but always contended that the power he used was too awesome and too frightening for normal men, that the uninitiated would likely be driven mad by contact with his device or the use of his spells.

It is known that Edgar wore a large ring with a crudely cut red stone affixed in its center. Some have speculated that this gem, or powerstone, was the seat of his magic. This hypothesis, however, was never able to be tested. It is rumored that on one occasion Edgar was waylaid by renegades and when they attempted to remove the stone from his hand they were all struck dead by its power. To this story, as to most of the others told about him, Edgar gave a sly smile and a shy wink but no further response other than his oft-repeated dictum that the power he used was more the power of death than of life and that anyone who chanced to possess his secret would probably die of contact with it.

The answer to this riddle will likely never be known, as, a few moments after Edgar's death, the

stone clouded, fragmented, and crumbled to powder,
pouring from its socket like red sand. In spite of the
passing of Edgar the Hartfords remained safe from
the Gogol menace due to the more recent advances
in wizardry by Englehardt and Emriss, students of
the great magician. Thus the Gogols were forced to
retreat far to the west and to halt their attacks on the
newly established Hartford villages.

Nothing, there was nothing here! Perhaps elsewhere,
other wizards, someone might be able to tell him how to
rid himself of the powerstone which must, judging from
his tortured dreams, soon drive him insane. Grantin
slammed the book closed, stood up, and walked to the
far corner of the library. He opened the great window
and leaned on the sill, watching Pyra ascend above the
horizon.

There before him lay the Eris Forest, and beyond, low
rolling hills. In the far distance was the hint of the Guardian Mountains which separated the realm of the Hartfords from that of the Gogols. Was a mere finger worth a
flight into such rugged country? Grantin looked down at
his hand. He bent back the index finger, hiding it, and
examined the result. Certainly men had lived with worse
deformities. Perhaps Greyhorn could be put off, delayed,
or convinced to consult other wizards more knowledge-
able than he.

A scrape sounded on the stone floor behind him.
Grantin turned and spied Greyhorn approaching him
stealthily. The wizard's left hand was extended, fingers
open as if ready to grasp a moving object. In his right
hand he clutched a long, gleaming knife.

"Uncle, please don't. There must be another way.
Can't we talk this over?"

Greyhorn made no reply but continued to advance on
his nephew.

Before Greyhorn's appearance Grantin had all but resigned himself to the loss of his finger. Now, with the
blade only a few feet away, the fear of its amputation
became overwhelming. In desperation Grantin raised his
right and left arms and swung each of them in counter-
rotating circles in front of him. From his lips issued a
broken stream of chants and incantations remembered

from his occasional attempts at scholarship. The spell had unexpected results. Instead of freezing Greyhorn's body into immobility, a great sphere of ball lightning was emitted from one of Grantin's whirling arms. This flickering missile raced to the ceiling, bounced off the beams, and ricocheted from wall to wall, leaving a sizzling path in its wake. Finally the sphere contacted the iron grille of the library door and exploded in a myriad of crackling fragments. The menace now gone, Grantin reappeared from under the heavy table. He spied his uncle also clambering to his feet.

"You idiot! That ring contains a bloodstone! Its magic is that of a hundred wizards. One wrong word and you could kill us both. It's too dangerous for you to have. Don't you know it will drive you mad unless you get rid of it? Your days are numbered."

Greyhorn regained his feet. Grantin saw that he still clasped the butcher knife. Highlights of the morning sun twinkled brightly on the polished surface of its blade. Grantin became almost hypnotized by the flickering gleams. Involuntarily he retreated back into the corner of the room up against the sill of the window.

"Stay back! Stay back, uncle! I don't care what you say, I don't want to lose my finger."

"You don't want to lose your finger!" Greyhorn yelled as he crept closer to his nephew. "What do I care what you want? That ring is mine, by God, and I'm going to take it if I have to cut off your whole arm!"

Grantin pushed himself up onto the window ledge and wondered if he could survive a jump. No—too high, too many rocks beneath him. Greyhorn was now only three or four feet away and still advancing. Without conscious plan Grantin shouted a keep-away spell which he had learned as a child, a simple incantation which slightly thickened the air around the person who pronounced it and hence tended to deflect an advancing individual off to one side or the other. But Grantin had not reckoned with the forces of the powerstone. Instead of Greyhorn being kept from Grantin, it was Grantin who was removed from Greyhorn. With a sensation of being grabbed by a giant fist, Grantin felt walls of force enclose his body, yank him through the window, and propel him out across the sky.

Tumbling, his body flew through space, gaining height and speed with each passing yard. Greyhorn's castle became a gray wall, a house, a distant toy structure, a spot on the horizon, then was gone. Below Grantin the landscape blurred and ran into a smeared impression of greens and browns. Villages, rivers, lakes, cities, all slid by. In the distance, Grantin saw the rapidly approaching towers of the Guardian Mountains, gigantic structures which seemed to soar even above the great height at which he flew. Tumbling out of control, in the spell's icy grip, Grantin flew onward straight at the heart of the rearing granite crags.

Chapter Fourteen

The snakelike path wound westward through a sea of mutated brambles. A league distant grew the Gogol fortress of Cicero. Pyra's russet edge had barely cleared the horizon, but already the Ajaj Grays had begun to trickle from their quarters in the tumbles and make their way to the trail head. Day after day, generation upon generation, so had the Ajaj come forth to render services to their Gogol overlords.

Ahead, behind, and to all sides grew the poison-tipped briars and sting-burred brambles cultivated by the Gogols as protection for this, the seat of their empire. Only through a few narrow trails could Cicero be reached, and these lanes were constantly watched by the jealous owners of the city's five gates.

Five walls had Cicero and five gates and five lords. Five trails led to the city, and into five departments were civil functions divided. The entrance at the Eastern point of the pentagon was the Gate of Dread, commanded, guarded, and watched over by Lord Hazar the Dread. Through this gate, down this trail, came the Ajaj laborers, servants, and empathers who staffed the city.

At the northeast point of the pentagon opened the Gate of Lust, commanded by Lord Bolam the Dominator. Over the path which terminated there came the slaves, both male and female, necessary to satisfy the more carnal pleasures of the lords and deacons and subdeacons. These being more or less a luxury item, Bolam's control of the gate made him the weakest and most lightly taken of the five lords.

Next, to the northwest, was the Gate of Mammon, guarded by Lord Zaco the Inquisitor. From the regions served by this road came the gemstones, gold, iron, minerals, powders, and potions sufficient to stock the city. For reasons not understood by the other lords, Zaco had entered into an alliance with Hazar—an arrangement much resented and feared by the other Gogol princes, for through Zaco's gate, from the lands he controlled, came the powerstones that were so crucial a part of Hazar's plans for empire.

To the southwest stood the Gate of Fear. Through this portal Lord Topor sent forth Ajaj nominally under indenture to Hazar to till the fields and tend the crops which provided Cicero with an abundance of food and drink. Because of his dependence upon Hazar's Grays, it was well known that Topor, in most events, could be counted on to do Hazar's bidding.

Lastly, to the southeast yawned the Gate of Pain, jealously guarded by Nefra the Cruel. Nefra was Hazar's most bitter and most powerful enemy. His kinsmen maintained the aquifers which supplied fresh water from Lake Nefra some ten leagues to the south. Hazar's control of the city's food and now apparent control of the powerstones as well as his domination of Cicero's labor force excited Nefra's paranoia to a fever pitch. Hazar planned to elevate himself from lord to king, of this Nefra was certain. With such an ascension Nefra's fate would be sealed.

Castor rounded another bend, whereupon the trail disgorged its travelers in a cleared semicircle some three hundred yards in diameter. Directly ahead of him the first of the three slabs which composed the Gate of Dread gaped wide. Shouts and curses greeted the Grays as they emerged from the wall of briars.

Sleep-dulled curses urged them forward across the barrens and into the space between the first and second panels of the gate. Castor, as much as possible, kept to the center of the group of workers, hoping to remain inconspicuous among his fellows.

Guards patrolling the face of the wall repeatedly snapped their whips over the heads of the Grays, causing them to press closer together. At last almost a hundred Ajaj filled the space between the first and second panel. Reluctantly, the guards in the watchtowers began to crank their great wheels. On rollers of seasoned oilwood the huge front panel crept forward, foot by foot, closing off Cicero's Gate of Dread from the outside world.

When at last the panel was fully closed the second portion began to move backward, sliding into the wall whence it came. Again the Ajaj crowded forward, stepping over the foot-wide channel which guided the ironbound wooden barrier.

After the Grays had cleared the middle door, it closed and the third panel opened into the streets of Cicero. A clerk checked off the names and duties of the Grays as they passed the wicket.

"Name, number, and classification?"

"Castor, 972, senior empather."

"Castor, 972, but senior empather no more. Now by the grace and wisdom of Lord Hazar you are allowed to enter into a new profession: scullery apprentice, fourth class, in the lord's own household. To your right along the outer ring past the entrance with the red and black flag, down the stairs, knock on the door; tell them you've been sent to clean the kitchens. Next!"

Numbly Castor stumbled forward, surprised, in spite of himself, that he had been allowed to live. A few yards past the clerk's desk he halted and turned back toward the gate. His pleasure at being alive vanished as he contemplated the scene before his eyes: burly copper-skinned soldiers patrolled the stone battlements above the gate. Gogols of various castes filled the walkways which paralleled the outer wall, beings who hated, distrusted, and loathed even each other. The depths of their insensitivity to the Ajaj could never be plumbed. The loss of a walking stick, the stain of a garment, upset them more than seeing a Gray gutted for its pelt.

With an anger more terrible than any he had felt before Castor turned and shambled forward toward Hazar's scullery. In the center of his rage Castor felt another emotion: fear, a fear that chilled him to the core—the fear of his realization that the only way that he would find peace was in Hazar's death or in his own.

Chapter Fifteen

Tears leaked from the corners of Grantin's eyes and his head bucked uncontrollably in the wind. Though the forces which propelled him protected Grantin from the full force of his passage, eddies and drafts and blasts of air penetrated the unstable shield. And the cold. Now that he was several thousand feet above the surface of Fane, Pyra's warmth had leaked away until the sun exuded only a thin, buttery light.

Grantin wrapped his arms around his torso and tried to orient himself so that he could view the approaching landscape from a more stable position. Loosening his left hand, he used it to shield his eyes. Through the cracks between his fingers he peered at the approaching Guardian Mountains. The band of the bloodstone ring pressed against his forehead. Images sporadically flashed into his brain. With each flicker a sensation like a high-voltage shock shuddered through his frame. Again and again these images displayed the scene of the imprisoned Fanist and the mad wizard who tormented him.

Grantin recognized none of the pictures, although it seemed to him that in addition to that of the Fanist certain other visions repeated themselves. Two or three times he spied an Ajaj Gray clasping a green, square-cut gemstone.

At last, unable to bear the continuous shocks, Grantin wrenched his hand from his forehead and removed the ring from contact with his skull. Half a league ahead of him and to his right lay the first pass between the Guardian Mountains.

Somehow Grantin had to turn his course. At first he flailed his arms and contorted his body, as if he could jerk and skitter his way at an angle across the sky, but to no avail. If his course did not change, in less than a minute he would shred himself against the granite outcropping which protruded from the side of the first peak.

Grantin's body twisted in a slow clockwise movement. He unclasped his hands and extended both arms straight out from the shoulder, but instead of slowing the maneuver increased the rate of his spin. Willing now to try anything, Grantin swung his arms back, and the spin decreased. He put both arms directly in front of him, and the spin halted. His course slowly veered to the right. The ring itself seemed to be the medium of control.

Grantin began a hasty experiment. He pointed the powerstone directly at the approaching jagged wall, and his movement away from the peak accelerated. Somehow the stone sensed movement around it and compensated by adjusting the field in which Grantin was carried. Grantin found that if he shook his fist up and down his whole body likewise oscillated. As if to prove his theory, the shattered palisade slid by a hundred yards to the left. Grantin freely rode the air through the pass.

Now he struggled to orient himself. Standing upright, he set his legs wide apart, right hand on his hip, left hand extended as if holding a searchlight which could guide his way through the tangled peaks.

Each time he detected a bulge of rock or escarpment impinging on his line of flight, Grantin solemnly pointed the powerstone at the obstruction. Like the north pole of one very weak magnet approaching the north pole of another, Grantin's line of travel shifted and he was repelled from those obstacles toward which he oriented the bloodstone.

After a few minutes Grantin gained a certain sense of

control, power, and even majesty. Like a minor god he bestrode the stone fortresses of Fane itself. One by one the battlements of the Guardian Mountains slid past. His twisting course at last opened to him a vista of the rich lands beyond.

There were the outer borders of the Gogol realm, the boundary lands inhabited no doubt by bandits, outcasts, and fugitives from Gogol justice. And beyond? Ahead lay the fabled settlements of Hartford mythology—the Gogol encampments of Mephisto, Styx, and their capital city of Cicero itself, all places which Grantin had no desire to investigate. But that brought up another problem: how to end his wild ride and still keep his bones in one piece and his organs in their normal resting places? Perhaps if he forced himself lower his speed would decrease.

Grantin extended his left arm toward Pyra. Could he obtain a repulsion from such a distant body? He sighted along his extended member to keep it fixed at the sun. After a minute or two he glanced below him to see what effect, if any, his experiment had produced.

His breath caught in his throat and his heart squeezed into a small icy lump. His scheme had worked better than he dared to hope. Now he sped at terrific speed only thirty or forty yards above the ground. Trees roared forward, their branches grabbing at him, at the last second to pass only a scant ten or fifteen feet below his dangling legs.

Now pale with fear, his heart racing in an adrenaline overdose, Grantin whipped out his arm and pointed it forward at an angle slightly below that of the horizon. After a few seconds he seemed to detect a decrease in his speed but suffered a corresponding increase in his altitude. Unless he was careful, in a few more minutes he'd be back in the freezing upper reaches of the atmosphere.

The ground was now composed of flatlands interspersed with a few rounded hills and humpbacked swales. Ahead these hummocks ended and a great forested plain stretched off toward the horizon. Summoning the last fragments of whatever courage he had left, Grantin adjusted his course so that his body now plunged directly toward one of the approaching hills. Grantin then pointed his arms skyward and lowered his level of flight until the top of the slope stood higher than Grantin himself. Finally he pointed his finger at the center of the hillside and waited.

His velocity did seem to slacken, but not enough. Now the hill was only a few hundred yards distant. Grantin saw that the knoll was covered by a copse of feather trees, their distended fronds resembling the terrestrial weeping willow.

Fifty feet, forty, thirty . . . Grantin's speed was too high and his altitude too low. In utter panic he pointed his arm straight ahead.

With a noise like a stone singing through a field of tall grass, Grantin smashed through the leafy tops of the feather trees. His arms and legs flailing, he whipped through tendrils and boughs. Leaves, stems, branches, bark, and bits of vegetation, together with a family of blue-crested squawk birds, exploded around him. He found himself tumbling downward. Instinctively his arms grasped at the limbs through which he fell. Grantin's grasp slipped from its last handhold. With a dull thud he bounced off the twisted trunk and collapsed in a bed of moss.

Dazed, head spinning, Grantin lay panting and gasping for air. So addled was his brain that it was several minutes before he realized that he had come to a halt. The nightmare flight was over. There ahead of him stretched out in a green-blue vista as far as the eye could see were the streams and forests of the borderlands. Beyond them lay the Gogol empire itself.

Chapter Sixteen

Commencing with his toes and working upward, Grantin began a cautious examination of his limbs. With mild surprise he discovered that his body, even if sore, bruised, and aching, was more or less whole.

Behind him lay wave upon wave of rolling foothills, and beyond them the granite vastnesses of the Guardian Mountains. To his left and right were scrubby tree-strewn barrens without a hint of water, cultivation, or settlement. Only in front did there appear to be habitation which might afford Grantin a few mean necessities of life. Off in the distance he thought he detected a crinkle in the forest which he took to be the sign of a meandering river.

Somewhat uncertainly Grantin stumbled down the hill and across the green-yellow grassland. The grass, tough desiccated fibers five or six inches long, bent and flattened reluctantly beneath Grantin's boots. Near its base the vegetation was interwoven into a tough springy mat.

Pyra rode high in the sky. Grantin estimated the time to be approximately the fourth hour. Soon sweat stained his forehead, cheeks, and palms. In response to the appearance of the salty fluid hordes of mites and flies arose from the soil.

Parched, hungry, and frustrated beyond endurance, Grantin carelessly swatted at the creatures and cursed them in a rasping voice. Quick as thought the powerstone seized the feeble energies created by Grantin's unplanned spell, channeled them, amplified them, then loosed them on the countryside in a nerve-shattering display.

The air was suddenly filled with an electric tension like the calm before a thunderstorm. In the air in front of him a vortex began to form, not the whirlpool of a tornado but rather a transparent cylinder stretched horizontal to the ground. Ten feet in diameter and seventy long, this tube of air began to rotate with ever increasing speed. In only a few moments its shape was sharply defined by the dust, twigs, bits of grass, and thousands of flies which it had sucked up along its length. Like a huge glassy spinning pipe it rolled ahead of Grantin in the direction in which he had been walking. As it moved it gained speed and power until, only a hundred yards distant, it ripped out the faded yellow grasses and proceeded to roll up a strip of the meadow as easily as a householder might take up the parlor rug. Shortly the juggernaut was more than a mile distant and, passing over a low rise, disappeared from view.

In equal parts pleased, amazed, and horrified by the powers he had loosed, Grantin ambled forward down his new vermin-free trail.

The powerstone was useful, but very dangerous. It occurred to Grantin that the tempest he had unleashed could just as easily have rolled backward over him. A sorcerer loosed a spell like a man pushing a rock over the edge of a palisade. Once freed it moved onward of its own mindless power, beyond control until its energy was spent. Grantin warned himself that he must exercise iron control over his movements and speech. A momentary slip, an instant of forgetfulness, and he might create a field of energy which would devour him. Chastened, yet pleased at the elimination of the bugs, Grantin walked over the rise and then down the visibly narrowing path toward the forest.

Once inside the glade Grantin noticed a tang of water in the air, the reek of mold and growing vegetation, the zesty pungence of gingerberry trees. Only a few hundred yards beyond the edge of the forest the trail opened by Grantin's cyclone became erratic in the extreme. The force of the wind spent itself against the sturdy trunks. The trail soon narrowed from its original width of seventy feet down to ten, then five, two, then none.

In its death throes the cyclone had meandered through the woods like a maddened snake. Less than half a mile from the edge of the forest, Grantin was confronted by a barrier of limbs marking the site of the expiration of the whirlwind.

Grantin struggled through the underbrush, determined to proceed forward in as straight a line as possible until he struck the river which he felt sure must lie somewhere ahead. In spite of his best efforts he soon found himself enclosed ahead and on both sides by a field grown rampant with thorns. Wheezing, he looked behind him. So thick was the underbrush that he could not even detect the trail he had broken.

Perhaps, Grantin thought, just the smallest, tiniest of spells might effectively clear the way for him again. Nothing so grand as the cyclone, of course; just a mild injunction to the thorns and branches to swing out of his way. His left arm extended, hand balled into a fist, the bloodstone pointing directly ahead of him, Grantin whispered the words "Out of my way!"

To the accompaniment of a great thunderclap a huge mallet of force smashed against Grantin's outstretched arm. The force of the blow lifted Grantin and propelled him backward, his body tearing a thirty-foot long tunnel through the underbrush. Stunned, scraped, and bleeding, he landed with a thud. Apparently somewhere ahead had stood a tree or a hill, or a boulder too massive to be moved, so instead of Grantin remaining stationary and the objects in front of him slipping aside, the objects remained stationary and it was Grantin against whom the energy of the spell was directed.

Resigned to his fate, Grantin stood, brushed himself off, and studied the foliage for some clue to the direction in which he should proceed. On his left a family of hoppers chittered as they searched the tamarack trees for clumps of fresh puffballs. Ahead and to his right he detected what might be the sound of rushing water. Pulling apart two small saplings, he edged off through the forest.

After he had advanced only a hundred yards or so the sound of the stream retreated, but Grantin's persistence was rewarded, for there he stumbled across a narrow but well-used trail. Almost a road, the ground was rutted, green at the humped center with grass and forest herbs.

Now so turned around that he had no conception of where he was going or where he had been, Grantin hesitated a moment and then, for no good reason, turned right and tramped on down the road. The noontime sun penetrated the clefts between the trees. Here the air was warmer and less damp than in the forest main.

Except for a renewed throbbing in the index finger of his left hand, Grantin's position seemed to have improved immeasurably since the beginning of his wild ride early that morning. He even happened past a jelly-apple tree and treated himself to six or seven of the immature fruits. True, occasionally the landscape wavered as if a silken curtain had been laid down in front of his eyes, but Grantin did his best to ignore those incidents.

By almost imperceptible degrees the trail grew wider and subtly assumed a more well-traveled appearance. By and by the trail entered a sweeping left-hand curve at the end of which the bordering forest fell away. The road debouched into a wide meadow dotted at the far end with a series of crude low huts. Beyond the huts swirled the river whose presence Grantin had sensed for several hours.

Increasingly conscious of the burning thirst in his throat and the yawning pit where his stomach once lay, Grantin increased his pace almost to a trot. For some reason the huts looked strange to him. The construction was crude, barely more than bundles of twigs cemented with mounds of dry mud and covered with leaves from the salad trees. The settlement seemed deserted, and a nagging fear began to play on Grantin's mind. Perhaps this was not such a good idea after all.

He slowed his pace, then stopped to scrutinize the town. Here and there he saw a few dogs but no inhabitants. One of the dogs, obviously a descendant of the original basset hounds brought down in the *Lillith,* waddled forward and entered a hut some hundred yards away. It was then that Grantin realized what was odd about the village. The structures were small, tiny by human standards. From a distance he had been unable to perceive their true size. Now he noticed that with the exception of one building at the far end of the lane, the biggest of the hovels was barely three feet tall. Each of them was in perfect proportion for its inhabitants, however. Here was something Grantin had heard about but never personally seen, a community of Fane's mutated, intelligent dogs.

Cautiously Grantin resumed his trek. As he neared the first hut a howling sounded behind him. At once four of the husky creatures bounded from nearby structures and arrayed themselves so as to bar Grantin's passage. At their highest point the dogs reached barely eighteen inches from the ground, but nevertheless Grantin came to a swift halt.

Grantin contrived to put as friendly a face on his appearance as possible.

"Good afternoon, friend dogs," he began. "It's a fine village you have here. What do you call it?"

One of the animals crept forward, his nose a few inches in front of the rest, and loosed a series of yips and low growls.

"I'm sorry, my friends, but you have me at a distinct disadvantage. I'm just a poor wanderer. If the truth be known I'm a bit lost. Tell me, though, do you understand human speech—perhaps one bark for yes and two for no?"

Only a stony silence greeted Grantin's remarks. No tails wagged, and on two muzzles skin pulled back to reveal gleaming ivory teeth.

"Surely, now, you wouldn't begrudge a hungry man a bite of food and shelter for the evening? Perhaps you have some chores I could perform in return? There must be quite a few tasks which even those fine paws of yours are unable to handle. Heavy work?" Grantin suggested, caricaturing a man lifting a weighty object. "Perhaps something that requires a bit of height?" Grantin stood on tiptoe and raised his arms above his head, pantomiming someone stretching and straining to place an object at a great elevation.

One of the dogs mumbled a few yips and whines to his fellows, and shortly the dogs' teeth were concealed. Apparently a bit of Grantin's message had penetrated, but still the tails did not wag nor did the bassets step aside.

On the other hand they made no move to chase Grantin away.

Resigned to the situation, Grantin lay down in a clump of moss at the edge of the road to see what would happen next. The vegetation was springy and soft and exuded a fresh scent of minty herbs. The air was clean and warm. Folding his hands beneath his head, Grantin lay back and for a moment closed his eyes. After what seemed only an instant a squawking voice startled him from his reverie.

"You there, fellow. What's your name and what're you doing here?"

Grantin jumped to his feet and whirled around, blinking his eyes, looking for his interrogator.

"I said, what's your name and what're you doing here?"

In the middle of the road Grantin spied a shriveled old woman; curled steel-gray hair protruded from her skull like handfuls of metal springs. Her face was all bulges and hollows, bulbous nose, sunken cheeks, bulging, protruding cheekbones and chin, sallow neck, huge Adam's apple, sunken eyes, and beetling brow. Though slightly more than five feet in height, the body under her soiled calico jumper seemed firm and well fleshed. All in all, an imposing, peculiar sight.

"Good afternoon, madam. My name is Grantin, and as I was telling our friends the dogs, though I fear they don't understand me, I'm a poor traveler who has lost his way. Spying this quaint little village, I had hoped for hospitality."

"Traveler, huh? And where might it be that you're traveling from?"

"Oh, over that way," Grantin said, waving his hand in a random direction. "When I entered the forest I became disoriented and I've quite lost my bearings. I come from a little town called Alicon where I live with my uncle. Unfortunately he and I had a minor disagreement, and I decided to see a bit of the world and, perhaps, return later when he was in a better humor."

"A likely story if I ever heard one. Where are you planning on going to?"

"No place special. Here and there. Hither and yon. Wherever an honest man might find work, excitement, new sights, knowledge. If the truth be known, my uncle thinks himself something of a wizard. I had it in my mind that I might take training with some master sorcerer and so upon my return I might show my uncle that he is not as great a wizard as he seems to think. I don't suppose there are any sorcerers in this vicinity to whom I might turn for instruction?"

The old woman fixed Grantin with a hard, calculating stare; then, apparently having come to some decision, she shrugged her shoulders and commenced a hoot-, yip-, and bark-filled conversation with Grantin's welcoming committee.

At the conclusion of her remarks, the lead bassett emitted two peremptory woofs; then he and his fellows stood aside, opening the trail to the center of the village. Cautiously Grantin stepped forward. The old woman walked by his side and, unbidden, began to speak.

"You'll have to excuse my friends the dogs; this be wild country, as you might well know. Strangers often carry bad luck with them like clouds bringing rain. My name is Sara, and in our tongue the dogs call this place Catlet. Why? Don't ask me, for I don't know. That's just the name they gave it—strange, queer creatures that they are."

"Do you live here, then?" Grantin asked.

"Yes, indeed I do. It's as good a place as an old woman like me can find in her final years. That little house down the end is mine, the only one in town big enough for a real person. Oh, the dogs aren't bad. I help them out with the things that they need a human to do: lifting, carrying, work too fine for their paws, and heavy jobs. There's always a human, someone like me, in any dog village. They couldn't survive without us. It's not too bad a life. They catch food for me and bring in firewood. They give me everything I need, and protection, too. They're fierce fighters, oh, yes, they are. You wouldn't know it just to see them there wagging their tails, but you don't want to get them down on you. Those teeth are sharp, those jaws strong; and their claws can take the bark right off a tree or the flesh off your bones. But, as I said, this is a wild place. The Gogols hold their councils not fifty leagues to the west."

"Where are we, then?" Grantin inquired. "I'm thoroughly turned around. In fact, I was hoping that someone here might have a map."

"A map! Ha, that's a good one. The dogs with a map. They always know where they are, and if they don't then they don't care. Oh, I'd like to see one of them draw a map, with a piece of charcoal in his teeth perhaps; that would be a fine sight. No, no—no map, but I'll tell you where you are. You're in the borderlands, the Grenitch Wood. This forest extends from eighty leagues to the south of us, thirty to the north, and another twenty-five leagues wide. That's the Black Pearl River there. Deep and silent and cold it is, too. These are the outlands where even the Gogols don't try to enforce their rule.

"In these woods you'll find every brigand, thief, and vagabond between Hartford and Cicero. Here they all come, between two worlds, too far for the Hartfords to pursue and not worth the trouble of the Gogols to wrinkle out of the forest. They've tried, they've tried; but there are more than a few wizards here as well. The woods are strong with a magic of their own. Many a deacon has met his end in these dark grottos. That's why I stay here with the dogs; they protect me, don't you know."

"I'm sure it's a satisfactory life here with the dogs, Sara, but tell me the truth: we're not really in danger now, are we? Surely there's nothing that you have that any of these minor bandits could want, no offense intended."

"I have my life, don't I? And my body. There's always a wizard who could use a replacement piece or two. No, there are dangerous men out there; but don't worry— you're safe here. The brigands leave the dogs alone. That's the order and the custom. Even the bandit Yon Diggery himself has decreed that the dogs shall be unharmed. They all know the value of the dogs."

"And what is the value of the dogs?" Grantin whispered conspiratorially.

"Why, the cats, of course."

"The cats?"

"Yes, indeed, the cats. Everyone knows about the cats. You mean to say you don't?"

"Perhaps I've forgotten. Why don't you tell me again?"

"Why, the cats are the spies of the Gogols. Sneaking, slinking around, they try to find out our secrets, discover our fetishes, our fanes, our talismans, the sources of our power. If the cats were left alone, they'd infest the area. With the knowledge they brought back the Gogols might make an end to us once and for all. No, the bandits are very much against the cats, and so the dogs have safe-conduct. As long as I help the dogs I, too, am just as safe. Well, what say you, young Master Grantin? How do you like Catlet?"

"Very nice, very fine indeed. I am most pleased that you have persuaded our friends to allow me to visit for a short while. By the way, do you suppose that we might make some arrangements for dinner? I'd be happy to help out in order to earn my meal."

"A guest work? Nonsense; don't think about it twice. Of course you're welcome to dinner. You can smell the stew boiling even now. A fine big stew, plenty for all."

"Stew. Excellent!" Grantin exclaimed. "May I inquire as to the type of stew it is—beef, or lamb, or ground hen?"

"What kind? Why, young Master Grantin, cat stew, of course!"

A sour grimace spread across Grantin's face. Still, his hunger being what it was, he continued with Sara down the main street of Catlet toward the fire where the stew bubbled in a large iron pot.

Neither Sara nor Grantin nor the bassets noticed anything unusual. No one spied the rustle of grass in the tussocks at the edge of the forest. The brief glitter of sunlight from a shiny lens went unseen. Slowly, inch by inch, the watcher, covered with scent killer, slunk backward deep into the thicket and out of sight. When she was sure that no one had seen her, the young sealpoint Siamese turned around and raced back through the underbrush to report to her Gogol masters.

Chapter Seventeen

Mara's usually neat brown tresses were tangled and askew. Absentmindedly she threaded her fingers through them in an attempt to remove the worst of the knots. Her black velvet robe was creased and travel-stained, her face and throat sticky with dried perspiration. But her appearance was the least of Mara's worries.

For the hundredth time Mara wondered if Hazar would blame her for failing to bewitch the messenger. But it wasn't her fault. A minor enchantress such as herself could never hope to beguile Greyhorn sufficiently to obtain a sample of his blood. The perfection of his disguise alone indicated the power of his magic.

Mara brushed out the folds of her gown and slapped the cloth to remove a dust stain here, a bit of dried grass there. Using a spell given to her by Hazar, she had flown to the edge of the Hartford kingdom, over the Guardian Mountains, all the way to Cicero. In spite of the speed of her travel a full day had passed since her delivery of the ring. Hazar might already have received confirmation of the delivery. Perhaps he had other spies who had reported her fleeing Alicon immediately after the transfer.

Again, as she had done many times before, Mara cursed the day her mother had taken a Hartford for a husband, vain, self-important hypocrites that they were. Had Glora married one of the People and remained within the boundaries of the empire Mara would have grown up as a normal girl rather than as a special courier familiar with the Hartford ways and apprenticed to Hazar the Dread.

With a muffled rasp the door to Hazar's outer office slid aside and a young acolyte stepped into the opening.

"Mistress Mara, Lord Hazar will now receive your report."

Nervously Mara got to her feet, then, taking a deep breath, walked boldly forward through the portal. With an air of self-importance the acolyte followed a pace or two to her left. The inner panel slid aside and Hazar scrutinized his visitor. He nodded to his clerk. The young man turned aside and Mara advanced into the office. Hazar reclined in a cushion-lined chair behind a horseshoe-shaped desk. Giving her a slight nod and a brief smile, he bid her be seated on the couch.

"Good afternoon, my lord Hazar," Mara began softly. "I return here having done my best to fulfill your commands."

Hazar's body displayed a sudden increase in tension. He had been expecting to hear the words "Good afternoon, Lord Hazar, I have done as you commanded." He sat up straighter in his chair and leaned forward a bit, both signs by which Mara discerned his unhappiness with her message.

"In what way have you failed to comply with my orders, to the best of your ability or otherwise?"

"My lord, I traveled across our empire through the Guardian Mountains and into the land of the Hartfords. I reached the village of Alican at the appointed time. There I met the messenger as instructed. After receiving the appropriate passwords I tendered the ring and saved the money he paid me in a tightly stoppered vial. I give it to you now, containing, as it must, the residue of his sweat and fibers from his pockets. All these things I have done as you commanded. I did not, however, seduce this man and take from him samples of his blood and skin and hair. In this regard I failed; but, my lord, I would have failed more terribly had I attempted to complete my mission. . . ."

"Go on, go on; let's hear your excuse."

"The man who appeared to receive the ring was Grey-horn himself. Clearly my wiles were not powerful enough to entrap a wizard of his experience. Had I tried to do so he certainly would have taken me prisoner. Then you would have had nothing, not even the tainted money, not even word that the ring had been delivered. Greyhorn might have claimed that the messenger had never arrived and demanded a second stone. Clearly it was better for me to return with my report than not to return at all."

"You're sure it was Greyhorn, then? Did you recognize him by his appearance?"

"No, my lord, he was in disguise. He wore the face and body of a young man of perhaps twenty or twenty-two years, brown hair, brown eyes, six feet tall—the guise of a strutting buffoon. It was a masterwork of subterfuge."

"But you, with your brilliant powers of observation, somehow penetrated this master disguise?"

"My lord, it could have been no one other than the wizard Greyhorn. The man to whom I delivered the ring removed it from its purse and slipped it upon his left index finger. Only a true wizard would put it there. The ring recognized its owner. I could see, even as we stood on the Street of the Artisans, that it had bonded itself to the wizard's flesh. Only Greyhorn would have done such a thing. Knowing that my powers were not strong enough to best him, I returned with his sweat and his coppers as fast as the spell would take me."

"Greyhorn himself, is it? In disguise? Your story does raise some questions; still, I am not at all convinced that it was our friend who received the ring. No, someone else has it, I think. Someone who now wanders loose with great power in his grasp. I will investigate further. Leave me. I will notify you when you are needed again."

Hesitantly Mara arose to leave. When she neared the door she paused and looked back at Hazar for some hint to her fate. She saw a brooding, saturnine face; puckered lips beneath a drooping black mustache; a man whose concentration had already turned inward, away from Mara, to other questions more substantial than that of her life or death. She slipped out the door while Hazar brooded.

The wizard sat in his chair hunched forward over the edge of the desk while he turned the possibilities over in his mind. How unlike Greyhorn, he thought, to pick up the item himself, in disguise yet! But Mara had a point. Who but a powerful wizard or an idiot would dare wear the bloodstone? An idiot? Could Greyhorn's nephew be that much of a fool? Of course, that had to be the answer. And Mara had ruined his plan! She had fled like a frightened ground hen instead of destroying both the stone and the nephew, and the uncle as well.

Something must be done about the girl. He'd be fair about it; he'd give her a chance; he would double-check his theory with Greyhorn—but he knew that it would prove out. If only someone else had enchanted Zaco he could be rid of the girl now—but no, no, restrain yourself, Hazar, he told himself. The girl controls Zaco, and Zaco the powerstones. Yes, he would have to wait until his scheme was complete and Zaco no longer necessary; then he would take care of her. He had never trusted her, in any event. Too soft, too weak. The Hartford blood in her was the reason. Blood can't be changed, as the old saying went, only spilt.

Hazar crossed the room and pulled back the drapes which concealed the lens. Automatically his hands performed the strokes while his lips whispered the incantation necessary to summon Greyhorn.

Hundreds of leagues away Greyhorn sat sprawled in his workroom, defeated and frustrated. All his attempts to trace Grantin had been to no avail. The ring was gone, gone forever, and there was nothing he could do about it.

In the back of Greyhorn's mind an idea began stirring: "Call Hazar on the lens; call Hazar on the lens." The merest unfocusing of Greyhorn's eyes conjured up a wavering transparent vision of Hazar's face. Greyhorn took three deep breaths, composed himself, and walked over to the plate. Reciting a four-word incantation, he passed his right arm, palm outward, across its face. Hazar's visage immediately appeared.

"Yes, Hazar; what do you wish?" Greyhorn asked irritably.

"I merely called to confirm delivery of the item. It meets with your satisfaction?"

"As a matter of fact, Hazar, it does not. There has been a difficulty with the ring, and I find that the one you sent is not suitable for my use. I need a replacement."

"You are the most unique of sorcerers, Greyhorn. You are the first I've ever known to complain that a powerstone does not sufficiently augment his talents. Certainly you don't need two of them."

"No, one would be sufficient, if I had one that was satisfactory. As I said, the one that you sent me is not suitable for my needs."

"Oh, really? Specifically in what way does it not fit your requirements?"

"The ring does not comfortably fit my finger, and because of its nature I find it impossible to adjust the band."

"How unfortunate. Hold it up to the lens and let me see; perhaps I can diagnose the trouble."

"That would not be convenient."

"No, I expect not, since the ring now adorns the finger of your nephew Grantin. I am surprised at you, Greyhorn. I didn't think that you were this weak. Had someone told me that you would let a little thing like a finger stand in your way I would have thought him crazy. Are you too tenderhearted to recover your own property?"

"As we both know, Hazar, a powerstone ring is not that easy to remove from an unwilling donor."

Hazar shook his head in mock sadness. "Very well, Greyhorn; if your magic isn't powerful enough to immobilize a worthless, ne'er-do-well young pup of a nephew I'll give you a spell which, if you catch him unawares, will stiffen him up harder than a frozen oak tree. Once it takes effect, he'll be unable to resist."

"I don't need any spell from you!" Greyhorn snapped. "I've got a freezing spell for every day of the week."

"Well, then . . . ?"

"If the truth be known, the problem is that my worthless nephew is no longer here. Early this morning I crept up upon him ready to do the deed, but at the last instant he awakened. Our ancestors' blood flows in his veins as it does in mine. When augmented by the power of the ring, even an imbecile like my nephew becomes formidable. The plain fact is that before I could reach him he managed to formulate a spell of miraculous transportation. He shot out of the library window like a stone from a sling. The last time I saw him he was tumbling out of control, heading for the Guardian Mountains. No doubt he's already smashed himself into a bloody pulp and the bloodstone has even now turned to sand. So, you see, you'll just have to send a replacement."

"Not at all, Greyhorn, not at all," Hazar replied with a sharp edge in his voice. Irritated now almost to the limit of his control, Greyhorn crept closer to the lens. His eyes narrowed into mean, angry slits, and out of Hazar's view his hands began to sweep back and forth in a potent spell.

"You *will* send me another ring or your plan will fail. Not only will I not cooperate, I will spread the word of your scheme. I and my henchmen will turn our powers against you. You agreed to deliver me a ring, and you owe me a ring."

"I agreed to deliver you one ring in exchange for your cooperation, and one ring I did deliver from my hands to those of your messenger. If your own nephew played you false and stole the ring right under your nose, then it's your loss, not mine. We have a bargain, and you'll rue the day you fail to live up to it. With or without your help I will rule Fane."

"Not without the ring. Give me my ring!"

"Your ring. Very well; your ring you may have. Not another ring. Not a second ring. But your own ring, the one stolen by your nephew. Yes, since you are unable to protect your own property, unable to control your own family, I'll get you your own ring back for you. I assume you don't mind if Grantin is damaged in the process?"

"I'll boil him in oil when I get my hands on him. I'll smash his fingers and then make every square inch of his body itch."

"I'll take that for authority to handle him my own way."

"Bah! This is pointless. He's hours dead, long gone."

"Don't be too sure, Greyhorn. In the hands of a sensitive, even an idiot sensitive, the ring is capable of amplifying the most subtle desires. Unless he had some wish for death the odds are high that the ring maneuvered him through the peaks more or less unscathed. I will inquire of my spies and agents. You, for your part, will keep your associates in readiness. I will delay the attack. It will begin in ten days."

"Not without my ring it won't! If I don't have a ring in ten days, I will rouse the Hartfords against you. Make it the one Grantin is wearing, if he is still alive, or another ring; I don't care. But you have ten days to deliver."

"If your nephew is here I will find him, and in much sooner than a week. Farewell, Greyhorn, and remember our bargain."

Hazar's image vanished instantly, as if he had detected Greyhorn's attempt to lay a spell against him. Greyhorn scowled at the empty lens. A few more long-distance discussions and he would complete his spell. Upon the proper final incantation he would turn Hazar's insides into mush and finish the scoundrel once and for all. But not before he got his ring!

Hazar pulled the drapes across the lens and opened the door to his chamber.

"Derma, come in here!" he shouted at his secretary.

The young man who had admitted Mara crossed the threshold and entered Hazar's office.

"Yes, my lord, how may I serve you?"

"Derma, check all of our spies, agents, operatives, associates, friends, and sycophants in the border regions from one end of Grenitch Wood to the other. Report back here at once if anyone has seen a young man, possibly a Hartford, six feet tall, with brown hair and brown eyes, someone with a slick tongue and a shifty eye, who might well be wearing a bloodstone ring. Don't just stare at me; go now, and come back as soon as you have news!"

Derma mumbled a hasty "Yes, my lord," then turned and raced through the outer office.

Hazar felt the fatigue and frustration deeply now. He knew he needed to relax. Summoning another messenger, he put out a call for Lord Bolam's staff to send to his office a particular twelve-year-old girl who had pleased him often these last few weeks.

Two hours later, relaxed and dissipated, Hazar was realigning his clothes when Derma knocked on the door.

"Yes, what is it?" Hazar called.

"My lord Hazar, I have news."

"Enter."

The door slid back and Derma hurried into the room.

"My lord, one of the outposts on the edge of Grenitch Wood has received a report that a young man such as you described has this morning entered the dog settlement known as Catlet. They believe he is still there now."

"Excellent, Derma, excellent! You have done well. Congratulate the captain and his cats on my behalf. Go and find Rupert. Send him to me at once."

A few minutes later Rupert pounded into the room, sweating heavily and out of breath. Again ensconced behind his horseshoe desk, Hazar was the picture of calm, snakelike power.

"Rupert! So you finally arrived?"

"Yes, my lord Hazar. At your command."

"Rupert, you remember that unpleasant business about the Ajaj?"

"Yes, my lord."

"You did not kill him as I ordered, did you?"

"No, my lord."

"Now, it's true he has supposedly recanted his heresy, but don't you think it would have been more of an object lesson to do away with him?"

"Yes, my lord Hazar."

"Are you a politician or a man of action?"

"A man of action, my lord."

"For a man of action you took a politician's way out, didn't you?"

"Yes, my lord, I suppose I did."

"Rupert, I have another job for you; a chance to redeem yourself. Do you want it?"

"Yes, my lord, I do. I think only of serving you."

"Yes, I bet you do, Rupert. Very well. This is a simple mission and one which I fully trust you to complete. I don't want to see you again until you have succeeded. Do you understand me?"

"Yes, my lord."

"Clearly?"

"I understand you very clearly, my lord Hazar. Whatever you command I will do."

"Very well. You are to travel to our outpost thirty leagues from the northern end of Grenitch Wood. You will seek out the captain of the guard in charge of the cats.

One of his cats has spied an enemy in the town of Catlet. That cat is to guide you to this settlement. There you will find a young man, brown-haired, six feet tall, a Hartford, wearing on the index finger of his left hand a gold ring with a polished scarlet stone. This man must be immobilized, but not killed; the finger, the hand, or the arm then removed, whichever is most convenient, while he is still alive. After the ring and the member are separated fill a small container with a portion of his blood; then bring me the ring, the blood, and his head—no more. I caution you, do not kill him before you remove the ring or you will destroy it. Take care with this, Rupert; he is a dangerous man. If you give him warning, if you give him a chance, he will bring potent spells to bear against you. Fail me not!"

"I will not fail you, Lord Hazar. I will bring you the ring, the finger, the blood, and the head."

"Very good, Rupert. I am pleased with your obvious devotion to this task. Off with you, now, to the borderlands. Quickly, quickly—he won't remain there long."

Rupert bowed slightly, turned, and sped from the room.

"I've got you, Grantin; I've got you now," Hazar mused to himself.

Chapter Eighteen

After a surprisingly pleasant cat-stew dinner Grantin retired to a rickety couch in Sara's two-room cabin. The strain of his crude sorcery and the deprivations of travel had weakened him more than he realized. Now, safe and well fed, he fell into a deep slumber and did not waken until late the next morning. He even enjoyed a respite from the worst side effects of the powerstone. Grantin could barely remember the five or six nightmares which had terrified his sleeping brain.

Bleary-eyed, Grantin reluctantly regained consciousness. It took him several seconds to lever his body into sitting position. His limbs felt numb and excessively heavy. Without a doubt he had to rid himself of the ring. Perhaps Greyhorn would forgive him if he managed to remove the bloodstone and give it to his uncle as a present.

"So you've come back to the living, have you, Master Grantin?" Sara called from the front door.

"Aajh, I . . . cough, eeech, cough, cough."

"The same to you, I'm sure. Is this how you normally greet people in the morning?"

"I . . . eemch . . . I don't feel quite myself just yet."

"Are you sick?"

"No, not exactly. I suppose I may as well tell you. A curse was laid on me by my uncle. Demons haunt me while I sleep. Sometimes it makes it hard to get up. If I could only find the right wizard I'm sure he could lift the curse and bring me back to health again."

Sara studied Grantin carefully, a calculating glint in her eye. He refused to meet her gaze. Obviously he could not tell her the truth about the ring. The last thing he needed was another person trying to fix his hand under the blade of a meat cleaver. All for her own good, Grantin consoled himself. A bauble such as this would only lead her to a bad end anyway. Still, for some reason, Grantin's duplicity bothered him.

"There wouldn't happen to be such a wizard in this vicinity?" he asked, focusing his eyes on a point above Sara's left shoulder.

"Maybe, maybe not. Wizards there are; but wizards such as you need, that's another question. Certainly none that will do it for free. Can you pay?"

"Only in heartfelt gratitude and a sincere promise to someday return tenfold any favors which are done me," Grantin replied with a poor imitation of sincerity.

"Goodwill means precious little to the outcast wizards here in Grenitch Wood. Have you no gold or silver? Gems or coins?"

Grantin shook his head.

"How about that trinket?" Sara asked, pointing at the ring.

Grantin considered the suggestion for no more than a tenth of a second. Without hesitation he replied:

"The ring—that is, I suppose, a possibility. I will say this: any wizard who cures me of my problem may have the ring for the effort of slipping it from my finger— though, to be honest, that might not be as easy as it seems. This lovely bauble is a family heirloom. In order to restrain my parting with it for some insignificant purpose, my father, when he put it on my finger, laid a powerful spell which prevents the ring's removal. Any sorcerer who is skilled enough to neutralize the injunction may keep it as his pay."

"Master Grantin, for some reason I am not convinced you are exactly what you seem. There's something about all this which doesn't seem quite right to me—but then, what business is it of mine? It's of little importance, in any event."

"Then you know of no such wizard?"

"Oh, there's a mighty wizard barely three leagues away. Skilled in all the arts, black and white. A man with magnificent powers, and interested in a new challenge, too. But he's not for you."

"Even with all his powers you think he could not do the job?"

"Oh, he could do it, I'm sure, if anyone could, but . . ."

"But?"

". . . but he's hopelessly mad. His mind's more twisted than an acre of briars. He thinks of nothing but his magic and power and revenge upon the world."

"Do you think he would kill me out of hand?"

"Oh, no; he's crafty and often displays great cunning, but he wouldn't kill you for no reason."

"Well, then, I should be safe. What reason would he have to harm me? All he need do is cure the nightmares and keep the ring as his pay. I go my way and he goes his. The worst that can happen is he can refuse to help me or prove unequal to the task."

"Aye, there's the rub. He's the most arrogant man alive. He's as sensitive to failure as a wound to salt. He boasts that he is the greatest magician in all of Fane. It would gall him to admit defeat. If he failed to remove your spell you would not leave his manor house alive. Oh, he's a twisted man. I think it has something to do with his size."

"He's very large and ferocious, then?"

"No, Master Grantin, a dwarf barely four feet tall. His physical deformity he can hide under wizard's robes, but his madness shows through his eyes."

"Still, if he's as powerful as you say, it is unlikely that he will fail. You don't know what it's been like these last few days since . . . since I've suffered under this curse. I have no choice. I must take the chance. What's the wizard's name? Can you give me directions to his house?"

"His name's Shenar. To reach his manor, continue on through the village and follow the river north for two leagues. You'll come to a small stream. Follow it one league to the east. It passes within sight of the big, dirty stone mausoleum where he plays his games and plans his spells."

"For someone who thinks he is a man to be feared you certainly seem to know a lot about this Shenar. How is it you are so well informed?"

"That's not so strange. You see, he's my son."

Sara paused at the doorway and shook her head in pity at the now chastened Grantin.

"Enough of all this, Master Grantin. It's your life, sure enough. Do what you think best. Don't take good advice when you hear it. I've got work to do. I have to earn my keep."

Sara turned away and walked out into the middle of the main street. A moment later Grantin, stiff-legged, trotted to her side.

"Why don't you let me help? When your chores are done I'll give you a hand with lunch and think over what you've told me. Shenar will still be in his house this afternoon if I haven't changed my mind."

With a nod of gruff assent Sara accepted Grantin's proposal. Both strode forward to the edge of the settlement.

The work loosened Grantin's muscles and to his surprise he gained a strange pleasure from the strain of physical labor. When Pyra was slightly past its zenith, dogs and humans alike ceased work, the bassets to retreat for their afternoon siesta while Grantin and Sara lunched on berries and salad, toasted puffballs, jelly apples, and thick slices of coarse bread.

Some two leagues away Rupert sat amid tussocks of tall grass, his back against a granite ledge, eyes closed. With the employment of one of his standard spells he had arranged to utilize the eyes of the Siamese scout. Hidden in the branches of a tree only a few yards from Sara's hut, the cat watched the humans finish the last fragments of their lunch. Bits of their conversation occasionally drifted in her direction. Though the animal understood little human speech, Rupert was well able to find meaning in their words.

"So, Master Grantin, in spite of everything you've decided to visit Shenar."

"How did you . . ."

"I can see it in your eyes. I'm not a wizard's mother for nothing. I, too, have my talents."

Only a portion of the conversation reached Rupert. What was that name again—Enar? Closer, cat, closer.

Reluctantly the sealpoint crept farther out along the branch. This was dangerous territory. Here in the tree retreat was impossible. Stealthily, step by step, the Siamese edged her way out along the branch until she was almost directly above the table.

"Do you mind if I come back here to spend the night after I finish with Shenar?"

"Why should I mind? The chances of your returning are almost nil, so what do I risk by saying yes?"

Grantin flicked his eyes down to the remnants of the meal on his plate. The old woman hated her son—and feared him too. Whatever the bitterness between them, it must have poisoned her mind. He wasn't gratuitously cruel, she admitted that. Only when he had a reason, a purpose, would Shenar be a bad risk. And Grantin would give him no cause. No, he would play to perfection the part of an ignorant peasant, his real motives hidden by the story of a nightmare curse.

A leaf fluttered down and landed at the edge of Grantin's plate; then a second leaf settled to the table two inches from the first.

Grantin picked up the second leaf and snapped it in half. Holding the sap-stained edges beneath his nose, he inhaled the wintry mint fragrance peculiar to the snaf tree. He tossed the pieces back onto the table.

A third leaf had joined its cousins. What was going on here? Was the tree diseased? Grantin tilted his head and scanned the branches above him. Something was not quite right, something out of place. The color was subtly wrong, not silver-green but more gray—gray like the fur of a cat!

Grantin jumped to his feet and backpedaled away from the table to view the limb at a different angle. Now Sara also arose and began weaving from side to side, trying to peer through the branches.

"Cat! Cat! A cat in the tree! There's a cat in the tree."

Instantly moaning bays echoed from several nearby huts. The dogs snoozed no longer, their siesta interrupted by the news of the interloper. They erupted from their hovels and sprinted forward to surround the tree. The cat barely had time to back off along the branch and reach the central trunk before four or five bassets were standing on hind legs, paws against the bark.

Grantin stood immobile beyond the circle of howling dogs. Sara hunted up a rock. She wound back her arm and threw the stone with great force, but the cat ducked behind a branch. The missile bounced off an intervening limb to land amid the baying dogs. Sara seemed to have expected that and was equipped with another stone. Only a second or two behind the first this rock whistled forward on a more accurate course. At the last instant the cat leaped aside, but in missing the stone she fell from her perch. Instantly the dogs were upon her.

Two leagues away Rupert raced to break the spell before the instant of death fed back into his own mind. He escaped the reaper's scythe, but not by much. His head rang and he could still feel the burning pain of sharp teeth puncturing his throat.

Panting, Rupert relaxed back against the boulder and composed himself.

"That's a bad sign, Master Grantin," Sara said, nodding at the carcass of the cat. "They never come this far without a good reason. I don't know what this is all about, but I'd wager that it has something to do with you. She must have overheard your plans. You'd be wise not to go anywhere near Shenar's castle now."

What should he do? Absentmindedly Grantin fingered the ring. In his nervous state he gave it a sharp tug. A hot spike jolted his nerves. He let go of the band.

"I have no choice. Shenar is my only hope."

Sara shrugged and walked Grantin as far as the river. There she bid him farewell, convinced that she would never see him again.

A few minutes later Rupert had recovered from the shock of the Siamese's death. He knew where Grantin was headed. By traveling in a straight line through the woods he would be able to intercept the youth before he reached Shenar's castle. Shenar—ah, that was a name out of the past. At one time he and his mother had been Zaco's deacons, before they had incurred his enmity and fled from Cicero in disgrace. Perhaps he would settle a score with Shenar as well, after he had finished with the Hartford. Rupert stood, brushed the moss from his pants, and then set out across the forest. He walked at a fast pace, keeping a steady beat by repeating over and over his instructions from Lord Hazar:

"The finger, the hand, the arm, the head, cut off the ring before he's dead. The finger, the hand, the arm, the head . . ." Rupert chanted as he marched through the woods.

Chapter Nineteen

By fits and starts the overgrown trail paralleled the river bank. Most of the time there was only the vaguest hint of a path, usually no more substantial than the absence of major obstacles along an imaginary line of travel. When he started Grantin had expected that he would reach Shenar long before dark, but as the afternoon progressed he became more and more unsure about arriving before Pyra set. The Black Pearl River meandered like a drunken caterpillar. The trail, such as it was, more or less followed the river's course.

On one occasion when the river slanted off to the left Grantin attempted to continue straight ahead through the underbrush. After only a few hundred yards he had lacerated his left hand on a thorn-studded branch, mildly twisted his ankle in a rodent burrow, and become totally confused about his true direction of travel. After a very few seconds' contemplation he turned one hundred eighty degrees and followed his broken trail back to the point where the river snaked to the left.

Having come equipped for cross-country travel, Rupert was not so handicapped. Before he left Cicero he had re-

corded from Lord Hazar's files both a map and a spell of
true direction and firm bearings.

The map showed the position of Catlet, the Black Pearl
River, and the stream to which Sara had alluded. Rupert
need only compute the angle necessary to take himself to
a point one league from the mouth of the stream, then
pronounce the spell while facing in that direction. The
incantation of true direction and firm bearings laid a
ramrod-straight corridor of psychic energy along Rupert's
line of sight. Until he released the spell Rupert would feel
a gentle wind blowing in the direction he wished to travel.
As long as this imaginary breeze remained on the back of
his neck he could not stray from his chosen path.

Equipped with the practical accouterments of heavy
leather boots, a stout staff, strong coarse trousers, leather
jerkin, and silver-studded black leather gloves, Rupert
was fully prepared to bull his way through the underbrush.

It was almost the ninth hour by the time Grantin
reached the juncture of Shenar's stream and the Black
Pearl River. There he paused for a few moments to rest.
Sitting on a rock by the edge of the brook, he splashed
cold water on his face and neck and treated himself to a
long drink of the sweet clear fluid. He heaved a heavy
sigh and glanced at the open sky above the river. By the
first hour Pyra would set. If he had not reached his destination he would be trapped alone without food or shelter
in the depths of Grenitch Wood. Cursing his fate, he
heaved himself to his feet and marched upstream.

The going was easier here. The stream was narrow
and fast flowing. Its course followed almost a straight line.

It was not quite the tenth hour—the dinner hour,
Grantin's stomach reminded him—when he caught sight
of a bit of stonework which he took to be a tower of
Shenar's manor. With renewed energy he increased his
pace. After traversing only a few yards he halted again.
Something was wrong. Nervously Grantin looked around
him but could detect nothing amiss.

Silly, what could be wrong? All he had to do was walk
straight ahead for another five minutes and then knock on
Shenar's door. Yet, for some reason, Grantin's legs refused to move. His skin tingled. His eyes stared intently at

one particular section of the underbrush. It was almost as if he expected to find some danger there.

Grantin decided to humor his new, highly sensitized powers of intuition. Bending over, he fished a fist-sized chunk of stone from the edge of the stream. Unlimbering his right arm, he hurled it into the thicket to which his vision had been so unerringly attracted. Leaves hissed as the stone sped through the branches. There immediately followed a resounding thud and an angry bellow of pain.

From behind the thicket erupted a portly, pale-skinned man dressed in dark, rough garments. Held high in his left hand he carried a staff which he waved at Grantin as he charged.

Grantin immediately picked up another stone, cocked his arm, and cast the missile with unerring accuracy. The rock ricocheted off the attacker's left hand, shredding skin and bruising bone. With a scream Rupert dropped the staff. Unintentionally Grantin had given the deacon a wound more grievous than he could know, for it was with his left hand, the fingers of which were now painfully bruised, that Rupert cast his most potent spells.

White-faced with pain, Rupert sucked his bleeding fingers while Grantin, taking advantage of the lull in the attack, scrambled to find another rock.

"You there," he called nervously. "You'd better leave me in peace, for I am a dangerous man."

"Dangerous man!" Rupert screamed after removing his ruined fingers from his mouth. "You are a dead man! You imbecile, you miserable misbegotten excuse for a man, you weak-kneed, soft-spined pup of a Hartford, I eat the likes of you for breakfast. Your life is numbered only in seconds."

"Stay back!" Grantin shouted as Rupert began a more stealthy yet more determined advance. "I'll do more than cut your fingers if you don't stop!" Grantin screeched.

His anger risen now to a fever pitch, Rupert cast a broken-fingered left-handed curse. The air between the two men shimmered. A blast of torrid air, like the draft from a kiln, washed over Grantin's body, charring his clothing and reddening his skin. Thoroughly frightened, he retreated two steps and sought to shield himself with his arms.

The spell had a great effect upon Rupert as well. Several times in the past he had used that incantation. On each occasion his victim had instantly burst into flame, but now here stood this whelp of a Hartford with barely his hair singed. The magic in the fellow's ring was powerful indeed. Perhaps he would not return it to Lord Hazar after all.

Rupert drew back his arm, prepared to cast another, more deadly bolt, but then stayed his curse. What was it Hazar had said? The finger must be removed before he's dead. No, he must wait to kill him. He had to get the ring first.

Rupert changed his aim and caused pits to explode in the ground around Grantin. Earth, stones, and leaves filled the air and splattered against Grantin's already disheveled clothing.

"How dare you molest a wizard of my great power!" Rupert shouted. "I could take you apart bone by bone if I so desired. Tell me now, while you still have a few moments left to live, what reparations do you offer me to dissuade me from this pleasant task?"

"Nothing . . . I have nothing. I apologize. Excuse me. Please, it was all a mistake."

"No gold, no silver, no precious stones?"

"No, nothing."

"What about your ring?"

"I can't; it won't come off. It's welded to my finger by a magic spell."

"Welded to your finger by a magic spell, is it? It happens that I have a solution for that." Rupert removed a razor-sharp dagger from his scabbard and tossed it at Grantin's feet. "Cut off the offending digit, throw it and the ring to me, and I give you my word that you may pass in peace."

"Why is it that everyone wants me to cut off my finger?" Grantin wailed as he stooped to pick up the knife.

"Come on, now, what are you waiting for? Get on with it or I'll make fast work of you."

Almost as if in a trance Grantin studied the mirrored highlights reflected in the blade. He brought it closer to his finger. Almost against his will he planned where he would begin his butchery.

Grantin juggled the blade clumsily. Its needle-fine point

pricked his skin just above the knuckle. A brilliant scarlet bead welled up in high contrast to the nut-brown hue of his flesh. The sight of the blood snapped Grantin from the spell which Rupert's threats had cast over him. He remembered the incantation he had tried while lost in the forest.

In the blink of an eye he again balled his fist and pointed the ring at Rupert. Before the deacon could utter a word Grantin screamed: "Out of my way!"

Like a stone flung from a slingshot Rupert's body was hurled backward, up through the trees, until in a moment it had passed from sight toward the far horizon.

Shocked by the effects of the spell, Grantin paced forward until he reached the spot which Rupert had occupied mere seconds before. Looking up, he could see the tunnel of broken limbs which Rupert's body had bored through the forest canopy. Perhaps a thousand yards ahead the trail reached an apogee and then slowly straightened and curved downward.

Off beyond the treeline Pyra was beginning its evening descent. Grantin had to hurry; he must leave the woods before full dark. Slapping his hands together, he brushed the dirt from his palms, then sprinted forward toward the portal of the castle of the mad wizard Shenar.

Chapter Twenty

Invisible gusts of heat rolled from the caldrons scattered about Hazar's basement kitchen. One human only was present to surpervise these, the most demeaned of the Ajaj. Obese and sweat-stained, Cockle, the chief cook, reclined on a stool near the far wall.

Higher than Castor's waist, the edge of the wort bin presented the Ajaj with yet another obstacle on this his first day of kitchen service. Straining forward to the limit of his reach, his fingertips touched the end of one of the cylindrical yellow-gray roots. The vegetable wobbled. Under the prodding of Castor's questing fingertips it bumped forward over its hair-fine filaments until it was fully within his grasp. Shifting his weight backward, Castor allowed his soft-furred stomach to slide across the edge of the bin until he had moved far enough for his feet to touch the floor again.

Wheezing heavily, Castor pushed himself back from the box and stood up straight. A momentary wave of dizziness rocked him. He shook his head, clearing it, then paced across the overheated kitchen to the caldron where the midday stew was already beginning to boil.

A few feet from the kettle Castor hesitated, then changed direction and headed for the cutting board. His tread made no sound except for the occasional clicking of his toenails against the stone floor. He raised his right arm toward a six-inch-long knife hanging from a peg on the wall.

A stunning buffet sent him spinning across the floor. "Just what do you think you're doing, you furry little sneak?" Cockle growled.

Castor turned and forced his eyes to refocus. Cockle stood aroused and belligerent in front of the preparation table. A roll of illusion-plant leaves hung from the overseer's mouth. His pale, sparsely haired belly protruded from the inadequate confinement of his shirt.

"I was merely going to trim the tendrils from the wort root," Castor said in a voice that seemed to him too calm to have issued from his own lips.

"For Lord Hazar you trim the tendrils; everyone else takes what they get. That stew's for the guards; they'll eat whatever's in there and like it. And while I'm about giving you a lesson, here's another: guards like wort root. As a matter of fact, they love it better than meat or anything else. They're always begging me to put more wort root and less meat into the stew, so you go back to the bin and get five or ten more. And don't never go near those knives again without asking me first. Well, what're you waiting for? Get to work!"

"There aren't any more; the bin's empty."

"Buster," Cockle shouted, "do I have to do everything around here? Have you let us get low on supplies again? What's this about no more wort root?"

An old Ajaj, crippled in the left leg, limped painfully forward. Head down, shoulders bent in what appeared to be a permanent cringe, Buster approached the kitchen steward. The grizzled white fur around his muzzle twitched with fear.

"Send somebody out to the depot to get some more, you old fool! It'll go hard with you if you don't return in time to finish dinner. Here, take this smart aleck with you." Cockle placed a meaty hand on Castor's shoulder and shoved him across the room, then grunted and ponderously reseated himself upon his overseer's stool.

"Yes, my lord, of course, my lord," Buster responded. "Come along, Castor."

Buster led Castor down the hallway and up the flight of stairs which separated the scullery from the alley near Hazar's quarters. With a nod from Buster the doorkeeper slid back the portal.

"Where are we going?" Castor asked once they had left Hazar's apartments behind.

"To Topor's supply depot," Buster replied. "Don't you know where the food bins are?"

"Until today I was a senior empather. The closest I got to Lord Hazar's food supply was the luncheons given to me during the term of my duties."

"Well, then, a bit of a lesson's in order, isn't it?" Buster limped along the outer rim street at a brisk pace. "This street we're on is called the First Circle, although it's not a circle at all but a series of five straight stretches which parallel the five-sided walls beyond. The five first lords, Hazar, Nefra, Topor, Bolam, and Zaco, retain for themselves the quarters bordering the city's five gates."

"Why are the most powerful Gogols housed at the edge of the city instead of its center?" Castor interrupted. "It doesn't make sense."

"It doesn't make sense to a Gray," Buster responded. Already he had lost some of the feeble appearance he projected in the scullery. Now, by indefinable means, his gait had become stronger, and his visage had taken on a sly, hardened aspect. "A Gray thinks only of security, of safety. The higher the status of a Gray, the deeper his tunnels, the thicker his walls, the more he hides himself from the outside world. The Gogols, on the other hand, think in terms of power.

"He that controls the gates controls the city. Also, if worse comes to worst, he who lives on the outside wall can flee. Ah, that's heresy to our people, the thought of fleeing one's home, running out into the open country. But not to a human. The lords' main enemies are within the city, not without."

"There now, up ahead, the street to the left, we go that way."

Castor turned his head and saw that at the angle where two walls of the inner pentagram normally would be joined there was a street which ran through the walls toward the center of Cicero. Two Gogols guarded the lane but let the Grays pass unmolested after Buster executed a gentle bow. Once out of sight of the guards Buster resumed his monologue:

"The guards know me as Hazar's scullery clerk and so let me pass without interrogation. Here, look to the right and left and you'll see a bit of Cicero's past. There and there," Buster said, pointing; "see the roughly chiseled stone, the crudely cut blocks? At one time there was a gate here, five gates in this ring of buildings between the First and Second Circles, and five more in the next, on into the center of Cicero.

"But the system proved unworkable, too much internal strife. Every lord and deacon and subdeacon and acolyte strove to control a gate and then use that position as a springboard to move outward until at last one of the five main gates themselves was under the wizard's sway. For two hundred years the energy of the Gogols was dissipated in internal struggles.

"Twenty years ago Hazar's father, for a brief period, accomplished a combination of all of the outer lords against all of the inner deacons. Thus they forced the destruction of all of the gates save their own. Now, as a courtesy, the residents of the inner walls are allowed guards in the corridors leading toward the center of town, but two guards only and no gates at all. The whole city is now under the sway of the five lords and the five lords alone. For the first time in decades the Gogols have the energy to turn their eyes outward and make new plans for conquest."

Buster halted at the junction between the First Spoke Road and the Second Circle.

"Now we go left, around the Second Circle, until we come to the next passage in toward the center. The street we just left was the First Spoke Road. There is a Second, a Third, a Fourth, and a Fifth Spoke Road between the First and Second Circles. Do you notice the pattern of these streets, by the way?"

"Five streets, five gates; it seems rather straightforward," Castor remarked.

"There's more to it than that, friend Castor. Notice, the five outer gates break the walls at their points. The Spoke Roads penetrate inward at the centers. The next Spoke

Road, the Sixth, between the Second and the Third Circles, again breaks the points of the pentagons; and lastly the Eleventh through the Fifteenth Spoke Roads between the Third Circle and the Central Plaza penetrate at the centers. In this way there is no one straight path between the outside of the city and its center. Neither an invading army from beyond nor a fleeing populace from within has an easy route.

"Come, now, I've babbled too much. Hurry. Cockle becomes most unpleasant if his whims are frustrated."

Picking up their pace, the two Ajaj quickly traversed the remaining byways to reach the center of Cicero. A huge circular building occupied the middle of the large paved area known as the Central Plaza. Like everything else in Cicero this structure was divided into five compartments. Limping more noticeably now, face twitching in an occasional grimace of pain, Buster led them around the plaza to a doorway overhung with a banner bearing the image of a loaf of bread. Buster in the lead, both Grays approached the guarded entrance. There Buster identified himself as Hazar's servant. A human clerk rudely questioned the Ajaj concerning their purpose, authority, and needs. Finally they were admitted and issued wicker baskets with straps so that they might be attached across their shoulders.

Around the room were situated bins, barrels, jars, and boxes. Here reposed the fruits of the agricultural Grays' toil. The lords of the city and their household retainers, staff, and guards were allocated a full half of all of the foodstuffs. Next, a fourth went to the inhabitants of the second ring of buildings, an eighth to the subdeacons of the third ring, and the balance to the guildless, patronless laborers of the tenements which dotted the central circle.

Castor marveled at the sheer, vicious efficiency of the system. The more powerful the lord, the more food was available to those in his service. Each individual, therefore, aspired to advance within the ranks of his own house. The head of each house desired to advance into the service of the lords in the next circle outward. Those who failed to cooperate ate poorly in good times and in lean times starved.

Castor and Buster filled their baskets, hoisted their loads, and, after allowing their supply of wort roots to be recorded by the warehouse clerk, trudged back through the streets toward Hazar's quarters.

"How long have you been here, Buster?" Castor asked after a long silence.

"How long? A lifetime . . . forever. How long is that?"

"Have you ever thought about . . . about doing something about all this?" Castor asked.

"Doing something? Bringing down the Gogol empire with my two bare hands? An Ajaj would have to be insane to even consider such a notion."

Another tame Gray, just like the rest. Clenching his jaws together to prevent an angry response, Castor grimaced and trudged ahead.

"Of course," Buster continued, a sly smile splitting his lips, "I never claimed to be very sane. I sometimes think the pain in my leg has affected my brain."

"Meaning?"

"I mean," Buster whispered, "ever since a group of the lords' children crippled me for a few minutes of sport, I have been crazy enough to believe that I'd like nothing better than to plant one of Cockle's wort stickers between Hazar's bony ribs."

For an instant a smirk of pure glee flickered across Buster's face, to be almost as rapidly replaced by a subservient expression as the bound wooden door of Hazar's scullery slipped into view.

Chapter Twenty-one

The stout bound timbers of Shenar's front door produced in Grantin their own particular brand of magic. For perhaps half a minute he stood immobilized before the portal, unable to overcome the deep sense of foreboding which chilled his bones. From somewhere far back in the corner of his brain a thin voice screamed, "Get away while you can! Danger! Leave while you can!"

Nervously, he turned to study the meadow, now flooded with the tawny blanket of dusk. Across the stream beyond a dense thicket of scratchberry bushes the squeal of prey in flight echoed through the early-evening air. No, there was no refuge for Grantin there. The throb of the bloodstone returned its pulsing beat to his index finger and, to a lesser extent, his whole left arm. Reluctantly he turned back to the door. Gathering up all of his courage, he propelled the knocker with two sharp thrusts.

There was no immediate response. After a minute's delay Grantin gave the door two more sharp raps. Almost instantly, as if the castle's owner had stationed himself just beyond the portal, a peephole opened. Shenar's high-pitched voice called out.

"Who are you, and what do you want?"

Startled by the sudden response, Grantin's own voice shot up an octave in pitch. He squeaked out his answer.

"Is this the manor house of the great wizard Shenar? I've come to seek his counsel and aid on a professional matter."

"Shenar has no time for the inconsequential problems of penniless vagrants. Be off with you!"

"I'm not a penniless vagrant, and this is a problem for only a great magician like the renowned Shenar."

"The wizard is very busy with spells of great importance. Briefly state your request so it may be decided if your errand is worthy of taking the time of the great Shenar."

Suddenly Grantin's tale about seeking relief from disturbing nightmares appeared flimsy and shopworn.

"Well, I . . . you see, I fell afoul of a great wizard, a matter involving his daughter, and . . . well, we need not go into the particulars. In any event, to vex me he pronounced a spell which now infests my dreams with horrifying nightmares. I have not slept well in days, and if I do not gain some relief soon I will shortly die."

"You dare bother Shenar for this, this petty trifle?"

"My death from malicious sorcery is not a petty trifle," Grantin responded with mock anger.

"It's a petty trifle to Shenar. Be gone before he hexes you himself."

"Wait, wait, there's more. My uncle is himself a great wizard, Greyhorn of the Hartfords. Shenar would earn his undying gratitude were he to rid me of this spell. Greyhorn . . ." Grantin detected the glint of the peephole being slid closed. "Wait, wait, one more thing—I can pay, I can pay. Look." Grantin held up his left hand, placing the bloodstone two inches in front of the now half-closed spyhole. "This ring, an ancient family heirloom of great antiquity and untold value, will be Shenar's if he succeeds in curing me of this spell. Look, look, see how it flashes with color; a finer stone has never been quarried."

The peephole slammed shut with a metallic clink. Shrugging his shoulders in despair, Grantin turned to leave before further arousing Shenar's ire.

Behind him sounded a scrape. A slight vibration passed through the soles of his feet. Turning his head, Grantin saw the great door slide open. Silhouetted in the glow from the room beyond, an imp in a baggy gown waved Grantin inside the manor.

Grantin advanced and the dwarf slid shut the door behind him. He studied the creature with frank curiosity. An aged face on what appeared to be, even beneath the gown, a shrunken, misshapen frame.

"I have the honor of addressing . . . ?" Grantin said, nodding at the midget.

"Shenar, grand wizard extraordinaire, at your service, young man. You say this ring will be my payment for ridding you of a few nightmares?"

"Yes, I—"

"A moment, a moment; let me examine my fee more closely." Shenar grabbed Grantin's left hand. Squinting and straining, his eyes barely two inches above the ring, Shenar studied the ornament from all angles. After a thorough inspection he clasped the band with his right hand, holding Grantin's palm in his left, and attempted to twist the ring free. After two or three fruitless attempts Shenar nodded his head sagely and let go Grantin's hand.

"The ring seems to be rather firmly affixed," Shenar suggested.

"As I said, it is a family heirloom. When it was passed down to me by my uncle he imparted a special enchantment to the band to restrain me from parting with it for some casual purpose. Naturally, for a wizard of your great powers, the nullification of this minor charm will be no problem at all, a trivial exercise at best."

"You seem to hold little respect for my powers, young man," Shenar responded slyly. "First you ask me to formulate a spell to rid you of a nightmare curse, and now willy-nilly you suggest I perform a second incantation and rid you of this ring. And all this for one fee? Two spells should require two payments."

"You have a brilliant mind, to be sure, learned Shenar, but I view this problem from a slightly different angle. The second spell, that of loosening the ring, is not for my benefit but for yours, for in so doing you free your property, the ring, from a site, my finger, inconsistent with your ownership. Without the second spell the first cannot be compensated. In a sense, it is I who bend myself to your needs by making my person available for the formulation of the enchantment of removal."

"Well, young man, there do seem to be several ways of looking at the situation. Perhaps a solution to this dilemma will present itself. But where are my manners? You are a guest in my home, and I keep you standing here in the entranceway. Come, come; let me show you to quarters where you can spend the night. Tomorrow morning perhaps another solution will present itself."

Waddling forward, Shenar led Grantin to the brass-bound door. In a trice the wizard had unlocked it and, waving his hand, bid Grantin follow him down the stone steps to the chambers beneath the house. To Grantin the doorway appeared no more inviting than the entrance to the pits of hell.

"Oh, there's no need to go to any trouble for me. I can sleep right here on this lovely rug."

"Nonsense; I insist. If you want me to help you with your ring—I mean, your nightmares—you must let me show you my hospitality. Come along." Shenar began to walk down the steps. Grantin reluctantly followed.

Reaching the bottom of the stairs, Shenar continued forward. At the end of the passage he threw back the last door and waved Grantin inside.

"There you go, young man, right in there. Now, don't be shy. Go right ahead, and we will talk in the morning."

Through the doorway Grantin could see bars marching across the center of the room. He stood rooted in place two feet in front of the portal.

"But . . . but . . . that is, ah . . ."

"Let us have no delays here, young man. Go ahead with you now." So saying, Shenar reached for Grantin with his open right hand. Because of his meager height the wizard's palm approached Grantin's body near the seat of his pants. When his hand was a few inches distant a spark leaped from Shenar's fingers and buried itself in Grantin's rump. With a cry more of surprise than of pain he leaped forward. His vision flickered, and Grantin found himself behind the row of bars. In a flash Shenar closed and locked the door.

"There, my young friend, you see how easy it was. Now, you just spend a pleasant evening, and in the morning I will get to work on that ring." Smiling, Shenar nodded politely toward Grantin's fear-ridden face, then, turning lightly on his feet, ambled back down the corridor.

How could this have happened to him? Without even so much as lifting a finger he had allowed a madman to imprison him. In frustration Grantin grabbed the bars and vainly attempted to rattle them loose from their sockets. In a few seconds his fury was spent, and, sick at heart, he turned to examine his new home. Only then did he spy a Fanist's gray form. With a startled gasp he leaped backward flat against the wall.

"Hello," the native said.

"Hello," Grantin replied uneasily. Fanists had never molested humans, although, in these borderlands, who knew what strange affairs took place? For the time being at least they both seemed to be on less than the most favorable terms with Shenar.

"Excuse me," Grantin said. "You startled me. It appears that we are both involuntary guests of the mad wizard." Grantin studied the Fanist carefully. Could this be the native from his dreams? And Shenar. Didn't he vaguely remember a nightmare in which such a man pranced and threw glowing bolts at a caged native?

"Are you . . . I mean, you seem quite familiar to me. Have you been here a long time?" Grantin asked.

"Almost two weeks," the native replied. "You have business with the small one?"

"I came to him for help in ridding me of a spell, but it seems that he has more than a simple business transaction in mind. I fear that he means to take advantage of me."

"I, as well; he asks questions for which there are no answers. You stare at me strangely; is there some problem with your vision?"

"No," Grantin replied hesitantly. "It's just that you look very familiar, like someone I've seen in a dream. Do you, by any chance—I know this sounds strange, but is it possible that you wear a blue jewel against your skull beneath the skin of your forehead?"

The Fanist leaped forward. Grantin cringed against the far wall.

"You know me? You know of my mission? These are secrets no human may share. Has Ajax sent you to win my release? Are you one of the Brothers?"

"No, I . . . I mean, I don't know. I don't understand what you're talking about. I had a dream. I saw you and, I think, Shenar. In my nightmare you had a blue gem beneath your forehead, and Shenar was torturing you. . . . It's this stone, this blasted stone. It's driving me mad." Futilely Grantin tugged at the ring.

Using the muscles surrounding his eyeballs, the Fanist increased the bulge of the lens until his telescopic vision gave him a clear picture of Grantin's ring. He studied the gem for just an instant and then relaxed his grip on the bars.

"I understand," the Fanist said, backing away.

"You understand! I wish I understood. Don't just stand there; explain it to me. Ever since I met that woman my life has been a waking nightmare."

"The stones all sense each other, the overflow of their energies."

Grantin met the Fanist's explanation with a quizzical expression.

"Your stone is a powerstone, a magic stone; my stone is the same for me. Red must be the stone for humans. Blue is the stone for my people. In sleep, in times of torment, apparently the stones of one race can sense a bit of the energy swirling about the stones of the other. Shenar wants the secret of our powerstones. I have refused to tell him. Naturally you may not tell him either."

"Powerstones, secrets . . . I just want to be out of here and home and free of this accursed ring. If I could just do away with all of this, I'd never complain about Uncle Greyhorn's chores again. Isn't there some way that we could pool our resources to escape from here?"

"Not I. The small one has enchanted me with a spell of great power. I am withheld from uttering the words and making the signs. And you?"

"Me? Has he put a spell on me? Well, we came in; we talked, and he led me down here. No, no, I don't think he bothered to. Do you think there's enough power in this ring to save us?"

"Perhaps. You are not a very good wizard, I can tell that. Certainly Shenar does not fear you. It's possible that you might be able to do something before he returns in the morning."

"You'll help?"

127

"As much as I can."

"Excellent. Perhaps we'll show that midget a thing or two yet. Let me just get a few hours' sleep; it's been a tiring day. Soon I'll be fit as a fiddle."

"No sleep, not now," the Fanist commanded.

"My friend—what did you say your name was?"

"Chom. You can call me Chom."

"Chom, I am absolutely exhausted. Just a few hours' sleep is all I need."

"I suppose each race knows its needs best. I would not interfere with a human, but you understand that an hour after sunrise Shenar will cut off your hand, and by lunch he will have made you ready for the pickup."

"The pickup?"

"Naturally Shenar will distribute your spare parts to the supplier for the Sawbones' Guild who will appear here tomorrow at the fourth hour."

Half a second later Grantin had leaped to his feet and reached the bars, ready to begin work. He bent over and with exaggerated care studied the joining between the iron bars and the floor of the cell. He could discover no crack or crevice at the juncture.

With exquisite deliberation Grantin clasped his hands around one of the rods and pulled back on it with slowly increasing force. Nothing happened. Beneath his fingers the metal was cool and remarkably slick.

Off to one side the Fanist quietly watched Grantin's exertions but made no suggestions of his own. After another minute or two of futile effort Grantin shrugged his shoulders and turned to Chom. "I suppose I'll have to take a chance on an impromptu spell."

Standing back three feet from the barrier, Grantin held forth his left fist, pointed the bloodstone at the base of the center bar, and sucked in his breath preparatory to casting an extemporaneous spell.

"If I may ask, friend human," Chom interrupted somewhat diffidently, "specifically what spell you plan to cast?"

Grantin held his breath for a moment, then let it out in a whoosh. "Since we are imprisoned by these bars," he replied somewhat waspishly, "I am going to command them to be gone from our way." Grantin turned away from Chom and again began to raise his hand, only to be interrupted once more.

"If I might make a suggestion before you start," Chom said while his lower right hand restrained Grantin from commencing the spell, "if you merely command the bars to be gone, they must go somewhere, and I would estimate that they will travel perhaps ten feet until they hit the far wall of the room. From there I calculate that they will rebound back toward us and will continue to ricochet throughout the chamber until they have reduced themselves to a state of molten metal."

Grantin opened his fist as if he clutched a red-hot cinder and immediately let his arm drop back to his side.

"Perhaps if I called up a tongue of flame to cut through the iron . . . ?"

"That would be a good idea except for the fact that Shenar has sheathed the rods with the energy of one of his most potent incantations. Any flame strong enough to burn through them would roast us both."

"Well, I might . . ."

"And of course an attempt to shrink the bars would pull the ceiling down around our heads."

"There's always . . ."

"I have considered bending them to one side, but their energy field has made them brittle. They would shatter and cut us to shreds."

"All right, I give up. What would you have me do?"

"Of course it's not my place to tell you how to use your powers," Chom began diplomatically, "but perhaps you know the incantation necessary to shrink us to a small enough size to fit between the bars?"

"That sounds rather complex. Do you think I could make it up as we go along?"

"That particular spell tends to give unreliable results unless recited perfectly. I fear that random attempts might result in a grotesque rearrangement of our internal organs."

"Well, what am I supposed to do, then? We can't cut the bars; we can't bend them; we can't shrink them; and we can't shrink ourselves. I don't know what to do, unless . . ." Turning away from the barrier, Grantin pivoted to study the other portions of the cell. "Can you tell if there's a spell on the walls?" he asked Chom.

The Fanist rubbed all four hands along the surface of the back wall. After perhaps a thirty-second investigation he looked back at Grantin and shook his head in a gesture copied from the humans.

"No, they seem to be mere stone," the native declared.

"Well, then, we'll ignore the bars. Let's see if I can use the ring to cut a tunnel through the wall."

"Possibly a workable idea. May I suggest that we begin over here?" Chom said, pointing to the right-hand edge of the enclosed area up near the bars. "When Shenar enters in the morning this is the place that will be most hidden from his immediate view."

Grantin nodded in agreement and approached the indicated section of stone. Holding the bulge of the bloodstone only a few inches from the juncture of two granite blocks, Grantin tensed his muscles and visualized a white-hot flame six inches long erupting from the surface of the ring. Forcing his eyes open while retaining the image, he spoke in a hushed voice.

"Flame, hot flame, jolting flame, burning flame! A torch to cut us free I order there to be."

A white-hot pencil of light appeared in the air a fraction of an inch above the surface of the ring and buried itself in the stone. Dust and fumes bubbled from the fissure, and globules of molten rock dripped to the floor. Scared and shaking, Grantin slowly lowered his arm and lengthened the fissure. In a few minutes the smoke and stench and heat had long passed Grantin's limits of tolerance and he commanded the flame to die. Staggering back, he collapsed in an untidy heap against the opposite wall.

Chom was apparently undisturbed by these adverse conditions and advanced upon the work site to examine Grantin's progress. Commencing at a point three feet above the floor, the line slanted downward slightly out of true for eighteen or twenty inches.

"Good, very good. Only eight or nine feet more and we will be able to escape."

"Eight feet more! I haven't gone two feet yet and I'm exhausted. I've got to rest."

"Plenty of rest you will get on the sawbones' shelf if we do not finish by morning," Chom replied.

Wearily Grantin pulled himself to his feet, approached the wall, and rekindled the flame.

It was just before dawn when a feverish, exhausted

Grantin cut the last inch of the escape tunnel, then promptly collapsed. Chom pulled Grantin to one side and, using all four of his arms for grasping and his two sturdy legs as levers, he began to worry the eight-inch thick plug from the wall. After several minutes' struggle the section fell clear.

Unceremoniously Chom grabbed the unconscious human by the shoulders and dragged his supine form out over the uneven stone base of the exit. He deposited Grantin in the unlighted chamber beyond, then crept back to maneuver the plug in behind them. Using his belt like a sling, straining every last bit of energy from his powerful arms and legs, Chom at last managed to guide the granite back into the wall in the hope that their method of escape would not be discovered until at least ten or fifteen seconds after Shenar entered the room.

After a minute or two of futile search Chom discovered a glowpod at waist height, which, he reminded himself, would be as high as the dwarf Shenar would be able to reach. Carefully removing the celluloselike pod from its cradle, he rubbed it gently until static electricity had excited it to a weak phosphorescence. In the torch's feeble glow he soon determined that he and Grantin had taken refuge in a storage chamber. He returned to the sleeping human.

A rough prodding of Grantin's shoulders failed to wake him. So deep was the human's exhaustion that finally Chom was forced to slap Grantin's face in order to bring him back to consciousness.

"Wake up! Wake up! Shenar will be coming any minute now. You must make ready to conquer him with your spells."

Grantin's eyes fluttered open and for a moment he forgot where he was. He had been dreaming that he was at home in his uncle's castle, asleep in his own bed and with no greater problems than finding a few coppers for the upcoming fair. All at once the terror of his predicament flooded back. Wearily Grantin levered himself into a sitting position.

"Grantin, we must devise a spell to conquer Shenar— something that will restrain his hands and his voice."

"A spell," Grantin said weakly. "I'll be lucky if I have enough strength to stand up."

"Hurry—he comes. I sense him approaching. You must do it." Chom helped Grantin to his feet.

The human ignored Chom. He studied the room in which they now found themselves, then lapsed into a deep reverie. At last, with Shenar's sandals scraping on the stairs, Grantin devised a plan and whispered it into the Fanist's earhole. The scheme required exact timing and perfect reflexes, two things which Grantin doubted that either he or Chom now possessed. Nevertheless, it was their only hope.

As soon as they heard Shenar begin to unlock the cell door Grantin and Chom slipped into the passage outside the storeroom. This hallway joined the corridor leading to their former cell. To the left of the juncture was the cell, to the right the anteroom below the castle entrance hall. Peeking around the corner, they saw Shenar entering the cell. Before the wizard had even closed the door Chom was sprinting noiselessly to the right toward the anteroom, weapon in hand, while Grantin slunk back down the corridor toward the utility closet.

In less than a second Shenar discerned the scars where the granite slab had been burned free from the rest of the wall. Outraged that any mere mortals would dare to try to escape from the great Shenar, the wizard slammed open the door and raced down the hallway as fast as his bandy legs would carry him. At the intersection of the tunnel leading to the storeroom he hesitated, then plunged down the small corridor to check the storage room before widening his search to the more distant portions of his manor. Sliding open the door, Shenar received a second shock to find Grantin, hands on hips, standing insolently in the center of the room.

"So, you've finally come. You don't move very fast on those shrunken little legs, do you?" Grantin taunted him.

The sorcerer's rage rose almost to apoplexy. He raised his right hand to cast a spell, but Grantin waved it aside with a casual gesture.

"Come, now; you don't think you can hex me, do you?" he asked Shenar. "I wear the bloodstone, and my power is that of a hundred ordinary sorcerers like yourself."

"You will die horribly!" Shenar screamed. He pulled back both hands in preparation for casting his most powerful spell of dismemberment. Fingers stiffened in a

V-shaped position, Shenar advanced. The wizard's gown rustled as he straightened his arm to cast the spell. The hiss of his sleeves hid the whoosh of air from behind as Chom brought down a mop handle full upon the wizard's skull.

Unfortunately for Shenar, Chom had little experience with the more intimate details of human anatomy, and, basing the strength of his blow upon Fanist standards, he badly misjudged the energy necessary to render the sorcerer unconscious. The mop handle shattered. Before he could finish reciting his spell, Shenar fell quietly to the floor, quite dead.

"I didn't mean to kill him," Chom apologized. "I forgot how fragile you humans are. What do we do now?"

Grantin shook his head, confused by Chom's question.

"Should we bury him in the garden to fertilize the plants, or do you humans prefer stuffing the remains into the fireplace?"

Grantin stared at the pathetic bundle of cloth and flesh that composed Shenar's mortal remains and shook his head in horror. At last he looked at the Fanist and replied in a quiet voice.

"I think planting in the garden would be appropriate, but not now. I've got to rest and then eat and then figure out what I'm going to do next. We can do it later. He's not going to bother anyone for the next few hours."

"Best if we left this place," Chom suggested.

"You can leave if you want. I'm going to get some sleep first. Besides, I came here for an answer. I need to find out how to remove this ring. Shenar's library may hold the key."

In a surprisingly human gesture Chom shrugged his shoulders, then helped the weak and shaking Grantin from the room. The former prisoners, now for a while at least masters of the manor house, proceeded down the stone corridor and slowly ascended the dungeon stairs. At the top Chom leaned Grantin against the wall, then reached out and threw back the foyer door.

Crisp early-morning daylight streamed through the opening and for an instant half blinded both beings. Through squinted eyelids Grantin was shocked to see a burly human in the center of the hall. The man turned to face the doorway and likewise registered dismay at seeing

Chom emerging from the dungeon. Instantly the intruder bounded back and raced out the front door. A few seconds later the disjointed rhythm of a Rex's two hooves and tail could be heard disappearing into the distance.

"What—who was that?" Grantin stuttered.

"We are in danger again," Chom responded. "That was the man who captured me and delivered me here to Shenar. In a day or two at the most he will get over his fear and return with his men. By then we must be gone."

"Who was he?" Grantin repeated.

"He is the human they call Yon Diggery, the bandit."

Chapter Twenty-two

Against the rustle of trees and the calls of the birds, the plop, plop, plop of softly dripping water was almost inaudible. The moisture made its way down between the fibers of the sodden tunic and passed as an invisible sheet over the slime-encrusted surface of the rough leather britches until at last it collected in large, graceful drops near the point of a mud-encrusted cuff. There it dripped back into the shallows at the north edge of the swamp.

At the beginning of his journey Rupert's back had snapped off protruding branches like so much dry kindling. In a second or two he reached the top of an arc which brought him clear of the uppermost branches of even the highest trees. There Rupert seemed to float suspended between heaven and earth. In a few seconds the propulsive energy was spent, and he sped earthward on a ballistic path. As the forest flew upward at him Rupert curled his hurtling body into a tight ball, all elbows, shoulders, and knees.

He snapped through branches, then rebounded from a limb too massive to break and shot straight forward on a course almost parallel with the ground. In the near distance the trees thinned and spread apart to make room for Stinkhole Marsh.

Gravity and the laws of aerodynamics overcame inertia, and Rupert's body angled downward. Still at high speed, he struck the surface of the water and skipped like a stone across the first two thirds of the swamp. Dense clumps of yellow marsh reeds finally brought a halt to his forward motion. Still grasping an armful of the rubbery vegetation, he promptly sank to the bottom of the pond.

With truly remarkable fury Rupert flailed his arms and legs until he reached the surface, there to take in great lungfuls of the foul-smelling air. Kicking off his waterlogged boots, he somehow managed to reach the shallows. Numbed and almost exhausted, he struggled forward. At last he reached the shore, where he allowed himself to fall backward on the muddy bank. There he now lay, wheezing like an exhausted pack animal on the verge of collapse. With each breath tiny insects were sucked through his open mouth, but even these were now beneath his notice.

Only two thoughts occupied the Gogol's mind: first, the knowledge that he had failed Hazar and that it would be death for him to return to Cicero; and second, the rageborn certainty that somehow, someday, he would tear Grantin's living body limb from limb.

After a few minutes the worst of Rupert's wheezing subsided, and he sat up to survey his location. Already he had begun to make plans.

He would find the river and clean himself. Using his Huntsman Spell, he would capture game for an evening meal. That night he would shelter in the forest, and the next day, clean and rested, he would set out to make a new life for himself.

Rupert recalled that some dozen years before another deacon had been forced to flee to the borderlands under similar circumstances. The man was now a bandit chieftain rumored to make his headquarters in this very vicinity. Rupert had little doubt that he would be allowed entry into the gang. If nothing else, he had valuable spells to contribute, together with information on Lord Hazar's incredible plans.

Rupert began to scheme with the utmost deviousness.

The outlaws would become allies in his search for Grantin and the ring—always the ring. Let his new associates take the brunt of Grantin's defenses while he, at the appropriate moment, cut off the Hartford's hand and appropriated the ring. Then how he would make the pipsqueak pay!

Rupert pushed himself to his feet and examined the sky. It was late afternoon. He would have to move fast to find shelter before full night.

And tomorrow, tomorrow he would search out his new-chosen comrade, the bandit chieftain Yon Diggery.

Chapter Twenty-three

Though it was not so fine as his uncle Greyhorn's manse, Grantin was, nevertheless, highly pleased with Shenar's Castle. A fine pigeon-fluff bed of truly immense proportions dominated the late wizard's bedroom, and a well-stocked larder provided Grantin and Chom with a wealth of food.

When their inspection had revealed no loyal retainers who might avenge Shenar's death Chom and Grantin returned to the basement. They unceremoniously tucked the wizard's body into a potato sack and carried it to the garden for burial. There beneath the blossoms of a great bush of saucerflowers Shenar was laid to rest.

Returning to the castle, Chom and Grantin barred the doors and took themselves to separate bedrooms. After only a few hours sleep, tortured by vague nightmares and a sense of tense weariness, Grantin awakened to search out Shenar's pantry. Slipping back easily into the duties he had performed for so long under Greyhorn's tutelage, he prepared a meal of cheese, fruit, bread, spiced meat, cookies, and cold marinated vegetables, to be washed down with a thick, bittersweet wine.

At about the time he finished laying out the meal Chom entered the small dining area just off the kitchen.

"We are in luck, my friend," Grantin called to Chom. "For all his faults our host set a nice table. Don't be shy. Come in; sit down; there's plenty for both of us."

With an expression of vague uneasiness Chom slipped into one of the high-backed chairs which bordered the table. Again the Fanist was confronted with the peculiar human customs regarding food. Also, after his first adverse experience with humans Chom had become a bit suspicious. Might these concoctions contain drugs whose very existence would be hidden by their peculiar seasonings?

Chom studied the fare with a critical eye. For a few seconds Grantin hesitated, waiting for the Fanist to eat but then hunger overcame his manners. Chom watched the young human load his plate with chunks, gobs, puddles, squares, and scoops of various substances and then shovel one after another into his mouth with the use of curiously constructed metal implements. Unlikely that the items were drugged. Well, Ajax said to experiment.

Following Grantin's lead, he loaded up his plate, then in a random fashion inserted the substances into his mouth. On a slab of dark yellow cheese he spread half an inch of crossberry preserves, then topped the appetizer with two slices of marinated potato. Next he ingested a molasses-brown cookie dipped in pepperroot relish and washed the lot down with a half-pint swallow of wine.

Chom was the victim of harshly contrasting sensations. His throat alternately burned and tingled while the organs which in Fanists passed for taste buds appeared to have been awakened from a millennia-long slumber. These sensations were beyond any of Chom's expectations. Thrilled with the effect, he began to prepare further mouthfuls with the coordinated use of all four of his hands. A slice of meat was wrapped around a chicken leg and eaten in two bites, bone and all. With his upper and lower left arms he drowned half a jelly-apple pie with spoonfuls of pickled beets, which concoction was conveyed in heaping spoonfuls to his anxiously awaiting gullet. Amazing! Chom decided that the human concept of food was an extraordinarily good idea after all.

With great deliberateness Grantin turned his eyes away from the nauseating combinations which the Fanist was ingesting. When the edge was off his hunger and Chom's devastation of the buffet had declined Grantin began a conversation with the native.

"Do you live around here?" he asked Chom.

"Nearby, no. My community is back beyond the mountains, in the land of the Hartfords."

"Then we're both a long way from home. I'm a Hartford as well, but as a result of various difficulties I find myself exiled here, for the time being at least. And you— were you expelled from your tribe?"

"Expelled, thrown out, no. I am, you might say, studying humans, a traveler, a tourist. Yes, that is a good description, I am a tourist. And you, you are an apprentice wizard?" Chom asked.

"What makes you think that?"

"The fact that you wear such a ring."

Grantin shook his head sadly and replied: "This ring is not enough to make me a wizard. If you want to know the truth, as of two days ago my occupation was that of apprentice factotum to my uncle Greyhorn. My greatest ambition was to survive long enough to inherit his properties. The ring is a mistake, a folly, a horrible error. It is one with my flesh and cannot be removed. It is a great curse."

"Certainly there must be a way of removing—" Chom began reasonably.

"You are not going to cut off my hand; you are not; you are not!" Grantin screamed and banged his fist on the table. "I'm tired of everyone wanting to cut my finger off!"

"I was not thinking about removing your finger," Chom replied pleasantly, "though I suppose that would be one possibility. No, I had in mind a counterspell."

"I have tried. Even Uncle Greyhorn's sorcery was insufficient proof against this blasted ring. Unless, of course . . ." Grantin's face visibly brightened. ". . . unless, of course, you have a spell . . ."

"No, but I understand a bit about such stones. There may be a spell which can coax the answer from the ring itself. Not only does such a gem project your incantations outward, but it gathers in energy as well."

"Do you think that such a spell might be contained in Shenar's library?"

"Library?"

"The books containing records of Shenar's sorcery."

"Books—I've heard about such things. We do not use them. Our magic instead is stored here," Chom said, tapping his forehead. "I think I would like to see this library. If you can read the books to me I will know if you find the right spell."

Leaving the litter of crumbs, bones, spilled wine, and fragments of food, the two beings, not yet friends but far from enemies, passed from the kitchen and down the corridor to Shenar's library at the back of the manor house.

On a workbench fronted by a low horizontal window, vials, canisters, and jars stood in comfortable disarray. The bench itself was stained with potent substances. Chips and mars tattooed its hardwood planks.

To the right of the table stood three ranks of cupboards ten feet tall. Along the back wall a much-used stepladder stood at ease. To the left of the workbench was a short wall fronted with low, open shelves. A doorway led to an alcove beyond. It was in this alcove. sealed off behind the left-hand wall of the wizard's laboratory, that Grantin and Chom discovered the library.

The paper in use on Fane was handmade, heavy, thick, and brittle; printing also was done by hand or, in rare cases, through the use of carved type laboriously set a letter at a time. Consequently books tended to be thick, oversize, and bulky. Shenar's collection was no exception. His library of perhaps a thousand books filled floor-to-ceiling shelves on three of the four walls.

Grantin sought to determine a pattern to the shelving, but if there were one he was unable to divine it. After fifteen minutes of fruitless study, he decided to read each title, and if the subject matter appeared to bear on the problem he removed the volume and passed it to Chom.

Some two and a half hours later, his back aching and eyes bleary, Grantin finished his initial examination. On the table, stacked in orderly piles, were the perhaps fifty or so books which might contain the sought-for spell. Grantin studied the table of contents in each of the books and, after another two hours, succeeded in marking chapters in fifteen of them.

By now night had come to Grenitch Wood. Chom brought food and tapers to the library, the glowpods for some reason refusing to respond to Grantin's command.

In one ancient book of Hartford origin, *The Sorcerer's Constant Companion,* Grantin found a reference to a spell which could be used to bind one's jewelry and personal effects to the person so that absentminded individuals could avoid their constant loss. Upon detailed examination, however, the spell appeared to be a simple one easily dissolved by a standard incantation.

Grantin studied the flyleaves on each of the ten books remaining on the table. Eight of these he dismissed out of hand as enterprises of Hartford origin. Two remained: one with no indication of its origin but apparently specializing in spells of physical prowess, athletics, and self-defense; the second a volume of obvious Gogol manufacture: *Black Arts and Sacred Fires.* With great interest Grantin now examined this last volume. Almost immediately he found a reference to the bloodstone and its Hartford discoverer.

Edgar of Illum repulsed our forces with spells of unheard-of potency. Over the succeeding years diligent investigation has revealed the source of Edgar's power: a transparent, hard, deep-red crystal known for its color as the bloodstone or for its energy as the powerstone. The crystal is mined in rock formations of as yet unknown types, and neither is the size of the raw crystals nor their depth below the surface generally known. The shape of the finished crystal is believed to have great importance. It is well known that Edgar of Illum's gem was cut in a faceted oval shape. More recent intelligence has suggested that the optimum shape for any given-size crystal is a smooth, polished oval with the major axis twice the length of the minor.

The stone, by rumor, may be employed in a number of settings, but each time one has been observed it has been noted that it was encased in a socket of gold, copper, or bronze. The exact composition of these alloys is a closely guarded secret.

In order to function, the stone, or at least the setting, must be in physical contact with the flesh of its possessor. The longer the contact, the more intimate the relationship between gem and wizard and the more powerful the spells. On the other hand, once the stone has become attuned to its owner it will become worthless unless removed from the owner before the wizard's death. For this reason those sorcerers who wish to pass the bloodstone down their family line must take care either to use it occasionally and then in the form of an amulet or to be ready to separate themselves from its power during their lifetime. In light of the energy and protection which a bloodstone gives its owner it is unthinkable that one would voluntarily part with it after the period of acclimation.

The power of the stone is in direct proportion to its mass, and therefore one which appears only slightly bigger nevertheless generates an exponential increase in power. Again, as with other aspects of the bloodstone, there is, however, a countervailing influence against obtaining an overly large gem. The larger the stone, the greater the power and the greater the danger for the wizard who seeks to use it. Brain burn, insanity, and suicide have all been associated with the bloodstone. A small stone allows very powerful spells with reasonably small risk to the skilled sorcerer. A very large stone provides spells of unheard-of power, with a huge risk of early insanity and death. It is, therefore, only the bravest and most competent of wizards who will dare to wear a ring containing a moderately sized bloodstone. The crystal itself creates a field of energy within any circular metal mounting in which it may be placed, be it ring, bracelet, or necklace.

As an aside it might be noted that Grundal, the great scholar, claimed to have evolved a spell which would allow the release of such a ring. Known as Grundal's Final Incantation, it is said that the effort of perfecting it so drained his energies that he died before it could be tested. It is set forth in Appendix A, pages 1 through 7. The hasty practitioner should note that on his deathbed Grundal claimed that his error in the spell was that it must be uttered by the one from whose hand the bloodstone was received.

The diseases which the bloodstone can cause, listed alphabetically, are . . .

Grantin slammed shut the book and went immediately to the appendices at the end. Regretfully he tore out the pages. As carefully as possible he folded the stiff paper and placed it in a pocket between the two layers of his belt.

"You intend to go through with this, then?" the Fanist asked.

"I have no choice. The nightmares torture me, and, who knows, I may go insane as the book predicts. Besides, I'm tired of having everyone who meets me try and cut off my finger. No, if I can just remove this ring I'll be able to return to my uncle Greyhorn. Perhaps he'll let bygones be bygones. But what am I thinking about that for? It's all hopeless unless I can find the girl."

"The girl who gave you the ring?"

"Yes. A lovely lady, obviously of the highest character. Long brown hair, sparkling eyes, magnificent figure. Mara, lovely Mara. She could be anywhere by now."

"If you are determined, there is a way to find her," Chom suggested.

"How? Do you know such a way? Tell me!"

"As I said, the stone both projects and collects magic. Since she gave you the ring, it would have formed a bond with her, weak but still there. If you concentrate hard enough perhaps you will be able to view her in the stone. Conceivably you might recognize her location."

Grantin made himself comfortable at the library table, gulped down the last of his wine, then, grasping his hands together in front of him, bent over and looked deeply into the ring. His forehead beaded with sweat. His hands clenched together so tightly that all trace of blood fled, leaving the flesh a sickly white.

At last Grantin sensed tenuous images taking shape within the stone. The more he concentrated on their line and form, the clearer the visions became. Eventually he could make out a red-faced Mara with red-brown hair in a red-walled room broken by only a slightly lighter red window. The vision paced ghostlike around her chamber. As she moved through the gem her features bulged and flattened, stretched and compressed, depending upon her direction of travel through the stone. Once she walked to the window, and for an instant Grantin had a view of a narrow curving street bounded by sheer rock walls on either side, with further curving walls in the distance, each surmounted and patrolled by armed warriors. At last Grantin's concentration slipped. The image faded to nothingness.

Grantin unclasped his hands, threw back his head, and, eyes closed, gasped great drafts of air. In a few moments he opened his eyes and leaned forward. Chom had risen from his position on the far side of the table and now stood at Grantin's right, looking down at him, a concerned expression clouding the native's face.

"You were right, but it did me no good. A few images, a flicker of a distorted face, a nameless room—it means nothing to me. I'll never find her."

"To the contrary, you did very well. Perhaps you have in your blood the power to be a great wizard."

"I did very well, except that I failed. I don't know where she is and I don't have the energy to try again."

"There is no need to look again within the ring. Her home is unmistakable. She could be in only one place."

"You recognized it? Where? Where is she?"

"Your Mara lives in the seat of the Gogol empire, the five-sided city of Cicero."

Chapter Twenty-four

Mara disliked enforced idleness and felt trapped and frustrated. Almost two days had passed since her interview with Hazar, and still she had not been assigned further duties. That in itself was an odd circumstance. Were Hazar of a mind to punish her, his vengeance would have likely touched her by now. On the other hand, it was not like Hazar to allow his coveted apartments to be occupied by nonproductive persons. If Hazar were not the most decisive of men Mara might have concluded that he had not yet reached a decision on her conduct, but the wizard was not a man to delay.

Each wall toward the center of town was slightly lower than the one which preceded it. From her room Mara was even able to glimpse a portion of the Central Plaza. Human and Ajaj commerce choked the narrow streets and imparted to Cicero a buzzing energy.

At last the dingy stone confines of her room became unbearable. Slipping out into the zigzag corridor, she made her way to the steps. Now, in this time of peace between the overlords, the first of the two sets of doors which led to the First Circle stood open. Only the outer portal was closed.

The sentry allowed Mara to pass with little more challenge than a leering glance at the bulges which swelled her gown. So long as Mara occupied the upper floor she could become the involuntary consort of no one below the level of overdeacon. Of course, should she fall from Lord Hazar's pleasure, he might assign her a stint in the guards' pleasure room. This happy possibility consoled the sentry and caused him to smile even more broadly as he watched Mara's retreating form.

Eventually Mara found that she had walked all the way to the Gate of Pain at the south wall of the city. Here Nefra's aquifers delivered their supply of fresh water. Pipes cut through underground passages guarded by Nefra the Cruel's personal staff branched out to all portions of the city.

Best not to tarry here. It was well known that Nefra was Hazar's most implacable foe. Perhaps even now Hazar's spies watched her for some sign of treason. For a brief instant Mara studied the Gate of Pain, then turned to her right through the Fourth Spoke Road and headed for the Second Circle. Reaching the end of the passage, she cut sharply to the right to place the bulk of the second wall between her and Nefra's gate.

Mara had barely turned the corner when a yielding object struck her in the waist, midthighs, and ankles. Abruptly she pitched forward wildly, grasping at thin air. The impediment fell with and beneath her and cushioned her fall. When she managed to right herself she saw that she had run into an Ajaj, who was now futilely clutching the open end of a sack of poundfruit. Several of the large yellow spheres had bounced from the bag during the collision and now rolled free on the pavement.

From the grizzled fur around his muzzle and the snappings of his uncoordinated arms, Mara discerned that this was an aged Gray. With painful, spastic motions he slowly raised himself into a sitting position, then, spying Mara, exerted himself with astonished horror. Many an Ajaj now adorned a Gogol matron's collar for a lesser insult than this. Heedless of his own scrapes and obvious pain, the Gray rushed to Mara's side and sought to help her to her feet.

"I am sorry, my lady; excuse me, please. It was all my fault; I didn't mean it. Are you hurt? Please excuse me. I'm sorry; really I am. Forgive me. Please forgive me." The Gray fairly cringed in abject horror at Mara's expected wrath.

"No, I'm all right. It was my fault. Accept my apologies," Mara said, rising to her feet.

"Your fault—oh, how gracious of you, my lady! How magnanimous, how wonderful! No, it could not possibly be your fault. The error was all mine. How fortunate of me in my clumsiness to chance upon a great lady such as yourself. Here, at least let me give you some small token of my sincere sorrow for this incident."

The Gray hobbled forward to his sack and removed a fine, mature specimen from the bottom of the bag. He picked up the unblemished fruit and hobbled over to the edge of the wall, where Mara now brushed out her clothes and rearranged her hair.

"You're limping. Are you badly injured?"

"Oh, thank you, ma'am. No. I've had this limp for many a year now. Please don't worry about me. I'll be fine. Here, allow me to make a present to you of this fine poundfruit. I hope in some way it will make up for the inconvenience I've caused. Perhaps after enjoying it you'll think kindly of poor old Buster."

"Buster—is that your name?"

"Yes, ma'am, and many a year I've served in Lord Hazar's scullery preparing meals for fine ladies such as yourself."

Mara hefted the fruit and smiled approvingly.

"Thank you, Buster. I will remember your kindness."

"Thank you, my lady. I hope to see you again under more pleasant circumstances. Good day."

Buster, with some effort, hoisted the sack over his shoulder and disappeared down the Second Circle. After a moment or two, Mara followed.

In a few minutes she reached the entrance to her apartments, again passed the grinning sentry, and made her way upstairs. The walk had cleared her head and drained the tension from her muscles. Also, she noticed, it had given her something of an appetite.

Setting the poundfruit down on her table, she brought forth a dirk and slit a wedge-shaped portion from the rough, waxy skin. After pulling back the rind she sliced more deeply into the meat and pulled out a dripping chunk, the inner edge of which was encrusted with small black seeds. After shaving off an inch or so of the section she was able to carve the remaining trapezoidal piece into bite-size fragments which she ate with great satisfaction.

Mara picked up the discarded rind and prepared to reinsert it into the fruit to keep the rest of the delicacy fresh. In a few minutes the skin would heal over, the cuts becoming invisible and airtight.

She had just succeeded in afixing the lower edge when she noticed an unusual addition to the core. There amid the seeds and the blushing pink meat was a white shape. Reaching inside, her fingers touched an object that was smooth and brittle. In a second she had extracted a folded piece of heavy white paper. She read its message:

> Mara, you do not sit high in Lord Hazar's favor, but a woman such as you has many friends. Allow me to extend my power and generosity to you. I offer myself as a friend in need. Should you wish, at any time, to avail yourself of my comradeship give your message to the one from whom you received this item.
>
> With great sincerity,
> Nefra

Chapter Twenty-five

At dawn Grantin made good use of Shenar's pantry. His eyes red-rimmed from the combination of bloodstone-generated dreams and a stomach-wrenching fear of what lay before him, he began his preparations. To one side he laid two loaves of coarse bread and a block of cheese. Rejected were the remnants of the crossberry pie and the roast chicken liberated from Shenar's coldbox. A packet of dried meat joined the bread and cheese as well as four barely ripe jelly apples and a sack of dried corn.

Grantin had almost finished his selection when Chom joined him in the kitchen.

"I know what you are doing," Chom announced proudly. "It's called 'packing,' is it not?—the ritual by which you gather together sacks of items which you must bring with you when you travel."

Not without cause did Grantin detect in the Fanist's announcement an undercurrent of derision.

"It's easier to carry food than to hunt for it along the way, and more conducive to regular eating as well," Grantin lectured as he busied himself wrapping the food-stuffs and placing them in a knapsack he had earlier discovered. "Surely you didn't travel all the way here without supplies of your own?"

"I have no need of them. There is always sufficient food available for me."

"You have special spells for hunting, then?" Grantin asked, halting his packing. Perhaps if the Fanist could teach him an easy incantation for catching game it would not be necessary to lug around the heavy pack.

"No, not at all. I mean we are not so picky about what we eat as you humans. Were you willing to follow my example you would not need provisions either."

"What things aren't you picky about?"

"Almost everything that is nutritious: lilypads, salad-tree leaves, wortgrass; and much nutrition is contained in bone, skin, and gut."

"You mean you eat the whole thing, everything? You don't even . . ." Grantin blanched as Chom gave affirmative nods to his questions. With increased fervor he continued to fill the pack.

"Is another one of those bags available?" Chom asked.

Grantin pointed to a partially opened drawer at the base of a set of cabinets on the north wall of the kitchen. Chom found another crudely woven knapsack folded in the back of the drawer and deftly removed it with his two lower arms. The Fanist then returned to the table and began loading the bag.

"I thought you didn't carry food. Don't tell me I've converted you to the human style of eating."

"It is pleasant, I admit, but, I am afraid, far too impractical for continued use. No, this is for you."

"I can't carry two packs. This first one alone is enough to bend my bones to the breaking point."

"No, I am going to carry the pack and you are going to eat the food." Chom stared fixedly at Grantin as one would study a slow-witted pet to see if it had understood a command.

"You're coming with me? You were going to Cicero, then, before Shenar captured you?"

"No, that was not my intention."

"But this is a very dangerous trip. Every time I let myself think about it I see visions of brigands gnawing on my bones. Why in heaven's name would you want to come along?"

"It is dangerous for you alone—have you not just said so? It will be safer with a companion. Could I allow you to undertake this journey alone? Did you not save my life? Are we not comrades? . . . By the way, do you want these broiled inknuts?"

For an instant Grantin fixed an astonished gaze upon the Fanist, who, at that point, held the box of inknuts in his upper left arm while the lower right grasped an extra loaf of bread and the bottom left and upper right were busily engaged in rearranging the parcels inside an already overstuffed sack. Not one to poke good fortune in the eye, Grantin quickly recovered his composure.

"Of course, my dear friend; roasted inknuts will make quite a nice after-lunch snack."

A few seconds later Chom's busy hands had filled the pack and, mindful of the danger of Yon Diggery's return, the Fanist and human slipped through the castle's back door.

"A moment before we leave, Chom; there is one further human ritual having to do with packing which you may take note of now. Before one departs one takes stock of the needful items. Food—well, that's taken care of. Money—" Grantin patted a pleasantly full pouch containing four silvers, fifteen coppers, and two irons which he had liberated from Shenar's personal effects. "Knife, lucifers—" Here Grantin touched the pocket of his tunic which contained several crude, handmade matches. "Let's see; what else, what else? Drink, of course, an appropriate fluid to complement our rustic meals. Chom, my friend, have you anything in your knapsack for us to drink?"

"Yes. I brought a container of liquid and two leather cups."

"Excellent. Lastly, then, there is this fine map so generously provided by our departed host, and we're ready to take our leave."

Sliding the rear door open a crack, Grantin peeked out. Detecting no hostile activity, he and Chom scurried across the meadow to a point where the westbound trail entered the forest.

Now, in the full light of early day, Grantin's fears seemed as insubstantial as the morning mist. He was now well fed, well supplied, and well protected both by the bloodstone upon his finger and by the strength of his newfound friend. The fears which had tormented him the night before had been magnified many times over by his belief that he would be facing them alone. Now, more than anything else, Chom's aid and companionship had reduced his terrors to a bearable level. In fact, in the midst of the pleasant smells of the sun-dappled forest Grantin experienced a feeling akin to that of thrilled excitement.

Grantin and Chom entered the forest. Above them the faint screeching caw of a broodhawk echoed through the woods. The call merged with the tapestry of yelps, cries, screeches, and chirps of the other forest dwellers. The bird's sedate circling glide went unnoticed by the two travelers.

Grantin and Chom disappeared from view where the trail plunged beneath a dense grove of cone trees. Anticipating their point of reemergence, the broodhawk steadied its wings and slipped forward to continue its lazy circle a quarter of a mile to the west.

The effortless thrill of unpowered flight was a new sensation to Yon Diggery. He felt what the hawk felt and saw what the hawk saw. With the merest thread of control he directed the creature along the desired line of flight. A few minutes later the human and the runaway Fanist slipped back into view.

What a wonderful spell, an exquisite spell! The incantation alone justified his acceptance of the Gogol defector. And Rupert hinted that he had other sorcery to share with his new comrades. True, the man was impetuous, overcome with a vindictive rage against the young Hartford; but Diggery and his men could keep that under control. Obviously Rupert intended to manipulate them for his own ends. He knew more than he was telling, but only a fool disclosed all he knew.

Rupert had wanted to capture the two at once. He accepted with ill grace Yon Diggery's insistence that the ambush must be delayed. They were dangerous, obviously; a caster of spells as competent as Rupert would have overcome the young man easily were he an ordinary person.

Today and tomorrow the two would make good time, but the next day they would reach the edge of the Weirdlands. Then their passage across that strange country would be slow and tiring. When they reached its far boundary, if they reached it, that would be the time and the place for the ambush. In the meanwhile Yon Diggery and his men would use the animals of the forest to keep the travelers under constant surveillance.

The bandit returned his attention to the landscape which rolled beneath his closed eyelids. While his concentration wandered the hawk slipped off course. Diggery sought to correct its path. In response to a sharp mental prod the great bird screamed, wheeled over, and dived down on the trail where the human and the Fanist walked contentedly toward Cicero.

Chapter Twenty-six

Within a few hours Grantin was again hungry and foot-sore, and he insisted on halting for lunch. Both he and Chom made a meal from the packs, although the native augmented the human food with several crickets, two dragonflies, and six pink flowers. When describing the Fanists, Grantin decided the word *omnivorous* took on an entirely new meaning.

Pyra's glow warmed Grantin's bones. He stretched out on the soft bed of grasses to take a nap, only to be roughly shaken from his rest. Sleepily he looked up to see that Chom had already strapped on his pack and was ready to resume the hike.

"Not now, Chom; I need to rest," Grantin said, rolling over onto his back amid the flowers.

"No, we must go," the Fanist replied, shaking Grantin anew.

"Chom, just a few minutes . . ."

"No, we must get away from the river before night," Chom insisted. "This is a game trail; animals use it to feed. Also, the nightbirds fly here. I have seen their signs, and the stingwings, too. We must leave now."

Reluctantly Grantin crawled to his feet and flung the pack across his shoulders. Again Chom led the way, setting a brisk pace.

"Chom, what's it like where you live? Your people live in the forest, don't they? Are the forests like this one?"

"No, not like this. There are no hometrees here."

"What's a hometree?"

"It's what we build our homes in, where we live. How we live together."

"You mean you hollow out the trees? Wouldn't it be just as easy to live in buildings?"

"Hollow out the trees? You mean kill them and live inside a dead shell? No; no Fanist could live that way. The trees are our homes, our friends, our protection, our companions. We care for them; they care for us. They are part of our life. We would not be what we are without them. We would be something different. The Fanist without his community, without his hometree, is an outlaw and renegade."

"You mean a criminal? I didn't know you had them. I've never heard of a Fanist going bad."

"Not a criminal, an outcast. Often they settle near human villages as weather predictors. They are out of harmony; ones who are so different, who think so differently, feel so differently, that they are not of us any longer."

"I don't understand you. You mean an outcast does not follow the rules? If he obeys the laws what does it matter if he lives in a tree or a house?"

"We are so different. I do not know if you can understand me or if I can understand you. Let me tell you about how we live, how a community is born, and perhaps you will see what I mean.

"A community exists. Call it a village or a town; it is not really either of those things, but, in any event, it exists. Like any other people we are born and we age. Each of us, when we reach a particular stage in our life, is overtaken by the urge to explore—but explore is not the right word. There are no exact human words, you understand. I simply translate into the nearest human equivalent.

"This urge ranges from a mild curiosity in some individuals to an all-consuming obsession in others. The individual discusses these feelings with an adviser or mentor or parent—again, none of the words is quite right. Each person looks to a particular older member of the community whose attitudes, learning, wisdom, whose entire personality for some reason appeals to and gains the respect of the young one. This person then becomes someone to whom he goes for advice.

"The mentor discusses the feelings of the young person with him and suggests several prospects—not just a particular place to explore but a philosophy of exploration: should the young one look for new foodstuffs, spectacular landscapes, dangerous adventure, the learning of a new craft or skill. You see, the mentor must find an area of challenge which will both satisfy the urge for exploration and also yield some benefit both to the individual and to the community.

"Once the path has been chosen the person commences the journey, the trip of life. For some it might be no more than a study of the berry fields a league or two from the community, while another might set off across the Island Sea for a trek into Hartland."

"Then that's what you're doing—you're on your trip of life," Grantin interjected.

"It is my time."

"Well, what is your mission? Surely you didn't start out with the idea of helping me?"

"A trip of life is a very personal thing which may not be discussed," Chom replied hastily, remembering Ajax's warnings of the need for secrecy. "Perhaps you will understand if I explain further. The more adventurous, strong-willed, and determined the individual, the more ambitious his trip of life. Those who are adventurous but foolish or unlucky or weak often fail to return. That is a good thing, for it improves the race. The dangerous, the weak, and the foolish do not return to found a family. Each of us is enjoined by the highest strictures to return with our report, and in this way we increase the knowledge and wisdom of the community."

"Your theory's not necessarily correct," Grantin said. "What about the timid ones who only go as far as the berry patch? They always return to breed. Doesn't that result in your becoming a race of timid weaklings?"

"An intelligent observation, but no. All those who return do not necessarily found a family. The more dangerous the trip of life, the more useful the wisdom returned, the easier it is for the individual to find a mate. Those who visit the berry patches often are unable to find mates and breed not at all. But who knows? Upon occasion startling knowledge has been obtained by quiet and contemplative individuals, and they have earned great respect by reason of their scholarly reports. Also, there is even a further benefit to our custom.

"Sometimes on the trip of life an individual finds a place which he prefers to his own community. After making his report the individual, if he is sufficiently bold, resourceful, and ambitious, leaves the community to found a new settlement in such a place. Upon the satisfactory establishment of a home the individual then takes a mate. If he is successful and the place is good a new community of strong stock is founded. If he has underestimated the hardships or picked a bad place he dies or fails to find a mate, and, again, the race is strengthened. In this way have we prospered through the ages."

"What about those who don't undertake the trip, who don't want to? What happens to them?"

"Those are the renegades, the criminals, the ones who wish to take no risks or to have a mate without earning the right; who give nothing back to the race. These are the ones who would destroy our whole world."

"What do you do with them?"

"They are forbidden to breed and removed from the community so that, through ignorance or error, they are not accepted as mentors by the young. They live out of contact with Nahra, the soul of the community, the empathy with the land."

Grantin's head was filled to overflowing with the Fanist culture, and still there were more questions. What did all of this have to do with Fanists living in trees? And how did they mate? Were only males expected to go on the trip of life? What was Chom really doing here in the Gogol kingdom? It was all too much for Grantin now. The afternoon was wearing on; the morning's high spirits had dissipated. No longer listening to Chom's lecture, he shifted his attention to the forest.

As if the Black Pearl River were a boundary between the outer reaches of the forest and its main domain, the character of the woods had changed. There was a subtle deepening in the green-hued sky as the leaves grew more dense. The trees themselves were closer together and their trunks thicker and more gnarled. Mosses of rust and deep green festooned many trees, as here the trapped air was humid and dank. The bushes and small plants had thinned greatly. The forest floor was dotted with mushrooms and other forms of fungi. The dominant color of the terrain had changed from green to the brown, white, and gray of dead leaf and mold. Though it was now only the eighth hour Before Dark, already a damp breeze presaged Pyra's setting.

By unspoken agreement Chom and Grantin increased the pace, as if in hope that the landscape beyond the next bend would be more hospitable. In point of fact the surroundings did change as the afternoon waned, but not for the better. By half past the ninth hour a twilight gloom filled the spaces between the trees. Although Pyra would not yet set for an hour and a half, Grantin and Chom had nothing like that much time to find a place to camp.

Uniformly covered with dead leaves, the trail could be discerned only by the fact that it provided an alley between the close-grown trees. Ahead the path curved to the right and, without warning, descended into a steep gully. Along the bottom of the ravine trickled a small, muddy stream. Chom's extra set of arms again proved their worth in ascending the far bank. Here the dead leaves made the walls slippery and Grantin found it difficult to obtain any purchase. Only after working his way fifty yards or so downstream was he able to make use of the protruding roots of a great jonquil and scramble to the top.

Grantin in the lead, the two walked northward along the far edge of the gully to again intercept the trail. In spite of their relatively minor detour, ten minutes later they had still not spied the opening into the forest.

"We should have come to it by now," Grantin said nervously. "Have we reached the point where we entered the gully?"

"I cannot tell. It is too dark to see a disturbance in the ground cover. We may have to camp here and look for it in the morning when the light is better."

Grantin examined his surroundings with obvious distaste. Here there was neither food nor shelter, and the water in the stream looked too black and forbidding to drink. Grantin suspected that when night came hordes of sting-wings would descend upon the stream and its environs. He halted and peered between the rearing trees to his left. Thirty or forty feet away the ground swelled upward to form a low hill. Perhaps from its top he might be able to spot the trail.

"Chom, wait here a moment. Let me climb that ridge and see what I can see."

The leaves crunched beneath Grantin's feet and gave him the feeling of walking on a deep, soft carpet. Unlike the banks of the gully this slope was tree-studded and of a gentler incline. From the top he had a surprisingly good view. The lower foliage of the surrounding trees had withered from the lack of sunlight. Ahead of him and a bit to his right, a direction which Grantin roughly reckoned to be the northwest, he spied a markedly brighter patch. The area was fifty yards distant, but it seemed to glow with the red-orange highlights of late-afternoon sun.

Grantin turned back toward the gully and waved for Chom to join him. A few moments later the Fanist stood next to him at the top of the hill. Chom agreed that the phenomenon was worth investigating. Both walked ahead briskly.

As if they had emerged from behind a thick curtain, Grantin and Chom found themselves on the edge of a brightly lighted, almost circular meadow ringed with a peculiar variety of short, stumpy tree. A hundred fifty yards in diameter, the parklike spot was open and inviting. With the sky open above them Grantin and Chom were able to estimate the true time. Grantin judged it to be approximately the tenth hour, as Pyra was already setting. In less than an hour it would be one o'clock After Dark and the meadow would be plunged into full night.

As excited as a child with a new toy, Grantin strode into the center of the clearing, obviously well pleased at its luxuriant ground cover. Chom hung back just within the boundary of the low trees. In spite of Grantin's signals he refused to proceed farther, and a moment later the young man returned to the Fanist's position.

"Chom, what's wrong? Is there something the matter?"

"Nothing that I am sure of, but I sense a strangeness here. I feel we're being watched."

"Watched? Are you sure?"

"No, it is just a feeling I have. I am not sure that we should spend the night here. Perhaps we should go back to the gully and find the trail to Cicero in the morning."

"Spend the night in that dismal gully with the sting-wings? No, thank you. Why are you looking at the trees like that? Is that what the problem is? Are they poison-ous?"

"No. I do not think so," Chom said, rubbing his hands over the smooth, dark blue bark. "But it is very unusual. I have never seen a tree like this before. Why should we suddenly find a whole community of them ringing this particular meadow? There must be a reason for it, but I do not know what it is. I have a feeling about these trees; something is not right."

"I think your time with Shenar has upset you more than you realize. I don't get any feeling from them at all. Come on, now; are you going to camp here with me tonight or not?"

Once more Chom rubbed the trunk of the tree. He inspected the architecture of its limbs. The deep bluish-gray bark sheathed the circular trunk to a height of five feet, whereupon two V-shaped branches sprouted upward from either side. The ends of each branch were encased in an egg-shaped mass of fleshy blue-green leaves. Another foot or two above the branching point, the tree's central stalk likewise exploded in a great inverted teardrop of the same thick intertwined blue-green leaves. This crown was four feet in diameter and six feet high. Upon close examination the leaves resembled fat corkscrews so tightly interlocked that not even Grantin's hand could be inserted between them.

For a few seconds longer Chom stared at the treetop with intense concentration; then he removed his hands and followed Grantin to a spot fifteen feet from the edge of the forest.

For dinner Chom hunted up some mushrooms which he assured Grantin were nontoxic. At the far edge of the clearing the human managed to find a tayberry bush heavy with fruit. These substances augmented the food from Grantin's pack, and the human enjoyed a pleasant dinner. For his part Chom completed his meal with various random animal, insect, and plant delicacies.

Not wanting to mar the meadow with a fire, the two curled up to sleep immediately after dinner, Grantin wrapping himself in a blanket while Chom trusted his comfort to his thick hide.

By the third hour A.D. both travelers were fast asleep. In their slumber they failed to hear the distant whinings of the night creatures, the chirps of the mating insects, the buzz of the occasional stingwing, and the plasticlike rustle and rattle of the life trees. With great care a budlike stalk pushed its way through the leafy surface of the tree nearest the travelers. Leaflike petals unfolded to reveal a functioning eye which focused unerringly on their forms.

Now satisfied that the two were indeed asleep, the rustle became louder and more agitated as inch by inch the life trees' shallow roots were plucked from the soil and slid forward. With the greatest deliberateness the trees moved slowly across the edge of the clearing to encircle Grantin and Chom where they slept.

Chapter Twenty-seven

Four days had passed since Grantin had fled, and still there was no word. For Greyhorn the first day was marked by anguished rage, the second by sour, heartsick defeat, and the third by a cautious hope that Hazar might yet find Grantin and the ring. Now, on the fourth day, Greyhorn lapsed into a state of numbed calm.

Since Grantin's departure the wizard had neglected his normal duties; he had skipped his usual Manxday seminar with the assistant commissioners of the Tectors and Artisans Guilds, thereby forfeiting his standard fee of a silver each; his appointment to cast a vermin-extermination spell over the rich acres of Elder Peabody had gone unkept. Even the day-to-day operations of his manor house and surrounding fields had succumbed to general neglect. So disheartened was Greyhorn by the loss of the ring and the consequent collapse of his plans for power that even Maurita's legendary charms failed to arouse him.

What was he to do? The commencement of the Gogol

attack had been delayed. Though originally scheduled for the following day, it had been pushed back until six days hence; but then what? In spite of his strong words, Greyhorn was paralyzed with indecision. Even without Greyhorn's support the chances were good that Hazar's attack would succeed. By opposing Hazar Greyhorn might only earn for himself swift disaster.

On the other hand, without the ring, without an important share in the plot, Greyhorn would be reduced to the status of merely another Hartford wizard to be dominated, and as soon as possible eliminated, by the victorious Gogols. And if Greyhorn opposed the devil-worshipers, then what? The small fragment of powerstone contained within Greyhorn's amulet would not be sufficient to protect him against the onslaught which would be launched by the Gogols against a traitor to their grand design.

The more Greyhorn pondered the problem, the more he realized that a favorable resolution could occur in only one of two ways: either he obtained the bloodstone before the attack commenced, or he disposed of Hazar and thus delayed the battle indefinitely. Charged now with a goal for which he could strive, Greyhorn shook off his apathy and made for his laboratory.

In a metal drawer in a metal cabinet bound to the stone wall with deep metal bolts reposed the amulet which Grantin had worn to Alicon. With a wave of his hands Greyhorn released the spell of impenetrable protection and slid open the drawer. From its cushioned bed he withdrew the necklace and slipped it over his head.

Carefully Greyhorn faced westward toward the Gogol empire. The wizard held the amulet in front of him so that he could stare into the stone set at its center. The thumb and index finger of his left hand pinched the left edge of the disk while his right hand grasped the right side in a similar manner. Now the energy of his body flowed across the disk and through the chip of powerstone.

With all his force Greyhorn cast a spell of location and focused his gaze upon the gem. As if of their own volition the pupils of Greyhorn's eyes began to dilate. The bloodstone swelled in hazy display until it filled Greyhorn's field of vision. Within its depths he was able to discern vague pink shapes, some of which seemed to be moving while others suggested trees or bushes, or perhaps mountaintops. The geometry of the splinter was flawed. The most he could hope for was a vague sense of distant forests and landscapes.

With a wail of psychic pain the sorcerer allowed the amulet to slip from his fingers and bounce against his chest. Though emotionally drained, Greyhorn found his nerves tightened to a high, singing pitch. He refused to allow himself to be defeated. He sat panting while frustration danced before his eyes like a haunting apparition.

Half an hour later, when he had recovered from his exertions, Greyhorn rose and approached his communicator lens. Carefully the sorcerer pulled back the drapes which sheltered the device, then moved to a cabinet high on the wall next to the window. Pressed against the left-hand edge of the cupboard was a folder which Greyhorn opened. Inside were two disks of shiny black, plasticlike material of the same dimensions as the communicator lens. With great care Greyhorn affixed one of these disks to the face of the lens, kneading and stretching it until it exactly conformed to every bend and ripple in the glass. A few seconds later and with equal care the other disk cloaked the bulging back side. No ordinary coverings, the disks were specially energized with a spell of Hazar's own construction so that when placed in contact with the communicator they filtered out the vision of the one who cast the spell while at the same time allowing the crystal to function as the focus of the transmitted psychic energies.

Greyhorn placed himself before his gray-black lens, checked his mental armory, and, finding all in readiness, at last passed his hand palm outward before the surface of the now blind eye.

In Hazar's laboratory two hundred leagues to the west his own crystal exhibited no more than a faint pearly glow now invisible in Pyra's ruddy afternoon light. Only slightly did Hazar feel the tug of magic drawing him to his lens; so faint was it, in fact, that he was unsure if he were being called at all. A quick glance at his crystal convinced him that he was mistaken.

Back in his manor Greyhorn was already enlarging upon his previously begun curse.

"In his stomach, in his vitals
find a canker and a worm.
In his guts and in his bloodstream
grows a tumor large and firm.
In his heart and in his brain,
softens mushlike the decay.
In his body gathers corruption;
when I command,
he'll die in pain."

Hazar stood with his back to the lens. Unbeknownst to him Greyhorn repeated his incantation a second time. While the Gogol wizard planned the next step in his rise to power over the black city of Cicero, invisible emanations poured from his crystal. To a great degree Hazar's own vitality and spells of protection warded off the deleterious effects of Greyhorn's curse. Even more important was the protection supplied by the bloodstone ring which now rode the fourth finger of Hazar's left hand. Still, augmented as it was by the fragment of bloodstone in Greyhorn's amulet, the incantation was immensely powerful. In spite of all his defenses Hazar's vitals were seized with a wrench at the conclusion of the spell.

Instantly, Hazar sensed the source of the attack. With a sputter of rage the wizard turned and hurled a bolt of force into the lens. Two hundred leagues away the energy flung itself against Greyhorn's shielded crystal. The communicator shattered with a cannonlike roar, its razor-sharp fragments cutting Greyhorn on the cheek, chin, and knees.

"Imbecile!" Hazar screamed as he felt the ripples of the destruction which his spell had wrought in Greyhorn's workroom. "Fool! That incompetent . . ." Standing, Hazar broke off his shouts as a new bolt of pain lanced through his stomach. Somewhat shocked by the potency of the spell which Greyhorn had managed, Hazar restrained his curses and walked stiffly to his chamber door. Time for the fool Hartford later, he warned himself. He had more important tasks at hand now.

"Derma," he shouted to his aide. "Go find Mara and bring her here, immediately."

Hazar slammed shut the panel and retreated to his couch. Zaco had again delayed shipment of the special powerstones which by the nature of their cut were subject to control through that worn by Hazar himself; stones that were needed to complete his plan of attack.

Zaco's excuses did not fool Hazar, not in the least. He was having second thoughts. Now was the time for Mara to prove her worth, to reestablish with even greater power the enchantment which she had woven around the Lord of Mammon.

Chapter Twenty-eight

Throughout the night Grantin had become accustomed to the clatter of the leaves. It was the absence of that sound which caused him to awaken. Sitting up sleepily, he needed a moment to remember where he was. Strange . . . he could not recall bedding down so close to the woods. Twisting his head, Grantin was surprised to see that he and Chom were surrounded.

"Chom!" he called. Chom awakened instantly. As soon as his eyes cleared the Fanist stood, turned a brief circle, and addressed the crown of the largest and oldest tree.

"What do you plan to do to us?"

"Who are you talking to? What's going on? Where . . ."

"These are not ordinary trees. I sensed something last night but could not interpret what I was feeling. Obviously they have some plans for us. What is it that you want, friend trees?"

A smooth, deep bluish vine terminating in thick palps which wiggled like a nest of worms slipped from the gnarled tree and snaked toward the Fanist.

"Pull back your arm before we are forced to employ our magic against you," Grantin warned in a nervous voice.

"We are magicians of great power, but we have no desire to injure you. Surely this is all a misunderstanding. Tell us what the problem is; perhaps it can be avoided without unpleasantness."

Already as he spoke Grantin began to point the power-stone. The tentacle waved for a moment, then pulled back a foot and slumped to the ground. The palps continued to writhe, but for the moment the vine halted its attack. Now a thicker, stubbier tube protruded from the base of the crown. A rhythmic pulsing convulsed the last two inches of the cylinder until its end became flattened and took on the appearance of a puckered mouth. Lastly a startlingly white eyeball surrounded daisylike by blue-green leaves emerged from the body of the tree and hung suspended above the newly created organ.

Dissonant moanings, grumblings, and squawks erupted from the tube. At last the tone settled back into a parody of speech.

"Such as you are never allowed to pass. You have trespassed on our meadow. Now you must join us. Prepare to be planted."

"Wait, wait!" Grantin pleaded before the tentacle could begin again to move. "We didn't know we were trespassing on your meadow; there were no signs or warnings. We are sorry, very sorry. We will smooth out the grass where we slept and leave immediately. You don't have to go to all the trouble of planting us."

"What do you mean, 'those such as us'?" Chom asked calmly.

"Men's evil desires, we have found, are cleansed by the transmutation. No longer does greed or lust burden them, nor are those like ourselves able to thirst for power. In this way we cleanse all of those who pass through our meadow."

"Surely you cleanse only those who need cleansing," Grantin replied. "We are both fine fellows, Chom and myself. He is a Fanist on his trip of life, a harmless, warm-hearted creature. I am but a poor Hartford who has been abandoned in this evil country. We have no need of cleansing."

"A moment ago you proclaimed yourselves to be great and powerful wizards. Obviously you are a perverted Hartford who is on his way to join the death-worshipers.

Your companion is a stranger story yet. We suspect that he is a renegade who has fled his tribe and hopes to sell his secrets to the lords of Cicero."

"No, no, you are wrong!" But as Grantin spoke the tentacle began to move once again.

"Hold for a minute longer and hear me," Chom said calmly. "This human is cursed. He has foiled some Gogol plan, diverted the ring he wears from the possession of a great wizard who would use it for evil. He would destroy the ring, but he cannot remove it without the help of her who gave it to him. This person lives in Cicero. We go there to somehow obtain her aid."

"And you, Fanist, why do you travel with this human on such a strange mission?"

"It is my trip of life. I am so charged by our elders. Further, it is my wish to help this human who has saved my life. If you end our journey here it will be a great tragedy for my community."

Again the tentacle hesitated, then went limp as the trees communed among themselves. At last the leader spoke again.

"My name in human life was Hans. Though I am not convinced that you tell the truth—in fact, it has been our experience that the more evil the person, the more ingenious the lie—we will give you a chance to prove what you say. Behind each of you are the materials for your test. If you turn you will see four young birds taken by us fresh from their nest. You both will put one in each hand, the Fanist leaving two hands empty and clasped behind his back."

Grantin and Chom took the seedbirds as directed. The chicks trilled merrily. Their bodies were covered with tiny soft yellow-brown feathers. Short-pointed, lemon-yellow beaks protruded from their tiny oval heads. In each of his hands Grantin's chicks hopped joyfully and twisted around to look at him with curious eyes. In his pleasure at their warmth and softness Grantin almost forgot Hans's brooding stare.

"Now do as I direct if you wish to save your lives. We, too, have our spells, and each of these birds has been given an enchantment of prevarication. Only someone who tells the truth will have the strength to breach the spell. A liar is impotent against this incantation. Do you, each of you swear that the explanations that you have given us are true?"

"I do," Grantin and Chom replied at once.

"Very well; each of you must squeeze your hands as hard as you are able. If you can crush the chicks, you are telling the truth. If you cannot, you are lying and must be planted."

Catching his eye, the little birds chirped happily at Grantin. He looked back at Hans and opened his mouth to speak, then, realizing the futility of further pleading, clamped it shut. He looked away and began to close his fingers. As he grasped the soft, furry bodies more firmly he became even more distressed and shut his eyes. In the darkness the chirping grew louder. He felt more intensely the vital movements of the fragile bodies in his palms.

Grantin's right fist was almost closed. The imprisoned chick squawked with alarm and thrashed against his fingers. With a cry Grantin opened both his fists. The birds hopped around his palms in a merry little dance. Carefully Grantin lowered them to the ground, where they played amid the stalks of the short, soft grass. With a sudden premonition of horror Grantin turned to Chom and saw that his hands were empty. At the Fanist's feet his chicks also hopped free. The native's upper set of arms now reached to clasp his forehead near the point where the blue jewel lay beneath his skin.

Grantin and Chom stood back to back, facing outward, ready to employ their powerstones in a fight to the death.

"We refuse to play your sadistic game!" Grantin shouted. "Do your worst!"

The crowns of the life trees began to rustle. Slowly roots withdrew and the trees began to move. Grantin and Chom stood their ground but were astonished to see that the trees moved not toward them but away.

"You are telling the truth," Hans declared. "No decent being would have killed the innocents. You may go in peace, but with this warning. Nearby there are evil men who stalk you. Ahead the trail is easy until you reach the edge of forest. There you will pass through the Weirdlands. If those who follow you plan an attack, that is where it will occur. Be on your guard. Farewell and good luck."

The tree backed off slowly to stand still and silent beside another tree, slightly smaller but equally old. There in Pyra's rich early-morning light the crowns of the two trees of life touched and entwined and slipped back into the somnolent peace of the deep forest.

Grantin and Chom walked a quarter mile to the westward trail. As they moved off and the small meadow slipped from view the former human Hans and the former human Ruda relaxed in the serene contentment of their life together.

Chapter Twenty-nine

At the main entrance to the Inquisitor's chambers Mara turned to her left and walked along the First Circle toward Hazar's apartments. When she reached the Second Spoke Road she turned to her right so that she might take a shortcut by way of the Second Circle. Above Dolos was visible as a small pink disk spinning across the sky. The other moon, Minos, was hidden by the high narrow walls which bounded the Second Circle. Around Mara the walls pressed tighter and seemed to become even more confining. What would it be like, she wondered, to be freed from bondage to Hazar and Zaco and the rest, to move from place to place unfettered, to make a life for herself instead of giving unending service to her overlords? But Hazar and Zaco would never let her go.

Go? Go where? What was she thinking about? It was all ridiculous. Mara tried to remember when her thoughts of escape had first manifested themselves. No matter how hard she tried she could remember nothing of the sort before today—or was it yesterday or the day before?

Had she caught some strange disease in the Hartford lands? Could one of those bucolic imbeciles have cast a spell on her without her knowledge? Nonsense, and besides, how could she escape? Would Hazar again allow her to travel across the Guardian Mountains? Not likely. Zaco? Impossible. She knew no other lords, except, except . . . Did she dare get embroiled with Nefra's scheme?

This was all silly, ridiculous. Mara didn't know what had come over her. What was she thinking about? Tomorrow her thoughts of defection would appear ridiculous. Tomorrow? What awaited her in the coming days and years? More Zacos, more selling of her body to vicious, disgusting men. What reward had she ever received for her services? Every day she balanced only one footfall from banishment to the guards' pleasure houses.

With a start Mara halted and placed her hands against the cold stone walls. Were these not the walls of her prison? She looked around her. On all sides she saw only confined space.

With sudden loathing Mara backed away from the wall and hurried down the First Circle. As she neared her apartment she found herself thinking about an Ajaj in Hazar's service, one twisted and bent. She began to wonder how she could unobtrusively contact the Gray known as Buster.

Chapter Thirty

In spite of Castor's unsuitability to kitchen work, Buster took a liking to him and smoothed his way whenever he could. He often took Castor out on errands, real or imagined. Usually these took the form of trips to Topor's market. Along the way Buster would lecture the young Gray on the history, politics, or geography of Cicero. Castor didn't quite know what to make of this behavior. Although he could tell that the older Gray sincerely liked him, he suspected an ulterior motive.

On the third day in the kitchen Buster made a request which strengthened Castor's suspicions. They appeared at Topor's market as usual and picked up a load of hazestalk and poundfruit. All went normally: Castor loaded the hazestalk into his knapsack while Buster carried the melons. Once out the door, however, Buster began to act strangely. Instead of leaving the Central Plaza by the Eleventh or Twelfth Spoke Road, Buster herded Castor through the Fifteenth Road. Once into the Third Circle he began to act even more peculiarly. He ordered Castor to halt by the wall and await his return. Castor reckoned that almost half an hour had gone by before Buster returned, sweaty and obviously feeling the pain in his leg but somehow strangely excited.

In spite of Castor's inquiries, Buster would offer no explanation for his conduct other than to hint dramatically that sometime in the near future he might be willing to take Castor into his confidence. That evening, after the dinner dishes had been cleaned and the kitchen put to rights, Castor and the other Grays left a nervous and excited Buster.

Castor's fifth day in the kitchen began as had each of the previous ones. All proceeded quite normally until the end of the second staff-level luncheon. At the conclusion of the meal—pickled water leeks, toasted zaff marrow, shredded salad-tree leaves, and red sausages boiled in water and beer—a young enchantress in Hazar's employ approached the refectory counter.

"Who's in charge of preparing this wretched salad?" she demanded, waving the bowl under Cockle's nose. "Was it you, or was it one of these filthy Grays?" she asked the startled overseer.

"Me? No. It was one of the Grays, of course. What is the problem, madam? If they've done anything wrong I'll flay the fur from their backs."

"Are you intoxicated?" Mara asked the frightened Cockle.

"Intoxicated? Me? Why, madam, no, of course . . ."

"Never mind. I'll handle this myself. You, was it you who made the salad?" Mara asked, pointing at one of the Ajaj. "Perhaps it was you; you look guilty to me. You, old one," she said, pointing at Buster. "Are you responsible for this outrage?"

Buster limped forward slowly and peeked over the edge of Mara's outstretched bowl. There slowly inching its way across one of the oil-covered leaves was a bright green worm.

"Yes, my lady. Don't blame the others; I am the one responsible. Master Cockle had nothing to do with it."

"There, you see, madam, it was the old crippled one who did it. Rest assured I'll punish him well for this. You leave it to me."

"Leave it to you! You can barely stand up without holding on to something. I'll handle this myself—unless of course you prefer that I report to Lord Hazar directly?"

"Oh, no, madam, that's not necessary. Take the old fool and do with him what you will—although I would appreciate it if you would return him in sufficient health to work for his dinner."

"Don't tell me how to handle a Gray. Obviously you coddle these Ajaj outrageously. I have a few chores in mind and a method of punishment all my own, so you keep your prying eyes away from my powers."

"Yes, madam, of course, madam. Take him and do as you please."

Mara stalked out of the refectory and imperiously waved Buster to follow her. Castor stared after Buster's limping frame. Cockle startled Castor from his reverie with a kick in the rump.

"Back to work, you lazy, good-for-nothing beast. You've got to clean all of this up and start dinner. Back to work, back to work."

The crew was now shorthanded. Cockle, being forced to run his own kitchen for a change, was denied the soothing pleasures of wine and illusion plant and so became more disagreeable than usual. For the next three hours Castor was kept too busy to worry about Buster's fate. Finally, at half past the eighth hour, the old Gray limped down the steps. He panted loudly, and his legs were obviously sore from great exertion. Cockle greeted him with a buffet to the backside and an order to take over the preparation of the evening meal. With a satisfied grunt, Cockle hoisted himself on his stool and gulped down a hearty cup of wine.

As unobtrusively as possible Castor worked his way over to where Buster directed the kitchen helpers' labors. When the other Ajaj had been sent out upon their tasks he tried to speak to him without success. Instead the Gray began to give him new orders.

"The scraps must be taken out; in my absence this place has become an absolute mess. You, Castor, you look to be the strongest of the lot. Clean all those leavings into the buckets and carry them out to the receptacle. What's the matter? Why are you standing there? Don't you know where the container is?"

Castor stood mute, too surprised by the command to speak.

"Well, if you don't know, it's about time you learned.

Come on, now; clean those up; fill the buckets. I will take you outside and show you."

Castor gathered up a supply of peelings, scraps, pan scrapings, grease, and the like. Buster in the lead, they trudged up the steps and into the alley alongside the kitchen. As the young Ajaj overturned the buckets into the bin Buster looked suspiciously this way and that. When he was sure that no others were nearby he whispered into Castor's ear: "Did you mean what you said before about fighting back?"

"Yes, of course I did."

"Are you willing to do something to help? Do you have the courage to take the risk, perhaps even be killed without achieving your purpose?"

"If there is a good chance of doing the Gogols some harm I'm for it."

"Very well; I must trust you. If you are a spy or a traitor to our people I am already dead. So be it. Lord Nefra and Lord Hazar are at odds, this I have already told you, but there is more. Hazar's enchantress Mara, the woman who accosted me this afternoon, has beguiled Lord Zaco into delivering to Hazar fifty bloodstones."

"What are—"

"Quiet! Empty the garbage and don't talk. The bloodstone is the human equivalent of our source gems. They are of great power. Zaco obtains them from a mine in the mountains west of the headwaters of the Mephisto River. With these gems Hazar and his allies will be invincible. First they will sweep across the Guardian Mountains. In league with traitors in the Hartford midst they will destroy the Hartford wizards and establish their own sycophants in control of the human lands. Next Hazar will return in triumph and overwhelm all the Gogol empire with his powers. If he succeeds he will be the supreme ruler of this world. Zaco is a senile old fool and, beguiled as he is by Mara, he does not understand the significance of the stones Hazar has ordered.

"The other lords know something of Hazar's plans but except for Nefra are too weak, too indebted to Hazar, or too allied with him in the project to oppose his plans. Nefra is not so foolish. He realizes that Hazar's success is his own failure. Nefra has a plan involving Mara and myself and such other Gray conspirators as I may locate

—a scheme which might topple Hazar before his attack can begin."

"You want me to help Nefra the Cruel? He is as bad as Hazar, if not worse."

"If we do nothing, Hazar wins and conquers the world. If we help Nefra, Hazar loses and life goes on as before. I count that as a victory for our people. We must return now. Tell me quickly, will you help?"

Castor hesitated a fraction of a second. "What must I do?"

"I am to prepare a special meal for Hazar. His tasters will find nothing; his spells will reveal no poison, at first. After he has begun to eat, the proper incantation will effect change as the food lies in his stomach. Shortly thereafter—death!"

"He will never let us get close enough to him to cast such a spell," Castor whispered as they approached the scullery door.

"We Grays, no; but Lady Mara, perhaps. As soon as possible I will send you out beyond the tumbles to hunt for herbs, the special plants which I need to brew the poison."

"Do you think she will actually do it, against one of her own?" Castor whispered as he slid open the scullery door.

"That is the question, but no point in wondering. In a few days we'll know for sure."

Chapter Thirty-one

Mile after mile Grantin and Chom trudged through the depths of Grenitch Wood. At the end of the second day they camped at the base of an immense ironwood tree, some two thirds of the way through the forest. The next morning they would break from the wood's western edge and enter the Weirdlands, an area about which Grantin's stolen map gave only the sketchiest information.

That night they slept uneasily and, mindful of Hans's warning, started nervously at the sounds of nearby beasts and birds. As soon as Pyra had risen high enough to penetrate the forest canopy, Grantin and Chom arose and took up a fast pace which they hoped would bring them through the Weirdlands by sundown. The exertion of the previous days had toughened Grantin. This morning he noticed that the aches and pains which previously had plagued him now seemed to be dissipating. For the first time he did not have to strain to keep up with Chom.

By lunchtime the forest had begun to thin. The terrain became more uneven, often displaying alternately ridges, then deep-cut gullies. It was clear that the land was becoming more rocky, less fertile. Small crumbling cliffs appeared, the edges of the formations displaying bright orange shale. The sun passed over the travelers' heads and as they neared the edge of the forest began to slant into their eyes.

"Chom, are you sure you've never heard any rumors about the Weirdlands?"

"None at all. All I know is what you read from Shenar's map."

"The map! A mess of hen scratchings and obscure names: the Twisted Reef, Shrinking Monster Gulch, Domino Grove, Mirror Scarp—what's all that supposed to mean?"

Sensing that the question was rhetorical, Chom made no reply other than to slightly accelerate their pace.

Near the sixth hour the trail descended into a gorge where it paralleled a shallow, swift-running stream. The walls on either side were composed of red sand and shale. The stream exuded a sulfurous mineral smell. Ahead the course bore first to the right, then the left; then, as it turned right again, the walls fell away to reveal a peculiar vista.

Water tumbled over a small falls fifteen feet in height at the base of which was a wide brown basalt pan. From there the stream meandered aimlessly in a hundred random channels to a stony meadow where its course was lost from sight.

To the left of the rocky plain began a field of boulders and shattered stone. Beyond the meadow the ground heaved and turned into a field of grotesque shapes. Grantin and Chom descended to the base of the waterfall across the rock ledge and meadow, there to halt in wonder at the eerie landscape beyond.

In all directions arose pinnacles, chimneys, towers, cones, and rocky protrusions. Their colors varied as widely as their shapes: mug green, deep purple, gray, black, rust red, and sandy ocher. Between these nests of stone lay a labyrinth of passages, tunnels, and trails. Grantin and Chom contemplated the barrier with sinking hearts.

"How wide do you think that is?" Grantin asked.

"Look again at the map and see if it gives a clue."

Grantin slipped off his pack and removed a cylindrical

roll of stiff paper. Carefully he spread it on the ground, using a small stone at each corner to hold it flat.

"As far as I can tell we're about here," he said, indicating a point at the western edge of Grenitch Wood a fourth of the way from its northern border. "Could this be the Twisted Reef? The map is not exactly to scale, but it must be at least a league wide. What do you think?"

"Once lost in there we could wander forever. Still, perhaps we could find our way by reference to the sun or stars."

"I don't suppose we have much choice, do we? Let's get started, then, while the sun's still high enough to follow."

Chom seemed not to hear Grantin's remarks. Instead he concentrated on the reef. When Grantin started to walk forward, Chom's lower arm gently grabbed his wrist.

"Wait—it is not what it seems. I detect subtle magic beyond. There are more than natural forces to contend with there. I suspect the Weirdlands were deliberately created by the Gogols as a barrier to keep their people from escaping into Grenitch Wood and through the mountain passes beyond. Let us make a test." From the side pocket of his tunic Chom brought forth a small hank of translucent string. "Tie this to your belt," he directed Grantin as he gave him the end of the thread.

Grantin quickly secured the line, then struck off into the pinnacles. He found the going surprisingly easy and penetrated the first hundred yards without difficulty. Though he endeavored to keep the sun always in front of him, occasionally it would slip behind a tower. Then he would be forced to circle the obstacle in order to get it back in sight.

Often the sun appeared in an unexpected quadrant of the sky, opposite from the point where Grantin had expected it. Whenever this happened he reluctantly turned from his planned course and headed again in Pyra's direction.

Without warning he was yanked to a stop. Had the thread run out already? Carefully Grantin turned around and backtracked along the string, winding it as he went. To his amazement he discovered a zigzag, twisted course, one which in fact crossed itself several times from different directions. It was a trail that might have been left by a blind, drunken snake. Carefully Grantin retraced his steps until at last with a sigh of relief he emerged from the edge of the reef to see Chom standing twenty yards ahead of him.

"It is impossible," he reported when he returned. "I ran in circles. We would starve to death before we reached the other side. I had better look at the map again." Grantin again laid out the parchment and tried to detect an alternative course. "A league or so to the north this shading might indicate the boundary of the Twisted Reef. There, to the north, along the length of the reef, seems to run the Shrinking Monster Gulch. What do you think?"

"It is no worse than sitting here."

Grantin and Chom paced northward along the ragged edge where the meadow joined the reef. From within the rock labyrinth sounds erupted, as if the stone pillars captured faint noises and amplified them by their passage. As they neared the northern edge of the reef, the scratching clatter of a group of Rex lizards trotting across stony ground could be heard. A few times Grantin even thought he heard garbled human voices. Once he detected the muffled words ". . . up ahead." Yon Diggery and his band had reached the pinnacles.

Grantin and Chom accelerated their pace. Shortly a ravine barred their way. The gulch appeared to be forty or fifty feet deep, with steep but not unclimbable sides. At the bottom the ground was smooth and broken by a trickle of muddy water. The edge of the gorge merged precipitously with the northern boundary of the reef.

Remaining in the lead, Chom moved to the border of the pinnacles.

"Not in there; we can make twice as much time by following the gorge," Grantin hissed.

"The bandits are mounted and have the advantage over us on flat ground. If we stay to the edge of the reef they will have to abandon their Rexes and come on foot. It is our only chance if we want to avoid a fight."

The clatter of the lizards' claws now sounded clearly from the near distance. With no time for further discussion Grantin jogged past Chom and entered the twisted reef. Standing sideways, facing the ravine, they inched along, careful not to pass more than two or three feet from its edge for fear of becoming hopelessly lost.

Behind them Grantin and Chom heard the voices of Yon Diggery's men. "They can't be far ahead of us; let's run them down," Diggery's Lieutenant Dukey shouted as he urged his mount down the trail into the gulch.

Grantin and Chom peeked around the edge of a jutting chimney to watch Dukey descend into the gulch. The bandit rode the lizard at full speed, yet his progress seemed slower than expected. As his eyes focused on Dukey's form Grantin's perspective pitched and changed. The farther the bandit progressed, the deeper the ravine became. Whether the gulch was hundreds of times deeper than it appeared or the rider shrank by degrees as he descended Grantin could not tell. It soon became obvious, however, that though he might ride for days Dukey still would not reach the bottom. The reason for the barrier's name was now clear.

Sounds issued from the eastern edge of the reef: clicks, snaps, and thuds as Yon Diggery and his remaining men entered the labyrinth on foot. With a new urgency Grantin and Chom resumed their frenzied sidelong flight.

At the end of the seventh hour they reached the western edge of the reef. From the sounds of the pursuit Yon Diggery was no more than five or ten minutes behind. To the southwest a trail stretched away from the reef across a meadow and into a twinkling yellow-red field beyond, the Mirror Scarp, Grantin decided. What could it be? Fields of mica-covered boulders, plains of silvered rock —another labyrinth in which they would be hopelessly lost, if not cooked by Pyra's reflected light? Directly ahead and to the northeast a second trail cut across the rolling meadow which a half mile in the distance ascended a gentle, forested slope to terminate at a thousand-yard-high rocky ridge.

"That must be Domino Grove," Grantin panted. "To the right is the gorge, to the left the scarp. At least in front of us the view is nice. If I am going to die I prefer it be under as pleasant circumstances as possible."

Chom made no reply but docilely followed the human's lead. Here, too, the perspective was deceiving. The ground became marshy and the travelers were limited to a narrow rocky ledge which crossed the swamp. Tall pea-green trees grew in copses at the edge of the trail.

Slowly the character of the land continued to change. The clumps of swamp grass grew taller. The stalky trees became more common. By nightfall Chom and Grantin found themselves in a thick forest. In the gloom of night further travel became impossible. The bushes and trees screened them from their pursuers. At last they straggled to a halt. Grantin pronounced an impromptu spell of protection. In theory, if anyone crossed an imaginary circle a thousand yards in diameter they would be warned by a keening in Grantin's ears.

By now the packs were almost empty, and Chom waded into a nearby pool to catch their dinner. Demonstrating exquisite coordination, the four-armed native tossed eight plump fish upon the bank. Chom was willing to eat them raw, but Grantin met that suggestion with a groan. At last Chom agreed that the thickness of the underbrush would hide a small fire, provided Grantin could find fuel in the swampy country.

After a few minutes' search the human discovered a peculiar variety of twisted shrub which solved the problem. He returned to their campsite carrying several of the plants, which he piled in a mound in the center of the clearing.

"What are those?" Chom asked him.

"I found them sprouting from the green-stemmed trees. I think they're a parasite. No leaves, no root system. They snap off at a touch, but they are hard and springy and seem thin enough to burn."

Chom examined the plants as closely as possible in the poor light. Their appearance suggested the work of a demented basket weaver. Each was spherical, about two feet in diameter, and composed of flat, shiny black strips. These ribbons twisted and intertwined with great complexity like a tangled skein of yarn. Still, none of the strips could be seen to split or converge. Each branch seemed to be constructed of one continuous tangled piece.

Chom wondered how they grew. Did they bend and turn upon themselves in response to some genetic code, or was each one patterned as uniquely as a snowflake?

Grantin struck a lucifer and thrust the flaming twig beneath the pile. He stood back to see if the shrubs would

catch. The result was astonishing. At first the ribbons re
sisted the fire; then, instead of bursting into flame, the
swelled like slowly inflating balloons. As Grantin an
Chom watched, the stems nearest the flames began t
bulge, followed by those more distant.

"Well," said Grantin after a moment, "it looks a
though—" A piercing howl interrupted him, and bot
turned back to the fire. The strips had filled to bursting
and now thin streams of gas hissed from their lowe
reaches. A jumping spark ignited one of the plumes, an
instantly it blazed with an orange-white glow. Soo
tongues of fire adorned the bottom strips. Their hea
caused the upper stems to swell. Grantin leaped forwar
and removed the bulk of the bushes before they turne
the camp into an oven.

"I wonder how it works," Grantin asked, fascinate
with the display.

"The branches seem to be composed of long, pliable fi
bers," Chom suggested, "giving the stems strength length
wise but no lateral support. With a little pressure the
inflate, and when the fibers can stretch no farther the ga
forces itself out at the weakest point. Obviously the fume
are flammable. Not the sort of thing we would want t
throw into a raging fire."

"It would probably go off like a bomb," Granti
agreed. "We should cut some short pieces and seal th
ends. You never know when an explosive might come i
handy."

The bush now burning easily, Grantin set the fish o
its upper surface and let them bake. Even Chom admitte
the benefits of cooking, although he disconcerted Granti
by consuming not just the flesh but additionally the hea
bones, skin, and tail.

Slowly the lantern bush, as Grantin named it, burne
out and the camp was plunged into pitch-black night. T
the south a mournful howl arose from the forest depth
a sound which Grantin hoped would keep Yon Digger
and his men close to their own camp a mile or two be
hind.

At first light Grantin collapsed his spell of surveillanc
and he and Chom sped down the trail. The character o
the land continued to change. The trees grew denser an
more uniform in shape; the ground began to slope u

ward, as if they were climbing the edge of a long, gentle valley. The forest was now composed almost entirely of tall, broad stalklike trees. The trunks had turned from pea green to sickly yellow and were of a uniform two-foot diameter. The surface of the stalks was covered with a horny, scaled hide unbroken by limbs or branches. Some fifty feet above the ground the treetops sported an egg-shaped crown colored an unattractive shade of greenish gray.

"It resembles a giant asparagus," Grantin said.

Vines and creepers seemed to favor the strange trees. With increasing frequency thick strands spanned the upper level of the forest until they gradually formed a canopy which filtered out the sun.

Bit by bit Chom slowed their pace, carefully threading a trail through the midmorning gloom. At noon they reached a small brook. As Grantin bent over to fill his water bottle a missile whizzed over his crouched body.

"Down!" he whispered. He and Chom dived to the earth. They waited tensely; but, except for a slight rustling in the underbrush, nothing could be heard.

After a few minutes Grantin rose and dodged through the brush to the point where the missile had hit the ground. There were no rocks in sight, but upon searching a bit he discovered a round, mustard-yellow object beneath a clump of ferns. About the size and weight of a small melon, it was covered with irregular spikes and barbs. In a moment Chom joined him and studied the object.

"It looks like a seedpod," he said, lifting it gingerly. "Perhaps the plants launch them somehow."

Grantin looked up at the bulging treetops. "If a treeful of these fell on us, we would be killed. We should leave here as fast as possible."

Grantin and Chom set off once more. A few minutes later another pod sailed across their path. Now they could hear snappings in the underbrush along the edges of the trail.

As the ground sloped more steeply the forest noises became louder and more constant. Spike melons became a familiar sight.

"What do you think?" Grantin whispered to Chom as

they picked their way around a large grassy mound. "Me
or animals?"

"The bandits," Chom answered.

"I'm afraid you're right," said Grantin, letting out h
breath. Another pod whistled through the air and glance
off Chom's pack. "And their aim is getting better." Th
travelers increased their pace.

"Do you notice anything different?" Chom aske
Grantin a few minutes later.

"No—yes, the sun is brighter." Grantin studied the fo
est canopy. "The vines . . . they're thinning out."

"And the pods are riper," Chom added. "They ar
huge now."

The pods in fact were dark and dangling from loos
strands at the treetops. The crowns themselves were swo
len.

Another missile flew at them from the bushes. With th
loss of the vines Grantin and Chom were now able to se
flashes of the men who flanked them, fifty yards to eithe
side of the trail. Apparently Yon Diggery was afraid c
using magic against anyone who had vanquished Shena
Instead he intended to harry them with the missiles unti
panicked to the point of exhaustion, they became eas
prey for knives, clubs, and crossbow bolts. His strateg
was working. Grantin's makeshift spells might be sufficier
to eliminate one of two of the bandits but not all of then
Chom's magic was mostly that of the practical variety
The Fanists had never developed spells for self-defens

Grantin and Chom struggled up the hill, hoping to ou
distance their pursuers. Yon Diggery seemed willing 1
pace his quarry until they dropped.

A few hundred yards farther Grantin was forced to res
His breath tearing at his throat, he leaned back against a
asparagus tree. Under his weight it began to wobble. Wit
a clatter, the ripest pods rained down around him. He an
Chom struggled up the slope away from the swaying tre
A few feet farther on Chom reached out and pushed ar
other of the growths. It wobbled back and forth as
merely balancing on a narrow base. He prodded a thir
It, too, leaned ominously.

Grantin and Chom looked down the hill and saw tha
the bandits were now growing bolder. They had tightene
their lines and were clearly visible as they moved throug

the underbrush. Chom once more studied the top-heavy trees.

"Grantin, I have an idea. Take from your pack everything you do not absolutely need and drop it on the trail. Do it as fast as you can. We must get to the ridge. Plundering our supplies may delay them for a minute or two."

Chom led them off at a slow trot, the best speed they could maintain against the grade. A quarter mile or so ahead rose the brow of the hill. Down below two of Yon Diggery's band, Luke and Spicer, pawed through the provisions and made a hurried report to their chief. Chom continued to set a grueling pace. Now a hundred yards to go. From down the slope came sounds of pursuit, and Chom urged Grantin onward. With a last surge of effort, gasping and sweating, they gained the ridge.

"Grantin, here is one of the stem bombs we made last night. Put it against the trunk of that tree—and hurry."

Grantin wedged the double-bent piece of lantern bush beneath the shallow roots of the asparagus tree at the top of the hill. An instant later Chom came rushing up, clutching dried leaves, twigs, and branches. These he heaped around the stem while Grantin struck a lucifer and set the materials ablaze.

"Now back," Chom commanded. For a heart-stopping fifteen seconds nothing happened. Yon Diggery's men could be heard scrambling up the hillside, only thirty or forty yards from the top. Exhausted, Grantin and Chom stood back from the edge of the ridge, their eyes transfixed by the fire at the base of the tree. They had almost given up hope when the sealed six-inch piece of lantern stem erupted in a ringing explosion. The trunk shattered; the asparagus tree leaned backward and toppled down the slope. As it fell it swayed sideways and careened into three other trees. In a slow-motion chain reaction each one fell against another and another and another. As each fell backward others in turn broke loose until, like gigantic dominoes, they created a path of destruction which raged down the grade. Like shrapnel their hard, barbed fruit sprayed in all directions.

Even Chom was startled by the violence of the reaction. In less than a minute the slope was littered with the fallen asparagus trees. Of Yon Diggery and his men no trace was visible.

Chom studied the scene critically and at last offered a comment. "This may be their normal means of reproduction," he observed. "As the fruit gets ripe the trunks grow hollow. The trees secrete a substance which kills the vines which normally steady them. Eventually they fall, spreading the pods. The new crop is fertilized by last year's decaying trunks. As they grow the vines reappear and tether them until the next generation of pods ripens and the cycle repeats. An ingenious if dramatic form of propagation."

"Just the same, I'm well pleased they are behind us. It looks as though we've reached the edge of the Weirdlands."

Following Grantin's gesture, Chom turned from the littered slope and looked to the west. Ahead the land dipped gently to a lush grassy plain. In the far distance was the glint of sunlight on water.

"The trees always fall downward and so have never been able to escape the valley," Chom said, studying the vista. "We will rest here and have lunch, then set off across the grasslands before nightfall."

Late that afternoon Grantin and Chom sheltered themselves in a copse of ironwood trees deep within the Gogol kingdom. A few leagues behind them, sap-stained, his skin scraped, Rupert struggled from a crevice between two fallen asparagus trees. Blood spilled freely from his gashed right arm, which now made a set with the smashed fingers of his left hand. As he emerged from the tangle of logs he spied Yon Diggery sitting on the ground, his back perched against a splintered stump. A large freely bleeding, purple-black bruise adorned his forehead. Like the Gogol deacon his body displayed the cuts, abrasions, and scrapes occasioned by the avalanche of trees and pods.

"Diggery, are you alive?" Rupert called weakly.

"More or less," the bandit responded in a husky tone. "Spell of impenetrable defenses, was it?" he asked Rupert.

"A charm of instantaneous miniaturization," the deacon responded.

"I thought as much. The rest of them, I suppose they're all . . ."

"Unless you've taken to giving your hired hands the power that only a deacon would have, they are. Your men lost, and the quarry too. A fine bandit leader you are."

"Not to worry. I have many associates, not all of them in Grenitch Wood. Obviously they're heading for Cicero. Tomorrow we'll contact my friends and prepare a reception for them both."

Chapter Thirty-two

"What special dinner?" Cockle asked suspiciously.

Buster cringed a bit at the question and contrived a look of mild surprise. "Why, the dinner for . . . it's just that I had heard that Lord Hazar had planned . . . well, it's just a rumor, but perhaps I should say no more. Excuse me for bringing it up, Master Cockle."

"You've heard something about Lord Hazar? Don't play games with me, old one. What is it that you know?"

"Well, master, it is only a rumor, mind you, but it's whispered that Lord Hazar has invited a guest to dinner in his apartments tomorrow evening. Naturally I assumed that you would want to plan a special fare for our Lord and his visitor; but of course," Buster added hurriedly, "it's not my place to say how you should perform your duties. I am sure the everyday provisions are good enough for them."

"Who are you to judge what's good enough for our lord and master? What do you mean, suggesting that I would stint on my duties? You be careful, Buster; you're not so old that I can't punish you for insubordination. Now, then, I must compose the menu. If you have any suggestions you may give them to me now and I will consider them."

"Well, perhaps a nice cold poundfruit salad."

"Yes, I've already thought of that. What else?"

"Broiled whitefish and toasted crown nuts with herb cheese sauce . . ."

"Of course, of course, I've already thought of that. What else?"

"Baked red tubers stuffed with pepperroot, shaved bean stalks fried in mint oil, and, for dessert, gingerberry cobbler."

"Well enough, well enough, except at the end I think throttleberry pie would be more to Lord Hazar's liking."

"Of course, Master, you know best."

"Blasted well right I do. Well, don't just stand there; hop to it! Get everything together. We don't want to be caught short. Is there anything we lack?"

"I think we have it all, Master Cockle, except I'm not sure about the herbs. Let me check." Buster hobbled off to a low cabinet, from which he extracted several heavily stoppered glass jars, three of which appeared to be empty. "As I feared, Master, we do not have sufficient herbs for the sauce or tubers. We lack zim root, sprite leaf, and chauger."

"Well, just don't stand there. Do something; get them from somewhere."

"I know a place where they grow, Master Cockle. The fresh herbs will make an especially delightful treat. Unfortunately with my legs the way they are I couldn't go myself. Perhaps, if you will allow me, I can have one of the other workers pick them tomorrow before reporting for his shift. The new one, Castor, seems strong, and we can afford to lose him for half a day. If he might be given leave to return at the fifth or sixth hour I could direct him where to go."

"All right, all right, anything; just you handle that meal and make sure it's right." Satisfied that he had now fulfilled his executive duties, Cockle retired to his stool and his wad of illusion plant. Buster turned back to the corner of the kitchen where Castor knelt scrubbing the floor.

"Castor," he said in a loud voice, "Master Cockle has directed that before you appear for work tomorrow you pick us a supply of herbs for Lord Hazar's evening meal.

Before you go home tonight see me and I will give yo directions as to where and what to harvest."

The first part of the scheme had come off flawlessl Castor now had official permission to scour the meadow east of the Ajaj tumbles. In addition to sprite leaf an chauger Castor would pick rot root.

After the evening dishes were cleaned and put awa Castor played out the charade. Nodding his head sagel he listened to Buster's directions concerning the natur quantity, and location of the herbs desired for the speci meal. After receiving his instructions Castor nodded po litely to Cockle and left the scullery.

That night in his apartment he double-secured all th apertures, yet still felt nervous and exposed. Sleep cam grudgingly and did not stay long. At the end of the tent hour A.D. Castor was already up and watching for sur rise through the crevices of his grate.

Sitting there in the darkness, more afraid and mor exhilarated than he had ever been before, Castor ra through the steps of the plan. In order to quiet his steadil increasing shakes and trembles he extracted his gree source stone from its hiding place.

The gem spread channels of cold fire through his bone: Calm now, Castor arose and removed the barrier. Hal way outside he hesitated. Should he return the stone to it hiding place? Castor halted, looking first back into th room, then out along the tunnel to the outside worl Overuse of the crystal was dangerous, but today h needed all the strength he could muster. He tucked th cloth-wrapped gem into the bottom of a deep pocket o the inside of his vest, then scrambled down through th tumbles to the beginning of the trail.

A narrow double band of trees paralleled Slicke Stream as it ran southwest to empty itself into Harridan' River. Beyond lay the rolling meadows and farmstead of the Gogol farmers, lands controlled in various quar tities by the lords, overdeacons, and deacons of Cicer

Though little better than slaves themselves, the igno rant, fanatic farmers formed one of the mainstays of th Gogol empire. Devil-worshiping was their pride and the pleasure. Should he be found crossing any of these fiel without Cockle's safe-conduct, Castor would be killed ou of hand.

Today the farmers seemed to be working another portion of their fields, for Castor saw no other beings during his passage across the meadows. Here only the livestock, descendants of the original seed carried aboard the *Lillith*, roamed the pastures.

Something over two leagues to the east and one league south of the tumbles Castor reached the spice grounds. Here were a series of small ponds, hardly more than swellings in Skull Creek. Clumps of feather and salad trees abounded. Under the shadows of the great leaves grew rot root interspersed with clumps of greenish-white fungus.

Getting down on his hands and knees, Castor inched across the soil, carefully digging out the roots which he then placed in a jar from his pack. In separate jars he stored several varieties of fungus, an item also entered on Buster's list, as well as sprite leaf and chauger.

By half past the second hour he had almost filled his quota. Castor knelt behind the trunk of a stately salad tree. He spied a tiny orange-tinged mushroom growing on a length of decaying limb, but as he scuttled closer an odd sound reached his ears—a series of deep modulated tones which, at the shift of the wind, resolved themselves into strangely accented speech.

Castor peered around the tree to the southeast, following the direction of the tree-lined creek. In the distance the light rippled, as if two bulky objects crisscrossed in front of the sun's rays.

A new voice sounded, younger, higher, definitely human. Transfixed, Castor stared in wonder as a Fanist and a bedraggled, travel-stained human paced into view. A Fanist, here? Could he be a sycophant of the Gogols? Not likely, but still in these strange times who could tell what schemes Hazar had at work? Best not to take any chances.

Castor ducked behind the tree, gathered up his bottles, and placed them in his pack. The voices stopped. He found it difficult to judge which way the travelers had turned. Ever so slowly he slung his knapsack. The bottles tinkled as he slipped on the straps. Castor dared another glance. The way looked clear. Light as a shadow he trotted across the open space to the next tree some thirty feet to the northwest. The bottles chattered softly as he ran.

Castor paused only long enough for three or four fast breaths, then set out again. The human and the Fanist had disappeared. He neared the edge of the meadow. Ahead the ground swelled upward gently, then dipped. Once over the rise he would be hidden from view.

A great barrel-trunked snaf tree stood sentinel directly between himself and the open ground. One more quick dash to shelter behind its bulk, catch his breath, and then up and over the rise. Several times Castor breathed rapidly in and out, then, fortified with oxygen, scampered on.

He rounded the tree at full speed and slammed into another tree which stood just beyond, hidden from view. This column, however, though rough-textured, was warm and softer than a tree should be. He loosed his grip and stepped back to view the obstruction. With a stunning bolt he saw in front of him not a gnarled trunk but the gigantic body of a gray-hided, four-armed Fanist staring down at him, smiling.

Chapter Thirty-three

Grantin and Chom slept late on the morning after their escape from the Weirdlands. Now deep within hostile territory, they would have to disguise themselves as best they could and continue their journey by night. When full dark had descended, they again took up the westward trail to Cicero. They made good time over the farmlands and by dawn were only ten or twelve leagues from the city's walls. Again they holed up during the daylight. Again Grantin foraged for food.

During the afternoon Grantin's nervousness increased. By the time they had commenced the last leg of their journey he gave voice to the concerns which troubled them both.

"Chom, I've heard that Cicero is surrounded by great walls. Is that true, do you think?"

"It has been so reported to me. It is a city of five walls and five gates."

"Do you think I will be able to slip inside?"

"I do not know, but it seems unlikely. If you could perform a spell of disguise you might take on the appearance of someone you observe leaving the city."

"I don't have such a spell, and even if I did the plan seems risky. I might be challenged by acquaintances of the person I imitated. And what about you? Do you think you'll be able to find a place to hide while I look for Mara?"

"Hide?"

"You don't expect them to let you through the gate, do you? Unless . . . tell me, do any of your people live near here?"

"No, they abandoned this country long ago, shortly after the arrival of the Gogols."

"Then you must find someplace to hide. If you are seen you will be taken and questioned."

"There is, of course, another solution to the problem," Chom suggested.

"Which is?"

"If you cannot go to the female, perhaps the female will come to you. If she could be lured outside the city, then various opportunities might present themselves."

Grantin considered Chom's proposal. Fragments of plans whirled through his mind.

During the night the character of the landscape changed, became more settled, thicker with farmsteads and tilled soil. Grantin and Chom were forced to take exaggerated detours around the habitations, careful always to pass through the gullies and not be silhouetted on the brow of any hills. By full morning they reckoned they were still two or three leagues from Cicero, with no secure hideout in sight. The best cover they could manage was that supplied by the tree-lined banks of a small stream which cut diagonally across their path.

Grantin and Chom ducked beneath the cover of the trees. They worked their way upstream in only marginal safety. Grantin assumed the lead, breaking trail, while Chom as much as possible fixed his eyeballs in their telescopic mode. While functioning in this way he was able to give warning of distant dangers yet had only the blurriest apprehension of details near at hand. He relied on Grantin to choose an easy trail.

Sometime after the second hour Chom tapped Grantin on the shoulder, signaling him to stop. With a wave of his upper right arm he indicated a point of danger three or four hundred yards distant. Grantin focused his eyes in the indicated direction and was able to make out a vague gray hump on the earth. The bulge moved in slow jerks, finally raising itself up to be revealed as the shape of an Ajaj Gray

Chom motioned for Grantin to continue his advance while the Fanist crossed the brook and broke from the line of trees on the far side. A few moments later the startled Gray sprinted for cover behind a nearby tree. Certain that he had been seen, Grantin broke into a full run, splashed across the stream, and pounded forward up the far bank. If the Gray escaped and warned his masters it would mean both their lives.

Grantin cut into the line of trees where the Gray had disappeared. Only a few feet ahead were the open farmlands. Grantin pounded around a last gnarled trunk and almost ran over Castor and Chom.

Castor's nerves had been stretched almost to the breaking point by his plot against Hazar, then his capture by the Fanist. Now Grantin's sudden appearance seemed sufficient to complete the process.

"What do you want of me?" Castor asked fearfully. Strangely enough, his terror was not for his own personal safety but rather that his pack would be searched and that he might weaken and betray his fellow conspirators.

Grantin was too winded to speak coherently, and so it was Chom who began the conversation.

"We only wish to talk to you, to gain information, and to ask of you a favor," Chom began. "We are strangers and know this country only by reputation. We do not wish to be killed out of hand. You might, we thought, give us helpful information about what we might expect upon reaching Cicero."

Castor examined Chom and Grantin critically. Could such an improbable story possibly be true?

"I have no money, no wealth. What is this favor you want of me?"

"Our lives," Grantin broke in. "You must give us your promise not to report our presence to your masters."

"Why should I wish to do that?"

"You Grays do their bidding, or so I've been told. Are the Gogols not your masters?"

"They are our masters only because we are too cowardly to live otherwise."

"Strange sentiments for a Gray," Chom commented.

"You are right, of course," Castor said as he sank weakly to the ground. "They say I am mad. I have defied the random factor and the Gogols and gained for my trouble only a stint in the scullery and my life hanging by a thread. Now I am accosted by two vagrants who clearly would kill me if they thought it necessary. Very well. As to the customs of the Gogols, I can tell you this: they are vile and a canker that should be removed from Fane. As to the favor which you ask of me, consider it done. I have no one to whom I would wish to report you. More than that I cannot do. So, now either let me go or do your worst."

Totally disarmed by the Gray's unorthodox behavior, Grantin and Chom removed their hands from the butts of their knives and joined Castor in sitting on the grass.

"We don't want to kill you," Grantin assured the Gray. "The Gogols are our enemies as well. You may leave if you want, though I would appreciate it if you would stay and talk with us a little more. You are almost right about us, you see. We are not vagrants; for myself at least, I'm a fugitive. For personal reasons I must find a girl who I believe is now in Cicero. If you were to tell anyone about our presence I would not last a minute.

"I am very sorry that we frightened you. If you hate the Gogols as much as you say, then we are allies against a common enemy. Isn't there some way that you could help me get into Cicero and find the girl? Or, failing that, take a message to her and ask her to meet me beyond the gates?"

"What about you?" Castor asked, looking suspiciously at Chom.

"My reasons for being here are complex. Part of my purpose is to help this human who saved my life. Besides that, I will admit to a deficiency of character as well—I am curious. I wonder what will happen to him."

Castor looked from Chom to Grantin; then, without speaking another word, he stood and walked out of the line of trees. The travelers made no move to follow. They were seized with apathy. By unspoken agreement they decided that this was as good a time as any to take a nap before pressing on to the conclusion of their foolhardy journey.

Ten minutes later Grantin was startled from his nap by a soft, pawlike hand on his right shoulder.

"I've decided that I believe you," Castor said. "We must hurry. I have to reenter the city before the end of the fifth hour. Come with me. I will hide you in my quarters. We will make our plans as we travel."

The Ajaj ran almost at a trot to keep up with Chom's long strides. "You say there is a human female whom you must meet," Castor said between gasps for breath. "Who is she? What does she look like?"

"She is fair and not too tall, not too short, well shaped, with a lovely face . . ."

"To me that means a female three feet high and covered with light gray fur," Castor snapped. "Can you give me a more objective description?"

"Long, straight light brown hair," Grantin began again, "light blue, almost gray eyes, pale skin, perhaps five and a half feet tall, and about my age, slender at the waist, but otherwise well padded in the normal places for a female."

"That could be any one of a hundred human women. How am I to tell them apart? I fear this is hopeless."

"Well, there is one other thing," Grantin said, catching Castor's eye. "When I met her she told me her name was Mara."

Castor suddenly halted and stared at Grantin, his face contorted in an expression of shock and fear. Mara was clearly much more deeply involved in the plot than had first appeared. What horrible conspiracy had he and Buster gotten themselves into?

Chapter Thirty-four

Nefra slumped in his chair and considered his schemes. Mara had agreed to join the plot. That very morning Castor had been observed heading east from the tumbles to hunt for herbs. So far everything was proceeding according to plan. With luck, by the tenth hour Hazar would be dead of a ruptured gut.

Nefra maneuvered his loose-limbed frame from the window seat and walked across his parlor to the entrance to his workroom. Unlike soft-fleshed lords like Zaco, Nefra was lean of both limb and spirit. No sumptuous draperies adorned his walls, nor luxurious carpets his floors. Bare stone surfaces were the hallmark of Nefra's apartments, an image into which fitted Nefra's own personal appearance and dress.

Tall and thin, with overlong bony arms and a horselike face, Nefra seemed the model of puritan rectitude. Dressed today as he was every day in an unadorned black blouse and black trousers, by his very presence he quelled all wayward thoughts of joviality.

With a furtive glance over his left shoulder Nefra bent to unlock his laboratory door. Opening his book of sorcery

—for Nefra was a careful and methodical man—he patiently recited the spell of communication; but, to his surprise, no results were forthcoming. Nefra readjusted the lens, called out Greyhorn's name, and tried again. Still no response.

Raising himself to a higher level of nervous energy, he repeated the incantation a third time and willed his powers to find a substitute receiver. Nefra became very warm. Sweat beaded on his forehead. With a feeling as if he had pushed his way through a yielding barrier, he saw in his crystal a distorted picture of Greyhorn's workroom.

In Greyhorn's laboratory Nefra's face bulged in miniature on the surface of a water droplet clinging to the edge of a flask. After several minutes Greyhorn sensed the summons and finally, after much searching, located his caller. A hideously distorted visage hung before Greyhorn's face. A gigantic maw bulged blackly, then disappeared as Nefra spoke. Soundlessly the words took shape within Greyhorn's mind

"Who calls me?" Greyhorn demanded.

"I do—Lord Nefra of Cicero."

"A Gogol! What do you want of me, evil one? As all know, I am a loyal Hartford and thus your bitter enemy."

"All do not know what I know about you, Greyhorn. My agents tell me that you schemed with Hazar, until he played you false. Now, I think, you need another friend."

"I don't know what you are talking about."

"You don't understand us, Greyhorn. Hazar does not speak for the Gogol empire or even for Cicero, only for himself and his sycophants. I, for one, do not choose to run my life under Hazar's orders. Nor, I think, do you. Do you understand the position you are in?"

"Talk on, devil; I am listening."

"Hazar's not delivered you your trinket, without which you are powerless to help him or oppose him. If he should complete his plan your days are numbered, unless of course you take action against him."

"What do you have in mind?"

"Fortify yourself. About forty minutes after the second hour A.D. Hazar should have completed his dinner. His meal will consist of broiled whitefish stuffed with seasoned tubers and shaved bean stalks. Concentrate all your energy upon transmuting those substances into an acid which

will melt out his innards. Do that and you might escape
your fate. If you fail, you are doomed, for your power cannot match that of Hazar."

Nefra's image had grown smaller and more circular as
the conversation progressed. Now the droplet's evaporation
was almost complete. As Nefra's visage shrank Greyhorn
imagined that the voice became more shrill, until at the
end, barely more than a squeaking whine, it faded off and
disappeared.

For a moment Greyhorn contemplated the beaker's
empty lip, then took himself to his couch to rest before the
evening's work.

Chapter Thirty-five

It was half past the third hour B.D. when Grantin, Chom, and Castor reached the tumbles. The jumbled mass of slabs and boulders appeared nothing more than a barren, rock-strewn palisade. That was the Ajaj way. Most of the Grays were in Cicero or tilling Topor's farmsteads. The aged and the cubs who remained kept to their apartments. Castor led them along a twisting path up the slope to the entrance of his shelter. The deserted appearance of the landscape notwithstanding, Grantin felt the eyes of unseen watchers fixed upon his back.

Castor halted next to a triangular opening formed by the intersection of two slabs of stone. Nervously the Ajaj motioned for Grantin and Chom to enter the crevice.

Grantin went first, crouching on his hands and knees, feeling his way along in the dark. The shaft lowered as it went and bent sharply to the right. Another foot or two and it jogged to the left. Grantin entered a pitch-black chamber which he sensed was large enough for him to stand upright.

Behind him came the grunts and scrapes of Chom's tortured passage. At each turn the native's shoulders jammed against the walls, forcing him to twist sideways in order to extricate himself. At last he, too, escaped the tunnel.

Castor was the last to emerge. The Ajaj circled his guests and released a set of shutters. Sunlight ricocheted through the chinks between the boulders, penetrated the grillelike windows, and patterned the far wall.

"You should be safe here for a short time," Castor said, already turning back to the exit. "Undoubtedly you were seen, but it is unlikely that my kinsmen will volunteer information about your presence, at least for a day or so. There is food in the pantry; take what you like. Above all, do not go outside. I will return sometime after the second hour and if possible will contact Mara."

So saying, Castor skittered from the room, leaving Chom and Grantin to fend for themselves. While Chom explored Castor's quarters Grantin laid out his blanket, curled up, and went to sleep.

Without pausing to rest or eat, Castor worked his way to the top of the cliff and trotted down the trail to Cicero. By the time he had passed through the gate and checked in at the clerk's wicket it was already past the fifth hour. The guard at the scullery admitted him without comment. Castor slipped inside as inconspicuously as possible.

The kitchen was deserted. Cockle and the rest of the Grays were now in the refectory serving lunch. Castor removed his pack and set the jars of spices on Buster's worktable, all except the rot root which he placed out of sight in the drawer. Next he stowed the backpack, then filled a water pitcher which he carried upstairs.

Castor contrived to enter the dining hall while Cockle's attention was concentrated in another quarter. Without making a sound he carried the flagon to the serving bar, then joined the other Grays in dishing up the meal.

Ever since the incident of the worm in the salad Cockle had forced himself to remain alert through lunch, a practice which he did not enjoy. Now he turned and looked truculently at the scurrying Grays but could find nothing amiss. To his rheumy eyes Castor was indistinguishable from his fellows; only Buster by his grizzled muzzle and limping gait had acquired a separate identity in Cockle's mind. Grumbling, the steward turned back to his duties. The meal proceeded without incident.

After lunch all retreated once again to the kitchen, where Cockle promptly bludgeoned his senses with a bottle of Hazar's wine. Once he was certain that the human had drunk himself into his usual afternoon stupor Castor sidled up to Buster's bench where the elder Ajaj worked on Hazar's dinner.

"As you see, Buster, I got the herbs you requested," Castor said in a somewhat theatrical tone.

"Yes, I noticed. Got all of them, did you?"

"Yes, all you asked for, plus some special delicacies besides; in fact, that's why I was late. I found some items more to the taste of us Ajaj than Lord Hazar, so I left them at my quarters before returning here."

"What sort of special items?" Buster asked with more nonchalance than he actually felt.

"They are difficult to describe. Here, let me sketch them for you in the flour."

Castor smoothed a thin film of flour over the workbench and hastily wrote with his fingertip: *A Hartford and a Fanist.*

"Can you draw that a bit more clearly?" Buster asked.

Castor wiped out the words, then wrote another message: *Mara gave the human a bloodstone ring. He must meet her. My quarters, after third hour A.D.?*

One of the other Grays approached the table, and Buster hastily wiped out the message.

"Can you help me prepare these rare items?" Castor asked.

"I'm not sure. I'll try, if I can get away."

Castor nodded and moved off. Numbly Buster resumed his preparation of Hazar's dinner. Theories, schemes, and fears raced through his brain while his hands automatically chopped, sliced, and scraped. The addition of the tiny fragments of rot root to the stuffing had become almost an anticlimax.

Chapter Thirty-six

Hazar made sure that the door to his office was secured. Satisfied that he would not be interrupted, he slouched back in his chair and allowed himself to relax. The bronze-hued face which, when animated, gave Hazar the appearance of mature vitality now, in slack-jawed repose, revealed something of the wizard's true age. Deep furrows plowed the flesh between the mouth and the edges of the nose; a maze of wrinkles flanked each eye. When the head was turned just right small wattles of flesh bulged beneath the chin. Even the glossy black mustache which at first glance seemed a badge of vigor now appeared out of place, incongruous, as if it were an artifice employed by a slap-dash thespian to give the appearance of youth to an aging performer.

Hazar tried to force his spinning brain to rest, to marshal his energies for the spells which in the coming days he knew he must perform if his plans were to succeed. For the hundredth time he considered adding a second blood-stone to his gem-encrusted left hand. Each time, reluctantly, he had rejected the idea as being equivalent to slow suicide.

Unbidden, new questions, schemes, and worries jostled for room on the stage of his mind's eye. Rupert's silhouette, grossly distorted, capered in a jungle of odd plants, sometimes trailing Greyhorn's bumptious nephew, at others prancing with glee, his bloodstained hand adorned with the missing ring. An instant later Rupert stepped through the wall of plants to emerge on the other side as a Fanist who walked arm in arm with the wayward young Hartford. The two approached a gigantic pile of rocks and, at the last second, twisted sideways to melt between a crevice and disappear from sight.

The face of the Ajaj leader Obron swam into view. The Ajaj's words echoed unintelligibly. She held up a piece of paper covered with writing which, no matter how Hazar strained and twisted, he was nevertheless unable to read. A clatter arose in the background and terrified the Gray. She turned and ran for the shimmering tumbles, but before she reached them the scene faded away.

Dimly background sounds at last penetrated Hazar's conscious mind. Tap, tap. "My lord Hazar?" Tap, tap, tap. "My lord, are you there?"

Hazar's eyes snapped open. He lifted his body to sitting position. His muscles ached. His skin was clammy and beaded with sweat.

"A minute—cease that racket!" Hazar croaked.

Removing a soft towel from his desk, Hazar dried his face and massaged the back of his neck. At last he rose, released the latch, and slid back the door. A nervous Derma, shuffling from one foot to the other, eyes fixed upon the floor, confronted him.

"My lord, I . . ."

"What is it, clerk? I told you I did not want to be disturbed."

"My lord, I am sorry, but some information has been received which could be important. I thought you might want to know at once."

"Very well; come in. For your sake you had better hope that you did not disturb me unnecessarily." Hazar settled again into his chair but now took pains to keep the weariness from his face. Ill at ease, Derma stood before the desk and made his report.

"My lord, as you know, Saschim, the tailor of the second wall, is known to have some contact with the bandit

Yon Diggery. For this reason, my lord, we have prevailed upon his apprentice Trecko to keep us informed of—"

"I know all that, clerk! You don't have to give me a lesson in who works for me. Get to the point!"

"Yes, my lord Hazar. To go to the heart of the matter, then: Trecko reported that yesterday afternoon his master received a communication from Yon Diggery to the effect that a certain young Hartford in the company of a certain native had crossed the Weirdlands and was making for Cicero. He prevailed upon Saschim to watch the Gate of Dread so that he might be informed if the two enter this vicinity. Not suspecting that Trecko is in my lord's service, Saschim, this morning, conveyed this information and charged Trecko to implement the plan."

"What's the rest of the message? What is Saschim supposed to do if he finds this Hartford?"

"Diggery charged the tailor to lure the Hartford into his apartments, there to drug him and cut off his hand. This accomplished, the body is to be hidden and the hand conveyed outside the walls and delivered to Yon Diggery."

"Yes, and what does the tailor get out of all this?"

"Upon delivery of the hand, my lord, he was promised ten golds plus a call on the bandit for future favors in time of need."

"Ten golds—a handsome price for a mere hand, provided you don't know the value of what you are selling. What of the Fanist who reportedly accompanies the Hartford? What were Diggery's instructions concerning him?"

"None specific, my lord. The tailor was given a free hand to do as he pleased provided he accomplished his primary goal."

"An interesting story, I'll admit—but why, why? Oh, stop fidgeting, clerk; you were right in bringing this to my attention."

Hazar transferred his attention to an oddment of metal and bone which rested on his desk. Idly playing with the instrument, Hazar mused over the possible motives for Grantin's trip.

"Why of all places would he come here? At first I thought that sanctimonious old fool Obron was making up the story about a human and a Fanist entering the tumbles. Now I'm not so sure. If that is Greyhorn's addle-

brained nephew, Cicero should be the last place he'd visit.
Why not return to Hartford lands or even remain in
Grenitch Wood? Why come here, and with a Fanist yet?
What could he want here? Money, riches? Not likely. I
can't believe he wishes to join our society. Do you sup-
pose his uncle sent him here? But no, not with the ring.
Greyhorn would never part with the ring."

"Perhaps he knows someone here, someone who he
thinks will help him," Derma suggested meekly. "Or perhaps it is the Fanist who has business in Cicero, and for
lack of a better purpose the human is merely accompany-
ing him."

"Even Greyhorn's nephew would not be foolish enough
to come here as a mere tourist; and as for meeting someone, that's impossible. He knows no one in Cicero. He's
never been out of the Hartford lands in his life. Except
for myself and perhaps a few of the other lords, none of
us have penetrated the Hartford boundaries. Only . . ."
Hazar dropped the demarcator as if it were red-hot and
riveted his gaze upon Derma. ". . . only Mara has visited
his homeland. He's met Mara, for a fact!"

"You think, then, my lord, that they are planning—"

"Don't be a fool, Derma! He doesn't have the brains to
plan anything like that, or the courage. Now his uncle—
No, that's not possible. Grantin has the ring, not Greyhorn. The old reprobate would never let the stone go voluntarily. I wonder if it could be love?"

"Love, my lord?"

"She's an enchantress, isn't she? She prepared herself
to enchant him when she delivered the ring, only she ran
off before she could find out how successful she was. That
little witch has laid a spell on him and doesn't even know
it. By Satan, he's come here to find her!" Hazar pounded
his fist on his desk.

"Derma, take down these commands: First, have
twenty of my guards surround the tumbles, quietly. The
Grays are not to be bothered, but Grantin and the Fanist
are to be kept there at all costs. The men are to stay out
of sight until further orders. Next, call my overdeacons,
Croman, Jasper, and Wax. They are to commence at
once to call up a Firebird, one big enough to carry a full-
grown man and strong enough to last through an entire

night. They must use all their energies. I want the demon readied for my commands by the second hour.

"Lastly, call my body servants; have them prepare my bath. Get my masseuse and have fresh garments laid out. Tonight I will thwart my enemies and make ready the attack."

The period of indecision was over, the questions banished from Hazar's mind. Hazar's lassitude had fled with his doubts. Now he knew what to do; a plan of action had presented itself. His energies renewed, he strode to his private chambers while Derma raced off to implement his lord's commands.

Later, bathed, his skin massaged to an invigorated tingle and coated with a thin, glistening coat of scented oil, Hazar joined Mara in the parlor. The ministrations of his servants had soothed Hazar to the point that while reclining on the masseuse's table he had enjoyed his first peaceful sleep in days. Now, somewhat past the first hour A.D., Mara the enchantress rose nervously to greet her lord.

Hazar detected the tense set of her muscles, the slight quiver of the tendons in her neck, the contracted tight black pupils of her eyes. Her attitude could be due to a number of factors: concern over Hazar's tardiness in appearing for their dinner engagement; fear that he might have planned some rebuke or punishment because of her failure on her mission to the Hartfords. Possibly, just possibly, Mara's uneasiness might be due to more personal factors. Was she interested in forming a liaison with him? Could she be planning on using her charms on him in the hope of obtaining an advantage? If that were the case she would be disappointed. Mara was far too old for Hazar's tastes.

They had barely exchanged greetings when a servant's knock announced that dinner was ready. With Hazar in the lead the two entered the dining room.

Chapter Thirty-seven

A little after the first hour A.D. Castor and Buster carried the steaming dinner to Hazar's quarters. A moment after the guard knocked, an eye appeared at the spyhole. It studied the supplicants, then reluctantly slid back the panel. Derma admitted the two Ajaj and one of the guards while the other soldier positioned himself outside the hallway door. The Grays conveyed the dinner service to Hazar's table and set three places, one for Hazar, one for Mara, and the last for the food taster.

Hazar's clerk, Derma, examined the dishes, then silently pointed to first one item, then another. In response to these directions Buster cut off a fragment of fish, a spoonful of tubers, a splash of wine, a portion of dressing, and conveyed each to the taster's plate.

From behind a curtain appeared a pale, sickly boy. The young man's cheeks were sunken and sallow. Dull brown hair hung thin and limp over his forehead. Selected for his susceptibility to disease, the food taster was kept in a constant state of ill health. A vigorous specimen might fight off the effects of a deleterious substance, whereas someone like this boy would easily be pushed over the line to sicken and die.

"You may eat, Martin," Derma directed.

Somewhat diffidently the young man seated himself before the plate and commenced stuffing his cheeks with food. Lord Hazar did not wish his dinner to grow cold while the taster savored the meal.

The rot root, not having been activated by the appropriate spell, caused the young man no discomfort. Five minutes later the meal was pronounced safe. Hazar feared no slow-acting poison, for his magic and that of his subordinates was powerful enough to counteract any harmful substance provided he was given adequate time.

Martin left the room and Castor removed his plate. Now it was up to the girl. If she successfully performed the spell Hazar would die. In the confusion Castor might even be able to deliver Grantin's message.

Immediately upon his passing, Hazar's overdeacons as well as the remaining four lords, together with the inhabitants of the second wall, would all begin plotting to take his place. There would be no lack of candidates to bear the responsibility of his death. Nefra, in fact, already planned to focus the blame on Greyhorn and thus divert attention from his own machinations.

Leaving the Ajaj under the watchful eye of the guard, Derma returned to the dining room. He crossed to the parlor door and knocked politely on the panel three times. Upon hearing Hazar's call Derma slid back the door.

"My lord, my lady, dinner is served."

Chapter Thirty-eight

Platters and cups of hot delicacies steamed on a table draped in glossy black cloth. Places had been set with fire-glazed scarlet plates, crudely handsome, twisted clear glass goblets, and utensils of silver and black enamel.

Hazar dismissed the guard and ordered the Ajaj to serve the meal. By long custom Gogol lords preferred the service of the Grays to that of humans. Being viewed as a cowardly and downtrodden race, the Ajaj presented less of a physical danger to their masters than a possibly traitorous or high-spirited human servant.

Secondly, the Ajaj by their very natures were deft and so judged less likely to spill hot soup in their masters' laps. Further, should such an unfortunate event occur a human servant might create an unseemly display, while an Ajaj would meekly endure his fate. Should the crime be severe enough to require the ultimate penalty, the Ajaj's cured pelt would provide a minor recompense for the inconvenience.

Castor noted with satisfaction that Hazar seemed to be in fine appetite, demanding large portions of almost every dish, including the tainted stuffing. Mara commanded smaller portions which she sampled sparingly, except for the stuffing, which she tasted not at all.

During the meal Hazar waxed expansively upon his plans for conquest. The more he spoke, the more Hazar's hunger seemed to be satisfied by the emotions to which he now gave full vent. Ten minutes after filling Hazar's plate Castor noted that the Gogol had eaten only a few bites. The stuffing had been left almost untouched.

"More wine—our cups are dry. More wine!" Castor scuttled forward. "Zaco's clerk brought word today that my stones are almost ready," Hazar said to Mara, "an announcement for which I suspect you are in large part responsible. In that you have done well."

"Thank you, my lord. I have done my best."

"Not always, not always. You made a serious error in failing to follow my instructions concerning Greyhorn's courier, but in light of your recent success I am disposed to overlook that incident. It is of little importance now anyway."

"Thank you, my lord. You believe, then, that the wizard Greyhorn will remain loyal to your plan?"

"Nonsense; trust no one. No, I have solved the problem in a different way entirely. With Greyhorn out of the way his assistant Maurita will take command of his associates. Of her loyalty, for the time being at least, I am assured. In any event there will be no one in that portion of the Hartford lands to oppose me."

"My lord's magic is great to overcome Greyhorn in spite of the ring he possesses."

"The ring he does not possess. You don't know how sadly your mission went awry, do you, Mara? There is no harm now in telling you. It was indeed Greyhorn's nephew to whom you delivered the ring."

"But he put it on. . . ."

"Exactly. He put it on his finger and then couldn't get it off. His noble uncle should have chopped the digit off, but he botched the job. The lad escaped. Greyhorn has no more than his ordinary powers with which to oppose me, and he dare not denounce the scheme for fear of implicating himself. I will bring him here tonight and under rigorous interrogation extract what advantage I can for the coming battles against the Hartfords."

"But what about the nephew with the ring? Could he not turn its powers against you? Where is he now?"

"That is where you come in, my dear. That is the marvelous humor of this whole series of events. You did your job better than either of us realized. You enchanted young master Grantin without even realizing it."

"I . . . ?"

"Yes, the idiot's come here to find you. Isn't that delightful? The report came in this afternoon; he's hiding in the tumbles east of the city. At this very instant my guards have the area surrounded."

In the corner Castor clamped his jaws together and cursed his fate. The significance of Grantin's hiding in his quarters could hardly be missed. Unless Hazar ate the stuffing all would be lost. Would Mara go through with the plan and perform the required incantation?

Castor studied the female. It seemed to him that Hazar's news had brought her near a state of shock. Mara put down her fork and dropped all pretense of enjoying her meal. Her fingers played idly with the napkin while she struggled to regain her composure.

"But, my lord, if he's there, hidden in the tumbles with that ring, won't it be difficult to capture him? Will not his powers do great damage to your men, perhaps even enough to allow his escape?"

"Certainly, if I were a fool. If I chose to send in twenty or thirty armed men to flush him from hiding I have no doubt some lives would be lost. Not that I quail at bloodshed, but I need Grantin alive, at least until I can separate him from his ring. But really, Mara, the answer to your question is so simple I'm disappointed that you haven't seen it for yourself."

"I don't understand, unless—you don't mean . . . ?"

"Ah, I see that you have figured it out at last. Don't be so upset; it is the simplest thing in the world. The young fellow has come all this way to find you, and I don't think we should disappoint him. You and one of the Grays— this fellow here will do as well as any other," Hazar said, gesturing to Castor—"will be directed to the Hartford's hiding place by the Ajaj Obron, who is even now in the company of the captain of my guards.

"You will contrive some way to embrace the fellow. I am sure that you can think of something along those lines.

When he's in your arms you will scratch the back of his neck with the edge of this ring. He will immediately fall into a deep sleep. You will then signal my guards to come and remove his body."

Mara looked at her plate and tried to organize her swirling thoughts. One thing was clear: if Hazar survived this dinner his plan would probably work. For a moment Mara considered abandoning her conspiracy but realized that she had no option. If she failed tonight Nefra would take his own vengeance on her. At best, her fate would be delayed until Nefra fell under Hazar's sway and bargained away the secret of her participation in the plot in exchange for some benefit to himself. Forcing herself to eat, Mara stabbed a light-brown morsel with her fork.

"Your plan is most ingenious, my lord, and no doubt it will succeed. Of course I will do everything I can. It appears that we are about to have a long evening. We will need our strength, and it would be a shame to waste this excellent meal. Let us finish our dinner, and then this Gray and I will go off to meet the Hartford." By way of example Mara thrust the fragment into her mouth and motioned to Castor to refill her plate.

"A worthy idea. I'll need my strength for the days ahead. Gray, more wine and another scoop of stuffing—this has gone cold."

Castor filled the goblet, then ladled a generous portion of the rot-root–laced compound onto Hazar's plate. The Gogol lord captured a heaping forkful of the rich brown mixture. Castor and Mara watched anxiously as he conveyed the stuffing to his mouth. Hazar's jaw snapped open, his lips pulled back, and the tip of his fork began to enter his maw. At that instant Hazar gasped and grabbed his stomach with both hands. Abandoned in midair, the fork clattered noisily to the enameled plate, spewing its load of stuffing across the table. Convulsed with a series of violent cramps, Hazar doubled over and clutched his midriff. Greyhorn's attack had begun.

Mara stared indecisively at the writhing form. After a few seconds' delay, she called to the guards. Derma and two guards raced into the room. For a moment they also stood frozen as they beheld Hazar's agony.

"Fool!" Hazar groaned through clenched teeth. "Call my overdeacons. Bring them at once!"

Derma sent one of the guards to fetch Hazar's associate wizards, then strode forward himself to attempt to aid his lord. By the time Croman, Jasper, and Wax entered the chamber Hazar, with Derma's assistance, had already succeeded in neutralizing the worst of the pangs.

Hazar moaned a series of instructions and Croman quickly called up an appropriate protective spell. The pains rapidly subsided. Hazar, although clearly shaken by the attack, returned, more or less, to normal. Livid with rage, he screamed at his underlings:

"Complete your incantations; call up the Firebird. I have work aplenty for the demon tonight."

At a sign from the overdeacons, Derma instructed the guards to clear the table. The ends of the tablecloth were pulled together to form a sack, upending plates, tureens, and goblets in the process.

Croman, Jasper, and Wax scratched a large chalk triangle onto the table's surface. Each seated himself at one of the figure's points. Satchels were brought forth. Each of the overdeacons extracted powders, vials, crystals, fragments of bone and flesh, and, at last, an ivory simulacrum of a great winged lizard.

The overdeacons worked rapidly, reassembling the implements of the spell over which they had struggled all afternoon. Soon the crystals were positioned, the powders spread in the appropriate patterns, their faces and hands anointed with the required fluids. In droning resonant tones each recited his portion of the spell.

As the incantation proceeded the room grew dimmer, as if the wizards were sucking the very light from the glowpods to energize their spell. As the moment of climax approached each extracted a blade and sliced the middle finger on his left hand. Their arms extended, bisecting the edge of the triangle opposite their seats; their fingers met in the center of the figure, touched, and dripped blood in a common stream, thick, red, clinging drops splattering onto the figure of the Firebird.

By now the glowpods had flickered almost out. The only illumination derived from a phosphorescent glow in the air above the triangle, a radiance which illuminated the wizards' faces with a pearly light. From beyond the outer wall of Hazar's apartments could now be heard the sound of a raging whirlwind tattooed with the snaps and scrapes of nail and claw.

"He comes," Jasper whispered.

A wild screech sounded, a howl which pierced stone and flesh as if both were no more substantial than paper.

"He is here," Croman proclaimed in hushed tones. "Your orders, my lord?"

"He is to leave this place, to fly east over the farmlands, beyond the Weirdlands, beyond Grenitch Wood, across the Guardian Mountains to the manor house of the wizard Greyhorn two leagues west of the Hartford town of Alicon. There, ignoring all barriers, he is to take possession of the sorcerer Greyhorn, to clutch the living wizard in his talons and return here with him at once. Now, set him free. Send him on his errand."

The overdeacons resumed their incantations. Lines of strain creased their faces as they joined hands and silently communed with their creation. In seeming climax to their spell the glowpods flashed briefly, went black, and then slowly returned to their normal illumination. The deacons slumped forward. In exhaustion, they released their hands. Wax muttered:

"It is done; he goes to Greyhorn."

"Excellent. Now to our other duties. You there, Gray— how are you called?"

"Castor," the Ajaj said, deliberately refusing to add the honorific "my lord."

"The famous Castor, is it—the Gray with backbone? Good; you're well suited to your mission tonight. Derma, get five guards and come with me; we'll follow out of sight just behind. Mara, Castor, go to the tumbles and bring forth Grantin's sleeping body and, if possible, the Fanist as well. Tonight I will conclude my dealings with the two Hartfords, uncle and nephew both."

Castor and Mara hesitated for only an instant, then, with no other course available, left Hazar's apartments and walked toward the Gate of Dread.

Chapter Thirty-nine

Mightily disturbed at the cruel fates which had dogged his heels, Grantin grumbled two or three sullen oaths and sought vainly for a comfortable position on Castor's stone floor. He thought it terribly unfair that a person of his breeding, intelligence, and tender sensibilities should be subjected to such repeated indignities. Were the world to function as it ought he would be back at Greyhorn's manor relaxing after a pleasant repast and planning his triumphs at the fair at Gist.

With the merest flip of his hand the doughnuts would float outward to center unerringly upon the winning pegs. So inundated would he be with marvelous prizes that within an hour or two he would be required to hire a sturdy lad to carry his winnings. Grantin smiled at the pleasant thought, then found his attention distracted by a knob of granite which poked insistently against the center of his spine. With ill grace he edged his lanky form slightly to one side and refocused his attention to happier circumstances.

The women, the lovely women; what a pleasant sight was that to imagine. When he was dressed in his smart new tunic, brushed leather trousers, richly adorned and manfully scented, the maidens would flock to him like stingwings to a flame. They should be tall, but not too tall; he found it awkward kissing eye to eye. Soft and shapely, but not overly endowed; that kind tended to run to fat. Long-haired, but not too long; hair of an excessive length became a nuisance on certain occasions.

The vision in his mind's eye rippled and adjusted itself as each new criterion was added to his list. Finally the picture was complete—a maiden striking, shapely, sensuous, yet soft, loving, complaint. The perfect girl. As the vision cleared, with more than a little surprise Grantin noted that the woman bore a striking resemblance to Mara. Somehow he found that disturbing.

A pebble crept stealthily forward and lodged itself beneath his calf. The image vanished. Grantin found himself wide awake and more uncomfortable than ever.

"I swear I was more at ease in the middle of the forest. How can the Ajaj sleep like this?" Grantin grumbled as he sat up and massaged several sore spots in his back.

"They do not," Chom's voice called out from the corner of the darkened parlor.

"Do not what?"

"Sleep like this. The open space disturbs them. Their beds are in niches carved into the walls."

"I should have known they wouldn't endure this discomfort. Doesn't this fellow have a guest niche or two where we could sleep?"

"We could," Chom answered with a gurgling laugh, "provided we squeezed in half our body at a time. It could become rather confining."

"Chom, do you think he'll be able to bring Mara? Do you think this is ever going to end? I'm so *tired* of living like a peasant!"

"I am certain that all of this discomfort will end," Chom answered reassuringly, "one way or another."

"I can think of one way. What's the 'another'?"

"There are several, really. They could chop your arm off and set you free, or they could chop your hand off and set you free, or they might execute you altogether, or—"

"Enough!"

"You asked for my evaluation of the possibilities."

"That was before you overwhelmed me with the optimism of your predictions," Grantin replied sulkily.

The termination of their conversation magnified the silence in Castor's apartment, a quiet which was soon broken by a new sound. From the jagged rocks beyond the parlor wall came the scratch and scrape of moving figures. Grantin heard the scuff of leather upon stone, then the soft chatter of pebbles skittering down the slope.

In the rock-walled darkness Grantin became disoriented. Though he was tempted to ask for Chom's advice, his fear of discovery would not allow him to speak. Minute by minute the sounds grew inexorably closer and more pronounced. At last Grantin heard the slab at the entrance to Castor's tunnel being dragged aside.

The scrape of the stone dissolved Grantin's paralysis. In an instant he jumped to his feet, crept to the tunnel exit, and slid his dagger from its sheath. Behind him Grantin heard the telltale hissing of Chom's horny feet against the floor. The scrapes and clicks were measurably louder now as their volume was amplified by the acoustics of the tunnel. A foot from the tunnel exit, a voice called out:

"Grantin, Chom, are you there? Don't be afraid; it's me, Castor."

Grantin let out a pent-up sigh and hissed into the darkness: "Why didn't you say something before? Poor Chom was extremely disturbed. He thought you were a Gogol trying to sneak up on us."

"Do not worry; his concern is not wasted. Hazar's guards will be here soon enough," Castor replied as he paced soundlessly across the room to where his glowpod hung.

Grantin could barely make out the Ajaj's form in the darkness. He turned to follow Castor's motion. From behind came a renewed patter of scrapes and clicks, sounds which so startled Grantin that, in turning, his dagger flew from his hand and clattered to the floor.

"The guards . . . !" Grantin squeaked. He found his limbs paralyzed with fright. He was able to do no more than stare stupidly at the tunnel's black exit.

Castor silently excited his glowpod to a weak yellow-green radiance. At the edges of its dim illumination Mara crawled into the room, then stood simultaneously straightening her garments and slapping the dust from the hem of her skirt.

"This is the female you asked me to bring," Castor announced, "the one called Mara."

Mara examined Grantin critically while the young Hartford was still searching for his voice.

"You are the same one after all," she whispered. After a brief pause she reached for Grantin's left hand. Pulling it sideways to catch the glowpod's feeble beams, she was able to discern the ruby stone which still adorned Grantin's index finger.

"Are you really the same Mara who gave me this ring in Alicon? Was it only a week ago? It seems like years."

"For me as well. Somehow I had not believed them, but seeing you here—did you really come for me?"

"Castor's told you, then? Yes, I've come a long way to find you. You have no idea of the indignities that Chom and I have endured. Oh, excuse me, I forget myself. Mara, allow me to introduce to you my friend and companion, Chom—as you can see, a Fanist of the highest order."

Now it was Mara's turn to be startled as she spied the native standing quietly in the shadows a few feet from her right shoulder.

"Do you know the danger you are in, Grantin?" Mara asked, turning back to the human.

"I can make a very good estimate, but I had no choice. It was so important that I find you. . . ."

"My mother told me that Hartford men were all worthless and untrustworthy. I see now she was wrong. To think of the risks you've taken on my account! So much love, and all for nothing." To his complete dismay Grantin noticed that Mara had begun to cry. "I cannot do it; I just cannot go through with it. Even if your love is foolish and misplaced at least it is sincere. To think that a man, especially a Hartford, could feel that way without me using my enchantments, could risk everything for me alone. I don't know what to do. You are so young to die."

"Die!"

"It is the Gogols," Castor explained. "They have found out that you are here. Hazar has ringed the tumbles with guards and sent Mara in to bring you out without a fight. The female was supposed to inject you with a drug which would put you to sleep. Then, with you and the power of your ring out of the way, she was to call for the Fanist to surrender."

"But how did they find us?"

"Obron, the leader of my people. She saw me bring you here. In order to protect my kinsmen from retribution she reported your presence. The shame is mine. As punishment I will share your fate."

"Is there another way out?" Chom asked.

"In an Ajaj's quarters? None that any of you could fit through," Castor said, nodding toward the tunnel. "That is the only way."

"Could we fight our way out?"

"Against one or two guards perhaps, but not the army that Hazar has poised—at least thirty of his soldiers. You might conquer a few of them, but you would never escape alive."

"What can we do? There must be some solution, some alternative, something."

"I see two choices," Chom announced. "Surrender, or defeat as many of them as possible before we are killed."

"Killed!"

"It's all right, Grantin," Mara said, throwing her arms around him and stifling her sobs. "I can't let you walk out there alone. I will die with you."

"Die? Are you crazy? I have no intention of dying over a stupid piece of jewelry. You can do what you want, but I am going to go out there and let them take the ring. Chom, are you coming with me?"

"It seems I have little alternative," the Fanist responded evenly. "Who goes first?"

For long moments the four figures seemed rooted to Castor's granite floor. At last Mara slipped forward, bent over, and entered the tunnel.

Chapter Forty

From behind granite boulders, abutments, and tip-sided slabs Hazar's guards peered through the darkness and waited for the signal to attack. Several of the men carried cocked crossbows, bolt tips swinging aimlessly back and forth across the center of the tumbles. These were the best weapons the common soldier possessed.

From time to time gunpowder had been formulated and pistols reinvented, but each such experiment ended in disaster. The chemical energy released by an explosion eventually was tapped by the combatants and incorporated, deliberately or accidentally, into fearfully dangerous spells. Time and again experimenters were horrified to see their guns explode. The last such disastrous experiment had taken place in Cicero only twenty years before, an object lesson in terror which would, no doubt, refer similar innovation for another twenty or thirty years hence.

It was one of the crossbowmen, one Huber by name, who first saw Mara emerge from Castor's tunnel. Huber steadied his crossbow and strained to discern the target more clearly.

A glowpod flickered to life in Mara's hand, and she swung it carefully over her head in the all-clear signal. Hazar's men cautiously advanced while Mara, then Grantin and the rest, picked their way down the rock-strewn slope. A semicircle of bowmen pocketed the prisoners at the bottom of the tumbles. Two members of the household guard, specially trained as hexmen, quickly released their spells of nullification, restraint, and deactivation, workmanlike incantations which, for a short while at least, would inhibit even powerful wizards from launching a magical counterattack. The group now physically and psychically secure, the captain of the guards signaled that Hazar might approach.

The Gogol wizard advanced briskly, his red-and-black gown streaming behind him. His feet picked their way unerringly over the rock-strewn sand at the base of the tumbles.

"You have restrained them?" he asked the hexmen.

"Indeed, my lord, they made no struggle."

"You did well, Mara, in arranging their capture. I seem to recall, however, that the plan called for this one"—Hazar jerked his thumb at Grantin—"to be drugged. But no matter. He is here and you have saved us having to carry him down the slope. You are Grantin of Alicon, I presume?" Hazar asked the young man politely. "Allow me to introduce myself. I am Hazar, Lord of the Gogols and Master of the Gate of Dread. And this being who accompanies you?"

"My human name is Chom."

"Both travelers from a far land. Allow me to show you our Gogol hospitality. I think you will find your quarters in Cicero somewhat different from those here in the Ajaj camp—and while I'm on that subject, there is business that remains unfinished." Hazar turned to the captain of the guard and issued a sharp command: "Bring me Obron, the leader of the Grays."

The soldier motioned to two of his underlings. A moment later Obron was escorted forward to Hazar's side.

"These two were given shelter in your city," Hazar began. "As you know very well, no unauthorized persons are permitted in our realm. Clearly your people are responsible. Why should I not make them pay?"

"They had nothing to do with it, my lord. The presence of these travelers was reported to your guards."

"Perhaps that is all part of a clever scheme to try and avoid the punishment which is due you. Very well; I will test your sincerity. You saw these people captured by my men?"

Obron silently nodded her assent.

"From whose lodgings did they emerge?"

"My lord, it is dark and difficult to tell from which—"

"Answer me or all will suffer the penalty of treason!"

Obron hesitated a moment then whispered: "Castor's."

Hazar whipped around and pointed a long, bony finger at the Gray who stood to Mara's right. "Aren't you Castor the troublemaker? Isn't that your name?"

"I am Castor and proud of it. Proud not to be a sheep like my fellows, or a traitor like Obron. Proud to oppose your evil madness. I am Castor your enemy. Kill me now if you will and have done with it."

The guards were shocked into silence by the Gray's incredible outburst. After a moment the stunned quiet was broken by Hazar's laughter.

"Now I have seen everything," the Gogol exclaimed, "the strangest of all possible sights, a Gray with courage. Don't be so hasty for the end; it would be a bad omen for me to precipitately eliminate such a rarity as yourself. No, I think I will take my own good time in finishing you. Perhaps we will put your courage to the test, but not tonight. Captain, bring them all to my quarters."

"My lord, if you need me no longer . . ."

"All of them, guard, the girl included."

The soldiers formed the prisoners into a line and, flanking them, marched the group up the winding trail back to the Gate of Dread.

In a few minutes Grantin, Chom, Castor, and Mara were ushered into Hazar's parlor. Already present in the small chamber were Hazar and his three overdeacons. At the far left-hand corner of the room wine-colored drapes billowed.

Mara noticed that the furniture had been hastily rearranged, the couch and chairs pushed back to provide an open area in the center where she and the prisoners now stood. In front of them, seated on the settee with his back to the outer wall, Hazar eyed the four critically. Huddled together to the right of the rippling drapes crouched Croman, Jasper, and Wax. Occasionally one of the over-deacons flicked a glance over his shoulder toward the window, as if nervously expecting the imminent appearance of another guest. Hazar concentrated his attention upon the prisoners. He commenced his interrogation with Grantin.

"Well, Master Grantin, so you are here at last. You have led us a merry chase. You know, of course, your uncle Greyhorn is quite displeased with you. No, no, you need not reply; his wishes are now of minor importance at best. More to the point, however, you have inconvenienced me. Do you have any idea of the trouble you have caused?"

Grantin shook his head.

"No? I will tell you so you will understand better what is to happen to you. It was I who sent the ring you now wear. The ring was your uncle's price for joining forces with me in my conquest of the Hartfords. He and his supporters were to nullify the defenders who normally man the main pass through the Guardian Mountains. Oh, not that I minded giving him the ring, you understand; I had dozens more coming, promised by my associate, Lord Zaco—another 'friend' of Mara's, by the way.

"But Zaco's promises have proved unreliable of late. I fear that the old fool has lost the control of his subordinates and that they tell him what he wishes to hear without any intention of following his orders.

"The ring was Greyhorn's price, but when you took it your uncle became petulant, obstinate, and uncooperative. Very well; by concentrating all my energy I could have taken the passes anyway, but Zaco hasn't sent me the promised stones. Still, matters could proceed with only one or two more rings such as the one you wear now. But you were gone with the ring, and Greyhorn had withdrawn his support, and Zaco's a senile old fool—and so here I sat committed to a battle without sufficient supplies, or at least the crucial support to be assured of enough when winning through the passes.

"And, as if that were not enough, my dear Grantin, your uncle took it into his head to oppose me, to actually commence a series of attacks against my person. Attacks which I could parry, but at what price? All because of you. Greyhorn's support gone because of you. A ring which I desperately need lost because of you. Greyhorn's opposition because of you. You blundering, stupid, incompetent, weak-spined, ridiculous, fatheaded fool, my great plans brought to a standstill *all because of you!*"

Grantin shivered and cringed from Hazar's screams.

"I see you are beginning to understand a bit about how I feel. Perhaps you may be able to imagine some of the things I have planned for you. . . . But you are trembling. How ungracious of me to so disturb my guests. Don't let me frighten you too badly. Perhaps you will think of some way to assuage my anger before the time for retribution arrives. I will let you think over the possibilities while I greet your associates."

Hazar now turned his attention to the Fanist. "And your name is Chom, you say. Why do you travel with this young fool?"

"He is what you humans call my friend," Chom replied in a neutral low voice.

"A friend? This pea-brained imbecile your friend? Only a fool has a fool for a friend. Is that what you are?"

"If I were truly a fool I would not know it and so would say no. If I were not a fool again I would deny it. There hardly seems to be another possible answer to your question."

"Don't play games with me, you four-armed freak. I'm not afraid of you Fanists like some of those weak-kneed Hartfords. You will die just as easily as anyone else; don't think otherwise."

Hazar turned his gaze on Castor and briefly addressed the Gray. "As for you, I need no answers, no explanations. You're a mutant, a freak, or at best insane. There is nothing I need from you except your death. Since you have chosen to befriend these two, to take part against your masters, then so be it; you will share their fate."

Now Hazar's attention slid slyly to his left, back to Mara.

"And last, my dear, delicious Mara."

"My lord, I haven't—"

"Calm yourself. I have accused you of nothing. To the best of your ability you have carried out my commands. You were sent to deliver the ring, and you did so. You were told to bewitch the person who received it from you, and you did so. You were told to make him your slave, and though you've not accomplished it exactly as I ordered, in the last analysis apparently you have done that too. And you have controlled Zaco as best you could. You have followed my orders, and it is not your fault that everything you have touched has turned to ashes.

"But when did we Gogols ever care about fault anyway? It is results that matter—success, usefulness—and here, Mara, you have failed miserably.

"In order to get Zaco's stones I must go to his mine myself and wrest them from his servants with my own hands. You are bad luck, Mara; perhaps you are fey. Under more normal circumstances I would simply banish you from my household, perhaps send you to the pleasure rooms, find you a task at which your ill luck would be of no harm; but these are not ordinary circumstances.

"This fellow appears to be in love with you. I don't mark him for a man of courage; but, still, who can tell about these things? Perhaps at the last moment he may choose to die rather than cooperate. Occasionally young idiots are gallant that way, so I think I will increase the stakes. If he cooperates and earns my favor, then you shall share his fate. If, on the other hand, he becomes obstinate and requires persuasion or elimination, then you shall also share his fate. In this way we will bend his noble urges to my bidding. Now for—"

Hazar's speech was interrupted by a moaning screech. The curtain flapped more vigorously, heralding an approaching gale. A high-pitched hissing shriek pierced the darkness.

"It comes. It comes," Croman moaned.

"Pull back the drapes; make ready for its arrival."

A great gust of air poured in. Borne on the gale was another raucous shriek embroidered with the undertone of huge flapping leathery wings. As the monster neared its destination its calls became more frequent. The sound of its flight rose to a fever pitch. A muffled thud echoed from the terrace, then one last cry, an announcement that its mission was complete. The beat of wings became softer, disappearing until, only two or three seconds later, the night was again still.

As if a trance had been broken, Hazar ordered his overdeacons to retrieve the demon's burden. Croman,

Jasper, and Wax scuttled onto the balcony and quickly returned, bearing between them Greyhorn's dazed form.

"Ah, now our little group is complete—uncle and nephew together at last. To show you that I stint no one, Grantin, I will throw your uncle into the bargain if you cooperate with me. You may have his life or his death as you choose. Well, what do you say?"

"Say to what? What do you want me to do? I don't understand. Why don't you just take the ring and have done with it?"

"If I only could—but that's right, you don't understand the powers of the stone. You've had it too long; it's been at least ten days. By now it has attuned itself to your mind. Though you might agree to cooperate the subconscious portions of your brain would take control. Anyone who now tried to cut off your finger would find the blade, his hand, his arm, probably his whole body, ablaze. There is not a thing you could do to stop it even if you thought you wanted to. In a sense the ring has a mind of its own. No, unfortunately, I cannot take it by force, but I can tell you the spells to pronounce, the words to say.

"If you follow instructions you can lend the power of your ring to my enterprise, in exchange for which I will give you the lives of your friends, the death of your uncle, your freedom, his property, and your life. Well, what do you say?"

"While I appreciate your offer, I don't really think I am well suited to the black arts. As an alternative, why don't we just— Ouch!" Grantin grabbed his left foot and hopped in a slow circle while he massaged the toes which had been suddenly caught beneath Chom's foot.

"I am clumsy tonight," Chom apologized. "I think it is because we are all so tired. Instead, could we not rest and discuss the matter among ourselves, since it affects us all? Grantin could give you his answer in the morning."

Hazar fixed a calculating gaze upon the Fanist. Then, after a moment's hesitation, he nodded his head and gestured for the guards to conduct the prisoners to their cell.

"I will give you to the third hour, no later. After that I will have no more time for you. I will have thirty bowmen take aim and fire at once. Master Grantin's not a good enough magician to stop all the bolts. I will see you all ground into fodder by noon."

The prisoners were led down into the cellars and sub-cellars of the outer wall until at last the four, Grantin, Chom, Castor, and Mara, were tossed into a stone cell with a hay-covered floor. Taking no chances on a resurgence of Greyhorn's powers, Hazar had the wizard conveyed to a separate chamber away from Grantin's sight and hearing.

Once the guards had disappeared Grantin slipped to Chom's side and whispered in his earhole: "Why did you "

"A moment." Castor waved his hands in an expansive gesture and silently mouthed an oath. The air in the cell seemed to thicken and congeal until a shiver ran through Grantin's body like the popping of a soap bubble.

"Now we can talk," Castor said. "They did not bother to neutralize my powers. I have pronounced a spell of secrecy."

"As I started to say, Chom, why did you step on my foot?"

"You were about to tell them about the spell which Mara could have used to remove the ring, were you not?"

"Yes, but—"

"If Hazar had learned of that spell, he would have removed the ring at once and had us killed out of hand. The bloodstone provides our only bargaining power."

"Then you think I should cooperate with him?"

"You can't trust Hazar," Mara whispered excitedly. "Once he has used you all he can, he will kill us anyway."

"Let me see if I understand this. If Mara removes the ring, he will kill us. If I do not cooperate, he will kill us; and if I do cooperate, he will kill us. Can you think of anything we can do so that he will not kill us?"

"We could escape," Chom suggested.

Grantin approached the bolts on the great door which sealed their cell. He pointed his bloodstone at the juncture of the metal. His forehead wrinkled in concentration, but no emanations appeared from the ring.

"It's no use. For the time being their spells have blunted my powers."

"I still have not recovered all my abilities," Chom said; "unfortunately my spells are not strong enough to destroy the door."

"Except for a spell of enchantment I can be of no help," Mara volunteered.

Now all eyes turned to Castor. The Ajaj carefully fingered the green cube in his pouch, then sighed in defeat. "I, too, have some skills, but of a defensive nature only. Alone I could never batter down the walls."

"Well, if I am going to be killed in the morning," Grantin said testily, "at least I am not going to be half asleep when it happens. Right now I am going to get some rest. Maybe an idea will come to me in a dream."

The prisoners lay down on the straw, Mara placing her body distractingly close to Grantin's. Nevertheless, in a few minutes all were asleep.

It was after the ninth hour A.D. when a tapping sounded outside the cell door. Groggily Grantin arose from his pile of straw and, as if in a dream, watched the portal slide open. The hallways were still dark, illuminated only by the faint lime-green radiance from the glowpods. With a scraping sound a small form came forward to be silhouetted in the opening. Grantin reached out and shook Mara's shoulders. The sound of her awakening disturbed Chom and Castor, and all sat up and stared at the shadowed figure.

"Hurry, hurry—what are you waiting for?" a small voice hissed. "Many lives will be lost tonight in helping you win free. Come on. Hurry—the least you can do is be successful in your escape."

Castor recognized the voice of their rescuer. He struggled to his feet and urged his comrades to follow his lead. Hesitantly, as if in a daze, Grantin, Mara, and Chom also rose. Together with the Gray all followed Buster's limping passage down the hallway to the dungeon exit.

Chapter Forty-one

It being Lord Hazar's custom to eat a late dinner, Castor had left the kitchen with the doctored meal a bit before the first hour. From that time on Buster had nervously paced the scullery with as frenetic a gait as his withered limb would allow. At the end of each pass across the floor he slowed his movements just long enough to cock an ear for the approach of heavy-booted feet. At any moment he expected to be swept up by Hazar's guards. By the second hour Buster had convinced himself that he was ready to accept his fate provided only that his plot succeeded.

It was a quarter past the second hour by the primitive water clock and no one came to shout the news of Hazar's passing. The droplets continued to trickle from the finely valved orifice, each one striking tiny spoon-shaped paddles and rotating the wheel a sixth of a revolution. The indicator crept forward at a snaillike pace until at last the clock registered half past the second hour. Still no alarm. Buster hoisted himself up on a stool and massaged his swollen knee.

The third hour came and Hazar's quarters settled into

their early-evening drone. Finally Buster could stand the suspense no longer.

Cautiously the Gray ascended the scullery stairs. He reached the main-floor corridor without incident and was surprised to see that the normal complement of household guards was absent. Though it was worth his very life to do so, Buster could not now restrain his curiosity. Painfully he picked his way up the next flight to the apartment level. There, as well, the guards were absent. Without a doubt something was in the wind.

Buster retreated to the first floor and made his way to the front entrance. There one of the Gogols remained on guard, but not a member of the usual complement. Instead a young subacolyte had been pressed into service during the emergency. Armed with an unfamiliar sword and oversized helmet and breastplate, the young man leaned uneasily against the entryway wall while his hands busied themselves tapping the hilt of his short sword against the granite blocks. Affecting his most harmless pose, Buster limped up to the guard and hazarded a meek question.

"Excuse me, my lord. I have just finished my duties in the kitchen and I see that the usual guards are gone. Is something amiss?"

"The doings of your masters are no concern to you, Gray. Go be about your business and leave me to my post."

"Of course, my lord. It is just that . . . well, I should be going back to my home. Normally one of the guards on duty escorts me to the gate and authorizes my passage back to the tumbles," Buster improvised. "I wanted to know if there were some problem that would cause me to remain here for the night."

"No, there's no problem, and I cannot authorize you to stay. Go on to the gate and tell them Garyl said to let you through; but, mind you, stay out of Lord Hazar's way. Spies have taken shelter in your beloved tumbles and Lord Hazar and some of the guards have gone to capture them. If they find you out wandering loose at this time of night they might slice you first and ask questions later. Well, go on. What are you standing there for? I have my own concerns to contend with."

Buster paused for a moment, considering the possibilities, then came to a swift decision. Exaggerating his disability for the benefit of the guard, he limped down the five stone steps to the First Circle, then made his way to the Gate of Dread.

The guards on duty visited upon Buster an extra ration of curses and obscenities for disturbing them so late but finally allowed him to leave the city. In a short while he reached the lip of the ridge which overlooked the tumbles. After only a few moments' rest he began his tortured descent. By the time he reached the bottom his right leg throbbed constantly. The Gray clenched his teeth and ignored the pain. Three yards in front of him in the flat sandy area between the base of the tumbles and the stream stood soldiers, underdeacons, and Lord Hazar himself.

Drawing on the racial knowledge of thousands of years as prey, the Ajaj moved soundlessly until at last he could hear Hazar's interrogation of the prisoners. All his plans had gone awry. Hazar still lived, while Castor, the human, and the Fanist had been taken prisoner. Even Mara appeared to be in custody. Of all the conspirators he alone, a withered, crippled old Ajaj, remained. Then Buster heard the cruelest revelation of them all, that their plans had been destroyed by one of his own kind. Obron had betrayed them all. A cold hatred washed through Buster's crippled frame. With it arose an idea born of the insanity which had long festered in what, for an Ajaj, was a distorted mind: the conviction that as soon as the Gogols left he would follow Obron to her apartments and there kill her with his bare hands.

Shortly the Gogols, Hazar in the lead, formed up their prisoners and marched them off to Cicero. As soon as the last soldier had disappeared Buster made his move.

With an agility that transcended his physical limitations Buster slipped noiselessly across the stream and followed Obron up the slope to her lodgings. A third of the way from the bottom the decision maker halted and made three chirping sounds. From within the pile of rock two chirps answered her. A few feet ahead and to the left a stone slab was pushed aside. Obron scuttled forward into the opening, but before the passage could be closed Buster, too, entered, his left arm hooked around Obron's throat and the point of one of the knives he had stolen from the kitchen scratching Obron's side. The Gray went stiff with fear, unable even to cry out against her attacker. Obron's mates were horrified and seemed rooted to the floor of the entrance tunnel.

"Push back the stone," he commanded. "Conduct us inside; I have business with our decision maker."

Terrified, Obron's mates led the way into the softly lighted, rock-walled parlor. There Buster pushed Obron away so that the two could see each other face to face.

"What do you want of me?"

"You betrayed our people, Decision Maker. For that treachery I intend to make you pay."

"I have betrayed no one. I merely reported a human and a Fanist who, without my permission, took up residence here in the tumbles. We owe them no duty of protection."

"The human and the Fanist came to us for help. They are the enemies of our enemy. You also betrayed one of our own into Hazar's hands. Castor was my friend, and it is you who have condemned him to a horrible death."

"I've done nothing other than to discharge my responsibilities. Our way is to serve. Castor knew that; he was warned. If he chose to break the rules of our people, then the consequences are on his own head, not mine."

"What rules of our people are you talking about? Our duty is to survive, not to serve. We were never slaves on Ajaj. Hunted, yes; threatened, yes; struggling against a hostile world, yes—but never slaves. The Pales across the mountains are not slaves. Never have the Ajaj willingly cooperated with evil. Never have they turned cannibal, feeding on their own, until now."

"What right have you to lecture me? I am the decision maker. The people have given me the power."

"You are the decision maker by the rules of chance. Thus were you chosen and thus now will you end your term, for I am the random element. I, Buster, and this Gogol knife will be the ill luck which separates you from your post at the same time it cleaves your head from your body. Perhaps it will change nothing, but the random factor must not be denied."

"No, don't! That is unnecessary. I did not ask to be decision maker. I was chosen. It was my burden, my duty. If you are indeed the random factor who is to remove me from my office, then so be it; I relinquish the post. I will re-move my token and those of my mates from the pile, and you may cast the stones again. Pick another leader and see if his decisions conform more to your own opinions. If so, that is the way of our people; but if not, then leave, for you cannot kill us all."

Obron's words buzzed within the old Gray's brain and he could not seem to make out their meaning. His body felt flushed. As if in a trance he limped forward, knife waist-high in front of him, its tip drawing a small twinkling circle in the air. Obron gasped and moved back, flattening herself against the wall. Her mouth hung open. She sucked in great drafts of air, causing her belly to palpitate as if it contained a living organism.

Buster moved closer, but as he approached his senses seemed to clear. He halted, then shook his head. Lower-ing the knife, he turned back and collapsed into one of Obron's woven chairs.

"Very well. I would do myself no honor taking your cringing life. Bring out the tokens and the stones. We will choose a new decision maker."

A panting Obron gestured to her mates, who, as if re-leased from a spell, raced to an alcove and brought forth a ten-sided chest. Inside, inscribed on polished stone disks, were the names and numbers of every Gray in the com-munity. The top third of the container was swung up on its hinges, and from within a small square wooden box was removed. In this box reposed three ten-sided stone dice, each face inscribed with a numeral.

"Go ahead, go ahead; choose whomsoever you wish," Obron commanded.

"No, we will follow the rules, such as they are. Is it not true that it is the outgoing decision maker who picks the successor?"

Obron did not respond, merely nodded dumbly.

"Pick them up, then; you know the routine."

Somewhat diffidently Obron approached the box. Swirl-ing her hand deep inside, she removed an inscribed stone disk. She mixed the clattering, clacking tablets until at last she had withdrawn fifteen tokens. She arranged them in descending numerical order, then took up the dice. These were shaken and released onto the chiseled floor. The topmost numeral of each of the dice was now read from left to right: 2-1-5.

Obron made a show of searching through the disks, then shook her head to indicate that no match had been found. The decision maker was about to pick up the dice again when Buster limped forward and restrained her hand. In double-checking the tokens Buster was filled with wry amusement to see that Obron had attempted to cheat him. Apparently Gray number 2-1-5, a certain Velo, was not to Obron's liking. From then on Buster carefully monitored each toss.

At the end of fifteen throws an amazing three matches had been found, a result far greater than that which would have been predicted on the basis of pure odds. Buster carefully examined the tablets once again. Those initially chosen were Velo, number 2-1-5; Hanther, number 4-0-8; and Brax, number 6-6-6. Buster clenched the tokens tightly in his right fist and ordered Obron's chief mate out into the night to collect the three. Together with Buster and his knife, Obron and the other mate remained in the parlor, hostage to the messenger's faithful completion of his errand.

Almost exhausted by his swashbuckling exertions, Buster slumped in a chair and massaged his throbbing knee. Time passed. The Gray's head lolled forward until the bump of his chin against his chest awakened him. In the corner Obron was stealthily making her way to the exit. She halted her motion upon a peremptory wave of Buster's knife.

For the next few minutes Buster strained himself to stay awake. Finally he heard the noise of visitors in the passage. The first to emerge was Obron's mate, followed by three undistinguished Grays. The first two were not familiar, but the third, Brax, he recognized as one of the laborers in Topor's market. The three Ajaj moved nervously to the center of the room and viewed Buster with expressions of mingled fear and curiosity. The old Gray painfully arose from the chair to address the newcomers. Noticing the fixed direction of their gaze, he slipped the knife back into his belt.

"I am Buster, formerly a servant in Hazar's kitchen. One of my helpers there was the Gray known as Castor. Each of you must have heard of Hazar's plan to send forth an army to conquer the Hartfords. In aid of this scheme he has obtained control of gemstones of great psychic power. If his plans are not disrupted the plot will succeed.

"Castor and I were determined to foil his scheme. Through a turn of fortune allies, a human with a bloodstone of great power and a Fanist, arrived here this morning. They would, I think, with some persuasion, have lent their strength to our cause. Unfortunately this one"—Buster pointed accusingly at the corner where Obron cowered —"saw fit to betray them to the Gogols in hopes of earning Hazar's favor. Not satisfied with condemning the travelers to death, she implicated Castor, guaranteeing a sorry end for him as well. In so doing she has betrayed us all and forfeited the right to her office. Tonight, at my bidding, she cast the stones fifteen times and immediately derived an amazing three matches, those three being yourselves. One of you shall become the new decision maker. To that purpose have I asked you here."

The three Grays seemed nonplused by Buster's announcement. They shuffled their feet, each one looking nervously at his fellows. At last, somewhat diffidently, Hanther spoke up.

"You say that Obron cast the stones at your command, but this is not the accepted way. If Obron wishes to retire, then she should call in the witnesses, make her declaration, and then proceed with the proper ceremony. I confess I don't quite understand what your meeting here tonight has to do with us."

"Obron has resigned. With or without witnesses it is no longer her wish to be decision maker, as she will confirm now if you ask her. She having resigned, the stones were thrown; your lots were drawn and you are bound."

"What do you ask of us, then?" Velo responded.

"First the stones must be thrown and our leader chosen. Then I have much to ask of him and of all of us."

"Obron, is that true? Have you resigned?" Brax asked.

Obron looked up and sucked in her breath as if about to make a speech; then, eyeing Buster's hand on the pommel of his knife, she nodded her assent. In spite of his twisted frame Buster's eyes were clear. He fixed a demanding gaze upon the three candidates. After a moment a shiver of resolution passed through the Ajaj. Brax shrugged his shoulders and spoke for the group.

"Very well, then; let us throw the stones and have done with this business." Brax knelt down, picked up the three dice, and made a show of offering them to Hanther and Velo, each of whom hurriedly signified that he was not anxious to participate.

Again Brax shrugged, juggled the tokens, and spilled them upon the floor. The uppermost numbers were a two, a four, and a six, a surprising correspondence with the first number of each Gray's token, a rare tie.

Brax again offered the stones to his associates, and, after some hesitation, Velo finally accepted. The dice rattled hollowly in the enclosure of his palms, then spilled out with a clatter. When they danced to a stop the result was a second tie; the stones refused to give a hint of whom the random factor favored.

A nervous glance passed between the Grays. Velo pressed the tokens into Hanther's unwilling hands. Stiffly Hanther bent to the floor and executed a clumsy toss. When the dice settled for the third time they revealed another tie.

Brax let out a long sigh and shook his head in bewilderment. "The stones refuse to choose," he whispered.

"Not so!" Buster declared. "The result is unmistakable. It is ordained that all three of you shall jointly share the post."

"No, we cannot," Hanther objected. "That is not the way. One only must be chosen."

"Our way is the way of the random factor," Velo asserted, displaying a newfound decisiveness. "Our brother is right. The stones have chosen us. They demand that we rule. I propose that the decisions of two of us on any subject shall become our law.

"Very well, Buster, we are the decision makers, chosen as you have demanded. State your proposal, and we will decide what must be done."

"Fair enough. What I have to say is precisely this: Hazar must be stopped before he conquers the humans and our brother Pales beyond the mountains. The Hartford with his ring and his Fanist companion are powerful allies in this enterprise. They should be freed to aid us in our struggle. Castor, our brother who was betrayed, is an Ajaj of vision and courage who should not be abandoned. The three must be rescued from the dungeon, hidden in a place of safety, and their aid against the Gogols requested. We should counsel with them on how best to spike Hazar's plans and each of us cooperate with the others in achieving this goal."

"An ambitious plan, to be sure, but practical? I hardly think so. You speak as if all we have to do to free them from Hazar's dungeon is snap our fingers. Where shall we hide them once released? How do we get them out of the city? It is all madness."

Buster was about to answer Hanther's objections but Brax spoke up first.

"I agree the task should not be underestimated—but madness? Of that I am not convinced. Hundreds of Grays work in the city; a few of them armed with simple blades could easily catch the guards unawares. As for getting them in and out, there are always the emergency caverns."

"The emergency caverns! That I would like to see. Some of the openings are barely big enough for us to crawl through. How do you propose to arrange for the passage of one as broad-shouldered as the Fanist?"

"That could be arranged, I think," Velo answered in an abstracted tone. "Most of the passages are natural caves, with more than enough room for the passage of the prisoners. At only two or three points do they narrow sufficiently to block a human. If we arouse the community possibly we could enlarge these points. It is a bold plan, to be sure, but not an impossible one."

"Madness! Madness I said before and say again. You would condemn the whole tribe to extinction with this act. Did we ask the human or the Fanist to come here? No, of course not. Their fate is their own. I say leave them to it."

"And what of Castor?" Buster shouted.

"Castor was a troublemaker—always has been and always will be. He was warned, but he went ahead anyway. He has no one to blame but himself for the trouble he's in. Why risk all our lives for his perversity?"

"You call stopping the Gogols perversity? One of our own is betrayed to the devil-worshipers and you want to throw him away like an overripe fruit? What's become of us that we can think this way?"

"Calm yourself, Buster. Hanther did not mean his words the way they sounded. Of course we are not insensitive to our brother's plight, but, not to put too fine a point on it, the truth is that the question is not whether or not we can rescue the three but whether we should. Is the chance of the safety of the human, the Fanist, and one of our own worth the risk? Of that we must be convinced before we can turn our backs on our instincts."

Buster took a deep breath and forced himself to relax. Passion and threats would not sway them.

"Very well; I will give you my answer as best I can," Buster began in an even, though strained, voice. "For the time being we will overlook the bondage under which we have labored for these hundreds of years, for even if we should succeed I cannot guarantee that our domination will cease. We will pass by the killings of our friends and mates, the casual tortures, the countless Ajaj killed for their pelts.

"All these tortures and terrors we will put aside, for the harm which this plan might wreak upon the Gogols will be too late to relieve the horrors already endured. I will not argue that to defeat Hazar's plans may improve our lot in the future, bring food to the bellies of those who have starved, or lessen those of our number who will die in the labor gangs when the Gogols decide that their city has grown too small and that they need a new wall beyond the one which now bounds Cicero. Hazar's defeat, the wrecking of his plans, the sowing of distrust and terror among the Gogol overlords, will no doubt distract them and turn them inward to feed upon each other, but I cannot guarantee that it will better our lot.

"Nor will I speak of abstract concepts. Not of courage, for we have not shown courage, merely cowardice, and thought to call it prudence. Not of pride or honor, for we have neither and have called their lack humility; nor of the strength needed to build a better life, for we have been content merely to survive to breed one more generation of slaves and thought to damn ourselves with the virtues of meekness and self-sacrifice.

"I will not praise the benefits to be gained from freedom or honor or the simple enjoyment of life, for none of us value these things. They are a burden too demanding to be borne. And lastly, I will not speak of the sweetness of revenge; of the extermination of those who glory in pain; of someday, after a struggle that might create terrors almost equal to those we face every day, expunging from Fane the curse of the worshipers of hell. Obviously none of these are important to you. If the lives of your-selves and your mates and your cubs, the prevention of your children's being ripped from your arms and disem-bowled as an offering in a Black Mass, will not dissuade you from your course, then surely these abstract concepts can have no effect upon your decision.

"No. I will only say that if we do nothing our lives and those of our descendants will, in the coming generations, be slowly ground out until the lust of the Gogols has rendered us extinct. If that is to be our fate, better to suffer it now with at least a chance of defeating them than to do nothing and wait for the inevitable extermination of our people."

No sound disturbed Obron's chamber. Buster stood, twisted, ignoring the fiery ache in his knee. As if he were a wax figure whose eyes alone were alive, he glared at the decision makers with a look of both rage and infinite sor-row.

Velo slowly turned his head to look at Hanther, then at Brax. Silently Brax extended his right hand and balled his gray-furred paw into a tiny fist.

"The prisoners must be freed."

Velo, too, held out his arm and in a more restrained voice declared the same.

Hanther hesitated, and all stared at him. At last, shak-ing with fear, he, too, brought out a fist and in a squeak-ing whisper announced:

"So be it. The prisoners must be freed, and Kaneb pro-tect us from the demons."

"Brax, rouse the Grays; get them into the caverns; break loose the bottlenecks. Remember, they must be wide enough for the Fanist. Open the box. We must choose a leader for the rescue party."

"No need there," Buster declared; "that job is already filled. It is my idea and my plan. I will be the one. Brax, lead me to the caverns. I'm an old Gray and it has been a long time since I've been out of Cicero. My memory fails me. Show me the way, and hurry. There's much to do before I can rest tonight."

Brax moved a few paces ahead of Buster, then halted and returned to the Gray. Placing his right arm around Buster's fragile waist, he helped the assistant keeper of the scullery limp to the hidden fissure which opened onto the secret ways to Cicero.

Chapter Forty-two

Buster led the fugitives at a hurried pace through Hazar's dungeon. He negotiated the darkened corridors with a sureness bred of many hours of studying illicitly copied plans. Grantin lost all interest in asking how their release was effected upon spying the first of the guards' bodies still leaking black-colored blood.

Just beyond a leftward bend in the corridor two figures appeared, but Buster ignored them. As they passed Grantin was able to identify the hunched forms of two Grays scrubbing a line of stain from the flagstone floor. Grantin's eyes followed the direction of the smear and saw that it led to an opening in the grime-encrusted wall. Obviously the body of a wounded Gray had been dragged back into a hidden entrance.

Grantin increased his pace until he reached Buster's side. He leaned over and whispered into the old Gray's ear:

"There was an exit back there; why didn't we take it? Why don't we escape while we can?"

"You can't; you wouldn't fit. We didn't have enough time to enlarge the tunnel. The only thing we can do is make for an old cavern under the foundations of the

246

northwest wall. Now be quiet! We must go up to the street level, waylay the guard, then make our way as best we can around the First Circle to the Gate of Mammon."

Buster increased his gait to a limping, pain-ravaged sprint. In a few minutes the fugitives had reached the end of the corridor. Ahead of them to the right were bare stone walls. At their left a twisting spiral staircase led to the ground level.

Buster climbed the first few stairs and halted there until the rest had crowded around the bottom of the well. Putting his finger to his lips, he pantomimed his intention to eliminate the guard. Buster, however, was not obeyed. As the old Gray adjusted the hem of his tunic so that it covered the dagger's hilt, Castor climbed to his side and removed the knife. Buster sought to regain the blade, but Castor pushed back his hand. He shook his head to indicate that the old Ajaj should remain with the others. Without waiting for agreement Castor loped noiselessly up the steps, followed a few paces behind by the other four.

When it had made one complete revolution of the spiral, the stairwell opened upon an identical hallway, this one also deserted. Castor motioned to his companions to follow him to the next level. Castor maneuvered up the last steps with the greatest caution until he was able to peek over the edge of the wall. Another corridor dead-ended to the right. Across from the stone spiral, a short passage led to a guardpost, then down several steps to a heavy wood and iron door, presumably giving entrance to the First Circle.

Taking a deep breath, Castor strode directly up the stairs, across the hallway, and down to the guard.

In this predawn hour the soldier was sleepy, more so than usual because of the extra duty. Castor approached within five feet of his post before he was noticed.

"Excuse me, my lord," Castor began before the guard could challenge him. "I have been charged to deliver a special message, but somehow I have become lost. If you could look at the writing on the paper perhaps you could give me directions." Castor immediately set about patting his pockets as if in search of the document. "I had it here a moment ago—yes, here it is in my belt. If you would just bend over, my lord . . . it seems to be stuck."

Castor grasped the dagger's hilt where it rode his left hip

beneath the cover of his tunic. The guard bent forward, curious as to the nature of the Gray's errand. When Castor could stall no longer, he whipped out the blade and swung it upward in a semicircular arc. The tip sliced effortlessly through the guard's bared throat. The Gogol slumped to the floor without making a sound. Castor wiped the blade on the soldier's sleeve, then ran back to the stairway and excitedly motioned for the fugitives to advance.

The five sprinted across the hallway and down the short corridor and, using the guard's keys, slipped through the door. Once outside, Castor relocked the portal and hid the keyring in a pile of trash.

The streets were dark, but the ribbon of sky above them showed a faint reddish hue, presaging Pyra's imminent appearance. Since the outer battlements were the most likely to be patrolled, the five crept along single-file as close as possible to the edge of the outer wall.

Their route required them to pass by Lord Bolam's Gate of Lust. If the guards were alert there, it might be impossible to pass. Castor and Buster would probably have no problem. Even Grantin and Mara might be able to brazen it out, but Chom's form could never be disguised or excused.

Keeping to the shadows as much as possible, Castor led the party to within twenty yards of Bolam's gate. His surveillance revealed two well-armed and alert attendants Castor slipped back to consult with the others.

"Two guards, and wide awake," he whispered to the fugitives.

"Maybe we should go back the other way," Mara suggested, but already Buster was shaking his head.

"Look at the sky. Pyra has begun to rise. It is too late for that. We have only a few minutes to get past."

"What if we just walked by and ignored them? Perhaps they wouldn't stop us," Grantin suggested.

"No. I am certain they would find my extra pair of arms an irresistible distraction," Chom replied. "The obvious answer is for the four of you to go ahead while will use another route and meet you at our destination.

Without pausing to consider his own self-interest Grantin surprised himself by blurting out an immediat no. Buster threw up his hands in bewildered defeat.

"A diversion might work," Castor said as he studied the rapidly lightening sky. "The four of us could divert the guards' attention. The Fanist might be able to slip past the opening without being noticed."

"Unlikely," Buster whispered, "but since I do not have a better suggestion, and since it is going to be daylight in a few more minutes, we may as well try it."

A plan was hastily agreed upon. The Ajaj and the humans set out, leaving Chom to creep as close as possible to the point where the wall was broken by the Gate of Lust.

Castor and Buster led the way, with Mara and Grantin following a few paces behind. The guards heard their approach several seconds before the four became visible. Grantin and Mara swung into view, then stopped and examined all aspects of the small plaza that fronted on the gate. Directing the Ajaj to walk in front of them and arguing loudly with Grantin, Mara approached the guards.

"Well, where are they?" she demanded of the soldier who came forward to meet them.

"Where are who, my lady?"

"What the lady means, guardsman, is, you see, we were expecting—"

"I know what I mean. Stop pampering these dolts! We are here for Lord Hazar's shipment. Where are they?"

"I know of no shipment for Lord Hazar, my lady."

"Incompetents, fools . . . !"

"I'm sorry, soldier; please excuse the lady. She is very tired. It has been a long night, and now this special duty. . . . This is the Lady Mara, Lord Hazar's chief enchantress, and . . . well, if the truth be known, he was less than pleased with certain of the companions with which he was provided. He roused my lady here and demanded that she immediately bring him the new shipment for his inspection. I am Grindle, one of my lord's underapprentices. Since my Ajaj and I had an early errand at Topor's market we agreed to travel a bit out of the way and accompany Lady Mara."

"Shut up, you yellow-spined fool! That's why you are only an underapprentice. Come over here and look at this and you will learn something." Mara strode past the guards and walked to the closed inner panel of the gate.

"Look at this; just look at this," she said, pointing at the iron-reinforced timbers.

"My lady, no one is allowed to approach the gate," ordered the guard as he turned away from the First Circle and hurried to restrain Mara from touching the panel.

"How dare you lay hands on me, you oaf!" Mara shouted as she elbowed the guard in the stomach.

Now the second watchman came running. Together both struggled to remove Mara from the forbidden zone. As they wrestled a blurred gray-brown shadow sped across the small plaza and merged with the other shadows on the far side of the gate.

"Unhand me, unhand me! Very well; I shall leave you and your miserable contraption, but I warn you, Lord Hazar will hear of this ill treatment." Mara broke free from the soldiers and stalked off toward the center of the First Circle.

"I am sorry. You must forgive her," Grantin reassured the guards. "She will calm down in a few minutes. We will continue on around the circle and down to the market. The walk will do her good. She can come by again on her way back to see about Lord Hazar's shipment." Grantin trotted off and made a show of attempting to placate Mara.

Thirty feet past the edge of the gate Mara and Grantin exhaled a sigh of relief, veered to the edge of the wall, and increased their pace almost to a run. A few minutes later they approached their destination. Buster called a halt.

On the far side of the street stood an alcove deeply recessed into the wall. At its back could barely be seen a worn plank door. Following Buster's lead, the escapees slipped into the recess while the Gray, using a tool which he carried slung inside his trousers, began to work on the lock. A few seconds later there sounded a metallic tinkle followed by the noise of splintering wood. They bolted inside the darkened opening, and Chom used three of his four arms to force the door closed.

"Everyone stand still until I can find a light." Rustles and scrapes sounded in the shadowed chamber. The sounds of Buster's fumblings ceased as a dim green radiance glimmered in the far corner of the room. Grantin could see barrels, bales, packages, canisters, and boxes lining the chamber's walls; obviously it was an infrequently used storeroom. Buster motioned the others to a point on the back wall opposite the window.

"Here," he whispered, pointing to an area piled high with wooden crates. "Under these crates the stones are loose. Beneath them is a metal plate which gives entrance to the caverns which lead to a cave in the hills a mile and a half northwest of the city. Hurry—we must move these boxes and be gone before the guards at Bolam's gate make their report."

The fugitives began work on the crates in shifts, as there was room for no more than two persons at any one time. Mara and Grantin soon tired and took their places at the end of the line while Chom and Castor spelled them, the Fanist's extra pair of hands making up for the Ajaj's diminutive form.

"How did you get involved in all of this?" Grantin asked Mara. "You seem like such a nice person. I can't picture you drenched in blood in one of the Gogol sacrifices."

"My mother was a Gogol," Mara replied somewhat defensively.

"And your father?"

"A Hartford, but being a Hartford did not mean that he was good any more than my being a Gogol means that I am bad."

"He was an evil man, then? Did he beat you? Is that why you came here?"

"No, he didn't beat me! What a thing to say! He . . . he loved me; I am sure of it."

"And how did you end up back here? Did your mother kidnap you?"

"No, we just had to leave. My father threw my mother and me out. He was going to take me away from her. He hated her, so she brought me back here to the only place that was left for us."

"I don't understand. You say that he threw your mother and you out but that he also wanted to take you away from her. It sounds as though he wanted to keep you and just wished to be rid of her. What happened between them? Why did he want to throw her out?"

"I don't know."

"Well, he must have said something."

"My mother took me away before he could do the evil things that he was planning. She told me that he was bad, that he wanted to hurt us, that all you Hartfords were the same."

"I don't wish to butt into your private affairs, but in defense of myself and my fellow Hartfords, let me ask, have you ever considered the possibility that your mother lied? Perhaps it was she who did not love your father and stole you away from him."

Mara's face contorted in a surprised expression, as if that possibility had never occurred to her. Just as suddenly a few seconds later she began to cry. Disconcerted by her tears, Grantin went back to the pile of crates and took over Castor's place.

"How much longer, do you think, until we get all of this out of the way?" he asked Buster, who, because of his crippled leg, now assumed the task of supervising the relocation of the boxes.

"With our four-armed friend here, perhaps only three or four minutes. I have almost come to believe that my scheme may work after all."

"Just the same, I will feel better when we have left this accursed city behind."

With Buster trailing a few paces behind, Grantin walked back to Mara at the far end of the room. By now she had stopped crying and was attempting to wipe away the traces of her tears with her velveteen cuffs. In the background sounded the scrapes and thuds of Castor's and Chom's labors.

"Mara, I am sorry I made you cry. It was none of my business. I shouldn't have interfered. Still, I have a favor I would like you to do for me."

"A favor? What is it?"

"You remember when you gave me this ring? Well, I'd like to take it off, but only you can remove it. It's a simple spell; I have it written down here. All you need do is read it and then pull on the ring."

"Remove the ring?" Buster hissed. "How will you do your magic without the ring?"

"I plan to do no more magic beyond a few elementary spells of self-gratification. This cursed ring has done nothing but bring me trouble. The sooner I am rid of it, the sooner I can return home and assume my normal station in life."

"But you must retain your powers—it is the only way the Gogols can be defeated. Mara can explain to you about Zaco's mine where the bloodstones are quarried. It is said that it is a place where in ancient times a huge meteor crashed into the earth and that the stones were formed as a result of the impact. Hazar will go there himself in a few days to pick up his last shipment. When he has it his forces will be unstoppable. I have pledged my life and those of all my people to freeing you so that you could use the energy of the ring to prevent Hazar from completing his plan."

"How could I do such a thing? It is certain death."

"This is far more important than the life or death of any one person. All our lives are hostage to Hazar's plans."

"Well, it is not more important to me than my life, because it is the only one I am going to have. I've risked my skin enough times with Hazar and his deacons. Now someone else can fight this battle. I'm going home to my uncle's manor while I'm still in one piece. If you want the ring you are welcome to it."

"Can't you understand? It will not work for me. It will not even work for another human until he has been accustomed to it. You have worn it long enough now. You can use it. Even if we had someone else he would never become attuned to its forces in time."

"Buster, I want to thank you for saving my life, if in fact we get out of here alive, but I'm not going to put my neck back into the noose after escaping from this trap. You'll just have to think of another way to thwart Hazar's plans."

"There isn't another way. We have risked everything to rescue you so that you can use the power of the ring against Hazar. It was on this basis alone that the decision makers authorized the attack. If you abandon us now, Hazar will slay half the tribe."

"Ever since I put on this ring I've been forced to do others' bidding. My uncle tries to cut off my hand; bandits pursue me; black sorcerers throw me into their dungeons; and now the Grays expect me to give up my life in a crusade of their own. Well, no more! Mara, if you please."

Buster looked on with frustrated impotence as Grantin motioned for Mara to commence the spell.

Reluctantly she held the ring with the tip of her thumb, index finger, and middle finger of her right hand and recited the incantation. With a gentle tug she freed the bloodstone. For a moment she looked at it strangely, then handed it back to Grantin, who, with no better use for it, dropped the ring into his pocket.

Buster's face was grim. With the removal of the ring all his plans were shattered. Grantin turned and saw that the last of the crates had been moved out of the way. Chom and Castor pulled the loosened stones from the floor. Mara wandered across the room to the window and idly stared out, searching the dawn-lighted street beyond. At the far right-hand edge of her vision a shape moved, then another, then another still. A squad of three soldiers came into view, then turned toward a door set into the outer wall on the far side of the street. The search for the fugitives had begun in earnest. Mara stood frozen for a moment, hypnotized by the spectacle, then turned back to the others.

"Soldiers!" she whispered. "They're making a door-to-door search. They're across the street now. They will be here in a minute or two. They will see the crates have been moved and find the passageway."

"Is there some way to stop them? Is there anything that we can do?" Grantin asked.

Mara put her arms around Grantin and stared solemnly into his face.

"Do you really believe what you said, about my mother lying to me, and about my father?"

"Mara, this is no time to——"

"Because if you are right, then I do not belong here with the Gogols. I am really a Hartford and I should be doing everything I can to save my people."

Mara abruptly released Grantin and stepped over to the door.

"What are you doing?"

"I have a plan, another diversion. Go ahead without me. You must escape to thwart Hazar's plans."

Before anyone could move, Mara opened the panel and slipped outside.

"She will need some help," Buster announced as he limped toward the door.

"Buster, come back," Grantin hissed.

"It makes no difference. If you don't put on the ring and defeat Hazar, my people are lost in any event."

"Buster, come back! We can still escape through the tunnel."

"No," Buster said over his shoulder as he slipped out the door. "I do not wish to outlive my race."

Buster disappeared through the door and closed the panel from the outside. Chom and Castor redoubled their efforts to free the trapdoor. Grantin ignored them and hurried to the window. Outside, Mara crossed the street, putting distance between herself and the storeroom. Of Buster Grantin could see no sign.

Mara ducked past the doorway into which the soldiers had been recently admitted, then turned around and began walking back. She halted fifteen yards beyond the door and waited for the guards to reemerge. In less than a minute the first soldier reappeared and Mara began to run down the center of the street in full view of the guards. The first one leaped after her. In an instant a second soldier reached her. She struggled in their grasp.

The officer appeared but stood well back from the skirmish. He eyed Mara and searched the street in the direction from which she had come. In a flash of inspiration the officer looked across the First Circle directly at the barred window from which Grantin now observed the fight.

The officer turned and walked purposefully toward the storeroom door. He was halfway across the street when a bundle of fur darted from the shadows and collided with his marching form. Buster could not hope to reach the soldier's throat. As he charged he held the knife high in his right hand and aimed for the officer's stomach. But the Ajaj was tired and lame and the soldier keyed to a sharpness of senses and acute reaction.

The officer drew his own knife. The blade pierced Buster's torso even before the Gray reached him. It was only through his momentum that the Ajaj succeeded in reaching the guard. With his dying hand Buster planted his dagger deep in the officer's stomach.

Both fell to the dusty pavement, Buster dead and the

soldier already losing consciousness. The guards saw what had happened to their commander and, convinced that the fugitives had avoided their initial search, dragged Mara back up the First Circle toward Hazar's quarters.

A groaning creak sounded behind Grantin. He turned to see Chom lift the iron door. Almost in a state of shock he stumbled forward and, gripped by the Fanist's four strong arms, felt himself being lowered into the darkness.

Chapter Forty-three

Inside the cavern a dim luminescence was generated by lichen-encrusted walls. While the radiation was too feeble to illuminate any features of the cavern, it did mark the twistings and turnings of the walls on which it grew. As the one most comfortable in cavelike surroundings, Castor led the way; then came Grantin, then Chom.

In the caverns hearing was an unreliable sense. Grantin found himself struggling to ignore the scrapes and rattles which reached his ears. Ahead of them he fantasized spiders and poisonous snakes, while from behind he feared attack from the pursuing Gogols. Each of Chom's footfalls, the rattle of pebbles, the scrape of arms or hips against protruding limestone walls, all echoed and reverberated; whispers in the distance were amplified and returned to terrify the travelers. Neither the direction, origin, nor cause of the echoes could be discerned, and so the fugitives tramped onward blind to the terrors which pursued or awaited them.

Grantin's original plan had seemed straightforward and definite: reach Cicero, find Mara, remove the ring, and return to the good graces of Uncle Greyhorn. Now his life bumped ahead aimlessly; his schemes had lost their anchor, and his mind was filled with conflicts which he found impossible to reconcile.

Mara was captured; what would happen to her? And didn't he still owe his uncle support because of the loyalty of blood to blood if nothing else? But wasn't Greyhorn lost beyond all hope? What about Buster's bloody end? Didn't he have some kind of obligation to the old Gray? Yet, on the other hand, dead is dead and nothing could change that.

Grantin suppressed all these disturbing questions and sought to focus upon the details of their passage. Slowly the character of the darkness changed. Ahead the air became suffused with a thin gray light which gradually grew more brilliant as the fugitives wound their way through a series of twists and turns. At last, a glowing clot of whitish gray burned through the center of the velvet screen. The rent in the darkness expanded until the fugitives found themselves standing at a brush-encrusted exit. With reluctant curiosity they advanced and studied the scenery beyond.

The mouth of the cavern stood halfway up a hillside overgrown with vines, springwood trees, and creepers. A procession of low, rolling hills marked the landscape ahead.

"Castor, do you know this place? Where are we?"

"I have never been here, but Buster lived in Cicero a long time and heard many things. He instructed me in Gogol geography. We are just beyond the northern edge of the city. To the west lies a great plain all the way to the Endless Ocean. These estates are farmed by the Grays under Topor's direction. To the east the country is poorer. There Gogol freemen have staked out their homesteads between Cicero and the edge of the Weirdlands. Directly ahead the foothills continue all the way to a group of peaks the Gogols call Satan's Chair. A bit to the east of us a major trail follows a winding valley between these mounds all the way to the headwaters of the Mephisto River. From there barges travel downstream to the city of Mephisto itself. To the northwest one can skirt the foothills and travel the boundary between Topor's estates and Satan's Chair. The country is by and large rough but not impassable. It is said that if one continues far enough he will reach Grog Cup Lake."

"Are you suggesting that we turn this into a tourist expedition?" Grantin asked.

"Buster said that Zaco's mine is to the northwest, at a place where a meteor had long ago smashed into the earth. It could be Grog Cup Lake."

"A lake?"

"Now it is a lake, but it might have begun as a meteor crater. It is said that in the middle of rolling country its walls rise hundreds of feet above the surrounding soil; that the cliff is perfectly circular, and the bowl within filled with clear water and dotted in the center with a stone island. Where else could Zaco's meteor crater be?"

"Where else indeed!" Grantin said testily. "You expect us to embark on a wild-goose chase across hostile, uncharted wilderness, racing toward a colony of evil sorcerers, on the word of some thirdhand geography lesson? For all you know there might be hundreds of places which could just as easily be the location of Zaco's mine."

"What else can we do? Surely we haven't come this far just to escape? Hazar must be defeated."

Grantin snorted in dissatisfaction. He turned to Chom, who had been studying the countryside below.

"Chom, you are very quiet about all of this. What do you say? Can you give me one good reason why we shouldn't wait until nightfall and then make our way home?"

"We each have our own goals. You must find your own reasons for doing what you do. Neither mine nor Castor's can properly be sufficient for you."

"And what does that mean? Tell me this—if I declared my intention to go home would you come with me or go running off on some wild-goose chase with Castor?"

"I do not wish to affect your decision. Assume that I will do what is in your best interest as balanced against the best interests of my people."

"Riddles! Double-talk! I'm in the company of a mad Ajaj and a logic-chopping Fanist. Castor, let me ask you this—how would you propose that we defeat Hazar if, in fact, we did find Zaco's expertly manned and guarded bloodstone mine? What am I to do—throw rocks at him?"

"It seems to me that with the great power stored in

your ring and with the assistance of Chom and myself a potent spell could be forged."

"Perhaps you have forgotten that I came all this way to be freed of that ring? Has it escaped your attention that I no longer wear it?"

"Your ring? Gone?" Castor grabbed Grantin's hand with a wild motion. "What happened to it? It isn't lost?"

"While you and Chom were clearing the passage I had Mara remove it."

"But you can't abandon us now," Castor shouted. "Does saving my people mean nothing to you? Can you stand by and allow the slaughter of the Grays?"

"What would you have me do?"

"Can there be any question? You must put the ring back on."

Grantin threw up his arms and paced a tight circle inside the cave's entrance. "Chom, what do you have to say about all this? Can you bring no sanity to this discussion?"

"I can say this: we should leave this cave at once. At any moment Hazar's guards may discover evidence of our presence in the storeroom. We cannot allow ourselves to be caught here. Whichever direction we go, we must move quickly."

Grantin seethed with frustration. He peered through the trailing network of vines in a vain attempt to locate a path to the Guardian Mountains far to the east. Why should he feel responsible if Hazar slaughtered the Grays? He hadn't asked them to rescue him. *But you didn't refuse their offer,* a small voice at the back of his mind reminded him. *And what about your uncle?* Grantin rejected his conscience's argument. His uncle had chosen to get involved with the devil-worshipers; his fate was of his own making. *And what of Mara? She sacrificed herself to save you. Can you do any less for her?* Mara, lovely Mara —but she wasn't the only woman in the world. With his uncle's property he would find plenty. Against his will the vision of Buster's murder and Mara's capture flashed through Grantin's mind. Blast! Blast! Why could not his life be simple, uncomplicated, and pleasant, like that of other normal men?

"Grantin, we must leave," Chom prodded. "You must make up your mind. Are you coming with us or going home?"

"He'll not go home like this. If I be a mad Ajaj, as they claim, I may as well be one to perfection. I'd sooner draw my knife here than let Grantin abandon us all to the Gogols," Castor said as he reached down to pull out his blade. Almost as if by lazy accident, one of Chom's forearms snaked out and grabbed the Ajaj's wrist.

"An unwilling wizard is worse than no wizard at all," Chom said quietly. "This must be a question for Grantin's own conscience."

"Chom, you're going with Castor no matter what I do?" Grantin asked.

"For what good it will do. Shenar's spell still binds me. My powers are still blunted. I had hoped that with the help of you and Castor we might be able to restore them. As it is"—Chom shrugged—"we will have to do the best that we are able."

"But this is madness!"

Castor jerked his hand free from Chom's easy grasp but made no move to withdraw his blade.

"Grantin, we must leave now. We wish you good luck," Chom said as he ushered Castor toward the edge of the cave.

"Wait! Apparently, Castor, your madness has contaminated me as well. Very well, then; we may as well march out of here together and all of us throw our lives into the very jaws of death."

"Why is it that the honest fellows such as myself are always sucked into the maelstrom of others' tribulations?" From his pocket Grantin absentmindedly extracted the patch of cloth within which was wrapped the ring. "Always it is the innocents who are called upon to hurl their bodies in the path of evil, ordinary citizens who like nothing better than a quiet evening at the inn, a harmless dalliance with a local maid, the simple life of genteel companionship.

"Why is it always we who are called upon to perform heroic deeds?" Without looking at his hand Grantin unwrapped the fabric and positioned the ring just beyond his index finger. "I am surrounded by reckless beings who urge me into a dangerous undertaking only to fulfill quixotic desires of their own. Ah, that is my flaw, my goodhearted nature! I am too easily taken advantage of. I know the error of my ways, but, alas, I am too weak to help myself."

A psychic shiver rippled through the cave as Grantin again slipped the ring over his finger. An inaudible snap reverberated through the ether as the band contracted and once more affixed itself to his flesh. "There, now I've done it! Are you happy? Are you pleased? Are you overjoyed at the position into which you have maneuvered me? Very well; lead me to my death! Forward to horrible trials and tribulations! Onward into the very maw of evil—but don't say I didn't warn you!"

"Does he always act this way?" Castor whispered to Chom as they picked their way down the hill below the mouth of the cave.

"Only when his conscience is bothering him," Chom whispered back. "But do not worry; generally with Grantin that is a rare and short-lived event."

Having overheard the exchange, Grantin emitted a loud "Hrrumph!" and slipped into a black sulk for an entire fifteen minutes.

Chapter Forty-four

Clerks scuttled busily up under the dome of Topor's market while overdeacons intent on sniffing out spells examined the walls. Below at the five doorways which led to the five stairways to the circular room above the market, ten of the Gogol lords' most vicious soldiers warily stood guard. By and by the frantic maneuverings of the clerks dwindled; the overdeacons expressed satisfaction at the absence of traps and talismans; the guards' narrowed eyes grew a fraction less suspicious. At last the appropriate coded signals were given and the five lords emerged from the steep-walled safety of the spoke roads surrounding the Central Plaza.

Surrounded by handpicked retainers, each crossed the plaza. Tall, thin, and in a state of extreme ill humor, Nefra sped across the flagstones as if driven by some inner rage. The next passage disgorged Topor and his retinue. The stocky, pedestrian Lord of Fear moved in a measured, businesslike manner and exuded an air of mild irritation that the operation of his vast estates should be disturbed by a meeting between himself and his fellow lords.

Zaco waddled to his entrance. By the time he reached the base of the stairs he had already become winded. He motioned to his two most stalwart guards, who advanced and clasped him beneath the shoulders, half carrying him to the conference room.

Bolam was the only one of the five who seemed unconcerned either for his safety or for the business of the conference. He ignored the activity around him and instead concentrated on the exquisitely arrayed and coiffured twelve-year-old boy who accompanied him to the edge of the market.

Lastly Hazar mounted his own set of stairs with a furious energy which left his two guards struggling to keep pace.

When all the lords had arrived, the five doors were closed and bolted for the duration of the meeting. No sooner had the guards withdrawn than Nefra brought himself to his feet and began the conference on a harsh and challenging note.

"As we all know, we are called here today to formulate plans for dealing with the dangerous situation which has been created by our associate, Lord Hazar."

"My dear Lord Nefra," Hazar responded, "perhaps that is why you are here, but I was not informed that the purpose of this conference was to call a council of war against me."

"Let's not bandy words, Hazar. I called the meeting, as we all well know. The others are here only because they have no intention of being left out of whatever decisions might be made between the two of us. The long and the short of it is that we are not about to surrender our power in aid of your plans of empire."

"I don't recall, Nefra, that I have ever asked you for your cooperation in my campaign against the Hartfords. And what would be the use, in any event? Satan knows you've no stomach for any activity more strenuous than hoarding your water."

"Gentlemen, gentlemen, let us have some decorum here," Lord Bolam interrupted. "We will accomplish nothing with bickering. Nefra, you have made various charges against Lord Hazar, charges which reflect upon the safety and prosperity of us all. If you would state your point without rancor we all could get about the business of making sense out of this situation."

Nefra gritted his teeth and struggled to control his temper. After a moment's silence he began again.

"Very well, Lord Bolam. Hazar has been planning to conquer the Hartfords on his own. As far as that goes, well and good. My information is that he made arrangements with a certain Hartford wizard named Greyhorn to use his powers against the defenders of the passes through the Guardian Mountains. Again, a praiseworthy plan. Unfortunately Hazar's scheme did not rest there.

"He has inveigled Lord Zaco, through the charms of an enchantress named Mara, to supply his subdeacons with a huge quantity of bloodstones. Through a string of blunders one has come into the possession of a Hartford named Grantin. Somehow or other this Hartford, together with a dangerous revolutionary Gray, a Fanist of unknown powers, and Hazar's own enchantress Mara, have entered into a vicious and dangerous cabal against us all. Now all save Mara have escaped and are loose in the city spreading dissent and revolution among our placid Grays and threatening from within the very basis of our power.

"If that danger were not sufficient for us to urge Hazar to abandon these plans, there is still the fact of the bloodstones he demands of Lord Zaco. Need I remind you, gentlemen, that should he obtain these, our own positions would not long remain secure? Should Hazar's bloodstone-enhanced army prove their skills against the Hartfords, is it likely that they would march meekly back to Cicero and abandon their gems at Hazar's door?"

"So what would you have us do?" Topor asked in a businesslike tone.

"I would have us all agree that Zaco will supply no more powerstones to Hazar. Further, Hazar must agree to distribute equally among the five of us the bloodstones which he has already received; and the rebellious Grays, the Fanist, the human with the bloodstone, and Mara must all go to the block as fast as we can round them up."

"Mara to the block?" Zaco squeaked. "No, not at all! I forbid it. I will take her into my household. I will see to it that she gets into no trouble."

Nefra, always the good politician, paused only half a second before agreeing to Zaco's demand.

"Very well, Lord Zaco; the girl Mara goes to you. The rest to the executioners."

"If I might interrupt you a moment, Nefra. Before you finish disposing of my property and my servants I would point out that you have no power over me or mine. Mara's fate will be as I decree, not you. As to the stones I already have, Lord Zaco has been well paid for them and I am happy with the bargain. Besides, as we all know, Lord Zaco, being a prudent man, invests his gems with secret inscriptions whose natures allow him to destroy the crystals upon the recitation of the appropriate spell. Is that not true, Zaco?"

"Of course; that is my practice. I am sure that I must have done so with your stones as well."

"A moment, Lord Zaco," Nefra interrupted. "Do you recall specifically carving these inscriptions?"

"No, I don't do such things personally. My servants—"

"Do you recall, then, instructing your servants to enter these inscriptions?"

"I can't seem to remember, but I am sure that I must have."

"How many stones have you delivered so far?"

"One ring, from my household supply, and fifteen loose stones directly from the mine."

"Loose stones! If they were unset, could not Lord Hazar read the inscription on the base of the gem?"

"I suppose he could."

"If he knew the secret symbols, could he not then formulate an incantation to protect the stone from your spell of self-destruction?"

"Perhaps, but still . . ."

"And before the stones were set in a ring or pendant, could he not alter the inscription by removing some portions and adding others and thus make the stone respond only to a spell unknown to you?"

Zaco became suddenly alert. "Yes, he most certainly could."

"I believe I have made my point," Nefra concluded, with a nod in Hazar's direction.

"Your mumblings do not settle this question, Nefra. The stones are the key to my conquest of the Hartfords. What of my noble mission? Would you forsake this victory merely to pamper your own paranoia?"

"If it is a question of choosing between supplying you with an all-powerful army or leaving the Hartfords to their own devices, then the choice is not a difficult one. I prefer to be a lord in a world that includes both Gogols and Hartfords than to be a slave in one that includes Gogols alone. In short, if you wish to conquer the Hartfords you must contrive a scheme without the use of bloodstones, or at least one in which each of our armies shares the power and the booty."

"Nefra, your whole argument rests upon the suspicion that after bloodying my army with a wearisome campaign I would return it here, footsore and bedraggled, to launch a new battle outnumbered four to one by the fresh and vigorous forces belonging to you and these other gentlemen. If anyone is at risk it is myself. What, in fact, is to stop you from taking advantage of the exhaustion of my troops and destroying me after I have lain the Hartford lands open to domination and tribute? It is you who should be giving me assurances of safety, not the other way around."

"Try and squirm out of it with your fancy words all you like, Hazar, but you won't get away with it. We all know what you are up to, and we are not going to stand for it. I call for a vote." Nefra glared at Hazar, then at the other lords, until at last Bolam, the unofficial secretary of the five, took up the job of stating the question.

"Very well, then; let us vote and make an end to this. Though of three parts, the question is essentially of one whole cloth: first, should Hazar surrender, for reasonable compensation, the stones which he had already received from Lord Zaco; second, should Lord Zaco be enjoined from selling further stones to Lord Hazar unless he sells equal amounts to each of us; third, in order to ease our minds about the danger of the renegades, should the enchantress Mara be given to Lord Zaco, in exchange for suitable recompense to Lord Hazar, and all our forces turned out in a citywide search for the Gray, the Fanist, and the Hartford whom Lord Hazar brought into the city and, by implication, has by his negligence allowed to escape? Have I fairly stated your proposals, Lord Nefra?"

"You have; let's get on with it."

"Very well, Lord Nefra. Presumably you vote in favor of the suggestions?"

"Yes."

"Lord Topor?"

Topor had made up his mind long before the meeting. Hazar's power had become too great, but Topor's dependence upon the Grays had made it impossible for him to protest. Now, as part of a joint action, Hazar's humbling would give Topor better bargaining power. "I also agree," Topor answered.

In light of the inclusion of Mara as part of the deal Zaco's vote was a foregone conclusion. He would lose nothing by reason of the arrangement; the other lords would pay him as much for his stones as Hazar, perhaps more if a bidding could be arranged. "I am in favor as well," Zaco answered.

"I, too, I am afraid, must agree with my associates, Lord Hazar. Please don't take this as a personal affront, but I think we would all feel somewhat easier if we maintained the balance of power which we have so wisely instituted over the years. Since I assume that you are against the proposal, it's four to one in favor of Nefra's plan."

"And if I do not agree?" Hazar asked in an offhand manner.

"Even the power of the stones you now possess is not sufficient to stand against all of us. You and your guards need Nefra's water, Topor's food; but of course we all hope it will not come to that eventuality. Why don't you consider the matter? Tomorrow will be time enough to send your messengers to each of our quarters with a proportionate share of the powerstones and your suggestion as to what would be a fair price for them."

"Very well, gentlemen; I will consider the matter further. Be assured that I will take action before tomorrow has passed."

Hazar rapidly descended the stairs. Once out the door he signaled his men. From various positions around the Central Plaza crossbows peeked out. Bolts flew at the soldiers guarding the exits of the other four lords. Within two seconds of Hazar's departure, eight guards were dead. Hazar's soldiers raced across the plaza and tapped wedges into the five doors. These mere physical restraints would not secure the portals against wizards with the powers of the four lords, but they were meant as only the briefest delaying tactic.

As quickly as they had advanced Hazar's guards withdrew, their flight accompanied by three sharp whistle blasts. Five seconds later another of Hazar's servants erupted from the main entrance to the market beneath the conference room. No longer did the underdeacon carry the shopping sack which had been in his possession when he entered the market.

Before the remaining lords of Cicero were even aware that their guards had been disposed of and the doors jammed, Hazar and his men had fled the Central Plaza. Inside Topor's market a crude gunpowder fuse sputtered as it ate its way through the lining of the underdeacon's pack. Chemical explosives had always proved too dangerous for successful use in battle, but Hazar, with a true genius for murderous schemes, had realized that they would function magnificently as an instrument of wholesale slaughter.

No more than fifteen seconds after Hazar had left the meeting the crude package of black powder and phosphorus exploded with a dull thudding roar. The roof of the market, which was also the floor of the meeting chamber, was blasted by a fiery bolt a yard in diameter, the aftermath of which explosion filled the room with sizzling fragments of wood and stone.

Ten minutes later the whole of Topor's market, the conference room and its inhabitants alike, were naught but a scattered pile of blackened, smoking fragments. In one stroke Hazar had become lord of all Cicero.

In triumph Lord Hazar strode back to his apartments, followed by a fawning retinue. At rapid intervals messengers and underlings approached him, were admitted through the cordon of guards, and delivered reports of unconditional success. Hazar had almost reached the entrance to his quarters astride the Gate of Fear when Derma caught his attention.

"My lord, you recall that you instructed me to have our spies watch Saschim the tailor in case he might receive information about Greyhorn's nephew?"

"Derma, that is ancient history. We captured the Hartford without any help from Trecko."

"Yes, my lord, but we never countermanded the order.

Trecko has continued to watch and now reports that Saschim has received a communication from Yon Diggery."

Hazar halted and gave Derma his full attention. "And what is the nature of this communication?"

"That Yon Diggery is on the Hartford's trail. The tailor is to keep his ears open and inform Diggery of any important events which might take place in Cicero."

"Specifically, Derma, was the tailor told where this Grantin is now?"

"Not exactly, my lord; only that he escaped the city with the Fanist and the rebel Gray, and that they travel through the wilderness on a northwesterly course."

"Northwesterly. . . . There is nothing there, nothing except Zaco's mine! For a bumpkin and an imbecile that one has managed to give us more than enough trouble. We must not underestimate him again. Tell Cranan, Jasper, and Wax to begin work at once on the spell of magnificent transport. If and when Grantin reaches the mine I must be there waiting for him. And tell them to make the spell strong enough to carry three."

"Three, my lord?"

"Myself, his uncle Greyhorn, who may be of some use after all, and the enchantress Mara. If he is really smitten with her, she may be just the lever I need to finish him off."

Chapter Forty-five

On the third day after the escape from Cicero the forest began to thin, its place now taken by isolated copses of ironwood and tamarack dotting the shoulders of low, rolling hills. Late that afternoon Grantin, Chom, and Castor crested yet another soft, easy rise and received their first glimpse of their objective.

The land fell away in a gentle slope for a mile or two at last opening on a fertile basin widening five or ten miles distant into a lush, forested plain. At the far border of the forest a huge rock escarpment, at least a league in diameter and almost a mile high, reared upward. The forest halted half a mile from the base of the cliff, as if the soil there were poisoned. The narrow band of yellow-brown earth which encircled the edges of the tower created a no-man's land.

Chom strained his telescopic vision but was able to discern few details. The Fanist reported pockmarks in the cliff which might be caves. They could not see the lake itself. None of the travelers doubted, however, that in the center of the tower was a great depression filled with water and centered with a barren island within which might or might not be found Zaco's mine.

"We will camp here tonight and tomorrow press on to the lake," Castor announced. "Assuming we can discover the trail used by Zaco's men, we should be able to reach the rim by tomorrow evening."

"And what do we do when we get there?" Grantin asked peevishly.

"If Shenar's spell can be removed from Chom, then between the three of us we have great powers. I suggest that we pool our abilities in the creation of one great spell."

"I did not realize, Castor, that you were an accomplished sorcerer."

"Before my dispute with the Gogols I was a senior empather on Hazar's staff. I have been trained to link my consciousness with the state of the psychic energy around me. Beyond that I carry with me my family's treasure, a source stone, which allows the projection of my spells in a manner similar to that employed by your ring."

Somewhat reluctantly Castor opened the pouch strapped to his waist and extracted a small bundle of silky white cloth. With delicate fingers the Ajaj unwound the material to reveal the milky green cube of his source stone. "We may yet prove more formidable than we appear."

Grantin had not forgotten the blue gem hidden beneath the skin on Chom's forehead and cast a sly glance at the Fanist's impassive form. For a few seconds Chom remained silent, pondering whether or not to reveal his own treasure. At last, with an imperceptible shrug, he reached his decision. Using all four arms, he kneaded the skin of his forehead until the two layers of the flap of skin split. Chom peeled the tough gray hide upward to reveal an electric-blue stone seated in a hollow in the horny flesh. The Fanist grasped the gem with two fingers of his lower right hand and delicately pried it loose.

"This," he said, holding out the brilliant blue marble in the hollow of his right palm, "is the companion given to me by my people in aid of my quest. It is a secret thing among us Fanists. Were it not for the awesome consequences which could flow from the failure of our mission, I could not allow you to know of it, but the fate of all the humans and possibly all of my people hangs upon our success. Should we survive I beg you not to reveal our secret."

"Should we survive? Do you mean you've come all the way out here assuming that we are going to be killed?"

"That seems to be the most likely possibility," Chom admitted, "but of course we have no choice."

"No choice! I have a choice. I am in the prime of my life! We could still escape back across the Guardian Mountains. Perhaps the Gogol attack will fail after all. At the very least we could alert the Hartford soldiers. The more I think about it, the more I think that we would be better advised to employ all of the powers we possess to defend the Hartford homeland rather than in a gallant but suicidal attack on Zaco's stronghold."

"No, the Gogols would merely delay their plans. They might wait a month or a year, but sooner or later, if allowed to continue to mine the stones, they would equip an invincible army. We must sacrifice ourselves if necessary to stop them."

Grantin threw his hands up in impotent frustration.

Less than half a league away, Rupert and Yon Diggery also debated their course of action, but with vastly different goals.

"I say we should attack them now, take the ring, and be done with it," Rupert argued.

"Rupert, you must learn patience. When you have lived by your wits as long as I have, you will learn to plan your attack so as to obtain the greatest reward possible. What do we gain if we defeat them now?"

"Vengeance upon those who have destroyed your associates."

"My associates, as you so politely call them, would have cut my throat had they thought they could get away with it and make a profit on the enterprise. Don't worry about them. There are plenty of freebooters back in Grenitch Wood."

"Don't forget the ring."

"Rupert, there is one ring and two of us. Assuming we kill them, the next thing that would happen is that you would kill me or I would kill you. Do not be so anxious to become my enemy. Think a moment. Where are they going?"

"Obviously they have some sort of mission. Perhaps there is a place up ahead for them to hide."

"If they wanted to hide there is no better place than Grenitch Wood. Out here they are ten times more vulnerable. And why even stay in the Gogol empire at all? The Fanist knows the passes through the mountains."

"Very well, Diggery, you tell me—what are they doing out here?"

"Have you ever asked yourself, Rupert, where the bloodstone in that ring came from? It had to come from somewhere, didn't it? You worked for Hazar; where did he get his stones?"

"From Zaco."

"Very good; and where did Zaco get them?"

"He has a mine someplace."

"Someplace?"

"Someplace northwest of Cicero. Do you mean— You think that's where they are going?"

"See! I knew if you thought about it hard enough you would come to the right conclusion. All this time they have made straight for Grog Cup Lake. What better place to get a powerstone than from such a site?"

"Very well; assume you're right. Suppose they are going to Zaco's mine. What good does that do us?"

"Rupert, think about it for a moment. They are going to break the trail for us. They are going to take all of the risks. Let them go; let them do our work. We will follow quietly behind. If they succeed in destroying Zaco's guards, we'll surprise them and take all the stones for ourselves. If they fail, they may still have weakened the defenses enough for us to complete what they have started. Now do you understand why we are not going to attack them tonight?"

"Very well. I agree to give them a day or so longer. But you understand me, Yon Diggery. No matter what else happens, within the next two days I am going to see that Hartford dead."

Chapter Forty-six

At first light Grantin, Chom, and Castor began the trek down the gentle slope of the basin. With a quarter of a mile remaining to the cover of a feather-tree copse at the bottom of the slope, Castor's panting reached an anguished level. The Fanist grabbed him with his upper two arms, lightly tossed him over his shoulder, and began to sprint for the small grove.

As soon as he and Grantin had slipped under cover of the feather tree's drooping branches, Chom dived to the ground and pulled Grantin down beside him.

"What's the matter?"

"Someone comes."

"Where?"

"From behind. Someone or something is coming very fast."

Grantin and Castor squinted at the hillside behind them. Though the grass was a lush green, at its deepest point it stood barely a foot high and offered little scope for a stealthy advance. Grantin studied the hillside but spied no pursuers.

"I don't see anything. Are you sure someone is there?"

"Wait, I think see something; to the right about a hundred feet above the top of the ridge there is a sparkle of some sort in the sky."

Chom sped forward, crawling on his four elbows and two knees. The Fanist's gray hide blended perfectly with the fallen leaves, branches, and bare earth beneath the feather trees.

"Chom, what is it?" Grantin asked, pointing at the approaching glimmer.

"I am not sure. I noticed it just before we reached the grove. I cannot make it out. It looks like a big glass ball with something dark inside. We will have to wait until it comes closer."

The object drifted closer. As the apparition neared the angle at which the sun impinged upon its surface shifted. The sphere became transparent. At last as it passed abeam of the feather trees its composition was clearly illuminated.

More than anything else the craft resembled a soap bubble twenty feet in diameter. Inside, at the center of the bottom surface, a vital bronze-skinned man was seated in a rich red-velvet chair. Hazar rode the winds like a king. On the transparent floor in front of the Gogol lord sat a disheveled Mara. To Hazar's left, a thin figure in a black robe and a wizard's pointy hat lay twisted, his body tightly secured with bands of coarse rope. Even allowing for the awkward angle of view, Grantin was certain the body was that of his uncle Greyhorn.

"Do you think he saw us?"

"No, I do not think so, but our troubles are not over. From now on there are bound to be guards, warning posts, deadfalls, traps, and alarms. We must devise a plan of defense."

"What do you suggest?"

"Grantin, your stone is capable of projecting great amounts of energy. You must work on a spell which could be used to destroy any missiles or physical attacks made against us. Castor, what sort of spells do you possess?"

"I can defend us against psychic intrusion and attacks by magic."

"Very well. Grantin, if you can neutralize Shenar's spell, for my part I will attempt to detect ambushes and traps."

"How am I going to do that?"

"Shenar's hex enfolds me like a blanket. Close your eyes

and visualize me through your bloodstone as if it were the window to your mind's eye."

Grantin sat cross-legged on the ground, eyes closed, his fingers caressing the stone. Chom's form swam into view, but hazily, as if seen through wrappings of dirty gauze. Shenar had been a master wizard indeed. His spell had survived even his own death.

Grantin visualized a pair of psychic hands which, under the control of his mind's eye, ripped away the gauze that swaddled Chom's form. A moment later Grantin opened his eyes and looked questioningly at the Fanist.

"I am free," Chom announced.

A few minutes later the three moved out with Grantin rubbing his bloodstone while Chom and Castor each fingered the powerstone appropriate to his race. Chom led the group a rough zigzag course through clumps of trees, back and forth across the stream, and at least once through a patch of immature razorbrush.

It was after the sixth hour when they reached the last bit of shelter before the mountain. Ahead a grassy meadow extended several hundred yards up to the edge of the mountain's sheer walls. The fugitives studied the clearing in the same way that a cliff diver stares at the sea beneath him.

"Why don't they do something?" Grantin whispered. "They must know we are here."

"Perhaps they don't have enough men to risk meeting us in the open," Castor suggested.

"No," Chom replied. "They are just waiting until they have us bottled up in the caverns where we will not have room to maneuver. A few men in front, a few behind, and they will keep us trapped until we fall asleep from fatigue. They know we cannot maintain a spell forever."

"In that case, why don't we avoid the passage and simply climb the walls?" the Gray asked.

"They would detect us there as well; and how long could we continue to repel the boulders they would drop from above?"

"Chom, couldn't you and Grantin construct a bubble like that which carried Hazar—something which would float us up over the wall?"

"Perhaps, but it would take all our energy. A hasty flotation spell might get us off the ground, but we would have no power left to repel Hazar's bolts and blasts."

"Why couldn't all three of us work together on the same spell?" Grantin suggested. "With the power added by the stones it should at least be equal to anything Hazar and his men can command against us."

"What kind of spell?" Castor asked.

Chom considered. "It must be something simple, an image all three of us can grasp at once. Any weakness, any imbalance, could cause a feedback and destroy us all."

"Why not just create a band of demons and send them on ahead to destroy Hazar's defenders?"

Chom and Castor considered Grantin's suggestion and agreed to give it a try.

"Each of us will create one demon," the young Hartford suggested, "and send them through the tunnels to clear the way."

Grantin closed his eyes and caressed the powerstone In the clearing a hundred yards ahead a misty red shape began to form. In a few seconds the apparition had congealed into an eight-foot-high biped each of whose arms was tipped with five long steel talons. From the beast's mouth protruded four great fangs which dripped great droplets of blood-red saliva. With sweat beading his forehead, Grantin opened his eyes and practiced putting the monster through its paces, causing it to march awkwardly left and right and slash the air with its taloned paws.

Grantin noticed that Chom had also completed his demon, but one of a wildly different sort: a hazy bluish six-foot mound of plastic ooze. From its upper portions a myriad of hand-tipped pseudopods flashed from its bulk, whipped the air with crazy strangling motions, and then retracted again.

Castor finished his creation last. It was as different from the others as they were from each other. Where Grantin's monster had two arms and Chom's hundreds, Castor's had none at all. Instead he created a snake fifteen feet long and four in diameter, with a massive head, twin foot-long poisoned fangs, and a gigantic hinged jaw which could easily swallow a man whole.

Grantin's demon, the first to be created, now exhibited the most lifelike movements, even down to the nervous whipping of its long, thin tail.

"Grantin, you seem to be the most practiced of us. Perhaps your monster should go first."

Grantin directed his attention to the beast and maneuvered it several quick bounds forward toward the mountain. Suddenly it slowed and stopped.

"What's the matter?" Castor asked.

"I don't know. It is becoming harder to control, almost as if it has a life of its own." As if to demonstrate the accuracy of Grantin's report, the creature turned back toward the copse, raised both claws high, and emitted a bone-chilling growl.

"I can't control it! It's getting away from me. It's angry with me for bringing it here; I can feel its hatred. The beast wants to kill us all," Grantin screamed as the monster began a purposeful stride toward the small grove.

Another shape flashed behind Grantin's creature. Just as the beast broke into a loping trot hundreds of translucent blue tentacles wrapped themselves around its body. The two demons rolled in epic battle, steel-tipped claws slashing deep into the puttylike structure of Chom's creation while the Fanist's monster sought to extrude itself into a wide, thin shape which might enfold and presumably digest the beast.

Castor by now was also losing control of his creation. The snake exhibited signs of extreme excitement at the sight of the writhing blue and red masses. At last, unable to be restrained any longer, Castor's demon slithered forward, opened its jaws to their fullest extent, and attempted to swallow both combatants whole.

More pseudopods shot out of the blue mass.

Before the writhing bundle could be swallowed completely, the tentacles extended themselves to their farthest limit. They whipped around and around the snake's great head, tying its jaws together with transluscent blue cable. The snake found itself unable either to regurgitate its meal or maneuver it into its stomach. Wildly disconcerted by this state of affairs, the demons whipped wildly back and forth and fled headlong across the basin.

With equal parts of terror and fatigue, a sweating, weak-kneed Grantin slumped to the ground, to be joined there shortly by his two comrades.

"What happened? Did Hazar turn our creations against us?"

"No, I do not think so," Chom replied. "We are not experienced at this sort of thing. We made our monsters too real. We called them up as if they were alive and visualized them having minds of their own. We created them with all the ferocity, savageness, and intelligence which we imagined a real creature of that sort would possess. They could do no less than become as we imagined them."

"Perhaps," Castor suggested, "the solution lies in imagining something without a mind at all—for example, a wall of flame which would travel through the tunnel engulfing all it passed."

"And what if there's something flammable in there?" Grantin protested. "What if they put Mara in the tunnel as a hostage? All they need do is stand back out of the way until the flames have passed and then attack us when we enter. No, it must be something which stops them and also protects us. A spell of some sort that doesn't necessarily kill."

"Perhaps Castor had the right idea in reverse. I propose that we surround ourselves with a wall of ice which will freeze anyone who attempts to penetrate it."

"Good, Chom—but not a wall of ice, a cloud, a transparent cloud. It should be a light mist so that we can see through it. Something so thin and delicate that Hazar's men will blunder into it unafraid. Something that does not kill but stiffens the victim, knots up his arms and legs, and numbs his brain."

"It is as good a suggestion as any. Castor, what do you think?"

"If you and Grantin think it will work, I am willing to try."

"Very well, then. We must work together; let us all visualize the same thing. Grantin, you are the most familiar with what this field should resemble. Describe it as you see it."

"It's a mist, a light, pale white mist the color of steam as it first begins to rise from a bubbling kettle. I see it as a shell, a sphere around us, penetrating the rock fifteen feet over our heads and ten feet on either side as we walk abreast. The field moves as we move, turns as we turn, and as long as we stay together it cannot touch us. I see a Gogol soldier running toward us. He walks through the field and is instantly frozen stiff. He turns and falls, his arms and legs still bent in the positions they held as he penetrated its edge."

"I see it!" Castor suddenly exclaimed. "Another soldier comes toward us; he has seen his comrade fall, but he does not understand the field and he extends his arm into it. The arm stiffens and becomes as immobile as a piece of iron. He stares at the member in horror; then he turns and runs from us, screaming."

"I see it, too," Chom declared. "A band of Gogols waits in a side passage, hoping to catch us from behind. We sense them and break into a run. The edge of the bubble races forward keeping pace with us. Our shield penetrates the solid rock and swirls over them, freezing them like statues. One of them has managed to fall backward out of the way and is unhurt. Grantin stands to my left and, seeing the soldier, he moves a few feet away from me. The bubble bulges in the direction that Grantin has moved, catching the Gogol in its grip."

Grantin, Chom, and Castor opened their eyes. Around them they beheld a shimmering sphere exactly as they had imagined it.

"Well, we seem to have done it."

"Yes, Grantin, it would appear so."

"What are we waiting for?" Castor asked.

Grantin ruefully shook his head and for the last time examined the sunny afternoon meadow and the sheer walls of Grog Cup Lake. "How do I get myself involved in these things?" he asked himself as the three advanced on the black crevice which led to the bloodstone mine.

Chapter Forty-seven

The chamber was abuzz with activity. From the tunnels behind Hazar's counting table emerged a constant stream of laborers. Clothing tattered, soiled, or nonexistent, the Gogol criminals and Hartford slaves trundled ore carts to a gigantic pile of fractured stone.

Around the edges of the mound bustled a second group of slaves. These latter workers, less vigorous, composed mostly of females, older men, and a few Ajaj, picked over the shards at the base of the pile, culling out the fragments which might contain crystals of powerstone. These pieces were carted to a huge semicircular table behind Hazar where twelve Ajaj carefully fragmented the rock with geologists' hammers. The Grays deposited the worthless scraps in another set of ore carts behind them, while the occasional bloodstone crystal was retained in a small bin affixed to the side of each Ajaj's chair. To eliminate any possibilities of smuggling the Ajaj were naked and the rubble in the carts behind them examined by Gogol supervisors before being disposed of.

In front of Hazar a hole five feet in diameter was bored

through the floor. Under the watchful eyes of Zaco's minions, the tailings were dumped into the pit.

Though none of the miners knew the terminus of the shaft, few who labored there were desperate enough to throw themselves down its maw in hopes of escape. In point of fact the opening was a garbage-disposal chute. The first section was a sheer drop to a point below the floor of the lake. There it bent at a forty-five-degree angle, eventually to protrude from the side of Grog Cup Mountain some two hundred feet above the level of the surrounding meadow. Day after day boulders, chunks of rock, stones, gravel, and occasionally a suicidal, infirm, or recalcitrant laborer roared from the garbage-chute exit to crash to the ground below.

Today all of these functions continued as they had over previous days, months, and years. But to these activities Hazar devoted only the smallest portion of his attention. Ore was removed, sorted, fragmented, checked, and discarded in a continuous process whose only important aspect, as far as Hazar was concerned, was the production of bloodstones. Each hour the overseer made his collection from the Grays' boxes, immediately thereafter depositing the raw gemstones on Hazar's table.

Hazar himself counted the stones and sorted them into piles by size, color, and shape. After entering a tally he personally carried the gems to the cutters' table to the left of the only entrance to the mine's main room.

Hazar carefully deposited three more dull red-brown crystals on the green felt of the cutters' table, then removed two polished oval bloodstones from the box of completed work. In another two days he would have enough stones to equip the key men in his army.

Hazar paused in his efforts long enough to instruct his subordinate, the subdeacon Nimo, to commence an attack against the intruders.

Nimo, who had supervised the mining operations for Zaco, bowed and sprinted from the room. The sight of his hasty exit pleased Hazar. He would have Zaco's lazy subordinates whipped into shape in no time at all.

Why stop at a mere fifty stones? Why not a hundred, two hundred? Each would have a special cut, a facet etched in its underside which would make it resonate to an incantation of Hazar's own devising. If any of their wearers opposed King Hazar—Emperor Hazar—he would pronounce the spell. The concentration of great magical energies within the lattice of the stone itself, a psychic harmonic resonance, would shatter not only the gem but the hand of the wearer as well. Yes, he had made a mistake in sending Greyhorn an undoctored stone, one of the rings he had received as a completed unit from Zaco. Was it possible that Zaco had placed such a grating in the bottom of Greyhorn's ring? Possible, but he would never know. Zaco was long gone and the exact components of the spell that would fit Grantin's ring could not be discovered by any haphazard method.

Hazar toyed with a new batch of crystals. Strange that such a dull and ordinary-looking piece of rock could, with a bit of effort, be turned into a magnificent scarlet gem. Hazar was so entranced with the flaws, bumps, and contours of the crystals that he failed to notice Nimo's approach.

"Uh, excuse me, my lord," Zaco's supervisor stammered.

"Yes, Nimo, what has happened to our friends? Have they been disposed of? Tell me, has the human been captured alive?"

"No, my lord, you see . . ."

"No, my lord, what? He is not alive, or he has not been captured? I don't see at all, Nimo; you had better explain at once."

"My lord, great magic protects the fugitives. The acolytes did their best, but even their most powerful spells were unable to reach them. They had no effect whatsoever."

"Well, don't stop; what happened?"

"Monsters, my lord, demons!"

"What!"

"Demons, my lord, in the meadow between the grove and the mountain. They just appeared: one like a great beast with fangs and talons, ten or fifteen feet high, standing on two legs. Another at least ten feet high, all blue, with arms and waving tentacles; and a third like a huge pale green snake, five, perhaps ten, feet in diameter. They just appeared there. And then they started walking and moving around. It was terrible! They began to fight with each other. The beast attacked the blue thing, and while they struggled the snake ate them both."

"And then what?"

"With the two of them struggling in its mouth the snake squirmed away across the meadow and vanished."

"You mean to tell me these demons appeared, fought with each other, and in the middle of the struggle all three of them disappeared?"

"Yes, my lord, yes. Our magic was as nothing against them. If they were to get in here we would be defenseless."

"Stop whining! They did not get in here, and obviously the fugitives cannot control them any better than you can. They are gone, and that is that. Now, return to your post and watch. I want to know what the three of them do next."

Hazar dismissed Nimo, then turned his thoughts inward. The fact that Grantin had apparently learned to manipulate the ring was not too much of a surprise, but there were other disturbing implications in the subdeacon's report. The three demons, each of a different color, indicated almost to a certainty that the Fanist and the Ajaj were also capable of manipulating formidable powers. True, their control was crude and clumsy, but the energy was there.

Hazar cast his gaze around the chamber, taking stock of the assets he might employ in the coming battle. Huddled against the wall on Hazar's left sat a bitter but cowed Greyhorn. Shorn of his amulet, half starved, frightened, and hexed to the eyeballs, the sorcerer had been reduced to a shadow of his former power and vitality. Did he bear his nephew enough enmity to oppose him? Possibly; but returning to Greyhorn a measure of his power was a dangerous proposition. Instead of attacking Grantin it was equally likely that the wizard would turn his waning energies upon Hazar himself.

On the other side of the room, opposite Greyhorn's position and only a few feet from the mouth of the disposal chute, Mara's form was restrained in a heavy ironwood chair. Thin, silklike cords fastened each of the girl's arms and legs to the frame.

Upon her capture Mara had displayed a notable inclination to uncooperativeness, intractability, and disrespect. Had he not been saving her against the possibility that he might have to use her as leverage, Hazar might have long since turned her over to his guards. Instead he had restrained his natural inclinations and had forced himself to be satisfied with more subtle forms of punishment.

The cords which restrained Mara were carefully but tightly tied in single strands so that each time she attempted to move her bonds cut deeply into her flesh. If she struggled sufficiently they would draw blood. Once she had been firmly settled in her chair Hazar had taken pleasure in shredding certain items of her clothing so that although more or less fully dressed the more intimate details of Mara's anatomy were displayed for the pleasure of his guards and the servants and slaves continually passing through the chamber.

A last-ditch plan formed in the Gogol's mind. A moment later he issued a stream of orders.

"Slaves—you, you, and you. Drop those stones and come over here. I have work for you."

Three sickly men released their burden and fearfully ambled forward to receive Hazar's commands. "You," he ordered, "against the far wall is equipment; fetch the bundle of linc. As for you two, one of you will stand on the other's shoulders and bore a small hole in the rock above the ceiling brace. Through this hole you will pass one end of the rope."

The first slave returned with a translucent coil. Hazar gave him a final set of instructions. "You take one end of the rope that has been run over the beam and tie it to the chair where the woman now sits. The other end you will tie to a stake which you will drive into the floor next to my table, being careful to leave enough slack so that the chair is positioned a few inches inside the disposal chute." The slaves hurried off to carry out their orders.

Ten minutes later the legs of Mara's chair hung six inches below the edge of the disposal chute, its weight restrained only by the cord fastened to an iron stake driven into the floor at the edge of Hazar's desk. Hazar removed a dagger from his belt, examined its gleaming blade, tested the razor sharpness of its edge, then placed the unsheathed weapon on the corner of the desk not two feet from where the line stretched up to the ceiling and down to the top of Mara's ironwood throne.

Hazar looked up from the crystals on his desk in time to

see Nimo, followed by another subdeacon, race into the chamber.

"My lord, they come!"

"The fugitives? All of them?"

"Yes, my lord, all three walking side by side. They are surrounded by a spell of great power."

"What kind of spell? What does it look like? What are they doing?"

"It is misty, my lord, transparent. It extends around them on all sides. Nothing stops it. It penetrates the walls as if they did not exist."

"The walls? You mean they are inside already? I ordered you to keep me informed of their movement. Why didn't you tell me this before!"

"My lord, at first nothing happened, so there was nothing to tell. They walked across the meadow very slowly. They took no hostile action, threw no bolts, and so we watched them to see what they would do. Soon it became clear that they were making for the southwest entrance. I immediately dispatched a squad of guards. I instructed the section leader to engage them and sent Goren here with the men to watch and bring back a report. He has just now returned."

"Stop making excuses for disobeying my orders and tell me what has happened!"

"My lord, I have never seen anything like it," Goren began. "They entered the tunnel as if out for an afternoon stroll. They had reached no more than ten feet inside the entrance when six fully armored soldiers attacked. The fugitives made no resistance. They took no notice of the swords and bolts aimed at them. The soldiers ran full into the field and then fell as if dead."

"And then what happened?"

"Nothing, my lord; that is to say, the fugitives continued to walk on down the tunnel immobilizing all who came near them."

"Why didn't someone stand back and fire bolts at them from a distance?"

"My lord, they did, but to no avail. As soon as they entered the field the arrows slowed as if proceeding through thick syrup. The fugitives easily moved out of their way. The bolts sailed harmlessly past." Goren gave a fearful shrug of his shoulders and was silent.

"Well, don't just stand there; what happened next?"

"Nothing, my lord. They come even now. Nothing stops them, not bolts, not fire, not rocks or knives. I used my spells, but they were as effective as trying to breach the walls of Cicero by throwing pebbles. They do not know the passageways, but surely they will be here in a few minutes, in any event."

"You are all a bunch of fools—cowards and fools! I can see that I can trust no one but myself. Nimo, I am going to give you an order, and you will follow it no matter what happens; do you understand?"

"Yes, my lord," Nimo answered a bit apprehensively.

"Stand by the edge of my desk and hold the dagger next to the line. Upon my command cut the rope. Do you understand?"

"Yes, my lord. I am to stand here and, when you give the order, cut the rope."

"And not before, Nimo. Goren, you go down to the bend in the tunnel. Watch for them. When they get there, if they get there, you warn me. Don't stand there like an idiot! Go! Go!"

More afraid of Hazar's wrath than the sorcery of the fugitives, the subdeacon raced down the corridor.

Alone now except for Nimo, the slaves having fled upon overhearing Goren's report, Hazar strode to the deserted cutters' table and retrieved the two largest of the finished stones. There was no time to set them in a ring or bracelet or amulet. He would have to do his work with them clasped within his palm, in contact with his naked skin. Hazar pushed his desk out of the way, then seated himself in his ironwood chair, a mate to the one in which Mara was imprisoned. The bloodstones trembled in the open palm of his left hand. Taking a deep breath, he clamped his right hand, imprisoning the stones in the hollow between, and then began to channel a spell of fiery death through the crystals and out into the ether, unerringly directed at Grantin, Chom, and Castor.

Chapter Forty-eight

The early stages of the attack were surprisingly easy. The protective sphere was mental rather than physical and thus presented none of the inconveniences associated with mass, weight, and inertia. Grantin, Chom, and Castor entered the Gogol caverns without the slightest difficulty. Above them and on each side the misty shield disappeared as it insinuated itself between the molecules of solid rock. Only in front and behind could its existence be discerned.

Suddenly a group of screaming soldiers raced down the tunnel, intent on repulsing the attackers. In less than five seconds the frozen bodies of the defenders littered the floor. Encouraged by this initial success, they increased their pace. Except for the distraction of being forced to dodge drastically slowed crossbow bolts, nothing except the intricateness of the network of tunnels hindered their advance.

"How long do you think we can keep up the shield?" Grantin asked Chom.

"I do not know. Perhaps hours, perhaps only a few more minutes. It may just slowly fade away to nothing, or it might disappear all at once. The only thing we can do is proceed as rapidly as possible."

"I assure you, Chom, I *am* proceeding as fast as possible."

From the bend in the tunnel ahead of them another flight of arrows was loosed at the attackers. In the dim light of the phosphorescent mosses the missiles flickered dully like a flight of peculiar insects. The arrows entered the shield and, as in each previous attack, slowed to a rate of one or two feet per second, imparting a brighter whiteness to the portions of the barrier surrounding the points of penetration. Almost absentmindedly Chom waved his four arms and plucked the bolts from midair.

The three reached the right-hand bend in the tunnel and increased their speed to a run as they made the turn. This tactic never seemed to be anticipated by the defenders, and always their increase in speed caught a few of the waiting soldiers by surprise. This time was no exception. They stepped over the immobilized defenders and continued at a rapid pace. Ahead of them the tunnel swung to the right, rising toward the central chamber.

Judging by the height of the tunnel and the number of turns already made in the spiraling passage, Grantin estimated that in another five minutes, ten at the most, they would reach the surface of the lake. As if to confirm his hypothesis, the tunnel seemed to be getting brighter, almost glowing with the illumination of reflected daylight. And it seemed to be getting warmer, too.

Grantin noticed that the front edge of the shield appeared thicker, frostier, while at the same time he detected within himself a great lethargy.

"Chom, something's happening. Do you feel it?"

"We are being attacked," Castor said. "They are trying to hex us."

For the first time in their relationship Grantin detected signs of weariness in Chom. The Fanist's head, neck, and shoulders glistened with a thin, oily film.

"We must make it colder," the Fanist rasped. "We must put more energy into our spell before their weapon defeats us."

Grantin's forehead became knotted in concentration, while Castor's tendons and muscles stiffened with the increased strain. Chom gave no outward sign of his redoubled efforts except for a thickening and spreading of his glistening second skin. Each of the three dredged up images of numbing cold, mountains of steaming ice, wintry vistas of bleak terrain frozen from horizon to horizon. Each visualized a blizzard driving sleet and snow through every tunnel, nook, and crevice of Grog Cup Mountain.

Two levels above the attackers their efforts made themselves felt. A burning shiver sliced through Hazar's body while, at the edge of the room, Greyhorn's flesh became as stone. The horror of Mara's suspension over the pit had caused her to faint before the latest attack. Since the sorcery achieved its goals through mental rather than physical power, her unconsciousness protected her from the incantation's worst effects.

Not so spared, however, was Hazar's servant Nimo. Even though he stood a bare ten feet from Hazar's protection, he received enough of a blast to remove from his members the power of voluntary movement. Sensationless fingers held the dagger and a frozen arm poised the blade a quarter of an inch above the rope.

Hazar alone of all the defenders survived the counterattack. The sorcerer squeezed his hands in a grip so strong as to be painful. The bloodstones forced deep indentations into his flesh. Hazar struggled to formulate a yet more potent spell.

Grantin felt that he could not keep up his strength much longer. The attack might even now have forced him to halt had he not noticed a sign announcing that the mine's central chamber lay just ahead. Grantin, Chom, and Castor turned another corner. Ahead of them on the right-hand wall Grantin spied a doorway which he hoped marked the end of their search. With blind eyes he stepped over the stiffened form of a Gogol subdeacon who had been waiting too close to the bend in the tunnel. They were almost there.

Twenty feet from the doorway a great hammerblow struck the three attackers. Grantin felt as if he had stood inside a huge bell while outside a sledgehammer-wielding giant struck the hour. Around him the field clouded almost to opacity. The three struggled to rebuild their defenses, but as they worked another massive blow crashed against their magic sphere. It seemed to Grantin that he could now see cracks and fractures on its milky surface.

Chom pressed his own stone tighter against his skull. At the same instant that Hazar loosed his third attack Chom released a bolt of his own. The two titanic energies met and, like a grounding of high-voltage potentials, their powers canceled in a display of sparks and flame and shards of ice.

The Fanist had employed great power in his beam but in so doing had exhausted his last reserves. He collapsed unconscious to the floor, with a consequent weakening of the protective shield. While Grantin struggled to rebuild their defenses Castor summoned his powers for what he hoped would be a triumphant effort. Energies flared in the corridor and spilled through the doorway into the main chamber, even so far as to singe the tips of Hazar's mustache. For a moment the wizard stood on the edge of unconsciousness. Grantin gave up all attempts to maintain the shield, and with a psychic pop the misty wall disappeared.

The atmosphere of the tunnel was hypercharged with magic. Grantin felt as if he were walking between two huge cats whose bodies were charged with static electricity. He dared not launch an attack by sorcery even if he had the energy. With the drain of the spell ended, a bit of Grantin's physical powers returned. He staggered ahead and turned through the doorway and into the mine's central chamber.

Grantin saw Hazar three or four yards in front of him, glassy-eyed and swaying on his feet but not yet beaten. To Hazar's right waited another man, knife in hand. The second man was frozen on his feet. The Hartford flicked his gaze around the room and in an instant spied Mara's bound form perched over the edge of oblivion.

The Hartford had not the slightest idea what to do next. He had not thought to remove a knife or sword from one of the fallen soldiers, and even if he had he doubted that he would be able to plunge the blade into Hazar's chest.

The Gogol's eyes blinked and became clear. The wizard shook his head, looked at Grantin, and brought himself back to full awareness. With neither word nor gesture of warning the Gogol leaped forward and extended his arms to clench Grantin's throat.

For half a second the Hartford stood immobilized, then

forced himself to fall backward out of Hazar's way. The two went down together. Hazar's fingers wrapped themselves around Grantin's throat. The Gogol summoned up all his remaining energy and channeled it to his hands. As he fell Grantin managed to double his right leg, which he pressed against Hazar's chest. With a wrenching kick he pushed against the sorcerer and propelled him away.

Both men rose to their feet and circled with arms outstretched. Grantin tried a kick at Hazar's stomach and barely avoided having his leg caught in an ankle-wrenching grasp. Hazar charged Grantin in a shambling run. The Hartford jumped to his left and struck at Hazar's onrushing head. Hazar's shoulder struck him a glancing blow. The wizard careened ahead and Grantin fell backward against the cutters' table. He put out his hand to steady himself, but instead of gaining firm purchase his fingers drove into the shallow, velvet-lined box at the edge of the table. His hand clenched automatically. As he staggered to his feet Grantin held in his palm eight of the finished stones.

Grantin pushed himself from the table, then backed across the room in hopes that he might be able to pull Mara's chair from the pit before Hazar attacked again. He was still ten feet from the edge, however, when Hazar returned to the attack. From his boot the wizard extracted a gleaming dirk. He waved the blade in small hypnotic circles.

Grantin tried to avoid watching the flickering highlights. Instead he concentrated on Hazar's eyes. For a moment he considered attempting to cast another spell but then abandoned the idea. Even with the amplification supplied by the gems the effort required would surely bring him to unconsciousness; best to get rid of the stones, they were only a distraction now.

Grantin opened his hand and allowed the gems to cascade to the floor. The sight of his precious bloodstones strewn about the chamber shocked Hazar. For an instant his attention was diverted.

In spite of his exhaustion Grantin was still a young man with a young man's reflexes. Instantly he seized the initiative. He grasped Hazar's left arm with both hands. Using all his strength, the Hartford turned the dagger away from himself and squeezed Hazar's wrist, hoping to break his grasp.

The Gogol was startled by the suddenness of the attack. Hazar tried to move past Grantin. The combination of Grantin's forward movement and Hazar's attempted maneuver snapped the wizard's wrist like dry kindling. In the blink of an eye the point of the blade was reversed and forced to the hilt into Hazar's torso.

Grantin released his grip. An observer would have found it hard to determine which of the two men was more astonished. Hazar stood on rubbery knees, his head bowed, eyes staring in dumb amazement at the dagger's protruding handle and the crimson ribbon which spilled down the front of his gown. In openmouthed surprise the Gogol sorcerer pitched slowly forward and sprawled upon the floor.

Grantin watched the wizard's demise with the same emotion felt by an innocent bystander who has chanced to observe a natural catastrophe. He staggered toward Mara, then, engulfed by a roaring in his brain, toppled over, three feet short of Nimo's menacing blade.

Chapter Forty-nine

An hour later the piercing cold of his rocky pallet forced Grantin awake. Groggy and disoriented, through bleary eyes he saw the still sleeping forms of his companions. Grantin pitched forward and crawled to where Castor lay.

"Castor, Castor, wake up," Grantin said, shaking the Ajaj's fragile body. The Gray moaned dully, fighting Grantin's attempts to awaken him. "Come on, Castor, you've got to wake up. Wake up; we must leave here."

"What . . . Grantin?"

"That's it, Castor! Come on; get up."

The Gray opened his eyes and forced himself back to consciousness while Grantin repeated the procedure, although with greater vigor, with Chom. In a few minutes the Fanist abruptly awakened, and the three stood up to massage their aching bodies. As they walked to the main chamber Grantin explained what had happened. Once inside he recruited Chom's and Castor's help in hauling Mara's bound form from the refuse chute. Nimo's dagger was wrested from his fingers and used to slice the cords which bound her to the chair.

Grantin awakened the sleeping enchantress as he had

done his two associates, but with gentler and more loving caresses than he had given either Chom or Castor. In point of fact Grantin struggled to restrain himself, as he found that the allure of Mara's tattered clothing strained him to the limits of his self-control.

Mara resisted Grantin's attempts to awaken her until at last he gently slapped her. Upon the first impact Mara let out a horrifying scream, leaped from the chair, and threw her arms around him. Instinctively Grantin wrapped his arms around her and caressed her back through the rips in her gown. He had begun to kiss Mara's neck when behind him he heard Chom ask Castor: "Will they begin mating now?"

The inquiry brought Grantin back to full awareness of where he was and the dangers which still confronted them. He released his grasp and jumped back a pace, his face burning with embarrassment.

"To answer your question, Chom, no, we will not mate now. Humans do not mate under these circumstances. I was merely comforting the young lady. My actions had no sexual connotations whatsoever."

Castor and Chom looked at each other and exchanged exaggerated expressions of skepticism and wry amusement. Grantin's cheeks colored an even deeper shade and he stamped off angrily toward the chamber's exit. Mara looked at Castor and Chom, then swept her gaze around the room, first noting Nimo's frozen body, then Hazar's punctured, bloodless form. A horrified whimper escaped her throat. She raced forward to again allow Grantin to comfort her, an activity which he engaged in with tender care, all the while presenting to Chom and Castor a look of exaggerated innocence.

In a few minutes Mara's tears slowed and with an exercise of willpower she managed to bring herself back to a state of more or less normal composure.

"How long will they be like that?" she asked, pointing at Nimo.

"We are not exactly sure. Several hours at least."

"Then you don't intend spending the night here?"

"By no means! Leaving here will mark the happiest instant of my life. In fact, I propose we depart the moment that we locate my uncle."

"The wizard Greyhorn? There he is, against that wall."

Grantin, Chom, and Castor turned as one to stare at the spot indicated by Mara's outthrust arm. At the far side of the room a heavily cloaked object sat huddled in a crumpled ball. Grantin walked to the figure and pulled back the edge of the cloak which shrouded the body's features. Beneath the cloak appeared Greyhorn's familiar thin visage, distorted now with a look of weary fear.

"Uncle, are you all right?" Greyhorn's eyes stared unseeingly into empty space. Tentatively Grantin poked the wizard's shoulder. Under his robes Greyhorn's body was hard and unyielding. Less restrained, Grantin pinched the old man's cheeks and slapped his face, but without response. The flesh had the gummy rubberiness that Grantin had felt in Theleb's mummified form.

By now Chom, Castor, and Mara had approached the wizard's rigid body. Chom bent over. Fixing his eyes three inches directly in front of Greyhorn's and clasping the wizard's ears and shoulders in his four arms, he attempted to commune with the sorcerer's consciousness, if any.

"Is he alive?"

"He sleeps."

"How long do you think he will stay like this?"

"Hazar has done something to him. Deep within him I feel a spark of life, but unknowing, unaware. I think he will stay this way a long time."

"A long time. . . . How long?"

"Years."

"Years? He is going to stay huddled up in this grotesque position for years? What am I supposed to do with him all that time?"

"You could leave him here, I suppose. He is your kin." While Chom's voice held no note of disapproval, Grantin sensed that somehow the Fanist was testing him. The young Hartford shuffled his feet nervously, his mouth downturned in a sour expression. Twice he seemed ready to take Mara by the hand and lead her from the mine, but each time, as he looked at his uncle's twisted shape, he relented.

"Why is it always me?" he asked petulantly. "Always it is Grantin, the easygoing, the softhearted, who is called upon to solve the problems of others. Why must I be the one to save the Hartfords, protect the Ajaj, rescue the maidens, defeat the villains, take on the labors of the world? I am too goodhearted, that is my flaw. Now I am expected to carry this heavy . . . object . . . halfway across the Gogol empire, through dangerous bandit-ridden forests, across treacherous mountain passes!"

Accustomed to Grantin's exaggerated complaints, Castor and Chom made no response other than the exchange of brief, knowing sidelong glances which, although retained for only an instant, contained overtones of skepticism, amusement, and weary resignation. Occupied as he was with his tale of woe, Grantin failed to detect the interchange and continued his monologue to its inevitable conclusion.

"Very well; I see that you will give me no peace until I comply with your wishes. No, you won't say anything about it; you will just treat me like an ingrate, like some kind of monster, if I refuse to strain myself to the limit for the benefit of one who would have cut off my finger and betrayed his own kinsmen into slavery. Very well, very well; I will yield to your accusation. Again, as usual, I act against my best interests. All right, Chom you win. We will take him with us for all the good it will do."

"As you wish. . . ."

"As I wish—hah!"

"However, we have some unfinished business before we leave."

"Such as?"

"The bloodstones. We cannot leave them here; they are too much of a temptation. Some other Gogol might come along and take Hazar's place; then all of our efforts will have been for nothing."

"Very well; as long as we're transporting my wretched uncle anyway, I don't suppose it will be much more of a burden to stick the things in one of his pockets."

"I think what Chom means," Castor suggested, "is more than just the removal of the loose stones. If we leave this place untouched, others might come here and reopen the mine. More than that, Hazar already has distributed several of the stones to his subordinates. When his death is discovered they will battle among themselves for supremacy. The winner of that struggle is certain to be someone who possesses one of the gems. He will still be a formidable enemy for my people as well as for you humans. Somehow we must destroy the mine."

"Destroy the mine! How do you propose to do that?"

"It is not absolutely necessary that we destroy the mine itself," Chom replied, "so long as we destroy the stones. We need only construct a spell which affects them alone."

"I know a spell," Mara said. "One of enchantment which one fixes upon an object in the possession of the victim of the spell. Perhaps we could adapt it to set a spell upon every bloodstone in the empire."

"That's a fine idea, except how do we protect ourselves from being killed in the process? If I were to project my energies into all the crystals in existence I would feel a feedback through my own ring as well."

"There is a way, I think," Castor suggested. "We know the gems amplify the power of our spells. Instead of projecting incantation into all of the gems at once, what if you formulated it so that it would take effect, for example, on one of the stones in this room, and that stone would, in turn, broadcast it to another stone, and another, and another, until the energies became so great that the crystals themselves shattered?"

"And my arm with it? No, thank you!"

"We could protect you, I think," Chom said. "The three of us could construct a force field around you that would prevent the energies from reaching your ring. We could pronounce most of the spell before we left and then, when a good distance away, create the protective field an instant after directing the final portion of the incantation back here through your ring. The distance and the shield should protect you."

"Should protect me! And if it does not?"

"We will be inside the shield with you. We'll all go together."

"That makes me feel a lot better!"

Three faces, three pairs of eyes, stared at Grantin. For a full thirty seconds there was complete silence.

At last Grantin threw up his arms in frustration.

"All right, all right; I will do it. I am putty in your hands. It will serve you right if I blow up the lot of you."

For the next half hour Grantin, Mara, Chom, and Castor discussed the possible contents of the incantation. Finally, after hurried preparations, all of the spell save the last line was recited.

A new tension filled the air. Grantin felt as if his body had been infused with gallons of stimulants. A high-pitched, inaudible whine prickled his ears.

"Something is happening. I don't know what it is, but I want to get out of here. If you are all quite ready, can we leave?"

"Yes, I think we should go. Grantin, you and I can carry your uncle."

Grantin and Chom groaned and hoisted Greyhorn's dead weight between them.

"At this rate it is going to be a long and tiring trip home," Grantin commented before they had even reached the doorway.

"Aren't we going to travel by the spell of magnificent transport?" Mara asked.

"I would love to, except I don't know the incantation."

"I do. I heard the overdeacons recite it just before we left Cicero."

"Excellent! Perhaps we will travel in style at last. Come, Chom, let us get Uncle Greyhorn outside, pronounce the spell, and be gone from this place before it comes down around our ears."

Grantin and Chom picked up Greyhorn once more and began to maneuver his unwieldly body toward the doorway. They had almost reached the portal when, in the passage beyond, they heard the clear, ringing sounds of heavy boots tramping down the tunnel.

Chapter Fifty

From their vantage point just beyond the ridge overlooking Grog Cup Mountain, Rupert and Yon Diggery had an excellent view of the battle. They rested prone on the ground, only their eyes peeking over the lip of the hill. Icy tingles rippled up and down their spines, but neither one would now turn back.

An hour after the fugitives entered the tunnel Rupert quested with his mind in an attempt to determine the situation within the mountain. The Gogol deacon was more than a little surprised when he could find no hint of activity.

"You sense nothing?"

"Nothing. No struggle, no spells. No energy being released, not even any conscious thoughts. You know what that means."

"If you're right. After all the trouble that Hartford has caused us, can our luck actually have turned this good? I don't know, Rupert; I don't like it. It might be a trap."

"A trap, bah! Stop being such an old woman, Diggery. They've killed each other off, and so much the better for us. Now, before someone else comes along or those guards down there wake up, let's get into the mine and fill our pockets."

Diggery's sixth sense told him that Rupert's answer was too pat, that there was something wrong, but he had no firm evidence for his conviction beyond the observation that in every free apple there is usually lurking at least one worm. With a rueful shake of his head Diggery relented. He and Rupert trotted down the slope and along the trail to Grog Cup Mountain.

Upon seeing the frozen bodies of Zaco's soldiers Rupert became elated, convinced beyond all doubt that his assessment of the situation was correct. Even Yon Diggery's innate suspicion evaporated as rank upon rank, level upon level, of guards was found immobilized. Swaggering, cheerful, and immensely pleased with himself, Rupert tramped into the main chamber, only to receive a rude surprise. There, not ten feet in front of him, stood Grantin and the Fanist, holding between them a frozen body and flanked on one side by an Ajaj and on the other by the girl whom Rupert recognized as the enchantress Mara.

Rupert's eyes bulged. He blurted out: "It can't be. Where is Hazar?"

Grantin inclined his head toward the place where Hazar's body lay. Rupert followed the direction of his gaze. The imbecilic Hartford had bested Lord Hazar? Impossible, but there lay the body.

Yon Diggery was anything but indecisive. The instant after passing through the doorway he drew his sword. Without conscious planning Grantin pointed his ring at the blade and visualized a white-hot plume of flame striking the metal. With a scream Diggery threw the weapon from him.

For perhaps a minute each group stared unspeaking at the other. Finally Grantin's numbed mind began to function. He lowered his arm and addressed the two bandits.

"Gentlemen, we seem to be at somewhat of a standoff here. I take it you have come for the stones?"

"That, and to see the color of your blood," Rupert answered.

"As you have already learned on more than one occasion, that's not an easy task. It's also an unprofitable one. Instead, let me propose an arrangement to our mutual satisfaction."

"What kind of arrangement?" Diggery asked through teeth clenched with the pain of his blistered hand.

"The best of all possible arrangements, one in which each side benefits. You get what you want, and I get what I want."

"Which is?"

"To be specific, you get the bloodstones and I get to leave."

"Why should you be willing to give us everything? What's in it for you?"

"Gentlemen, I already have a bloodstone. I certainly don't need two of them. Additionally, I have these two trusty associates to act as my personal bondsmen and this nubile beauty to keep me company. Together with the proof of my uncle's demise—this is he you see here, turned to stone—I will inherit all his lands, his properties, his wealth. What else could I want?"

"It does seem a not unreasonable proposition," Rupert said, greedily eyeing the bloodstones scattered about the floor.

"There's something wrong here," Diggery responded. "I don't like it. I don't know what game he's playing, but no one gives away this much wealth."

"Gentlemen, as you can see, I could easily destroy you. As you well know, I have powers beyond those of all other wizards. But I am weary; it has been a long day. Disposing of you two would be quite tiring; besides, a stray bolt might injure one of my slaves, or perhaps scar my new mistress. In order to avoid these minor inconveniences I am willing to give you your life and the stones that remain. I assure you, I have more than enough wealth for my own purposes."

Instead of soothing Diggery's misgivings Grantin's speech only seemed to increase them. Against all logic he was certain that the young Hartford was practicing some great deception. Sensing Diggery's suspicions, Mara decided to add some color to Grantin's story.

"Oh, please, don't let him take me with him, I beg you. He's a beast! You don't know what he plans to do to me! His perversions are worse than Hazar's. I beg you, strike him down and free me. Look at those two," Mara said, indicating Castor and Chom. "He has turned them into mindless slaves. Even if he kills you, you must try. You can't allow an evil power like his loose on the world."

Grantin grabbed Mara's arm and roughly pulled her back from the doorway. He allowed a sneering smile to crease his lips.

"Well, what is it to be?" he asked with a nasty edge to his voice. "Are you going to sacrifice your lives to do the bidding of this enchantress? Make up your minds. Move aside or prepare to die." Grantin raised his left hand and pointed the bloodstone menacingly at Diggery and Rupert. The two bandits stood frozen in position for a moment; then, by unspoken agreeent, they slowly and carefully moved aside.

Grantin motioned to Chom and Castor. Trancelike, they picked up Greyhorn's body and carried it out the door. Mara followed stiffly behind, with Grantin bringing up the rear.

Rupert and Diggery stood at the edge of the doorway, their muscles tensely coiled, waiting to spring. Grantin slipped by them and out into the hall. Once out of sight of the mine's main chamber, the fugitives raced through the passages. It was after the eighth hour but still light enough to put substantial distance between themselves and Grog Cup Mountain before sundown.

Castor and Chom deposited Greyhorn on the ground. While Mara waited to one side, the three followed the spell Mara had repeated and brought into being the bubble of magnificent transportation.

Ten minutes later they floated effortlessly a hundred feet above the countryside, making their way toward the northern pass through the Guardian Mountains. By sundown they had maneuvered through the first range of peaks. In a few more minutes sight of the Gogol empire would be lost.

"I have been thinking. Perhaps if we just waited a bit, Rupert and Yon Diggery might trigger the spell on their own and save us the risk."

"Need I remind you, Grantin, that if they do so you are not protected and yours will go up with the rest of the stones."

Grantin instantly leaped to his feet and began making preparations for the hex. "Well, don't just sit there; let us get this over with before they kill us all."

Grantin, Chom, and Castor visualized a protective shield similar to that which had served them in their attack on Zaco's mine. In one edge of the shield they left a tiny hole which pointed directly at Grog Cup Mountain. The four clenched hands and recited the last line of the hex.

At the instant the last syllable was uttered they patched the hole which they had left in the screen. For one second, two, three, nothing happened. Then far to the west there was a flicker of light, then another, then a third, followed by a brilliant red-orange fireball which, for a brief instant, illuminated the entire sky.

"Gone, all gone. The mountain blew itself to bits, and Diggery and Rupert along with it."

"Probably."

"What do you mean 'probably,' Chom? No one could have survived that explosion."

"They could have filled their pockets with the blood-stones and left with the slaves before the explosion."

"But wouldn't the bloodstones they carried with them have exploded as well?" Mara asked.

"I am sure that all the bloodstones in the Gogol lands, whether at Grog Cup Lake or in Cicero or anywhere else, were destroyed, but whether they exploded with the violence of the mountain I cannot say. They might have just melted. Do not forget, the crystals in the mountain were locked beneath tons of rock which acted to compress their energies. Carried loose in a pocket, they might have done no more than burn the skin or break a few bones as their energy diffused into the open air."

"Chom, I refuse to think any further on such a depressing topic," Grantin said. "Now, have I performed all of the miracles which you two have asked of me? Have I not vanquished the Gogols, saved the human race, protected the Ajaj, bested the villains, rescued the fair maiden, liberated my misguided uncle, and set the world to rights in less than a month? Am I not now permitted to return home in peace and enjoy the fruits of my labors? Can we not now, at last, think of happier topics?"

Castor and Chom made no reply other than to exchange their now familiar looks of resignation. They turned their backs on Grantin and advanced to the most forward part of the bubble. There they sat, side by side, to watch Pyra's rays dapple the peaks with ocher, scarlet, and russet beams.

Grantin was satisfied with their response, which he took to be an acknowledgment of the validity of his claims. With a slight mental kick he urge the bubble forward and was rewarded with a gentle lurch, followed by a soft pressure about his thigh, waist, and upper torso.

Mara slipped her right arm around Grantin's waist and cuddled her body against his. Again Grantin became acutely aware of the rips and tears which Hazar had so strategically placed in her costume.

"And what of me, Grantin? Are you going to abandon me homeless and penniless?"

"Abandon you? How could you say such a thing? Only an unfeeling cad, an insensitive rogue, would do such a thing."

"Then, even knowing that I was Hazar's enchantress, you still want me?" she asked, pressing her ample figure even more tightly against his body.

"Want you?" he exclaimed, increasing the pressure of his arms. "How could any man not want you? Your past means nothing. It is the future which is important. A future which belongs to us. Naturally you will stay with me. My uncle's properties must, of necessity, come under my control during the period that he is indisposed, no matter how burdensome the administration of so much wealth might be."

"You mean it, then? You are sincere? You want me to come with you, live with you in your house, minister to your needs?"

"I absolutely require that you live with me and minister to my needs," Grantin replied fervently.

"I don't know what to say, Grantin. You truly love me, then? I will give you this one last chance to change your mind. Tell me what you wish me to say to you."

"Say yes," Grantin moaned as he nuzzled Mara's left ear.

"Very well, then; I accept your proposal. I will marry you."

Chapter Fifty-one

In some indefinable way Greyhorn's stodgy old manor house had changed over the preceding six months. It now seemed lighter, airier, washed with more brilliant colors, adorned here and there with subtle feminine touches.

From his position just inside the second-floor broom closet Grantin could hear the clatter of Mara's retreating steps. She had searched for him in the kitchen, the parlor, and Greyhorn's downstairs study, and now she was making a tour of the second-floor library where the adventure had all begun. By now Grantin could detect the subtle echoes of frustration in the snap of her steps and the thumpings which accompanied her movement of the chairs as she searched beneath the library table on the off chance that he might be hiding there.

Three weeks before, Grantin had discovered the false panel in the broom closet. During the intervening days he had made good use of the hidey-hole for those increasingly frequent occasions when Mara had dreamed up another task for him to perform.

Initially he had not minded cleaning the manor house, the occasional repair here and there; but of late Mara's ambitious homemaking had pushed him to the brink of his patience. Dear, sweet woman that she was, she had an annoying ability to formulate tasks whose number always exceeded by one those which Grantin could perform during normal waking hours. As a result, except for last Trueday evening when he had managed to slip out before dinner, and, of course, Amisday when he had sent Mara on an errand, and then Playday afternoon while she was out picking berries (but that didn't count since it was a day of relaxation anyway), Grantin had been unable to spend sufficient time in the local taverns and gaming rooms to make even a small dent in the prodigious income from Greyhorn's many properties. Why, it was getting so he had to spend five or six days out of ten working like a slave, and he a moneyed and respected wizard and landowner and the savior of the Hartford kingdom.

Grantin slid back his panel and peeked down the hallway. The coast seemed clear. Holding his sandals in his left hand, he tiptoed on stockinged feet to the library and slipped noiselessly inside.

Grantin wandered back to the window through which he had begun his adventure into the Gogol empire. Before him spread the green and golden afternoon landscape, serene and lovely. Off to his right just a few leagues over the rolling hills was the easygoing community of Gist where Castor and Chom probably still reclined at their ease.

After their perilous journey Grantin had naturally invited his friends to remain in Greyhorn's manor house, and for a while they had accepted his invitation. After the wedding, however, the situation had changed. Soon both took their leave to visit surrounding Hartford communities.

"Stay, stay. There is room and food enough for all of us. Let me show you the countryside. We could have a jolly time of it."

"Thank you, friend Grantin, but things are different now. You have a new mate and you should spend your time with her. We will learn more on our own, in any event."

"You're staying together, then?"

"Yes," Castor answered. "I would like to visit my fellow Ajaj who live among the Hartfords, but I would fee more comfortable traveling with a stalwart companion."

"And I have not finished my trip of life. There is much more that I must learn about humans before I can return to my community. Castor and I are well suited to each other. I feel that our relationship will be a harmonious one."

"But you will come back and visit with me. We have been good comrades, all. This is no time to break up a fine friendship after what we have been through together."

"Of course we will come back. We have planned a great circular route, first south, then east, then north, and then back this way. In a few months we will return to Gist for the biannual fair."

And so they had left. Now the fair was only two days away, but Mara was proving obstinate.

"Let you go to the fair alone, so that you can drink and carouse with those tavern friends of yours? Why don't you take me to the fair? Is there some reason why you can't be seen in public with your own wife?"

"No, my darling, of course not; it is just that . . . well, a man enjoys a chance now and again to get together in the company of other men. You would feel out of place, I'm sure."

"The company of other men, is it? You wouldn't be thinking of some of those bar wenches, now, would you? I've seen the way you look at that serving girl at the tavern. I'm not going to let you run loose on a binge to Gist even if there weren't a fair going on. You, taverns, celebrations, and money in your pocket are not a good combination. We can go to the fair together next Trueday and see who wins the ribbon in the home-jelly competition."

"Yes, my dear," Grantin had mumbled meekly.

What was that? Did he hear a sound in the hallway? Quick as a snake Grantin sprinted around the table and peeked through the crack in the door. No, all was quiet. Grantin turned away from the portal and then stubbed his toe on an obstruction. Looking down, he saw that in her fanaticism for cleanliness Mara had again moved poor Uncle Greyhorn out of position.

Grantin bent over and shifted his uncle's body six inches away from the door. Over the past six months by dint of great effort Grantin had been able to unlimber Greyhorn's two arms, which now protruded straight up, the fingers spread open. On the little finger of the left hand hung Grantin's stylish new beret. No doubt about it, Greyhorn made an extremely functional hatrack. Who knows, perhaps in another year or two his legs might be unbent to the point where the wizard would be able to serve as a life-size sewing dummy for Mara's domestic pursuits.

Grantin gave his uncle a jolly salute and made his way to the bookcase against the left-hand wall. As quietly as possible he removed a heavy leatherbound volume and carried it over to the table by the window. He quickly found the spell he needed.

In a hushed whisper Grantin recited the appropriate incantation, then stared into his ring's scarlet stone. In only a few seconds shapes began to take form. Shortly he was able to make out Chom's and Castor's visages. His two friends reclined in soft comfortable chairs on a sunny patio. A great circular umbrella shaded them from the harshest of Pyra's rays. At their elbows stood tall, foaming mugs of beer. In the background Grantin thought he spied an enchanting hostess.

Without conscious thought Grantin's fingers leafed through the volume of spells. Unbidden, his eyes leaped down a weathered wrinkled page to one special incantation:

Spell of Magnificent Transport

Through the use of this spell an accomplished sorcerer may be transported quietly, safely, and in absolute comfort to any nearby location which he can clearly visualize. The greater the power of the wizard, the more distant the destination, or the more rapid the speed of transition. To call up the vehicle one must embark upon the following steps in order. . . .

Grantin greedily scanned the page and convinced himself for at least the tenth time that he had properly committed the spell to memory. Guiltily he closed the book and replaced it on the shelf before returning to the window.

Outside, the golden sunlight painted a lovely picture of

peace and harmony. How easy it would be to slip away to Gist for a visit with his old friends. Perhaps in their travels they had discovered other wrongs which needed righting. For a fact, Grantin's recent life, which a year ago he would have deemed idyllic, now seemed somehow stale.

But what about Mara? Could he just run off and leave her like that? Grantin felt a pang of guilt. He really did love the girl. He couldn't just abandon her. What if she took solace with another man in his absence?

Still, still . . . absence makes the heart grow fonder. A few days away from her, a week or two, would not be so bad. He could leave her a note so that she would not worry.

In the distance Grantin heard Mara's heels clicking up the stairs. He turned back to the window. Straining his eyes around the edge of the castle, he hoped to catch a glimpse of a plume of smoke or the glitter of sunlight on glass which would mark the location of Gist. He still had time to recite the spell. What should he do?

84